DOUBLE-CROSSED

Praise for Ali Vali

Answering the Call

Answering the Call "is a brilliant cop-and-killer story…The crime story is tight and the love story is fantastic."—*Best Lesbian Erotica*

"Is there anything better than a smoking hot butch woman in uniform?… If you enjoy stories with stakeouts, gun-slinging butch cops, meddling family members coupled with murder and mayhem around every corner, then this story is certainly for you."—*The Lesbian Review*

Lammy Finalist *Calling the Dead*

"So many writers set stories in New Orleans, but Ali Vali's mystery novels have the authenticity that only a real Big Easy resident could bring. Set six months after Hurricane Katrina has devastated the city, a lesbian detective is still battling demons when a body turns up behind one of the city's famous eateries. What follows makes for a classic lesbian murder yarn."—*Curve Magazine*

"The plot is engrossing and satisfying. A fun aspect of the book is the images of food it includes. The descriptions of sex are also delicious." —*Seattle Gay News*

"In *Calling the Dead*, Vali has given us characters that are engaging and a story that keeps us turning page after page."—*Just About Write*

Beauty and the Boss

"The story gripped me from the first page…Vali's writing style is lovely—it's clean, sharp, no wasted words, and it flows beautifully as a result. Highly recommended!"—*Rainbow Book Reviews*

"This was a story of love and passion but also of surprises and secrets. I loved it!"—*Kitty Kat's Book Review Blog*

The Romance Vote

"Won by a Landslide!…[A] sweet and mushy romance with some humor and spicy, sexy scenes!"—*Love Bytes*

Balance of Forces: Toujours Ici

"A stunning addition to the vampire legend, *Balance of Forces: Toujour Ici* is one that stands apart from the rest."—*Bibliophilic Book Blog*

Blue Skies

"Vali is skilled at building sexual tension, and the sex in this novel flies as high as Berkley's jets. Look for this fast-paced read."—*Just About Write*

Beneath the Waves

"The premise…was brilliantly constructed…skillfully written and the imagination that went into it was fantastic…The author managed to insert a real fear and menace into the story and had me totally engrossed…A wonderful passionate love story with a great mystery."—*Inked Rainbow Reads*

Second Season

"Whether Ali Vali is writing about crime figures or lawyers, her characters are well drawn and extremely likeable. Indeed, writing so the reader really cares about the main characters is a trademark of a Vali novel. *Second Season* is no exception to the rule…This is a rich, enjoyable read that's not to be missed."—*Just About Write*

"The issues are realistic and center around the universal factors of love, jealousy, betrayal, and doing the right thing and are constantly woven into the fabric of the story. We rated this well written social commentary through the use of fiction our max five hearts."—*Heartland Reviews*

Carly's Sound

"Vali paints vivid pictures with her words…*Carly's Sound* is a great romance, with some wonderfully hot sex."—*Midwest Book Review*

"It's no surprise that passion is indeed possible a second time around."—*Q Syndicate*

"*Carly's Sound* is a great romance, with some wonderfully hot sex, but it is more than that. It is also the tale of a woman rising from the ashes of grief and finding new love and a new life. Vali has surrounded Julia and Poppy with a cast of great supporting characters, making this an extremely satisfying read."—*Just About Write*

Praise for the Cain Casey Saga

The Devil's Due

"This is an enthralling, nail biting and ultra fast moving addition to the Devil series...once again Ali Vali has produced a brilliant story arc, solid character development, incomparable bad-ass women in traditionally male roles, leading both the goodies, baddies and cross-breeds."—*Lesbian Reading Room*

"A Night Owl Reviews Top Pick: Cain Casey is the kind of person you aspire to be even though some consider her a criminal. She's loyal, very protective of those she loves, honorable, big on preserving her family legacy and loves her family greatly. *The Devil's Due* is a book I highly recommend and well worth the wait we all suffered through. I cannot wait for the next book in the series to come out."
—*Night Owl Reviews*

The Devil Be Damned

"Ali Vali excels at creating strong, romantic characters along with her fast-paced, sophisticated plots. Her setting, New Orleans, provides just the right blend of immigrants from Mexico, South America, and Cuba, along with a city steeped in traditions."—*Just About Write*

Deal with the Devil

"Ali Vali has given her fans another thick, rich thriller...*Deal With the Devil* has wonderful love stories, great sex, and an ample supply of humor. It is an exciting, page-turning read that leaves her readers eagerly awaiting the next book in the series."—*Just About Write*

The Devil Unleashed

"Fast-paced action scenes, intriguing character revelations, and a refreshing approach to the romance thriller genre all make for an enjoyable reading experience in the Big Easy...*The Devil Unleashed* is an engrossing reading experience."—*Midwest Book Review*

The Devil Inside

"Not only is *The Devil Inside* a ripping mystery, it's also an intimate character study."—*L-Word Literature*

"*The Devil Inside* is the first of what promises to be a very exciting series…While telling an exciting story that grips the reader, Vali has also fully fleshed out her heroes and villains. *The Devil Inside* is that rarity: a fascinating crime novel which includes a tender love story and leaves the reader with a cliffhanger ending."—*MegaScene*

"*The Devil Inside* by Ali Vali is an unusual, unpredictable, and thought-provoking love story that will have the reader questioning the definition of right and wrong long after she finishes the book…first time novelist Vali does not leave the reader hanging for too long, but spins a complex plot of love, conspiracy, and loss."—*Just About Write*

"[T]his isn't your typical 'Godfather-esque' novel, oh no. The head of this crime family is not only a lesbian, but a mother to boot. Vali's fluid writing style quickly puts the reader at ease, which makes the story and its characters equally easy to get to know and care about. When you find yourself talking out loud to the characters in a book, you know the work is polished and professional, as well as entertaining. Ever just wanted to grab a crime boss by the lapels, get in their face, and tell them to open their eyes and see what's right in front of their eyes? If not, you will once you start turning the pages of *The Devil Inside*." —*Family and Friends Magazine*

By the Author

Carly's Sound

Second Season

Blue Skies

Love Match

The Dragon Tree Legacy

The Romance Vote

Girls with Guns

Beneath the Waves

Beauty and the Boss

Call Series

Calling the Dead

Answering the Call

Forces Series

Balance of Forces: Toujours Ici

Battle of Forces: Sera Toujours

Force of Fire: Toujours a Vous

Vegas Nights

Double-Crossed

The Cain Casey Saga

The Devil Inside

The Devil Unleashed

Deal with the Devil

The Devil Be Damned

The Devil's Orchard

The Devil's Due

Heart of the Devil

Visit us at www.boldstrokesbooks.com

DOUBLE-CROSSED

by
Ali Vali

2019

DOUBLE-CROSSED
© 2019 By Ali Vali. All Rights Reserved.

ISBN 13: 978-1-63555-302-4

This Trade Paperback Original Is Published By
Bold Strokes Books, Inc.
P.O. Box 249
Valley Falls, NY 12185

First Edition: September 2019

Credits
Editors: Victoria Villaseñor and Ruth Sternglantz
Production Design: Stacia Seaman
Cover Design by Jeanine Henning

Acknowledgments

A new series is both a daunting and exciting thing to start. Daunting because you want to do the story justice and exciting because you're entering a whole new universe where new characters are waiting for their story to be told. That there are a few familiar characters, murder, mayhem, and romance are added bonuses.

Thank you to Sandy Lowe, not only for all you do but for the gentle shove to start another adventure and for the idea of the title. As always, thank you to Radclyffe for all your support from that very first day. Thank you to my BSB family for all your support and advice whenever it's needed.

New adventures are also better shared with friends and new editors. Lucky for me I got both in the awesome Victoria Villaseñor and Ruth Sternglantz. Thank you, Vic, for everything you taught me in this process, for your friendship, and for making this a book I'm proud of. Ruth, thank you for all the hard work in finishing the process, and for all the things you do that go beyond editing as well as your friendship. Thank you to Jeanine Henning for the great cover.

Thank you to my first readers, Cris Perez-Soria, and welcome back to one of my real first readers, Lenore Beniot. You guys were great and I value your input. To all the readers who have supported me and followed my work, every word is written with you in mind.

Thank you to C for the greatest adventure of all, and I look forward to all the ones yet to come. *Verdad!*

For C

For all the readers
Thank you

CHAPTER ONE

A re you fucking listening to what I'm saying? I don't give a good goddamn how much it costs. Get it done, and *don't* make it look like I have anything to do with it." Sofia Madison's disembodied voice sounded as if she was trying to downplay her anger, but she was failing miserably.

What Sofia was asking for was something Reed Gable totally understood. She wasn't the first woman to request the exact same thing once the reality dawned that her marriage was a total sham. Some people made mistakes, but Sofia's husband had more women than an old sultan with a harem. A feat he seemed pretty pleased about, from what Reed could tell. "It's ten percent of the total. Are you sure about that?"

"He's probably going to offer me less than a percent of the fucking total in a divorce," Sofia said, going from angry to exasperated. "You think ten percent is going to bother me?"

"I need a few days to figure out a timeline, and I'll get back to you." Reed stood in the den of her home in Henderson, Nevada, and gazed out at the empty golf course beyond the pool. It was incredibly early, so the hardcore golfers weren't out yet. The house had plenty of space between the two neighboring properties and was exactly like all the other houses on her private street. That was the main thing she loved about the place. It didn't stand out. Homogenous wasn't a dirty word in her world.

"I want to meet." Sofia tried again. Like a forgetful old codger, she'd asked for this every time they'd spoken.

"It's your right to insist, but if you can't proceed without that, you need to find someone else." She hung up and tapped the burner phone against her chin. There was another contract offer she was considering, but she'd put them off because Sofia's job was more of a challenge. It might be time to give them a callback.

"Fuck it. Not my problem, and hopefully she'll be okay with getting screwed in the divorce." The phone rang before she could remove the SIM card and destroy it, so she took a moment before answering to watch the first golfers of the morning playing by the fourteenth hole. She found the sport boring, and it seemed aggravating, if all the cursing she heard was any indication.

"How do I know you're not a cop?" Sofia asked without preamble.

"You don't, and you can choose not to believe me, but I'm not. I'm willing to help you, but meeting people isn't my thing. What you're asking for is something you might not be able to do without laying eyes on me, and I understand that. If you decide this isn't something you can stomach, this conversation will never come back to haunt you. On that you have my word."

The problem with most people was that they were too emotionally invested even when they declared loudly and repeatedly that they weren't. Emotions, or more precisely an overabundance of them, weren't Reed's problem. She patiently waited for Sofia to either talk herself in, or out, of what she was asking—that wasn't Reed's job.

She stared at the guy whacking away in the sand trap and figured his time would be better spent gardening. At least at the end he'd have something to show for it. By the time the ball had rolled into the tall grass, Sofia seemed to have come up with more to say, and she kept on rambling. Reed sighed away from the phone; this was by far the most aggravating part of the job, and she rolled her shoulders to try and relax. Long, unproductive conversations had a way of tensing her up more than the actual job.

"I gave Victor *my* word, as well as everything else, including our children. He turned them against me first. My sons want nothing to do with me because their father has told them repeatedly I'm a bitch who's fucking crazy." Sofia stopped and took a deep breath. "All I wanted was a faithful husband, but when I complained too much when he slept with half the women in this town, he started stripping away the life I've enjoyed and the things I love about it." Sofia's voice finally softened and she sounded like a woman set adrift in a sea of uncertainty.

"Has he contacted an attorney that you know of?" An impending divorce was the fastest way to an impending police investigation, and that's not what her client needed. She promised quick and easy closure, and that's what she'd deliver.

"Unless he went behind my back, no." Sofia sounded sure, but she'd droned on at first about how solid her marriage was, saying she just wanted to make totally sure. But that had been a month ago.

The fantasy world Sofia had existed in for so long was destroyed after Reed had followed Victor for two days. All Sofia had wanted at first was to convince herself the rumors about Victor weren't true. That simple plan had turned on the proverbial dime when the truth was staring at her in nice glossy pictures.

"Do you want me to find out?"

Reed wondered if the golfer trying to put his little ball in the hole knew his pants had torn down the seam, showing his dingy tighty-whities. The lesson from this little story was: become a better golfer and avoid sand traps if your pants are at least a size too small.

"All I need you to do is tell Victor and your kids you're going to New York to spend time with your family. Once you're out of town, turn your phone off and relax. Don't complain about Victor or your sons to anyone, but answer the inevitable questions of why you're there with you needed a break before you came back to work on your marriage. Do not raise any questions with Victor or anyone else about divorce. You don't want that in someone's memory when the cops start asking questions."

"You know who my father is, right? He'll never believe that I'm in New York for a break, and I don't want him blamed."

"Your family has its favorite personnel for jobs like this, and none of them are in Vegas. Forget about me and everything we've talked about. That is, if you're sure. Once this call is over, there's no going back. This number won't be available, and I'll be in touch like before." Once the job was done, Sofia would use the burner phone she'd have delivered by courier and they'd finalize things.

There was only a moment of hesitation. "Promise me you'll humiliate him as much as he has me."

"I'll do my best. You have fun in the city, and once things are done, answer the phone you'll get as a gift. Destroy the one you're using now somewhere not near your home or the airport. If you decide to keep it and you get caught, you're on your own."

"When do you want me to leave?" Sofia asked, not sounding as upset.

"Today," she said. A little space from his wife would deny Victor the chance to do something not in his usual routine she couldn't overcome. She'd been following him for a month and he was a shit bag, but a fairly consistent shit bag. "Depending on what's going on, I might be done in the next couple of weeks, so try to be on the next plane to solidify your alibi."

Reed hung up, trashed her phone, and grabbed her overnight bag. It was still early, but she needed to make a trip to one of the buildings she owned. The money she'd made was mostly invested in ways that would take time and effort to trace back to her, and she'd made enough of it to retire and not have to deal with the Sofias of the world.

Anonymity from her clients and the world was something she'd learned coming up the ranks, and it was a solid way to keep her freedom. Retirement, though, wouldn't come until the game lost its allure, so she'd keep at it and continue to diversify her investments.

A big portion of her real estate portfolio was made up of strip malls and warehouses, which weren't huge moneymakers, but like everything she did outside of work, they were safe bets. The small place on the way to Red Rock Canyon was being rented by a lawn maintenance company, and one of the only ones she'd had built. The young guy who leased from her had no idea what was right under his feet.

The ministorage next door was another spot she'd constructed, and the car in the middle unit had Georgia plates from her last job, so she switched them for Oregon ones and placed the proper paperwork in the glove compartment on the off chance she got stopped. She then went through the opening in the false back wall of the unit and took the steps to the tunnel that led next door. It was the only way into the basement of the warehouse.

It took an hour in her little studio, but when Reed was done, her dark hair, blue eyes, and slim waist were gone. The image in the mirror was a blond scruffy-faced man with a prominent paunch—totally believable as an accountant from a small town in Oregon.

"Hopefully you were serious, Sofia." She put on the glasses and combed her hair to the side. "Victor's about to lose big."

❖

"Would you have a problem working after-hours every so often?" Dean Jasper, the accounting manager at the Moroccan Casino, asked Brinley Myers.

Brinley was still settling into her apartment in Las Vegas, but the opportunity her neighbor had told her about was too good to pass up, even if she wasn't quite ready. That was, if she could actually get hired. Vegas, she was starting to understand, was all about the Strip to some people, but there was more to a casino than the actual gambling. This job was pretty much a nine-to-five gig with awesome benefits and salary, and she'd probably never see the gaming floor.

"As long as you give me a heads-up so I can arrange a sitter," Brinley said and nodded for more emphasis. This job paid almost three times the one she'd left in New Orleans, and considering that had been in her mom's firm, this was a sweet deal.

"You have children?"

Dean's question made her wonder if that was going to be the thing that sank her chances. "Only one." She held her finger up and smiled. Finn was her reason for the move.

A fresh start seemed in order after the biggest mistake of her life had been convicted of drug trafficking and would be a guest of the State of Louisiana penitentiary for the next thirty-eight years. Being incarcerated should have stopped the loser's demands about Finn, but no such luck. A collect call seemed to come every few days, and the more she declined, the more persistent the idiot got.

"My son Finn—he just turned one."

"Here." Dean took a card out of his top drawer. "This is the day care I use for unexpected work stuff, unless you have someone set up. They're really good, and they have those cameras throughout the place, so you can check in on him if you want. They're open twenty-four-seven and will accommodate last-minute stuff. My kids love it."

"Thanks." She placed the card in her wallet and took it as a good sign. "Do you have any more questions for me?"

"Can you start Monday?" Dean closed the folder in front of him and held his hand out.

"Thank you, and yes." She shook his hand and stood. "I really appreciate the opportunity."

"I think you'll be a great fit, so I'll hand you over to Naomi Williams. She'll navigate you through HR, and she'll also be your office mate." Dean picked up his phone, and a few minutes later a beautiful African American woman with a pencil stuck behind her ear entered and waved her out.

"Nice to meet you," Naomi said as they headed for the elevator, "but please tell me you're not a Republican religious nut with a sequined pin of Mitch McConnell hidden away in your underwear drawer." Brinley couldn't be sure, but Naomi sounded totally serious.

"No way." The inside of the car was completely mirrored, like some throwback seventies decorating, and the lighting made her skin wash out against her blond hair, even with the red highlights. Her coloring was a combination of her parents', and her green eyes were something both her mom and dad had in common, at least according to her mother. Her father was someone she didn't remember, and he'd never been a part of her life. She didn't feel the lack of his presence, except for moments when she saw something in herself she supposedly got from him. "It's a George W. Bush pin or nothing."

"Jesus Christ, I hope you're joking. Being stuck in our box of an office with that last woman was like spending my days trapped with Jerry Falwell. She thought my soul was beyond saving, but that didn't stop her from going on and on about it. The old bitch finally got fired when she hosed me down with holy water."

"You're kidding, right?"

"I have a silk blouse with water stains to prove it, so no, not kidding."

"I doubt you're that far gone, and no to the rest of your list. With a one-year-old, I never have time to watch the news, much less join a religious cult." They entered the second floor where HR and the security center of the casino took up the entire space. "Wow, that's a lot of cameras."

"Don't believe the commercial, girl. What happens in Vegas is filmed for eternity, and if you try to pocket a chip that doesn't belong to you, one of these goons will break your fingers." Naomi stayed with her as she got her paperwork done and they issued her an ID badge. "Here's my phone number. Call me if you need something, and I'll see you Monday. Maybe your little one will eventually be interested in a playdate with mine."

"That'd be great. Do you have a boy or girl?"

"Amelia's two and a handful." They shared pictures as they headed to the employee lot so Brinley would know where it was. "Your badge will get you in, and all you need to do is pick the first spot that doesn't have someone's name on it."

"Thanks for all your help," she said taking Naomi's hand. "I have a feeling you're going to make this fun."

"Thank the gods Dean wised up this time. The job is boring—accounting, after all—but the town's a blast. If our kids like each other, maybe we can split a sitter and go out some time." Naomi gave her a one-armed hug, and it made Brinley feel good about her decision to interview. "It'll be nice to have a new friend to blow off steam with. See you at nine on Monday."

"I'll be here." She walked back toward the entrance where they'd valeted her car at Dean's insistence. "Well, Brinley, this will certainly be different," she whispered to herself when she handed her ticket over.

All the mistakes she'd made over the last three years had played in an unending loop in her mind as she'd driven west, and she was ready to stop binge-watching. The woman she'd been totally committed to had broken her heart, but that had been no reason to completely upend her life with massive changes. Not that one night of heavy drinking and then sleeping with a loser was completely upending your life, but the residuals that had come from that experience had sent her down a different path.

Her ex had taught her that a woman could be a bitch. The kind of bitch who would not only sleep with a couple of your friends but mention a few things she didn't like about your body on the way out the door with *your* luggage because the bitch didn't own any.

That delightful rundown of all her shortcomings, combined with way too much alcohol and betrayal, had made her think jumping the fence back to men was a genius idea, and she'd ended up in bed with the tweaker Jarrell. But—and there was a big-ass but in this story— there were mistakes like putting the Hubble telescope into space with the lens in backward, and then there was Jarrell. Granted, she had Finn, and she wouldn't trade him for anything, but Jarrell had latched on after he found out she was pregnant and convinced himself it was his.

Finn was *hers*, and she put *father unknown* on his birth certificate, not wanting Jarrell anywhere near either her or her son, but that'd been wishful thinking. That hadn't stopped the unending calls, and she'd had enough. One night of bad sex shouldn't have been an invitation to have to deal with Jarrell and his family for the rest of her life.

"This isn't exactly the quiet town I was going for, but it's a great place to get lost in."

CHAPTER TWO

Robert Wallace reclined in his office chair and loosened his tie. He'd been up for most of the night, a responsibility he'd thought he'd put behind him when he took over at the Moroccan, but it was a big night and he stayed to make sure everything went off with no hiccups. The Moroccan had been a pit when he got in the top spot, but now the local paper reported they were the *it* spot for boutique casinos. Never mind he'd paid the reporter to write the article, but it would generate business eventually.

They were sandwiched between the Bellagio and the Cosmopolitan, and their room census was full for the next four months. The only kitschy thing about them was the tiki bar at the center of the casino floor. There were no fountains, pirate shows, or volcanoes up front, but his tables were full because of excellent service and the perks they offered that had nothing to do with free rooms and buffet dinners.

"You going home soon?" his assistant, Alex Bell, asked.

Alex was the only one aside from him who knew all the secrets the Moroccan held, and he trusted him enough to let him live with those secrets.

"I've got a meeting, then I'm heading out." He really wanted to drink, but he needed to be clearheaded for the next hour. "You got that bitch out of my house?"

"We put her in one of the premier rooms next door. Victor said he'd take care of getting her on the plane when she realizes there's no going back." Alex poured him a cup of coffee and dumped three teaspoons of sugar in it. The drink probably wasn't manly, but it was how Robert's father always fixed it for him after his mother died.

"Still too close for me, but Victor probably thinks he's got a chance now that she's vulnerable. She's good in bed, but the bitch is crazy."

"Victor's a great swordsman in his own mind, fucking all these young airheads who fall for his hype. But he's fucking with fire playing this game." Alex fixed another cup and sat across from him. The extremely handsome young man did more than help him run the casino—he was his personal fixer. "You don't drop Diego Moretti's daughter and try to leave her penniless without blowback."

"Diego's family has no muscle in Vegas, so I get how Victor thinks he can chance it." He closed his eyes and savored the hot coffee as it went down. "Sofia's become a broken record about the things she wants, and it's not his *hype*, Alex, it's his wallet. Fat old fuckers are gorgeous only when they have money. Remember that." September in Vegas was always stifling but the casinos were always kept a cool sixty-eight. That and the constant flow of pure oxygen kept the money flowing.

"Don't count out the Morettis so fast, Bobby," Lucan Terzo said, coming in without knocking.

The young arrogant asshole was the son of Francesco Terzo, and Francesco's money was what had turned the Moroccan around. That was the only reason he tolerated these damn meetings and Lucan's use of the nickname *Bobby*. He hated it and had given enough beatdowns in his life to have earned being addressed as *Robert*. Putting a hand on Lucan or anyone in the Terzo organization was the fastest way to be shown the dumping grounds in the desert he was sure the Terzos used to rid themselves of problems.

"I never discount anyone, Lucan, but Sofia Madison is Victor's problem." He stood and opened his arms for an embrace he disliked as much as his nickname. He waited for Lucan to sit before retaking his seat.

"Diego and me are second cousins, so thanks for the heads-up. A problem keeping marriage vows sometimes becomes a problem keeping any vow." Lucan laughed and patted himself on the crotch. "Thinking with your dick never did anyone any good, my father always says. There's a time and place for that, and it's not ever while you're doing business."

"That's why I'm not married," Robert said, smiling.

"This is a place full of beautiful women, so I sympathize, but my father also says real men eventually marry and have families. It's our responsibility to the future." Lucan had two men with him who nodded like idiots at whatever the young genius had to say, and the sight made him tired. "Enough about that. You got something for me?"

Robert took a ledger out of his safe and handed it over. "It's all distributed like Mr. Francesco wanted."

"He'll be back in town later today—he's swamped, but he wants to talk to you this week. We need to double what we're doing now, and he wants you to handle it. Have a plan in place to show him when he calls." Lucan stood and buttoned the jacket of his linen suit. The cut reminded Robert of the sixties, but it was stylish enough to make Lucan appear more like a model than a thug.

"I never want to disappoint, but—"

"Bobby, think before you say anything"—Lucan cocked his head to the side—"well, disappointing. Have Alex here suck your dick if that's what it'll take to clear your mind, but get your plan together. Papa isn't after excuses. He doesn't tolerate them well, and you don't want to see what happens if you disappoint him."

"Thanks, I'll work something up." He stood as well and shook Lucan's hand.

"Sorry about the dick joke, Alex," Lucan said, patting Alex on the chest on his way out. "You got a week, Bobby."

The door closed and he dropped back down and reached for the whiskey after dumping his coffee in the trash. "There's no fucking way we can double what we're doing now and get away with it. We're at the max. It's like these fuckers want to get caught, and if that happens, we're all going down. I'm not taking the rap for them and their stupidity no matter what they threaten me with."

"You want me to talk to Lucan and see if I can reason with him?" Alex asked after he called down for Robert's car. "If not, we'll think of something. Like, working our way to double, but not all at once."

"Don't get ahead of yourself," he cautioned. "I make the deals, not you. Besides, we got other shit to worry about." He swallowed the whiskey and moved quickly to Alex, forcing him to his knees. "Maybe that little shit had a point about reminding you what your position is."

"Think before you start something you might not like the results of," Alex said, getting back to his feet. "You wouldn't want anyone to question your manhood."

"Get the fuck out of here, and keep your ideas to yourself."

❖

Reed took her valet ticket and rolled her bag inside to check in to the cheapest room Bellagio had. The lanyard around her neck for the accounting convention hosted by the hotel had the name *Bill Smith*, and she wasn't the only one in line wearing that particular fashion statement. Accountants weren't exactly party animals, but Vegas seemed to bring out everyone's wilder side. The call girls working the check-in line were subtle but seemed to be doing okay with the conventioneers. That was probably the only reason the security team hadn't cleared them out of the lobby.

"You want to grab a drink later, honey?" The young blonde was pretty, but not someone she'd met before. Not that the girl would recognize her. "I know a great place if you can afford it."

"Maybe later." She stopped the woman's wandering hands and smiled. "I just drove twelve hours and I doubt I could get it up, even for you." Reed reached in her pocket. "How about a down payment for later? Here's my card." She handed over a card with her number and six hundred bucks.

"Are you sure? You shouldn't be so trusting, honey." The women pressed the money back into Reed's palm but kept the card. "Here's my number."

"What's your name?" She really didn't have time for this, but sometimes lost sheep were hard to ignore, and unless her instincts were way off, this woman was new to the game. It was obvious from her clumsy flirting and her trying a little too hard. Too many of the kids she'd grown up with had left the system too early and ended up where this woman was, or worse. If she was here at the urging of a bastard boyfriend, maybe she could offer her peace for at least one night.

"Jayden," she said, moving along with her in the line. She toyed with a loose thread on her skirt, as though needing a way to keep her hands busy.

"Keep it, Jayden, and believe me, I'll call. It'd be nice if you weren't busy later." She took out another four hundred and kissed Jayden's temple. "Go have lunch and wait for me to call you."

"This is enough for two days."

"Lucky me then." She kissed Jayden when she pressed her lips to hers and hoped Jayden simply went home. "I'll call you."

"Don't go throwing all that cash around, or you won't live out the week. Sometimes this town isn't full of nice people, so don't follow the lead of your friends and get all crazy. Crazier, anyway." Jayden kissed her again and walked out.

It took another twelve minutes before she made it to the front and handed over a business credit card for the room. The young woman made small talk as she processed the card, then handed over a map with the room keys. "Enjoy your stay, Mr. Smith. All the conference meetings will be held here." She circled the spot on the map and smiled. "Please call if you need anything."

The route to the room was through the casino, and she ignored the conference goers lured by the slots. She wanted to get set up to see where Victor Madison's car was. The tracker she'd put on it was still there. Sofia's exit had kept him at home longer than usual, but the bugs she'd placed in the Madison home had yielded a simple explanation. Victor was free to entertain his secretary at home while Sofia was away.

If Sofia knew her scumbag husband was screwing one of his many mistresses in her bed, she'd probably have shot the bastard herself, but Reed would save that information for later in case her client showed any kind of remorse. She hadn't mentioned the bugs to Sofia or anyone else. Right now, all that was important was to keep him out of the office until she was ready for him.

"You're running late," Oscar Dawson said as he got into the elevator with her. "Though, you look hot for a middle-aged guy with a desk job. How many beers a day do you think it would take to get that beer belly?"

"Fuck you too, buddy." She laughed.

They'd been friends since they were nine, when she'd saved Oscar from a beating. He'd been surrounded by the bullies who ran the facility they were in. Both of them had grown up under the state of Nevada's neglectful eye, orphans of circumstance, as they'd been told over and over, which translated into unwanted and useless. Reed had been big for her age and Oscar had exactly the opposite problem, so he'd stuck with her from that day on.

"And Bellagio doesn't know Bill Smith, so I had to wait in that long-ass line. You got what I asked for?"

"Please. When have I ever let you down?"

They walked to the room that was as far from the entrance as possible and had a view of the parking lot and the tops of the mountains in the background. She'd manipulated the selection because of the elevator bank just down the hall. Two floors below were the executive offices, including Victor's office with his perfect view of the Strip and his private gardens. Supposedly, it was one of the most beautiful spots in the city. The top floors above them were where the best suites were. One elevator was electronic-key-access only, and Victor's most convenient route if he was entertaining.

"We need to start this afternoon," she said. "The first part of this has to be finished before we move to the big finale."

"You sure tonight wouldn't be better? We were on schedule for two weeks from now, so what's the rush?" Oscar took the computers he'd need out of her suitcase and started setting up.

"I had Sofia scatter some stuff around the house that should keep him at home looking for clues as to what she's up to, so now's good. Victor's obviously not expecting this, but then neither is Sofia, so it'll help with the surprise response when the cops call her this quickly." She took off her suit jacket and rolled her sleeves up. "All you need to do is monitor security and give me some warning if anyone comes my way."

Oscar was strictly a behind-the-scenes kind of guy, but he was good at getting into places she couldn't. As far as hackers went, Oscar was one of the best. "Get going and I'll be ready."

She walked out and headed for the elevators. All but one opened onto guest rooms and the casino floor. But the sixth elevator, the keyed access one, had back doors that opened toward the executive offices. It was used at times by the security chiefs who had offices on the fourth floor, but it was mostly for Victor's convenience, so he could come and go as he pleased, bypassing anyone he wanted to avoid outside his office.

"Wait for it," Oscar said into her ear. The middle car on the right opened and she noticed this one was plusher than the one they'd ridden up in. "Get in and don't worry about the camera. It's on a loop."

"Thanks." She got in and stared at her shoes out of an overabundance of caution. The camera was never your friend, whether it was on or not. The elevator opened outside Victor's private office and his secretary's desk was empty. "Are you ready?"

"You're invisible until you reach the door. The inner sanctum is the only spot that's a camera-free zone. It's probably contributed to his marital problems," Oscar said as she picked the lock to Victor's door. "If there's a couch in there, don't go anywhere near it."

"Trust me, that's not part of the plan."

"Shit," Oscar said as the door gave way.

"Problem?" she asked as she studied the space. "Talk to me."

"His assistant must've not been in the mood, or Sofia fucked up her part. His car is headed our way."

She glanced at her watch and figured she had twenty minutes tops if she wanted to be cautious. This part of the op had to be done in less than fifteen if she didn't want to get stuck in here.

"Give me updates." She headed to where Sofia thought the safe was—bingo. It was larger than the ones in the rooms but had the same digital readout. She attached the passcode breaker to it and moved on. Her gut instinct was Victor didn't keep what she was looking for in a safe any petty thief or maid could get into. "And I'm in no way petty," she said softly as she searched the space for what she knew in her gut was there. Somewhere…

"Did you say something?"

"Nothing important. Talk to me, Oscar."

"He's still en route, so concentrate."

"Working on it." The picture in the bathroom of dogs playing poker made her laugh. Whose bright idea was that in the decorating department? The trip wire attaching it to the wall, though, made it the one thing she was looking for. If she'd simply moved it, severing the wire, security wouldn't have given her the time to escape.

It took a few minutes to get past all the security measures the tacky velvet painting came with, but she smiled when she saw what it covered. The American Security safe wasn't the best on the market, but Victor had obviously factored in the safe's location and the security he had. Those two factors alone would keep anyone from actually getting this close, so he'd saved himself some money.

"He's passing the Cosmopolitan," Oscar said as she stuck the earpiece in and attached the amplifier to the safe, right by the dial. She left the Earwig in her other ear so she could still hear Oscar.

"Give me a few minutes." She cleared the dial, stopping on zero after four spins, and blew out a breath.

"That's about all you have."

She started turning slowly to the right with her eyes closed until it clicked on twenty-two, then turned to the left—longer since it clicked on eighteen, and then back to the right to twenty. That one she almost missed since it came so quickly. The safe held stacks of cash, a bag of diamonds, four ledgers, and six different bankbooks. The stockpile of loot was tempting but the bankbooks and ledgers were all she was interested in.

"Reed, he's in the building, and he's walking really fast toward his office."

Reed could almost hear his heart pounding. His tendency toward panic was why he was up in the room and not here.

"Do I have time for the elevator?" she asked as she rigged the painting back up.

"He's a hundred feet from the executive offices. Can you flush yourself down the toilet?"

"I could totally do that, but it'll mess up my hair." The safe in the office was open now and the folder on top captured her attention. The business card attached to it was from some law firm that specialized in divorces. That she had to chance taking, but it added a job for the night.

"He's at the door," Oscar said, his voice higher than a prepubescent boy's.

She locked the smaller safe again and headed back to the bathroom with one more glance back to make sure nothing was out of place. This hadn't been in her plan, but she was good at improv. She started formulating a plan as she heard the office door open and people entered.

"Get my villa ready and take off. You can take the boys with you," a voice she recognized as Victor's said.

"You want me to stay with you tonight?" a woman asked. "This afternoon wasn't enough time."

"I've got meetings. Take the night and the morning off."

From the way the door slammed, Victor's assistant was pissed about something, and it was probably with Victor. Reed listened as he poured a drink, the ice cubes rattling in the glass. From the whoosh of air, he must have fallen into his office chair.

"Let me talk to him," Victor said, and since there was no answer, he was clearly on the phone. There was an extension in the bathroom but she refrained from using it. "Then fucking tell him there's no way we're in on this." The phone slammed down.

The office door opened and closed again, and Reed waited to see if she had to take drastic measures. Her pulse was steady, but she damn well wanted to get out of there.

"Did you talk to Robert?" a man asked, but Reed didn't recognize the voice.

"Little Bobby's got himself in deep, and he's drowning in his own shit." There was movement but they stayed away from the bathroom door. "No way in hell is he stinking up this place to save his own ass."

"You told him that?"

"He's not answering the phone, but the fucker can't hide forever," Victor said, slamming something down. "Have you heard from my fucking wife?"

Reed smiled at how articulate this guy was. How in hell he'd gotten to where he was with Bellagio was a true mystery.

"Sofia isn't your problem right now. You have until tomorrow to clear your head, but then these guys want an answer, and I would highly suggest it's not no." Someone grunted and Reed figured it was Victor. "Get whatever's in your head worked out because this is no fucking joke. Having the big office won't save you from these guys."

"Let's go have a drink and mingle with all the beautiful people." The door opened and slammed shut again.

"Oscar?" she said softly once the office was empty. "I need to know who that was." She took a minute to breathe and to give them time to get to the elevator.

"I'll tell you later. Get out of there. You're clear."

"Great advice, my friend."

CHAPTER THREE

Y ou should call and ask a few questions," Brinley's mom, Wilma, said after congratulating Brinley on her new job. "This sounds like a great opportunity and you want to show you're eager."

"Disrupting someone's weekend might be too eager, Mom." After the interview and job offer, the rush to finish unpacking had been Brinley's main focus.

All the scattered boxes in her apartment were a visual analogue of her life. There had been a restlessness since Finn's birth that made her anxious for the first time in her life. Sure, she had worries like a normal person, but anxiety and its multitude of wonderful side effects, like lack of sleep, weren't her favorite things in life. Maybe once all this was put away where it belonged, the shit in her head would do the same thing.

"But don't worry. I'll get there extra early on Monday to show my eager-beaverness." She wiped down the inside of the cabinets before putting her dishes in. The sight of Finn's Spider-Man plate made her sigh in relief since he'd pointed at his paper plate during dinner and refused to eat.

"Are you sure you don't want me to come and take care of Finn for a couple of months while you two adjust to the new place and job?"

Her mom was the true definition of persistent—especially now that she was semiretired. "Mom, he has to get used to day care. We talked about this, remember?"

Wilma—a name her mother hated with a passion usually reserved for terrorists and people who were mean to cats—had run her own small accounting firm in Metairie, Louisiana, for over twenty-five years. The job paid well enough and afforded her the flexibility to work from home as needed. After Brinley's father abandoned them both when she was four, her mom raised her as a single parent, and the job flexibility had allowed them to spend plenty of time together.

But for years, Wilma had poured all her time and attention into her and her job, which had left no room for dating. And she and her mom were the best of friends, which meant her move to Vegas hadn't been met with any sort of enthusiasm, but her mother understood the necessity.

"I'm going to keep trying, so grin and don't try to stop me," Wilma said.

"Isn't that *grin and bear it*?" Finding the wineglasses was surely a sign the moving gods wanted her to take a break.

"My version is much more accurate. I miss you and my little guy."

"Believe me, we miss you too, and once we're settled, we'll have you out for as long as I can talk you into staying." She poured herself a glass of the white wine a courier had delivered with flowers and a note welcoming her to the Moroccan family. The gift surprised her, but it made her positive she'd made the right decision in accepting. "Is Crystal bothering you anymore?"

Finn's loser father, Jarrell, was locked away in Angola, but Jarrell's drughead mother, Crystal, kept threatening to take Brinley to court to prove Finn was her grandson. Brinley was sure they didn't actually want anything to do with Finn—the threat was a ploy to somehow extort money from either her or her mom. They both promised to stay away if she could help with their quote-unquote *bills*, code for *I want you to work hard to keep me in drugs*.

If she could have paid for them to stay away, she would've, but Jarrell's best talent was upping the ante, and a little money was never going to be enough. There was no way she wanted her son around Jarrell or any of his family. It was a miracle her little man was born healthy, considering the drugs Jarrell had consumed. She'd die before she allowed Finn around any of that.

"She came by last week, and one of my guys finally threatened to call the police, and she left quietly." Wilma stopped and laughed. "Well, as quiet as Crystal ever gets. According to my new associate, she smelled like she'd bathed in whiskey before she got there."

"Believe me, Mom, I love Finn more than life, but I've said it before and will say it again, we can both admit I really fucked up on this one. I'll regret that night until Finn can make his own decisions about knowing his father. Even then, I'll really have to think about telling him who the guy is."

"I don't regret anything, my darling. You and I had the same kind of luck—life didn't exactly deliver Prince Charming, but we both ended up with great kids. Concentrate on all the good stuff that's happening in your life, and forget about Jarrell and his family and all their scheming."

"Thanks, Mom," she said, missing her late night chats with her best friend. "And you can come whenever you want."

"I'll give you a couple of months to settle in. That should be enough time for me to feel comfortable leaving the office." Her mom was dedicated to her family, but her clients also got a lot of her attention. "Do you need anything before you get started? Are you set for money?"

"Mama, please." She raised her wineglass. "Your paying for our move out here was generous enough."

"You're my child," Wilma scoffed. "If I don't spend my money on you and Finn, who the hell am I going to spend it on?"

"We're fine, so make sure everyone's trained so you don't have to hurry home when you come for a visit." She finished her wine and went to put her glass in the sink. "I love you."

"Finish up, but don't stay up too long." Her mom's voice softened, and it made Brinley crave a hug. "I love you, my sweet girl, and I'll call you later."

She put the phone down and finished wiping the inside of the cabinets so she could unpack the last of her boxes. The memories she fought hard to forget always appeared when she talked about Jarrell and his mother. Her pregnancy had been horrific, and then Finn had sucked up all her free time. She wouldn't change the outcome or give Finn up, but she sometimes missed the fun of a night out with friends.

"Get used to a boring life for a while yet," she said as she started placing dishes away. "With any luck you'll remember what to do if you actually get hit with some excitement."

❖

Reed headed down to the casino floor and played slots while Victor sat at the bar at the highest stakes poker table and talked to one of his floor managers. It was after six and she had another stop to make, but the guy in Victor's office was still a mystery and she wanted a name from Oscar before she left. Victor and mystery guy had been talking about Robert Wallace, top dog at the Moroccan, and everyone in Vegas knew of Victor's hate for the putz in the big chair next door.

"Victor's visitor was Benito Lucassi." Oscar could see her but she could only hear him, and his disembodied voice answered one question but spawned others. She had to keep her expression from showing her surprise. Benito Lucassi wasn't someone she'd have put anywhere near Victor.

Benito ran one of the largest bookie operations in the city and was successful because he never tried to play favorites, no matter how much money was involved. Vegas was a place where any kind of bet could be placed, but there was still plenty of action that the gaming commission didn't control. Benito was the go-to guy for the Mob on the East Coast as well as the West Coast. Interesting that he was with Victor talking about the Moroccan CEO.

"Oscar," she said softly, since there was an elderly woman on each side of her.

"Yes, Master?"

"I'm glad you're learning," she said, tapping her chin with her middle finger.

"I'd tell you to bite me, but you'd probably enjoy it. What's up?"

"Keep an eye on our friend and I'll be back." She tapped the play button and hit a three-hundred-dollar score, so she printed the ticket and pocketed it.

"Are you sure you don't need me to come with you?"

"Don't lose Victor, and I'll be back. Throwing Benito into the mix has me curious, and I'd like to know if anyone else interesting shows up."

"Any insight on that?"

She shook her head as she headed for the entrance. "Benito has to be a middleman for someone, but I doubt he'd go out of his way for anyone in Vegas. That means there's someone in New York yanking on his leash, and we need to find out who that is. And why they're connected to Victor."

She had the valet bring her car around and she parked two blocks from the building where Victor's attorney had an office. The place looked to have about twenty floors, and the place she was after was on the eighteenth. There was a parking lot next door, and she walked through it to get to the back of the building. She left her jacket behind and carried a tool bag with a cable company logo printed on the side.

The utility box was right inside the service entrance, and it didn't take long for her to completely shut down the security system for the entire building by running a diagnostic and resetting it. Every job seemed to be a race against the clock, and this particular one could only last forty-five minutes. She pulled her ball cap lower and headed for the service elevator. The eighteenth floor was dark, but she walked the entire length of the hall to make sure she was alone. This time she wanted to leave absolutely no sign she'd been here.

At the end of the hall was a kitchen and a set of bathrooms, but it was the unmarked door to their left that got her attention. Since the law office took up the entire floor, it made sense that the building management would've made it easy for employees to access this area. The lock was simple and she took a few moments to acclimate to the darkness when she made it inside the offices.

The area she was in was open-plan and full of desks—assistants and paralegals. That meant the files wouldn't be far, and she quietly opened doors until she found a room with row after row of filing cabinets. It took her twenty minutes to find Victor's and Sofia's names. Holding a penlight in her mouth, she removed only the information that pertained to their divorce, and nothing more.

All she needed now was access to a computer. "Let's see who doesn't follow company protocol," she said, searching for a computer that hadn't been shut down for the night. All the ones in the open area were off, so she headed down the hall and stopped when she thought she heard voices. She crouched beside a wall and listened. It definitely wasn't a radio.

"You worry too much," a woman said.

"I love sex as much as anyone, but I don't want to die because of it," a man replied.

Reed smiled and moved closer to where the voices were coming from. The size of the office suggested this somewhat reluctant participant was one of the attorneys, but not a partner. The sound of a zipper gave her the opportunity to look in, but she was careful. No point in getting caught looking like a voyeur.

"Fuck," the guy said.

"That's exactly what I had in mind." The woman was the aggressor, and from the way the guy was moaning, she was getting her way. "You want me, baby?"

"Fuck yeah."

They weren't visible from the hallway, but whoever this guy was, his secretary's computer was on. She sat down and typed quietly but quickly. Her search yielded quite a few results, which she sent to a private folder on a public computer at one of the branches of the public library, which Oscar had rigged for her use. The place didn't have any security except a nighttime alarm with no cameras, so it was easy to break in if she needed immediate access to information gathered during an op.

"Baby, you're so hard," the woman said, and Reed hoped the guy had some stamina.

"Fuck yeah," he said, and Reed smiled. Hopefully the guy was more articulate in court and didn't just repeat inane things over and over. She finished sending what she needed and got up to leave.

"You want me?" The guy grunted at the question but didn't answer her. "You want me more than Lucan?"

That question stopped Reed. The likelihood he was talking about Lucan Terzo was like winning the thirty million dollar progressive at the slots, but hey, someone had to hit it every so often. The opportunity was worth the risk, and she dropped to her stomach and slid to the door. Her phone recorded action on the sofa, and she made sure to focus on the faces. If this was Lucan Terzo's wife, it was a chip Reed would save for the future.

"Harder, baby," the woman said, and the man grunted in response.

Reed shot a bit more footage, then calmly walked out. There was only one thing left to do for the night.

"What's happening, Oscar?" she asked when she got back in the car.

"He's still drinking at the bar. The older son came by to see him and left with a girl and a lot of cash. I think Victor's hoping for father of the year."

"He should be so lucky. Although that wouldn't pay very well." She drove back to the valet at Bellagio and headed to her room. It amazed her that people had children for all the wrong reasons, and the kids were always the ones who were thrown away and forgotten when they no longer served a purpose.

She knew from experience that from the moment you were tossed aside, only the strong survived. She flopped onto her bed and let herself remember…

Juvenile Court 1994, Las Vegas, Nevada. The room was packed with people who in no way appeared happy. Rebel Jones sat and swung her legs, since her feet didn't touch the floor, and took a bite of the peanut-butter sandwich the woman who drove her away from her mom had given her. All the crying, screaming, and kicking hadn't done any good, so she sat and waited. Her mom had probably figured out she was gone by now and would come looking for her.

"Do you want some milk?" the African American woman who'd told her she had to go with her asked, as she opened her big purse and took out a thermos. "I have another sandwich if you're still hungry."

"When's my mama coming?" The lady said she needed to tell the truth, so she might as well try since they'd driven around so much there was no way Rebel could find her way back now. The only place she really ever went was the small store close to their apartment to buy cereal and milk when her mama had money. Sometimes, though, her mama forgot because she slept a lot.

"Sweetie, your mom's at the hospital. She's really sick but she'd be proud of you for calling 9-1-1. You saved her life."

"I couldn't wake her up, but when she's up, she'll come for me. She needs me to take care of her." The sandwich made her thirsty so she accepted a cup of milk. She didn't know what peanut butter was, but it was good. All they ate was cereal, and burgers sometimes, but her mama had told her not to complain. She didn't know what *hell* was, but that's what Mama said she had to pay when she forgot and did complain. She didn't like hell.

"Rebel Jones," an old man dressed in black said loudly.

The woman raised her hand and screwed the cup back on the thermos. They went through the fence at the front and the woman with her started talking. "I recommend foster care placement until Ms. Jones is finished with mandated rehab. The minor child was living in squalor, and there was no food in the house. My office rushed all the welfare inquiries and the minor hasn't been enrolled in school, which puts her a year behind. This is a real case of neglect, Your Honor."

Rebel figured they were talking about her, but none of the words made sense. All she could do was try and remember for later.

"Rebel, do you go to school?" the old man asked.

She wasn't sure what that was so she shook her head. "When's my mama coming to get me?"

"Not for a while, but we're going to take care of you until she's better." The old man spoke softly and smiled. "Go ahead and place her with an available family and we'll review in six months."

He called some other kid's name before she could ask about her mama again, and the woman took her hand and walked out. They went to a big office next door where everything was beige, and that night she was in a place with lots of kids, beds, and bad food. Rebel waited until it was dark until she cried, but she did it quietly. The big woman who'd given her a big T-shirt to sleep in had told her she'd be punished if she was too loud or kept asking about her mama.

"Please, Mama, come find me," she whispered and didn't repeat it when someone close by yelled for her to shut up. She clamped her jaws together and tried not to think about how alone she was. *Please, she thought, too afraid to open her mouth.*

Six months had turned into thirteen years, and the foster families until she'd turned nine were too many to remember, and then it was a state-run facility for kids no one wanted. Once she turned eighteen the state didn't want her either, and they'd put her out with a high school diploma and a trash bag of whatever she owned. It took exactly three months for Rebel Jones to get arrested for armed robbery, and she again became a ward of the state.

Those four years of prison weren't a total waste. They were a better education than all the years of school, and when she was paroled, she killed Rebel Jones and buried her right alongside the life she could've had with her mother. She became Reed Gable, as well as the dozens of other identities she cultivated, and getting caught wasn't something she'd ever let happen again.

CHAPTER FOUR

A re you back?" Oscar's voice came through the Earwig, and she stopped her spiral down memory lane.

"I am, and I'm on my way down. I stopped by my room to pick up the bag I needed."

Dwelling on things no one could change was useless, but she still missed that kid who hoped to be rescued from the shit life she'd endured. Only problem was, she had no idea who her father was, and her hooker and junkie mother had fucking OD'd the night her caseworker, Mrs. Speck, put her in the system. Eventually, she learned the only person who was going to save her was herself. And she had.

Thankfully, the elevator didn't take long and she mentally reviewed the rest of her night. All that was left was getting to Victor without leaving a trace.

"Any problems?"

"Not a one. Did he go up yet?" She stopped to admire Chihuly's Fiori di Como on the lobby ceiling, and to make sure nothing strange jumped out at her.

"He's still sitting in the high-stakes area with a woman who isn't his assistant, and they're really cozy."

She headed for the slots near the bar and put in a hundred. She was starting to see there was so much more to Victor than the cheating. He was in deep with something much bigger, and she wanted to know what it was. He wouldn't be around much longer to clarify everything she wanted to know about him, but the download from the attorney's office would be a start. A quick glance at his position gave her the scenario she needed for what came next, and she smiled as Victor discreetly handed the woman a small bag.

"What room, Oscar?"

"It's one of the so-called villas out back. They're short a few dozen rooms for true villa status, but that's never stopped Vegas from making everything grandiose. It's more secluded, and it sounds like he enjoys his privacy." She heard Oscar typing something, so she pressed the max pay button a few times. "It's number four, and I'll guide you whenever you're ready."

"I need to beat him there."

Victor and the woman were ramping up, so Reed stood and cashed out. It was time to give Sofia what she wanted. All she could hope for was that the result would still be what Sofia wanted when it was done. Death wasn't something she could undo, and Sofia changed her mind as often as an adolescent.

"Head for the spa."

The path Oscar led her on was one where he could manipulate the cameras along the way, so she didn't walk too fast. She didn't run into anyone else, which was a blessing. Anyone with a comp for this area was either at a high-stakes table, or a private one.

The villa Victor had reserved was situated down a flagstone walk in the dense garden and had a private pool. All the lights were dimmed, and a bucket of champagne chilled next to the bed. "Very romantic, this guy," she said as she entered the bathroom.

All couples in which a guy in the late stages of middle age was paired with a very young beautiful woman had one thing in common. It centered around a small blue pill, and she was willing to bet her ten percent of this job that Victor had some. Sure enough, the bottle of pills was right next to the champagne. Classy.

"Are there flowers?" Oscar asked. "The happy couple is getting close to the spa."

"Champagne and Viagra, buddy, but no flowers," she said, emptying Victor's bottle and replacing them with some from her bag. She put in the same number in case Victor was a guy who noticed small details.

"Ah, the combination of champions." Oscar kept typing and hummed even though it drove her insane, and she knew he knew it. "They should reach the door in about two minutes."

"A lot of his stuff is here, which means this is where he comes when he's supposedly working." The wingback overlooking the pool was in a dark spot so she turned it slightly, sat down, and waited.

"It'll be like dying at home then."

She chuckled. "I'm going to deliver every man's dream."

"Robert Redford, when he was twenty-five?" Oscar said, but the door opening prevented her from answering.

"Get on your knees and show Big Daddy how much you missed him," Victor said.

Reed almost gagged. Big Daddy? Really?

"Let me share my candy with you," the girl said as she sucked the head of his dick, then spread some of the powder he'd given her on it. She massaged it in with her finger, making Victor laugh. "You promise what you said?"

"Yeah, baby. As soon as the bitch gets back, it's over. The guy will make it look like an accident." Victor headed for the bathroom before the woman could get her mouth back on him.

Nothing like a blue helper to get the magic wand to respond, Reed thought. The woman wet her finger, dipped it in the powder, and rubbed it on her gums before stripping her dress off and heading to the bed. Whoever this was didn't have a problem with Victor killing his wife, but sometimes whatever you threw out into the universe boomeranged on you tenfold. Victor was about to learn that lesson. Killing him before he killed his wife might bring repercussions, but there was no way to link it back to her. Hopefully Sofia had a great attorney.

Once the happy couple were in the bedroom, Reed put on some latex gloves and got what she needed from her bag. She wondered if Victor was surprised how fast his last erection came up, but it sounded like he didn't care as the sound of skin slapping on skin started in earnest. He didn't last very long before he started gurgling slightly, and then there was silence.

"Baby?" the woman said, but there was no response. "Come on, this isn't funny."

Reed stood in the doorway and cracked her neck as the woman pounded on Victor's shoulders, but he wasn't moving. Victor's date was now trapped under him, making Reed's next step easier. She came in and pressed her fingers to her lips when the woman opened her mouth as if to scream. The gun in her hand must've been deterrent enough for the sound to die in her throat. "Spread your legs for me."

"What?" the woman asked, not taking her eyes off the gun.

"Slowly spread your legs, and don't make me say it again." She slid her finger into the woman, next to Victor's penis, and inserted the pill that would dissolve quickly. Another pill went on the tip of the small dildo she'd brought for Victor. The rest wouldn't take long at all, so she got to work staging the scene.

Reed replaced the bag of coke Victor had given his date in the casino with the one she'd brought, which was coke mixed with fentanyl. She entered the bedroom again and sat by the bed. The woman's eyes were open but they were vacant of life, and Victor wasn't breathing. When she felt no pulse, Reed opened the woman's purse and got her information from her wallet.

It was Victor's bad luck that the twentysomething beauty in his bed was really nineteen. The address on her driver's license bordered an affluent area that boasted plenty of the headliners on the marquees around town. Someone was definitely going to miss this girl and be pissed she was dead. She was young, but the address meant she was in no way an escort.

She paused and stared at the hollow faces and reflected on her feelings. These people were dead by her hand, and yet she felt nothing. The part of herself that should've had some sense of shock or horror had started its slow death the day that old judge and Mrs. Speck spoke a lot of words she didn't understand, then dropped her somewhere she didn't want to be. All those lost years had emptied her soul and left her only with the keen drive to survive and to never be the victim again.

Granted, plenty of people went through foster care and came out to find success in business, or maybe a marriage, and went their whole lives without killing a spider, much less a person. That was true, but she'd chosen this life for the fast money and to have enough to take care of herself. She probably needed to spend time on someone's couch spilling her problems. No shrink would ever understand that she'd do whatever she had to in order to keep from relying on anyone ever again, and that playing on the far side of the law gave her a rush no desk job ever would.

The young woman's eyes were open, as if she was staring into some unknown abyss, but she had only herself to blame for a death that was years too early. When you got mixed up with the wrong people, shit went bad. That's how the world worked, and yeah, it was a shame, but it was part of the job. No witnesses. What the hell was a nineteen-year-old doing with Victor, and where the hell had he met her?

Facial recognition unlocked the young woman's phone, and Reed scrolled through the calls, texts, and contacts to see if some answer popped out at her. Every single message was the typical bullshit people this young exchanged, with the exception of one thread. From the number of explicit texts she'd shared with Caterina Terzo, they were much more than phone buddies. This woman had been in way over her head and probably hadn't even realized it.

She stopped at one message and reread it four times before photographing it. Fuck but this job would have some complications if it found its way back to her.

Make sure you get him to commit on Sofia and I'll handle it from there. Do whatever to get the asshole to make the call, and I'll make it worth it.

The Terzo family was targeting Sofia, but Reed doubted it had anything to do with the state of her marriage to Victor or any concern over Victor's bedmates. Reed had done work for the Terzo family, and the old man, Francesco, had raised two pit vipers. Their rule was simple: anything or anyone that came up against them got eliminated.

The text message made her take more time than she'd planned to check the rest of the device, and she searched Victor's as well. His led to a number Victor was supposed to call to solve his divorce issues without an attorney, but his call history showed he hadn't committed yet. She wrote the number down and placed the phone back in Victor's pants.

She glanced outside. "Oscar, can I move?" she asked from outside the door.

"There's a couple headed to five, so walk slowly to avoid them. I need to hit the next camera."

She made her way back to the elevator that led to the room where Oscar was waiting. Even if someone saw her, they'd describe Bill Smith, and that person didn't exist. The only thing she wanted now was to head home and relax before she had to deal with Sofia. From what Victor and Caterina had planned, it might be the smart play to get Sofia's family involved even if they had no real presence in Vegas. Victor was dead but that didn't mean the Terzo family might not still want Sofia dead.

When she took Sofia's job thinking it'd be a quick challenge, she'd had no way of knowing all this crap. Whatever the reason for the Terzo family's interest, Sofia would have to figure it out while she was under the watchful eye of her father and most probably the police.

"It's done?" Oscar asked.

"Like I said, I gave him every man's wish. He came and went," she said and Oscar laughed. "It's done." She picked up the phone and punched the number on her valet ticket. "Could you bring my car around please?"

Oscar would stay and deal with monitoring the response. She was curious to see how the cops handled the investigation since Victor was someone people didn't expect to die with his dick in a nineteen-year-old who was helping him plan his wife's murder. His public image revolved around charitable events and business organizations. But while it didn't matter to her how her current employer stayed alive, Sofia was going to be interested in a detailed account before she started spending her inheritance.

"Thanks for all your help, buddy, and call me if something goes south." She kissed Oscar on the top of his head and smiled. Oscar would handle the luggage when he left. "I'll be home by tonight."

"Relax," Oscar said, taking her hand. "We've got something else at the end of this week, and you have to have a clear head."

"It's always something, but no matter what, it's not anything we can't handle." It was true—and the secret to success was stopping when you didn't believe that with your whole heart.

The silence of the room under the warehouse was comforting, and a refuge Reed needed to put her thoughts on hold. It was something she'd craved from an early age, but until recently she'd never had a chance to really let her guard down. She closed her eyes and took a few deep breaths, but no meditation known to mankind would keep the past from haunting her.

The fear that had gripped her for so long was something she fought against, but it was always simmering right out of her reach, taunting her. She was determined to beat it, though, which is why she loved jobs like Victor Madison. That scrawny kid from all those years ago would've never had the cojones to pull it off, and every time she did, it was like a dagger through the heart of the fears of that pathetic mutt no one wanted.

"Stop wasting your time on dead subjects," she said out loud and opened her eyes. If she didn't regain control, every single idiot who'd ever touched her without consent, beaten her, or tried to take what little she had would parade through her mind in an effort to chip away at her sanity.

The facade of Bill Smith from Oregon didn't take long to wipe away, so she changed into her jeans and white T-shirt and tried her best to decompress. Victor was dead, but there was still work to do. She opened the first ledger and started going through it as she made a peanut-butter-and-jelly sandwich. Peanut butter was the only thing aside from cold milk that she'd kept from her first day in foster care.

It took most of the night, but she managed to crack all of Victor's codes and had to whistle at the total. "My, my, Victor, you've been a productive little bastard, haven't you?" The fucker had to have been skimming, along with all the screwing around he was doing. No one accumulated ninety-six million running the Bellagio alone.

Her contract with Sofia said ten percent of whatever Reed could find, and she'd found a fuck-ton. Whatever he'd done or wherever he got it wasn't her problem. All she cared about was the 7.2 million dollar payday, and the 2.4 million for Oscar. Their deal had always been a seventy-five–twenty-five split, since Oscar never ventured out of the shadows. In the beginning he would've been happy with ten percent, but he made her life so much easier that she'd talked him into the larger cut.

Sofia would be set with her eighty-six million, plus whatever Victor owned legitimately. The house alone was probably worth more than five million, plus the life insurance, and the perks coming from Bellagio. If she wasn't satisfied with her take, that, too, wasn't Reed's problem. Once the transfers were made, and with Oscar's wizardry, they were untraceable. It was time to move on.

"Hello," Sofia said, and the noise in the background meant she was somewhere public. In case the police checked Sofia's phone, Reed was spoofing a number tied to a clothing store Sofia frequented. She probably should've waited until the police had contacted Sofia, but hopefully the warning would prepare her for what was coming.

"I'm sorry for your loss, Mrs. Madison, but your gains might bring you comfort," Reed said softly, using a program that would bounce the signal around the globe, since she didn't feel like leaving her safe room. "I'll call you in two days."

"Wait," Sofia said but didn't raise her voice. "I'm coming home as soon as I can manage it, so we can meet sooner."

"Two days, Mrs. Madison, and again, I'm sorry for your loss."

She hung up, moved to the bed, and turned the lights off, bringing the room to total darkness. The small bear her mom had given her was under her hand, and she took a few moments to think about the woman who'd given birth to her.

Penny Jones had been a simple country girl from Kentucky who'd come to Vegas with her best friend, thinking they'd make a fortune working for a casino. It took them six months to fall victim to the city's multitude of vices, and to continue to pay their way and avoid going back to their boring lives in the hills, they had to start turning tricks.

To dull the pain and shame of too many men, Penny had turned to drugs, but somewhere along the way she'd gotten sloppy, and pregnant. Reed had no idea who her father was, but she'd loved Penny despite the abuse and neglect. She hadn't known till much later that the day she'd gone before the judge for the first time, Penny was already dead. That was the only reason she'd forgiven the case worker responsible for the hell her childhood became. Not that Penny had been Mary Poppins, but at least she'd had a home.

The phone she'd used that day rang and she sat up, wondering who was calling the number. "Yeah."

"Hi, baby," a woman said and she could hear slots in the background. "You promised you'd call."

"Jayden?" She turned the lamp on and swung her legs off the bed.

"Want to come out and play?"

"I actually had to leave, but my sister took my place. If the offer's still good, she might want to play with you."

"Really? Is she like you?" Jayden asked and Reed couldn't be sure, but Jayden sounded relieved.

"We're twins, so it's like we're the same person, and we both like beautiful blondes."

"It's your money, baby, and if you have her number I'll call her."

Five minutes later another phone rang, and Jayden sounded even more seductive. Her tone was enough to get Reed to change clothes and head out the door, anxious to blow off some of her pent-up energy.

She parked her car herself and pocketed the keycard to the room upgrade Oscar had gotten her. The bar close to the high-stakes tables was where Jayden was waiting, and Reed watched her nurse a glass of wine as if she was using it to pass the time. The dress Jayden was wearing made Reed want to peel it off slowly.

"Jayden," she said as she sat next to her and raised a finger toward the bartender.

"Hey, you guys really do look alike in the face," Jayden said, putting her hand on Reed's thigh. "And don't tell your brother, but I'm more into women."

"Lucky me." She stopped to order a vodka on the rocks and pointed to Jayden's glass. "You want another one?"

"More than one makes me clumsy, and I don't want to be that tonight."

"Never mind," Reed said to the bartender as Jayden's hand moved higher. She dropped some money on the bar and helped Jayden to her feet. "Let's get more comfortable."

They walked to the elevator and she held Jayden's hand. These were the only kinds of encounters she allowed herself, since she'd never have enough to offer anyone except the few hours it'd take for the need for human contact to be satisfied.

The suite was high enough that they could keep the curtains open, but low enough to give a good view of the Strip. She put her hands on the first button of her shirt, and Jayden stopped her.

"Please, can I do it?"

Reed dropped her hands and nodded.

"What's your name?"

"Rebel," she said and smiled at Jayden's arched eyebrow. "My mother's idea of a joke, I guess."

"I like it," Jayden said as she slowly moved down her chest, undoing buttons and kissing exposed skin. "Can I admit something to you?"

"If it's that you're a cop, you're a really friendly one."

"No, but I'm new to this." She stopped at her belt, tucking a few fingers into the front of her pants. "The fact that I'm getting to fuck you doesn't seem fair."

What an interesting thing to say, Reed thought as Jayden tugged her toward a chair by the window and gently pushed her into it. "Unfair how?"

"Baby, have you glanced in a mirror lately? I'd do you for free."

"You'll be successful if you decide to stick to this," she said as Jayden moved to turn some music on and started to dance for her. "You're really good at flattery."

"If you don't think you're good-looking, I don't believe you."

Jaden dropped the straps of her dress, and it fell to the floor when she wiggled her hips. The sight of the black underwear made Reed lean back and spread her legs. The woman was beautiful in the curvy feminine way she loved.

"The same could definitely be said of you." She raised her hand and held it out. "Come here."

Jayden stepped out of her dress and heels to walk over and knelt when she was between Reed's legs. Without asking, she unbuckled Reed's belt and unzipped her pants. "Do you want me, baby?"

She'd paid good money for the conversation that was totally contrived, but right now, she didn't give a shit that none of this was real. The relief she needed was calling the shots. "Yes, I do," she said, wrapping her hand around Jayden's blond hair and pulling her head back to kiss her.

"Lift for me," Jayden said when their lips came apart. She tugged at the top of Reed's pants. The way Jayden yanked them down almost convinced her that Jayden was enjoying this, money or no. Jayden left Reed's shirt on, but spread her legs wider and put her mouth on her without another word.

Jayden sucked her clit hard enough to get her attention, and she put her hand on the back of Jayden's head. She might've been new to the escort game, but Jayden really knew what she was doing. "Fuck," she said, suddenly winded as Jayden stopped sucking and started making flicking motions with her tongue. It was enough for Reed to feel the orgasm start to build to the point of no return. "Harder." Talking during sex wasn't something she was comfortable with.

"Don't worry, I'm going to take good care of you," Jayden said and went back to what she was doing.

"Goddamn." Reed came hard enough to stop herself from thinking. That was a rarity.

Jayden sat back on her heels and smiled before moving to straddle her hips. Reed smiled back before Jayden leaned in and kissed her softly as if they were lovers. She froze at first, not used to such intimacy, but Jayden was so nice she relaxed into it. The kiss came to an end, and Jayden leaned back and pressed herself into Reed's abdomen, apparently seeking her own relief.

"I'll give your brother some of his money back if you touch me."

Reed reached around Jayden, unfastened her bra, and kept her eyes on Jayden's chest. The woman was perfect, which wasn't a strange thing in Vegas since there were more plastic surgeons in the city than showgirls, but all of Jayden's body seemed totally unenhanced.

"And where do you want me to touch you?" she asked as she pinched Jayden's nipple and pulled her forward.

"I want you to fuck me."

She stood with Jayden wrapped around her and laid her on the bed, taking a moment to look at her. Jayden really was new to this, and for some reason she hoped she found another way to support herself. She wasn't stupid enough to have feelings for an escort, but somewhere in her brain she couldn't help but think about what her life would be if she'd had to resort to this.

"What's wrong? Come on, baby," Jayden said, holding her hand up. "You don't have to be shy—I want you to touch me."

Brought back to the moment, she hovered over Jayden and sucked her nipple in as she put her hand between her legs. Jayden was dripping wet, and the feel of her slick pussy was a major sign she wasn't just playing at her role of devoted lover. "Is this what you had in mind?"

Jayden nodded and held her other breast as if begging her to suck on the other hardening nipple. "In my bag…please."

This woman had a talent for saying interesting things, so she rolled off her to see what else she had planned. She lay on her back and watched Jayden head for the purse she'd dropped by the door. There was little chance Jayden would do anything to harm her, but she tensed in case she had to move fast.

Jayden held her hands behind her back as she knelt on the bed, and Reed steeled herself not to overreact. She almost laughed at herself when Jayden showed her the harness with the flesh colored dildo attached. She shifted so Jayden could slide the harness up and over her hips, and the look in Jayden's eyes suggested just how much she wanted to be fucked.

"You ready for me, baby?" Jayden asked as she stroked the cock and pressed the base down on Reed's clit, making her exhale. If she didn't take a few deep breaths, she was going to embarrass herself by coming too soon.

"Let me take care of you," Reed said as she placed her hands on Jayden's hips.

Jayden didn't need a lot of encouragement, and she moved up and drew the head to her sex, rubbing it against her own clit. Jayden threw her head back and closed her eyes. She really was beautiful. "If you want, you can use your hands instead, but I really want your cock in me," Jayden said, but she was already tilting her hips forward, taking in the entire length. When it was in, she stopped and took a breath like she needed a minute to get accustomed to the fullness.

"You okay?" Reed asked as Jayden threaded their fingers together and gazed down at her.

"Feels good," Jayden said and gasped softly when Reed pumped her hips. Then Jayden started moving. There really wasn't much in life sexier than a woman claiming her pleasure, and Jayden certainly seemed to know how to do that.

Reed let go of Jayden's hands so she could slide hers up Jayden's body to her breasts. She pinched Jayden's nipples, and the action sped Jayden's hips, but Reed rolled them over before Jayden could get carried away. With Jayden under her, she fucked her hard while holding herself up and off her. She liked looking at the ecstasy on her face, the passion of a woman being taken. Control in all situations was paramount.

The way Jayden wrapped her legs around her hips and locked her feet behind her back made Reed speed her movements. They both came at the same time, and Jayden pulled her down, seeming to want her covering her.

"You're incredible," Jayden said as she combed her fingers through Reed's hair.

"You're pretty incredible yourself, and thank you for your time." Reed rolled off her and sat on the side of the bed.

"I can spend the night," Jayden said, pressing against her back. "Your brother was nice enough to pay for it."

"Actually, go ahead and keep the room and get some sleep, but I've got to go."

Jayden appeared to understand their time together had come to an end, and that Reed really wasn't a big cuddler. She backed off and pulled the sheet over herself.

"Thanks for everything."

Reed headed for the bathroom with her clothes in her hands. She wanted to get dressed and get out of there as soon as she could. The lure of being at home with nothing to do or think about was the only thing on her mind now that Jayden had drained her. The girl was sweet, and that kind of sweetness didn't belong in the world Reed lived in.

"Will you call me again?" Jayden asked when Reed stepped out of the bathroom and sat on the bed, about to put her shoes on.

"I've got your number, but you should think about doing something else. I could be way off, but you don't seem cut out for this life. Quit before it sucks the good out of you," she said and tolerated the kiss Jayden placed on her neck.

"Thanks for worrying about me, baby, but this is all I've got." Jayden stood naked before her and was truly stunning. "There's no other job I can get that'll pay me enough to keep my car and condo."

"Then keep my number in case you need something." The comment came out before she could censor it.

"You're sweet, but I'll be okay. I've got someone watching out for me." Jayden stopped her by claiming her shoe, then tugged her from the bed and back into the bathroom, where she started the shower. "Let's enjoy ourselves a little more before you've got to go."

"Sure," Reed said, but she was anxious to leave. The good thing, though, was she was going to walk out of here without any extra baggage. Whatever possessed her to offer Jayden anything would go back in its box, and she'd go back to her unencumbered life.

After she dressed again, she put another five hundred by Jayden's purse and left without saying good-bye. She could still sense Jayden on her skin and in her head, but they'd never see each other again. If Jayden really did stick with this, then hopefully there would only be boring accountants and the like in her future. No one deserved a life like Penny's.

CHAPTER FIVE

I'm so sorry," Brinley said, mortified she was twenty minutes late on her first day. "I didn't expect this much traffic on a Monday morning."

"Don't sweat it." Naomi handed her a cup of coffee. "Usually Mondays are dead unless you take the Strip, that's always a mess, but the cops are still next door jamming traffic. There's enough rubbernecking out there to make you think this town is full of old gossip hounds."

"Did something happen?" The kitchen was fully stocked so she dropped a bagel in the toaster before adding cream to her coffee.

"I forget you're like me, and it's cartoons in the morning instead of the news," Naomi said and laughed. "The head guy next door was found dead in a private villa with a rubber dick in his ass, and his dick in a woman who wasn't his wife. They got too carried away with their partying and OD'd by putting drugs where you really shouldn't have any, not prescribed by a doctor."

"That was on the news? The media here must be way more progressive if that's how they reported the story."

"The maid found them, called her supervisor, who called security, who called management." Naomi ticked the list off on her fingers. "There's no way it stays quiet after all those people got a peek at the dead pervert, which complicates things if the cops or the family want to keep it quiet."

"I guess there really are no more secrets these days." She spread cream cheese on her bagel and followed Naomi to their space. "I'll be shocked if we don't see pictures soon."

"Victor Madison was the shit in this town, as in a big deal, but you're right. Vegas—for some things, anyway—is still very much a small town. Rumors fly fast, especially about someone who liked to rub your face in the fact you weren't him." Naomi snapped her fingers and cocked her head. "Mr. *I'm the shit* couldn't have picked a more humiliating way to die."

"How old was the girl?" Brinley sat and started changing the passwords on the computer per IT's instructions.

"Nineteen, but my contact over there said she could've passed for thirty. That's probably what fooled Victor, but that's still going to be a problem for the grieving Madison family."

She'd done so much research before uprooting Finn and bringing him here, so this news on her first day of work wasn't welcome. Not what she had in mind as a safe environment for him. Maybe she would feel safer outside the city, but a year's lease would be hard to break now. Yet another thing to feel guilty about.

"Did he have kids?"

"Two boys, and the older one was about the same age as the dead girl." Naomi sat across from her and started sorting the stack of receipts someone appeared to have dropped haphazardly on her desk. "We'll finish our gossiping later. All these weekend deposits can't wait."

They worked for two hours, talking occasionally about their own kids and life in general, and finished entering deposits and footing the books from the weekend haul. Brinley found the numbers staggering but knew they also accounted for the reason the pay was so good, so she wasn't complaining. Before lunch their boss, Dean, came in and sat in the only extra chair they had in the small space.

"Are you settling in okay?" he asked Brinley.

"Naomi's been the best, and thanks again for this opportunity." She meant it, but Dean appeared to be the kind of guy who thrived on a lot of compliments, so she wouldn't scrimp on them.

"Just remember to make me look fabulous and we'll be good," he said, slapping his hands together. "The top guys want a complete audit of the books from our usual accountants, and I want you to make sure everything is in order before it goes to them. I'm going to hand off your day-to-day stuff for the next few weeks and give you two that responsibility. Do you think you can handle it?"

"Sure," Naomi said, shooting Brinley a subtle warning look. "It's been a while since I've done an audit, but I'm sure we can do it."

"I did a couple at my last job." Brinley tapped the eraser of her pencil against her thigh, already thinking of the work plan. "Are you sure you don't want to bring someone from an outside firm in, even just for the pre-work? That's what most folks like doing, especially in case you're looking for wrongdoing."

Dean raised his hands and laughed loudly, but it sounded forced. "Whoa, no one said anything about wrongdoing."

His reaction made Brinley think he was hiding something, and it definitely didn't answer the question about why they weren't bringing in someone from the outside. She glanced at Naomi, interested in her reaction since she had more experience with Dean. Maybe this was his normal, but her gut said otherwise.

"We'll gather the information and start today after lunch," Naomi said, her voice steady. "Let us finish the weekend stuff since we're already in the middle of it. Whoever you put on that will appreciate not having to backtrack."

"Great. I've already gathered all the stuff you need to begin. I'm moving you to a larger space, and the faster you finish, the better." Dean stood and made a rolling motion with his index finger. "Think two weeks is enough time?"

"If it's just the two of us, it'll be a stretch, but we should have some preliminary reports by then," Brinley said, wanting him out of their office so she could talk to Naomi.

"And this audit," Dean said with his hand on the doorknob, "is strictly need to know. You report to me and no one else."

"You got it, boss," Naomi said.

They were both quiet after the door closed, and as if by mutual consent, they waited to make sure Dean wasn't outside listening in. She opened her mouth and Naomi shook her head and discreetly pointed at her ear. "Do you want to tackle the journal entries from Sunday? I've already started on Saturday."

"Yeah, then let's go to lunch before we have to move. Hopefully, wherever our new digs are, we'll have a nice big window with a view."

"Here's hoping," Naomi said.

Brinley wondered what the hell this was about. Had she made a terrible mistake in moving to Sin City after all?

❖

Caterina Terzo opened her eyes when she felt a shadow across her face. The early morning was the only time she indulged in some sunbathing, before her forty laps in the large family pool. Everyone on the staff knew better than to disturb her, and she held her hand over her brow when she saw her brother Lucan looming over her.

"Get out of my sun," she said, not liking the expression on Lucan's face. Her brother was quite the alarmist over things that always seemed to be her fault, and the habit sent her father into a lather at times.

"What the fuck were you thinking?" Lucan asked, not moving. "I haven't gone to Papa yet, but you better come up with a good story if you don't want him to slap you back down the ranks."

"Am I supposed to know what the hell you're talking about?" She sat up and put her shirt over her suit. The last few days had been busy, and she hadn't heard from any of her crew that there was a problem big enough to warrant this kind of reaction.

"Victor Madison's dead," Lucan said, biting off each word like *she'd* shot the fucker on the Strip. "They found him in bed with some girl, and if it's who I'm thinking, she's yours. If that's true, you better pray nothing they found with the stupid little bitch can be traced back to you."

"She's dead?" The young woman was one of many, but she needed her alive.

"Don't give me that you don't know shit. Dammit, Caterina, we needed Victor for the deal we've got going. Killing him is going to bring heat we don't need while we're trying to ramp up. If Papa gets blamed, he's going to want to take it out on someone."

"I'm not a fucking idiot. The *girl*, as you put it, had a job, and it wasn't fucking dying. All I needed her to do was to get Victor to commit to offing Sofia, and then you could've named your price on what we're after. Believe me, blackmail was the fastest and easiest way to get him to do whatever we wanted. There was no way he wanted to go down for Sofia's murder, and if he'd used my guy with the help of my friend who died with him, that's what we would've had." She stood and went inside for her phone. "She had a date Friday night, and she said she was close."

"That makes sense," Lucan said as he followed her into her rooms. "Our contact with LVMPD said Victor's dick was about to rot inside her. They had a bitch of a time getting them apart. You think Sofia offed him?"

"Sofia probably wanted to, but her father knows better. He's got no muscle here, and he doesn't need a war back home. She's not stupid enough to go against her father." She turned the TV on for him and headed for a shower. "Do you know anything about what happened?"

"All I know is he died with his dick in someone, and a fake one up his ass. Who knew Victor was so progressive."

"Believe me, I'm sure he would've sucked his own dick to keep the girl interested." She picked a suit and stopped before closing the door. "Wait for me?"

"Sure, but we have to break this to Papa. I'm going to have to go back and talk to Little Bobby. I'm positive whatever plan he had centered around Victor picking up some major slack."

"This could be an opportunity for us."

He sat on her bed and settled in front of the TV. "How do you figure?"

"If we can influence the selection of Victor's replacement, we'll be set for years." She closed the door, positive Lucan would take credit for that brilliant idea, but it wasn't worth the effort of getting mad, considering they had bigger issues. She'd have to pay her respects to the girl's family. She wouldn't have kept her around after they got what they wanted out of Victor, but the kid didn't deserve this. Her death, though, brought about some new problems if her association with Victor could be traced to Caterina.

Lucan was half asleep by the time she was ready, and they headed for the other wing of the large house. Their parents had added it in an effort to keep them both at home. The slight separation gave them the privacy they wanted while still keeping them all under one roof.

The dining room overlooked the pool and the mountains, and there was always someone over for every meal, no matter the day. Francesco Terzo thought he'd earned the right not to have to go into the office every day, so the office came to him. He was an understanding man unless something—or someone—screwed with his plans.

"Good morning," she said, kissing her mother's cheek first, then her father's.

"Do you want to explain what all this is about?" Francesco pointed at the television. Pictures of Victor at various events flashed across the screen. "Start talking, either of you."

Caterina poured herself some coffee and sat next to him. "Give me an hour and I'll be able to answer that, but I didn't have anything to do with this. I know how important Victor was to us." She knew his question was directed at her. Lucan never made a move without their father knowing first. He didn't have the spine.

"The cops and the gaming commission are going to be all over this bastard and his associates. You all know how they like to run off the rails when an idiot gives them the chance," Francesco said loudly, but nobody flinched. Timmy White, her father's bodyguard and assistant, and Gino Roca, his top lieutenant, were common fixtures at this table and were used to her father's rants.

"You know Victor's reputation," she said as a maid served her. "He fucked anyone with a pulse and a little interest. He could have pissed off any number of people who wanted him dead."

"Caterina, please," her mother, Serra, said, clucking her tongue. "Such language at my table."

"Sorry, Mama, but this is important. I'm going to find out exactly what happened and take care of anything that needs taking care of. You can trust me, Papa."

"I trust you both, but we need to work together," Francesco said, stopping to finish his toast.

"I'll send Timmy over there and he can ask questions." Lucan finally spoke up now that he knew he was in the clear.

"Papa, I think I can handle that," she said, stopping when Francesco put his hand up and glared at her.

"I know you can, but today you're going to let Timmy do it. You're going with Lucan to see Bobby one more time, and you're going to explain the facts of his life like only you two can. I know he can't handle the entire load, but he can start taking on more." Francesco spread butter on his toast like he had all day to do it. "Until we know what this was about, you all lay off the Bellagio." He pointed his knife at Gino and narrowed his eyes. "I mean lay off completely. You understand me?"

"Yes, sir," Gino said, lowering his head. "I'll talk with the guys and let them know."

"Do you have plans for another site if we need to persuade whoever the new guy is at Bellagio?" Lucan asked.

"The Gemini would be my first stop, but we need something on that bitch Remi Jatibon and her father." Francesco finished with the butter and started with the fig preserves.

Caterina shook her head at her father's defiance of his doctor's advice. The great Francesco Terzo wouldn't die from an enemy's bullet, but because of his diet. "Remi is in New Orleans, Papa. The Gemini is Mano's operation."

"You think I'm stupid? Mano might run the operation, but the right hand of God calls the shots. Her little brother is not the kind to make waves." Francesco sounded like his patience was at an end.

"Should be easy then, if he's that much of a pushover." Lucan shoved a too big piece of sausage in his mouth.

"You try to browbeat Mano Jatibon, and his sister Remi will fly here and cut your balls off before I can do anything about it," Francesco said, exhaling loudly. "Once she's done, and you're lucky enough to survive, their business partner Cain Casey will scoop your brains out with a spoon and force-feed them to your sister."

"Let's go, Lucan," Caterina said, not wanting to aggravate her father any more. The Jatibons were a thorn in his side, and that wasn't good breakfast conversation. "Let's do what Papa said and go to the Moroccan." That would appease the old man, but it wouldn't hurt to ask some questions along the way.

Chapter Six

Mano Jatibon stood in his office and stared down at the Strip. His family's casino was next to Caesars Palace, which gave them a good view of all the flashing lights in front of Bellagio. He'd never cared for Victor Madison, and while his death didn't surprise him, it was time to shore up their operation just in case. At times like this, the authorities used the opportunity to dig where no one wanted them.

"Hey, brother. You're up early," Remi Jatibon said after answering on the first ring.

"I'd much rather be getting my kids off to school, but they found Victor Madison dead this morning. I don't have all the details yet, but it sounds like a stupid accident."

Remi whistled. "Did he shoot himself in the head cleaning his gun?"

That made him laugh. "It was more like he shoved a dildo with coke and fentanyl up his ass. From my contact's initial report, he had traces of the same two things on his dick as well, and the girl he was with died along with him." The coroner's van drove slowly down the street between Caesars and Bellagio, and hopefully it meant the cops wouldn't be much longer.

"What a fucking idiot—may he rest in peace."

"The girl was nineteen, so maybe he should be glad that combo killed him. She's young enough to make the media swarm like killer bees." The lights on the cruisers out front went out as the police started to leave. "I just wanted to give you a heads-up."

"Hang tight and let me know if we get any heat on this. We're finally up and running at full steam after the storm, and we need the Gemini in Vegas and the casino in Biloxi so we don't get a bottleneck of cash." Their offices in New Orleans had been partially destroyed by Hurricane Katrina, and the rebuilding had taken what seemed like forever because of the Historic Society's rules about anything in the French Quarter or near it.

"How's Dallas?" Remi was their father's heir, and Mano was fine with taking orders and being her number two. Plus, he was enjoying seeing his twin in love. Like his wife Sylvia, the actress Dallas Montgomery had accepted their rather unorthodox business ventures.

"She's learning to play craps for a new role, so she's been keeping Papi busy. The first couple of scenes will be shot in Vegas, and I'm coming along as a groupie."

"Plan to stay with us," he said, imagining how happy his kids were going to be with the news. Ramon Jatibon III, or Tres as they called him, and Lilia, his little sister, loved their aunts Remi and Dallas. "And bring your glove. Tres is practicing for Little League and my arm's getting tired."

"It'll be a month or so, but I'll let you know. If the star doesn't have any production meetings, maybe we'll come up early and bring Papi and Mami."

"We have plenty of room, and we'll be waiting."

His intercom buzzed and the secretary announced there were two detectives to see him. "What's that about?" Remi asked, having obviously heard.

"I'll call you back after I figure it out." He pocketed the phone and smiled when his crew came through the side door. Dwayne St. Germain and Steve Palma had graduated law school with Remi, and they'd joined the family business before their graduation. They were usually at the studio with Remi but had relocated to Vegas to be closer to their Hollywood operation until the offices in New Orleans were done. "Any clue, guys?"

"If we're all guessing," Steve said, sitting at the small conference table in the corner, "it's got to do with the pervert down the street."

"All our stuff's in order, but I'm sure Las Vegas's finest don't care about that," Dwayne said.

"You can handle this guy, but we'll stay for moral support," Steve said. "If that's okay with you."

"Sir?" his secretary said.

"Send them in." Mano leaned against the front corner of his desk and waited.

They came in looking like tired, worn-down cops. Nothing new there, then. One of them did, anyway. The other looked a little more eager. "Mr. Jatibon," the older man said, holding his hand out. "I'm Detective Andrew Wamsley, and this is my partner Corey Grant. Thank you for seeing us."

"We always have time for dedicated public servants, but I'm at a loss as to what this is about." He shook hands with both of them before taking a seat at the head of the table where his guys sat.

"I'm sure you spotted the action down the street from this great perch," Grant said in a tone that meant he was obviously playing the role of bad cop.

"I did, and while I'm curious, the Bellagio's business has nothing to do with us. Is there something we can help you with?"

"Victor Madison OD'd last night with a young female," Wamsley said, placing his hands flat on the table. "Most probably this was an accident brought on by some very bad judgment, but we have to cover all our bases. You understand."

"Actually, I don't," Mano said flatly.

"Cut the shit," Grant said loudly. "You're Ramon Jatibon's son, and Remi Jatibon's brother, and you honestly don't know why we're here? Do we look stupid to you?"

"If you want brutal honesty, you don't sound like a very sharp pencil," Mano said in a low voice. "You want to accuse me of something, go ahead, but let's hope you have more than my family tree to back it up."

"Getting rid of your competition can't be bad for your business if it leaves their business in disarray," Wamsley said.

"How many tourists—or locals for that matter, Detective Wamsley—can name the CEO of any casino on the Strip?" Steve asked.

"What's that got to do with anything?" Grant asked.

"It doesn't matter who's at the top," Steve said. "The Bellagio's tables and slots will be open today and every day after. Their big show will go on, and the buffet will be full no matter who's at the top, so it would take blowing up the building to mess up their business enough to, as you said, send them into disarray."

"Now that you've gotten your business lesson for the day, I'd like to know how many other visits like this you plan to make during this investigation," Dwayne said. "My client is a respected businessman, and a productive member of the community."

"Your client is also a member of an alleged Mob family and—" Grant snapped his mouth shut when Wamsley put his hand up.

"Time to go, gentlemen," Mano said, "and Detective Grant, we'll need your precinct and contact information."

"It's too early for my Christmas wish list," Grant said, laughing.

"If anyone gives you an early holiday gift, I'd use it to retain an attorney," he said and Grant opened his mouth but his partner placed his hand on his forearm.

"Corey's new and enthusiastic," Wamsley said. "He doesn't fully understand the way things here work yet."

"Nothing like a slander suit to welcome him to the force then," Steve said.

"It's my word against yours, and who's the judge going to believe?" Grant sneered at them, looking every inch like a caricature of a cop.

"You should know by now you're always on surveillance video when you step into any casino in Vegas, Detective," Dwayne said. "By walking in, you've given consent."

"Not in the management offices," Grant said quickly. "No one puts cameras in there."

"There's always an exception to every rule, so smile for the camera," Mano said, pointing to the corner where the camera that was only turned on for meetings like this showed a blinking red light. "I wish you luck finding something to back up your accusations before you're due in court."

"The boy said alleged," Wamsley said. "No one's reputation has been damaged here, so you've got no grounds. We just wanted to ask you if you knew anything about what happened at the Bellagio."

"Then you got no problems," Steve said with a smile that meant what was coming would be fun for them. "Leave now while you think you're still ahead."

"We're not done," Grant said, his jaw clenched.

"And we're going to be late for a meeting with the police commissioner," Dwayne said. "That makes us done. Unless you'd like to call him and explain why you're here about something we had nothing to do with. We can discuss my client's family tree and the zero indictments against them."

"We'll be back if anything ties this to you," Wamsley said.

"Thank you for the warning. Next time you're going to need either a warrant or appointment," Steve said. "Good luck getting either."

Mano could practically feel the vitriol vibrating from Grant as he slammed the door behind them.

"Go ahead and cut the feed," Mano said, moving back to his desk. "What did Victor have going on the side?"

"Who knows? We didn't keep tabs on him. Do you think that's what those two are doing here?" Dwayne asked.

"You know Papi's philosophy about stuff like this. When someone goes down, the police start shoving pitchforks in the hay to see if they can find any other needles in the haystack. Waste of time—like all of us are in bed together. It doesn't make sense to us, but it does to someone, and it might be the beginning of something we want no part of." Gemini existed to launder money from the family's illegal gambling businesses, and from their partnership with Cain Casey. The Casey family had run illegal liquor and cigarettes in New Orleans for generations, and their new partnership in the casino in Biloxi and in the movie studio in LA accomplished the same thing for their joint operations. They didn't need to get involved with the other Mob families in Vegas. It wasn't their style. But while they didn't have anything to hide with regard to the Vegas happenings, they still didn't want the police poking around their business, either.

"Dwayne, make the meeting with the commissioner a reality," Steve said.

"Good," Mano agreed. "Let's see if we can figure this out before we bother Papi or Remi. Don't get too handsy with this because I don't want to get ambushed by the cops or any other family. But knowledge is never wasted, and I want information on what's going on out there before it can come knocking at our door. Just to be safe."

"Do we have enough contacts here if this turns into something?" Dwayne asked.

"Reinforcements are never too far away," Mano said, and they all laughed. If someone wanted to start something with their family, they'd never live long enough to ponder their mistake. "But send some of the guys out and discreetly ask questions about Victor that have nothing to do with his interesting sex life." He put his jacket on and called for his bodyguard, Hugo Padilla. "On second thought—I want to know about the woman who died with him. That could lead us somewhere."

"I doubt a nineteen-year-old will yield anything useful, boss," Steve said.

"Humor me," he said as they headed out. "Sometimes treasures can be found in the unlikeliest of places."

❖

Diego Moretti held the telephone and listened to what the man was saying, but he was having a hard time hearing the words thanks to the rage going through him like fire in a dry field.

His daughter Sofia had come home to get away for a little while, but she was going back to work on her marriage. Just a little break from problems that weren't at all serious, she'd said. This phone call meant that was all bullshit, and the guy hadn't introduced himself yet, but Diego had taken the call when the maid said it was from LVMPD.

Cops calling his house, no matter where they were from, wasn't something he ever welcomed—especially without a heads-up from someone he trusted.

"Sir, can I speak to Mrs. Madison?" the officer asked for the third time.

"Who is this?" He knew the secret to survival was control. The other families had tried to move in on his territory, but knowing his business had kept him on top. This, though, felt like the complete opposite of control.

"This is Detective Andrew Wamsley with the Las Vegas Metropolitan Police Department." It seemed like a lot of information but it wasn't.

"What do you need with my daughter?" The door to his study opened and his son Paolo walked in and dropped onto the sofa.

"Sir, I just need to talk to Mrs. Madison."

"She's out with her aunt, so you can tell me what this is about, or you can go back to whatever busywork takes up your day." Cops were all the same. The assholes always thought they were the smartest people in the room when that wasn't the case about ninety percent of the time. "I ain't got all day."

"Sir, can you bring it down a notch," Wamsley said softly. "It's imperative that I speak to your daughter about an important matter. I'd rather her hear it from us, but if you're her father, I can give you the message."

"Are you accusing her of something?" It would take less time for him to do a complex long division problem in his head than for this guy to spit out whatever he had to say.

"No, sir, but her husband Victor was found dead this morning at Bellagio. From the coroner's estimation, Mr. Madison passed away around ten o'clock last night."

"Damn," he said, more from shock than grief.

Victor Madison was a nobody Sofia had fallen for who'd used

Diego's connections to get where he was. The problem was, Victor wasn't a grateful man, and even worse, he was a forgetful man. A man with no respect had no place in their lives, but Diego had ignored the bastard's shortcomings because of his love for his daughter. And Victor had finally become useful as well, which made this particularly irritating. "What happened?"

"It's a rather delicate situation, sir, but from the preliminary reports, he and the young lady he was with OD'd."

Diego closed his eyes and took a deep breath. Victor was lucky he was already dead. "What young lady?"

"We're running down some leads on that, but I hope you see now why it's important for me to talk to Mrs. Madison."

"I'll make sure she calls. Have you located my grandsons? Do they know?" Pietro and Gabriel Madison were his family, God help him, but he didn't really care for those little assholes much either.

"According to the housekeeper, Mr. Madison sent them to visit his parents. We haven't contacted them yet."

"Good, don't. I'll handle that, and I'll also accompany my daughter back to Las Vegas. Thank you for calling." Diego hung up before the cop said anything else about wanting to talk to Sofia.

Detective Wamsley wasn't going to fill in all the information he needed, and he had to find someone who would. He picked up the phone, and Lucan Terzo gave him the whole story, or as much of the story as he knew. Diego wanted to drive a knife through his son-in-law's eyes even though he was dead. "What kind of sick fuck his age beds a nineteen-year-old with a rubber dick in his ass?" he whispered as he waited for Sofia.

"Papa." Sofia came in, her heels clicking on the floor, and kissed his cheek. "Is something wrong?"

He sat her down and told her everything the cop and Lucan had told him. The truth, he figured, would save her from mourning the piece of shit. "You have to go back, but me and Paolo are coming with you."

"Thank you, Papa." Sofia had yet to shed a tear.

"Tell me, *cara*," he said, "did you know he was cheating on you?"

Sofia nodded and finally the tears came. "I only knew about a secretary, and I begged him to stop. He promised he'd take care of it, but I couldn't stand it anymore so I came here. I just didn't know how to tell you."

"Why didn't the boys come with you?" He already knew the answer, but he wanted to hear it from Sofia.

"It hasn't been good between us, and Victor's done everything he could to turn them against me." She put her hand over her mouth and shook her head. "They're going to blame me for this."

"Cara, go start packing and I'll take care of everything." He held Sofia for a moment and kissed her forehead. She left, her face covered by her hands.

"Get on a plane to Reno and go get those two little fuckers," he told Paolo once they were alone. "If Victor's parents or my grandsons give you any shit, tell them I'll come and take care of it myself. If that has to happen, tell them I'm not going to care that we're all related."

"Sofia gave Victor too much influence over those boys. It's not a surprise they have no respect," Paolo said, hitting his palm with his fist. "If it wasn't for you, Victor would've ended up in a trailer park selling bait somewhere."

"Trust me, I won't mourn him, but we need to find out if Sofia had anything to do with this. Victor was an asshole who died with no honor, but you know what we had in place. If we rock the boat on that deal, the Terzos aren't going to give a fuck about Sofia's bad marriage, and we'll make the perfect punching bags when it comes to blame."

"You think she put a hit on him?" Paolo asked, laughing as if the thought was ridiculous. "You're joking, right?"

"Paolo, remember that Sofia is a Moretti. If Victor flaunted this woman, I wouldn't expect her to take it. I raised both my kids with more pride than that." Diego rubbed his chin and nodded when Paolo held up the decanter on the bar. "I didn't agree with her choice when she brought him home, but I gave my consent anyway."

"What if she did have something to do with this?"

"I'll tell her she did what she had to do—that I understand. She'll have to understand, though, that whoever did this is a loose end, and that, along with lying to me, is unacceptable." He downed his drink and kissed Paolo's cheek. "That's a lesson the two of us know well."

"True, Papa, but if Sofia did do this, don't give her too hard a time. It's saved us from having to kill him."

"Let's go pack. Vegas isn't my favorite place, but our future is there. It's time to make sure it remains bright."

CHAPTER SEVEN

W hat aren't you telling me?" Robert Wallace asked Dean as he looked over the preliminary reports of the audit he'd ordered. He'd been able to postpone the meeting Francesco Terzo wanted until this was done. It was the only way he could think to start slowly breaking away from the Terzo family and all their connections. He had something much bigger in the works and needed more time to implement his plans.

"I needed help getting this done," Dean said hesitantly.

"What the fuck are you talking about? I told you to take your time and do it yourself." Robert listened when Dean told him exactly who was doing the work. "I don't have time to explain to you what a screw-up you are, but remember this when you have to live with what has to happen."

"What do you mean?"

"You really want two bitches walking around with a complete picture of what's going on here?" He got in Dean's face and poked him in the chest. *"Your* laziness sealed their fates, Dean."

"Are you sure?" The whine in Dean's voice meant he didn't have the stomach for what came next. "They don't see the total picture every day, and they both have kids. They'll totally go back to what they were doing with no problem when I assign them back to their regular duties."

"And what happens if the gaming commission or the Feds want a real audit and start asking questions? Do you think these two women are going to toe the line when the agents show them the fake books? I don't think so." He was tired of having this conversation, and from what he was seeing, he couldn't fathom going forward with Dean in charge since he wasn't man enough to be convinced of the hard truths the business demanded.

That made getting the Bellagio job important. The Terzos could keep this dump and do whatever they wanted with Dean—he wouldn't be his problem anymore. "Remember, your ass is on the line here too. We get caught, and we're all going to jail."

"I don't want to be involved in this. I'll keep the books and twist the numbers to whatever you want, but this is too much."

"Get them to finish and I'll take care of it. They're just doing this year, right?" He glanced up from the folder when Dean didn't answer. "Tell me you're not that fucking stupid."

"My instructions were this year, but Naomi accessed the records from a couple of years ago. I'm sure it was for comparison purposes, which isn't out of bounds for an audit. But…" Dean told him about the lunch Naomi and Brinley had shared across the street, and how they had their heads together through most of it. "I can't prove it, but it didn't look right, and Caterina met me to talk about the meeting with her father. The only good thing was Naomi and Brinley didn't see us."

"Did you tell Caterina they were doing the audit?"

"No way. I fucked up but I'm not that much of an idiot."

"I don't know about that. Get back to work, and fucking finish even if you have to do it yourself. I need it by next week."

Dean jumped up and left quickly.

"If I didn't need that fucker to keep everything straight, I'd kill him myself," he said as he called for Alex, and it went to voicemail again. After he'd tried to make Alex give him a blowjob, his assistant had made himself scarce around the office, which was really pissing him off.

"Hey, you need something?" Alex asked, entering from the back door to his office.

"Where the hell have you been?"

"I sent you a text message," Alex said defensively. "We had a fire in the kitchen and I've been dealing with the inspectors to get us back to full steam."

"Don't we have people who do shit like that? It sounds a little beneath you."

"There's plenty that's beneath me, but like you tell me, it has to be done." Alex sat across from his desk and folded his hands on his lap. "What can I do for you?"

"Are you pissed that I wanted you to suck my dick, or is it that you think you won't get the chance to do it again?" He laughed but stopped when Alex glared at him.

"Lucan called me and offered me a job managing the club he owns close to the Rio," he said, his tone devoid of emotion.

"You'd walk out on me? The gig next door might be a real possibility and you're right there with me. Lucan's never going to be as loyal to you as I am." He slammed his fist on the desk, hating the Terzos more than ever.

"I doubt he will, but I need respect as well as loyalty," Alex said.

"You know I respect you, and I also don't want you to go." The sick fact was, he really didn't want to lose the one person who knew him best. It would be a pain to train someone new to do all the shit Alex did for him.

"Then treat me like a man you want and not some trick you can use to scratch that itch none of your women can touch." Alex put his hand up to keep him from interrupting. "I'm not stupid, and you can't publicly embrace me, but there has to be some common ground. If you can't find it, I'll understand, but I'm going to take Lucan up on his offer."

"Alex, you know I care for you, but I'm not—"

"What, gay?" Alex laughed mockingly. "You don't put your dick in some man's mouth more than once if you're not interested. From what I hear, straight men don't do that."

"There's always exceptions to every rule. I trust you with all my secrets, and you understand what I want." He stood and walked around the desk to get closer to Alex. "I need you, so don't make me beg."

"You need me how?" Alex asked, standing up and unzipping Robert's pants so he could put his hand inside. He laughed when he found him hard. "You need me to take care of this? Or should I call in the airhead who answers your phone?"

"Come on, don't be cruel."

Alex dropped to his knees, taking Robert's pants and briefs down with him. He swirled his tongue around the head of his dick and Robert closed his eyes. They popped open again when Alex sucked him in and simultaneously shoved two fingers up his ass. Every bit of him wanted to protest, but the surprise move almost made him come. This wasn't what he had in mind when he'd called Alex in, but he wasn't complaining.

He came faster than he wanted to, and before he could do anything to stop Alex, he turned him, bent him over the desk, and fucked him. He didn't exactly put up a fight, though.

"You ambushed me," he said once Alex came but was still inside him.

"Don't lie." Alex reached around and found him hard again. "I mean you can try, but this guy hasn't gotten the memo that you didn't love that."

"This isn't how I planned to spend the afternoon, but hopefully you're staying," he said once Alex got him off again. "Like I said, I need you."

"Don't disrespect me again and we won't have a problem."

"You have my word, but we do have a big problem." They straightened their clothes, and he told Alex what Dean had reported, then gave Alex the two names in question. "Use two different contractors so no one has the ammunition to give us any shit later. I don't want to sabotage our chances of moving up in the world."

"I'll take care of it," Alex said, placing the slip of paper with Naomi and Brinley's names in his wallet.

"If everything falls into place we can screw around in the villa where Victor died to celebrate. We owe it to him to finish what he was too fucking stupid to do."

Alex gazed at him as if not knowing whether to believe him. "Are you sure?"

"About what? Moving up or fucking around with you?"

"Both," Alex said, placing his hand on his chest.

"Trust me, you're with me all the way in every aspect."

"I'll take you up on that."

"Count on it. I want you with me for years to come." He smiled, knowing once he had everything he wanted, he'd drop this conniving cocksucker in a hole in the middle of the desert. For now, though, he'd make Alex believe he was the center of his universe, but there were plenty like Alex in Vegas just waiting for their chance. With the threat to go work for someone else, Alex had proved he couldn't be trusted completely.

❖

Diego Moretti glanced out the plane window and studied the Vegas Strip, a glowing oasis in a sea of darkness. He didn't care for this place that had no real character or history. Granted, the Mob had brought the idea to life, but those guys' true homes weren't here. The city, to him, was for wannabes like Victor who were all about the flash, but had little to back it up.

He reached over and took Sofia's hand. "We're almost there, cara. Are you okay?"

"I'm fine, Papa. The truth is, I don't know if I should be more mad than sad. He went out of his way to humiliate not only himself but the whole family, so it's hard to mourn him."

"Once we see what all this is about, you and I need to have a talk. Victor's death might be humiliating, but it's going to be a big problem to some people." He tried his best not to put any judgment into his tone. "If there's something you haven't told me about all this, you need to, before things start to get out of hand. You know I won't blame you, but I want to avoid any type of shit if I can help it."

Sofia studied him with the long silence she used as a child when she was formulating an answer in a way that wouldn't piss him off. "Was Victor doing something for you?"

"Not just me, and starting over is going to upset some friends who are better kept happy. In this case, unhappiness might put you in enough danger that it will be hard for me to protect you. That's especially true if you knew this was coming." He squeezed her fingers when she opened her mouth. "I'm not accusing, cara, but I need all the information you might have before I meet with Francesco Terzo. He's a business partner, but he's an animal."

"Papa, I was embarrassed that my husband preferred his stupid secretary to me, but he's the father of my children. You can't believe I'd do something to cause him harm."

It wasn't a denial, which was as good as an admission. "Do you remember our talk before you married Victor?" She hesitated but nodded. "I gave you my warning, but I didn't want to stand in the way of your happiness. It's not your fault you were in love and didn't want to see then what kind of man Victor was."

"I know, I should've listened to you, but you're right, I was in love." She glanced down at their hands and took a deep breath. "My life would've been different if I listened to you, but now all I can do is move forward."

"You'll be fine, but remember, I can only protect you if you're honest with me. I'll keep saying that until you believe me, and the consequences of lying to me sink in."

"Papa, I've told you the truth." Sofia finally made eye contact with him, and he knew she was lying.

This was going to turn into a fucking fiasco, and if it did, there was only so much he could do without calling in some major muscle. That would be an excuse for Francesco Terzo to hit him hard for trying to move in on the territory he thought was his alone.

The plane landed and he glanced at Paolo but didn't say anything. They had to talk, but he needed at least a couple more guys than the guards they had with them. Traveling with a small number of personnel was his way of not attracting attention, but the cops had already called them, so…safety first.

"Boss, you go out to the car with Sofia and Paolo, and I'll grab a porter for the bags," Diego's guard said, pointing to the exit. "I arranged for a ride."

"Thanks," he said, cocking his head at Paolo's guard so he'd drop back to stand with Sofia and Paolo. "Have you heard from my grandsons?"

Antonio nodded, but from the set of his mouth, Diego wouldn't like whatever was on his mind. "Not now, sir, if you don't mind."

"Take everyone to the car," he said, not wanting to wait on whatever Antonio had to say. "Tell me."

"I know they're your grandsons, but you might want to brace yourself for these guys. They might or might not be at the house when we get there. If they are, they said their father left everything to them, and you and Sofia aren't welcome."

Disrespect. The one thing he wouldn't ever tolerate. "Call Lucan and tell him to take Sofia and Paolo somewhere for dinner, since he called and offered. You and me are going to catch up with my grandsons."

Antonio took the wheel of the second car they'd gotten and followed the GPS directions to the large house outside the city that looked like some modern monstrosity. It was one more example of why he thought the city had no soul. Who fucking built something this hideous?

The gates were locked, their code didn't work, and there was no answer on the intercom, which made him laugh. "I hope you got the insurance for this thing," he said as Antonio turned the car around.

They drove to the other side of the street, and Antonio gunned it, knocking through the gate with the back of the large SUV. He didn't slow down until they reached the door. Diego noticed the movement of the curtains where the living room was but no one came to the door when Antonio rang the bell.

"You want me to put my shoulder into it?" Antonio asked.

Diego shook his head and took Sofia's key ring out of his pocket. He held one up, handed the ring over, and pointed to the door. "Open it, but with your gun in one hand."

When the door swung open he stared at seventeen-year-old Pietro pointing a shotgun at them from the grand staircase, and fifteen-year-old Gabriel doing the same thing from the living room. Their backup, holding a pistol, was Victor's father, Todd.

After the initial meeting of the families, when Sofia met Victor, Diego realized that every bit of Victor's arrogance he'd inherited and learned from Todd. The uneducated bartender hadn't been one of Diego's favorite people since he'd gotten drunk at his daughter's wedding and totally embarrassed himself. A man with so little self-control was no man at all.

"We called the cops, so leave now and we won't have you arrested," Todd said, lifting his gun higher and holding it to the side as if he'd watched one too many gangster movies. "This is my grandsons' property and none of you are wanted here."

"Antonio, let's take a seat," he said, motioning for Antonio to holster his weapon. "These motherfuckers saved us a call."

"Papa," Pietro said, not lowering his gun. "We're not fucking around. Dad told us everything belongs to us, and Mom only made him miserable. That bitch isn't welcome here."

"That misery is probably what killed him." Gabriel's shotgun wavered slightly. "He gave her everything and all she could do was bitch constantly."

Diego glanced toward the window and smiled when he saw the flashing lights. The two police officers entered with their guns drawn and it didn't take them long to make everyone drop their weapons. Right after that Todd started yelling to the cops about how Diego and Antonio were trespassing.

"Sir, do you have anything to add?" the young patrolman asked.

Diego glanced at his watch and smiled. "I have plenty to say, but if you give me a minute, we can wrap this up."

Another car drove up and a well-dressed young man came in with a folder. "Hello, I'm Ezra Brayden, and I'm Mr. Moretti's attorney." Ezra took some papers from his briefcase and handed them to the police. "This house is the property of Mr. Moretti, as you can see on the deed. It's impossible for him to be trespassing somewhere that's legally his. The other form you'll find there is Victor Madison's will. Mr. Madison was the prior tenant but is now deceased."

"How do you have that?" Pietro asked, moving forward and trying to grab the papers out of the cop's hand.

"Mr. Madison was also represented by our firm, and with his written permission should anything happen to him, we're able to share it with you. That's in there as well."

"How is this your house?" Todd asked, holding Pietro back to keep him from getting arrested.

"Your son blew all the money he had on women and bad investments. My daughter asked for my help so they'd have a decent place to live, and I said yes. Knowing Victor and his loser ways, I kept the property in my name." He stared at Pietro and then Gabriel. "Your father wasn't who you thought he was and who he claimed to be, but your mother isn't to blame."

"He said you'd come here blowing smoke. Crawl back into your hole, old man. My father was the head of the biggest casino on the Strip," Pietro said, and Todd placed his hand on his shoulder with a large smile. "He was an important man who didn't need your fucking help."

"The great man died with a rubber dick in his ass, and his dick in a nineteen-year-old girl. That's a real role model. The only thing I give thanks for every day is your name is Madison and not Moretti."

"You fucking liar," Todd screamed.

"Ezra," Diego said, and the attorney produced pictures.

The glossy colored evidence was one favor Francesco Terzo was more than happy to do for him. "The truth fucking hurts, so take these two disrespectful little bastards and get out of my house."

"You can't throw us out of our house," Pietro said.

"I'm crawling back into my hole, which in this cesspool of a town is this ugly fucking place. From now on, count on Grandpa Todd here because the Moretti money is finished for you and Gabriel." He stood and buttoned his suit jacket. "You want nothing to do with me or my daughter—fine, but the cars and all the other shit I'm paying for stays here. If you decide to test that theory, I'll report all of it stolen, and when you're in court, I hope Todd can afford decent representation."

"We'll be in court all right," Todd said, dropping the pictures on the floor. "I'm suing you for slandering my son."

"Slandering?" he said and laughed. "There's the old saying about what a picture is worth, but in this case, they'll be worth a thousand laughs. Maybe the three of you can comfort each other by shoving something up *your* asses. Might be a Madison family thing this old man doesn't understand."

"Fuck you," Todd said.

"Believe me, I prefer beautiful blondes of the female persuasion."

CHAPTER EIGHT

Tuesday morning started with unusual cloudy skies, and Reed sat in the diner close to the funeral home she figured Sofia would use. The scanner Oscar loved to listen to had clued them in to the trouble at the Madison home the night before, which had made her glad she hadn't removed the bugs she'd planted. From what she'd heard, Diego Moretti wasn't a man who let family relationships get in the way of what he wanted or who he needed to beat down.

"So why are we here?" Oscar asked as the waitress brought their coffee. "It's nine in the morning, and it's Tuesday. I don't ever wake up this early no matter what day it is, but especially on Tuesdays if I can help it."

"Wait," she said as a line of black SUVs drove by and turned in at the funeral home. The courier service she'd hired was a few car lengths behind, and the delivery guy waited for Sofia to get out like she'd asked. "It turns out our favorite breakfast spot is perfectly located."

Diego immediately got in front of Sofia but relaxed when the driver held up the package from the Bellagio. It was the only way Reed could think to make the Moretti men stand down.

Oscar ordered breakfast for both of them and waited for the waitress to leave. "Is there something wrong? From what I can see, this job is over."

"Diego and Paolo Moretti arrived last night, as you know," she said as Sofia waved her family inside and then opened the small box. "It made me curious about why his grandsons would've called the police to bar him and Sofia from the house. Diego doesn't have muscle or influence here, but he's the shit back east. Ordering him out of anywhere is a death wish depending on who's doing the ordering."

"I agree that was a gutsy call on the dynamic duo's part," Oscar said, pouring what looked like a pound of sugar in his coffee. "They're lucky the old man didn't have them shot for their blatant disrespect, even if they call him Grandpa."

Her burner phone rang. "Hello?"

"When do you want to meet?" Sofia asked.

"I don't, but you've got some stuff to do. Finish all your business and do your best not to call attention to yourself."

"If you try to screw me, believe me, you're dead."

She laughed, especially when she saw how pissed Sofia was. "I know my job, Mrs. Madison, and my word is what'll give me all the work I can handle once I'm done with you. Your money can wait, so stop worrying about me, and bury all your problems."

"Did you even do anything? From what I know from the damned cops who called me, Victor was enough of a scumbag to have died all on his own. It doesn't seem like you had shit to do with it."

"The young lady was all his idea, but believe me, fucking her to death wasn't his idea." She hung up and turned the phone off since she wasn't a fan of circular conversations. Trust Sofia to think Victor had died on his own after she'd hired someone to kill him off. The waitress dropped off their order and winked at her as she walked away.

"Why didn't you just give her the codes? All you're doing is poking the bear with a thousand sharp sticks. Sofia won't kill you but her father will."

"They have to find me first, but never mind about that. Last night made me think we need some leverage, and it won't kill Sofia to wait a few days. The hit on Victor wasn't sanctioned by Diego or anyone of importance, and that's not going to go over well if Sofia cracks." She put her fried eggs on her hash browns and broke the yolks to mix it all together. It was a habit both she and Oscar had developed early on. "Besides," she said as she shoveled in a mouthful of sausage, "we have an in now." She held up an Earwig and smiled as she handed it over.

"Wow, I'm impressed," he said as he listened to the conversation going on in the funeral home.

"I learned from the best, and we need to monitor this and the house until we can put Sofia in a rearview mirror and be sure she stays there. If she's got a nasty surprise in mind for us, she's going to wish she'd done as she was told." The other phone she carried rang, and she tried to think if she'd ever seen the number before, but it wasn't familiar. The only clue was the Vegas area code. "Hello."

"I'm looking for a fix for my problem," a man said.

"I can take a message." She wasn't worried about a trace, but she didn't like to linger on the line any more than she had to.

"This isn't something for a flunky, so I want to talk to you."

"That's fine if you don't want to leave a message, but I'm not the one who needs something fixed." She hung up and showed Oscar the number. It probably wasn't traceable, but they might get lucky. It didn't take long for it to ring again.

"Are you trying to lose business?"

"You're obviously new to our service, but you leave a message and we get back to you. That's nonnegotiable, but it's also voluntary on your part. If you pass on the rules, don't call back."

"I need to get rid of a problem, like, right now," the man said and he sounded pissed. "And I mean permanently get rid of."

"Send all the particulars to this address." She gave him an email address and waited. These things sometimes took turns she never expected.

"Do you think I'm brain-dead? I send you that and you pick me up when you get a warrant."

"You got this number from someone who's already a client. That means they trusted us enough to hire us, and I'll repeat that I did say *voluntary*. The next move is yours." She hung up again and Oscar pointed to the funeral home.

"I'm beginning to see what you mean." Oscar tapped on the window. Diego had a grip on the top of Sofia's arm and he didn't appear happy. "He's suspicious about all this, and he's worried about the Terzo family. He mentioned them more than once in the last fifteen minutes."

"It's well known Moretti doesn't have business in Vegas, so why would he be worried about Francesco Terzo?" The video on her phone came to mind and she kept staring across the street. On the surface, an attorney fucking Terzo's son's wife didn't have anything to do with Moretti, but life was strange at times.

"Do you think there was something more to Victor that Sofia didn't know? Something that's not jumping out at us?" Oscar asked.

"If she put us in the middle of a turf war, then all the precautions we put in place might not be enough." She was finished eating, pushing her plate away before she was done, her appetite gone. "We need to dig and find out what Victor meant to people other than Sofia. I might've fucked up on this one because it was a challenge, and by rushing to finish I ignored everything else."

"It's not anything we can't fix, and nothing we can't beat if it gets hot." Oscar placed his hand over hers. "Was there anything else you left behind in his office that we might need?"

"A pile of cash and some diamonds," she said, distracted. "Maybe, though, the real answers aren't in the office, but someplace he was free to be himself."

"The house, you mean? That's not going to be empty until well after the funeral." Oscar motioned for the check.

"He wouldn't have risked Sofia finding anything he was going to use to cut her out of his life." She stared at the retreating cars and shook her head. "No, Victor died with his secrets."

"If you say so, but we could always take a vacation and wait this out."

That was probably the smart play. All the security measures they put in place would slow someone down, but if they had a real hard-on for you, nothing was totally safe. The problem with running was it was a weakness you couldn't easily overcome.

"I'm not living with a target on my head, buddy. This is our home and none of these fuckers are going to take it away from us."

The lesson here was that Sofia killed Victor, the one man she was supposed to be loyal to—not because he was a lousy husband, but because he was the father of her children. Reed wasn't fucked in the head enough to think Sofia would feel some deep-seated need to be loyal to her, a hired gun, which meant this whole job might have been a total screwup on her part. Panic wasn't the smart play here either, though. No, what was called for now was standing her ground and killing anyone who tried to take what she'd built.

"Vacations are for celebrating a job that's done, Oscar, not for hiding out."

Nope, she was staying. She smiled, thinking of the coming days. What the hell was the purpose of playing this game if you didn't play to win? The rush of living to play again was better than anything in her life. No amount of money or sex could touch the thrill.

"This job's not done."

❖

Brinley kissed Finn good-bye as he went into her neighbor's apartment. Her neighbor—a blackjack dealer at Wynn, who'd told Brinley about the job opening at the Moroccan—was also a single mom, and she dropped Finn off with her three-year-old son once day care was open. It was a godsend for Brinley since she couldn't be late for work.

The job had quickly become all-consuming as she and Naomi worked through lunch every day and brought stuff home to try and have the bulk of the audit done in the two weeks Dean Jasper had given them. The numbers were still hard to grasp. The bulk of her mom's clients had been small-business owners and oil field service companies, and while some of them made millions, they were dwarfed by the cash flow the Moroccan brought in.

So far the average take on a daily basis was forty-eight million, and the payout was close to the same, minus ten percent. What she'd been looking for in what Dean had provided, but hadn't found, was the average number of gamblers. Considering the steadiness of the take, the Moroccan had to have the lousiest rich gamblers in Vegas. They lost, but only the ten percent, consistently.

The marquee outside advertised their around-the-world buffet and some comedian she'd never heard of, and she cursed her lack of expertise with the gaming industry as a whole. "I have to find a nonconfrontational way to ask Naomi about all this so I can get up to speed," she said to herself as she sat in the ever present Strip traffic. The traffic light turned green and someone immediately blew their horn to get her to go, so she made the turn onto the street where the employee lot was.

She lucked out and found a spot close to the door, which was nice even though her walk now was shorter since Dean had moved them. For once she'd beaten Naomi to the office and juggled the box she was carrying to get the door unlocked. As she dropped the finished files on her desk, she noticed there were a few more boxes since last night and she wanted to groan. If they kept piling work on them, they'd never finish.

"Girl, nothing can be that bad," Naomi said, dropping another box on the table and handing her a coffee cup. "I saw you turn in, but that light only lasts a nanosecond, which means you just got here. If you're already looking pissed, it must be something you carried in with you."

"Those ten weren't here last night," she pointed to the other end of the conference table.

"That fucker Dean is trying to bury us in paperwork," Naomi whispered in her ear.

That was something else that was off. Naomi acted like the walls had a multitude of listening devices, and she'd get fired if she said anything about Dean or their other bosses. That day at lunch Naomi had pointed out that asking questions wasn't a smart career choice, and her only advice was not to make waves. Vegas was now civilized according to all the cute commercials, but there were hints of that seedy underbelly in everything she was doing, and she was having a hard time coming up with excuses to ignore it.

The money was what had tempted her, but was it worth whatever this was? Things that were too good to be true had a way of blowing normalcy to shit, and if you tried to get back to where you were, your mistakes would lock you out of a better place forever. She could accept the consequences if it was just her, but Finn deserved better.

"I finished everything through March, so those have to be the summer files," she said, taking the top off the closest box. It contained all the financial reports from May first through the twelfth. Strange way to break up the months, since there was more room in the box.

"I have about a quarter of the April files done," Naomi said, "but Amelia got sick last night. So I spent the night cleaning vomit instead of doing more. My life is so damn glamorous."

"That totally sucks," she said knowing exactly what that was like.

"Do you mind helping me with the rest, and we'll try the same cut of files for tonight if we're not finished by this afternoon?"

"You brought coffee and scones," she said, opening the bag, "which means I'll do anything for you."

"Maybe if we concentrate, we can actually get out for lunch. You can tell me all your secrets for making kids stop vomiting."

She laughed and took what Naomi handed her. They sat side by side and were done with Naomi's unfinished work by noon. Brinley made no comment as they walked across the street to Paris and Naomi got them a secluded table inside at Mon Ami Gabi. Naomi told her the French bistro was usually packed, and Brinley joked that her friend was sleeping with the hostess to score this table if that was true.

"Get your mind out of the gutter, girlfriend," Naomi said as she arched an eyebrow at her. "I do the girl's taxes for free in exchange for whatever table I want no matter how crazy busy they are. I love this place, but it's always full, so I'm the winner in this deal."

"You might want to introduce me to the other hostess after lunch then," she said, laughing. "Do you want to check on Amelia?"

"She's fine," Naomi said, staring at her as if trying to decide something. "I wanted an excuse to get out of there and not make anyone suspicious."

"Make anyone suspicious about what?" They stopped talking when the waiter took the order Naomi gave him. Since it was her first time, she didn't mind Naomi picking for her.

"What do you think about our new assignment so far?" Naomi leaned in and spoke softly like they were in some kind of spy movie.

"I wish I knew how to answer that without sounding incredibly naive, but I have no experience to make a reasonable assessment." Naomi tilted her head like she didn't understand. "When I worked for my mom, her biggest client's company cleared about one point eight million a year. If you combine him with all her other clients, you're looking at roughly fifty million."

"Sounds about right for a small firm," Naomi said.

"It does, but in the first quarter of this year the Moroccan took in an average of forty-five million daily for the months I finished. If you got something different, then I performed the work wrong." She said it all fast and in the same low voice Naomi was using. "Since I was convinced I was off, I did a little research and compared that to last year, and the year before that."

"What'd you find?" Naomi asked.

"Two years ago, the average was twelve million with a payout ratio of between thirty-two and thirty-nine percent. That's good since you're still in the black, but it drastically jumped in this year, and it's stayed consistent."

"One of my months was fifty-two million with a ten percent payout ratio," Naomi said, which made Brinley happy—she wasn't crazy. "We've become the most successful casino in the history of casinos with an uncharacteristically steady level of return. For no apparent reason."

"Or maybe their business really picked up and we just don't see it," she said, shrugging. She had a feeling there were things she didn't want to know.

"Or maybe they're doing something else—" Naomi straightened up and stared at the door.

"Ladies, does this mean you're finished?" Dean asked as he entered with a woman Brinley recognized as a secretary.

"We've been locked in there for a week, including Saturday and Sunday, and I decided we needed air, Dean. Don't worry, we'll be back in our cage in less than an hour," Naomi said.

"Just remember that Mr. Wallace and I are counting on you," Dean said and left to join his date.

"Who's Mr. Wallace?" she asked.

"Our CEO and fearless leader, but he's more of a closet perv if you ask me," Naomi said, keeping her eyes on Dean. "Shit, that's Caterina Terzo," she said when another woman came in and joined Dean at his table.

"Is she famous?"

"Eventually, when her picture goes up at the post office under a wanted sign, she will be," Naomi said and smiled. "Sorry, you're a newbie, and you don't know all the players yet. Caterina is Francesco Terzo's daughter, and Francesco is head of the Mob here. That's not someone you expect to see your boss having lunch with."

"Like in the movies?" The concept sounded ludicrous.

"What, there's no bad guys in New Orleans?"

"More than our share, and from what I understand, they're mostly bad *girls*, but I doubt I could point them out in restaurants." She glanced at the woman Naomi had mentioned and was surprised to find her staring at them. She quickly looked away. "What's your guess as to what Dean is doing with her?"

"I really don't know, and I think it's best if we forget this conversation. Let's finish so we can go back to our box of an office with no window. Whatever you do, don't access any other files from previous years. Neither of us wants to be someone Caterina Terzo gets to know well, and if they're in business together, we want to stay far away from that stuff."

"Okay, and thanks for the warning. My ex and his mother are bad enough. I don't need any other problems."

The waiter put her lunch down and it looked delicious, but her stomach was queasy. This was too much change too fast, and it had a way of clarifying there were certain things worse than her ex and his mother bothering her for money. She missed her mother, the green spaces of Louisiana, and her uncomplicated job and life.

The little voice in her head was suggesting she run before it was too late, but she'd made the decision to start over, and she owed it to herself to see it through. Besides, it wasn't like they could kill her and get away with it. This wasn't the movies, after all. Real life wasn't that exciting.

❖

"Anything?" Remi asked after getting all the niceties out of the way.

Mano was at home, the phone pressed to his ear, having left the office early to practice throwing the ball around with his son. Six-year-old Tres was pumped about playing baseball after finding Mano's old yearbook and seeing him in his uniform. This was the first night he hadn't worked late, and he'd spent the afternoon wearing Tres out. Watching his boy run around the backyard made him wish the rest of his family was closer, but Remi and his father had trusted him with Gemini, and he'd vowed to do the best job he could.

"We got some stuff from our police contacts, but according to them, Victor's death will be ruled an accident. If someone did off him, they were good enough not to leave any traces of themselves behind." He accepted a drink from Sylvia and squeezed his wife's hand as he sat behind his desk. "That's a dead end for now, so Steve and Dwayne are concentrating their efforts on the girl."

"I'm giving you a raise if you find something interesting about a woman who wasn't old enough to drink legally," Remi said.

"Hey, Mano," Dallas called out from somewhere behind Remi, followed by kissing noises.

"You heard that?" Remi asked and he could see her smile in his mind.

"Give her a kiss for me."

"That won't be a problem, but finish telling me about the woman Victor was with."

"The most popular number in her phone, the number she sent the most texts to, belongs to someone we both know." He flipped through the copies of the phone numbers and texts he'd paid for and was disgusted that this young woman had been used like this.

"As long as they're not on our payroll, it won't shock me."

"I doubt anyone on our payroll is a scumbag the likes of Caterina Terzo."

He took a sip of his drink as he waited for Remi to formulate a reply. It was best to let her think.

"What is a nineteen-year-old doing planning a murder for hire, and how is that related to Caterina?"

"Maybe they were kissing cousins," he said, and Remi snorted. "I'll email you these texts in case you're interested in a sideline as a lesbian erotica writer. This kid certainly got around, and it's clear she slept with Victor as a favor to Caterina."

"The cops know that and they don't find it strange that Victor's dead? And why aren't they questioning Caterina?"

"I'm working on the answers to those questions, but for now all I know is they have another theory of the crime. The texts that weren't filled with all their sexual desires were about how Lolita was supposed to get Victor to commit to hiring someone to kill his wife."

Remi laughed and he had to join her. "Isn't Victor's widow Diego Moretti's daughter?"

"The one and only Sofia. Diego and Paolo are in town and already had the cops call on them."

"I don't know that family well, but they aren't known for their finesse."

"No, but that's good for everyone. With the addition of the Terzos and the Morettis, it gives the detectives investigating all this some enticing targets that aren't us. It does open up the question of why Caterina wanted Sofia dead, though."

"The only thing that comes to mind is Caterina wanted Victor under her thumb, and we can all guess why. The Terzos are moving plenty of product for the drug cartels and their bosses, but they're also on the radar for the meth labs the family personally owns. They're producing enough product to supply Nevada and the neighboring states, and they're using the biker gangs to move all that. The rumor even here in New Orleans is they're close to cornering the market."

"You're like the Encyclopædia Britannica." He gave his son a thumbs-up when he raised his glove to show he'd caught a ball he'd thrown into the air. Tres frowned when Sylvia came out and got him. That meant his fun was over for the night and a bath and bed were in his future.

"I'd like to think I'm more up-to-date than that." She laughed.

"Don't worry. I've had some of our guys keeping an eye on those operations in case they get out of hand. The problem is Caterina and the Terzos are good at making inroads here and south of the border, which means if they get any bigger, it'll be next to impossible to overcome the juggernaut. All that cash, though, has to be washed somewhere, and Victor must've been Caterina's plan for that big problem. The Moroccan is just low-key enough not to get the authorities' attention, but big enough to wash the money. If their operation gets bigger, though, they'll needed someone else, and that's where Victor probably came in."

"Let me see what Dallas's timeline is, and if she's not ready, I might come up early."

"We've got it under control, so wait for her. A couple more days might give us time to get a better idea of what all this was about. My money's on Sofia if this was a hit."

"You know the players better than anyone, so I'm keeping my money. And if it was a simple hit ordered by the wife, things should cool down pretty fast unless it becomes a turf war. Call if you need anything."

"You're number one on my speed dial." Mano hung up and called his guard. "Have you called it a night yet?"

"You need to go out?" Hugo asked, sounding as alarmed as he always did when Mano went somewhere alone.

"No, I'd like to save myself from Sylvia kicking my ass if I left the house tonight. I just got off the phone with Remi and wanted to see if you got anything new." He walked around and made sure all the doors and windows were locked.

"Our contact at the gaming commission says they've heard rumors that Robert Wallace is trying to position himself to take over for Victor. He barely waited for Victor's body to get cold before he called the Terzos." The background noise dimmed as Hugo went somewhere quieter. "Those cops seemed to have moved on and are going to close the investigation. Victor will go down as a dumbass with questionable morals, but they don't think there was any foul play."

"Remi and I have our doubts about that, especially after the text messages I read. It did look like an accidental overdose, so their next play will probably be to question Caterina about those texts about the wife. There's nothing to confirm Victor made any move on that, but there's plenty to tie Caterina to that planning even if her accomplice is dead."

"No one can accuse the cops of complete genius all the time, but then, that's why we're so successful. I agree with you, though, and I think they're putting that word out so whoever's responsible will trip themselves up. Right now I'm at Bellagio talking to some old friends to see what else shakes loose. I'll be there in the morning to pick you up, so don't leave without me."

"I wouldn't dare." The night was warm, and he stared at the thermometer Sylvia had hung outside close to the door, but he didn't mind the heat of Vegas as much as most. He hung up and listened to the cicadas buzzing.

"Want to pretend we don't have two kids sleeping in the house and go skinny-dipping?" Sylvia wrapped her arms around his waist from behind.

He turned around and kissed her. Sylvia was a true partner, and he couldn't imagine ever betraying her like Victor had with Sofia. "I love you, and I never turn down any opportunity to see you naked."

"You have a silver tongue in that mouth, lover." Sylvia ran her hands down his chest and unbuckled his belt. "Time to prove it."

CHAPTER NINE

The doorbell rang, rousing Brinley from her sleep on the couch. She opened the door—"Mom?"—and thought for a moment she was hallucinating from the stress she was under, but her mother smiled and opened her arms. The familiarity of it came close to making her cry. "Oh my God, thank you for never listening to me."

"You're not mad?" Wilma tightened her hold and kissed her temple.

"Are you kidding? I'm so glad you're here. I feel like I'm either crazy or in over my head." Brinley didn't let go right away, needing the safety she always associated with her mother. The disorienting feeling of losing everything that was familiar to her as well as the uncertainty of what she was doing had set her adrift.

"Baby, you're the smartest accountant I know, so I doubt you're either of those things." Wilma stared at all the ledgers and open files on her kitchen table and sighed as if in disapproval.

"I'm telling you, Mom, there's something fishy about all this, and my work partner acts like someone is listening to everything we say. Jarrell and his crazy mother are starting to look better and better."

"You haven't talked to Naomi about all that?"

"All she keeps saying is not to ask questions, and she doesn't appear too anxious to give me any answers about any of this. It's like she's truly scared about something, but she won't say what it is. For now I figure the answers are in there"—she pointed to all the paperwork—"but the numbers keep leaving me with more questions."

"Okay, how about this." She took Brinley's hand and patted it. "You look beat, and nothing makes sense when you're this tired, so you go to bed and get some sleep. I'll take a glance at what you have."

"Trust me, I'd rather spend the rest of the night catching up with you."

"I would too, but you really do look tired. Take me up on my offer. Back home we worked on stuff together all the time, and no one was the wiser. Besides, I won't make any changes to your work, and I'll follow your flow for any reports you need to finish."

"Are you sure?" Brinley couldn't think of anything better than her pillow.

"You're exhausted, honey, and I slept on the plane. Go to bed and let me do what I came for, and that's to help you." Brinley didn't protest being led to her room and getting tucked in. "Get some sleep, and we'll talk some more in the morning."

"Thanks, Mom, but come get me if you have any questions. I feel horrible for dumping all this on you right off, but I love you."

"It's not dumping it on me if I volunteered, and I love you too. All you need to believe is there are plenty of jobs out there if this one doesn't work out. You're good at what you do, and any company would be lucky to have you." She kissed Brinley's forehead and combed her hair back.

"I'm sure you're right, but part of me really wants to know the answer."

"Let's see what the hell all this is about, and I can help you decide what the best move is." Wilma stood and kissed her forehead again. "Get some sleep and it'll make more sense if you're not exhausted."

Five hours later, feeling more rested than she had since her arrival in Vegas, Brinley hugged her mother again. "I still can't believe you're here."

"I'm your mother, and I'll always know when you need me, but I'm glad I'm here too." Wilma handed Brinley a cup of coffee and pointed to a chair. "We need to talk about this place you work."

"What do you think?" Brinley tapped her finger on the ceramic mug in her hand and chewed on her bottom lip.

"The only way any of that makes sense is your bosses are laundering massive amounts of money. It's the only reasonable explanation for the unpredictable part of gambling that's become more than predictable in those books."

"That's what I thought too, but I didn't want to overreach by having an overactive imagination. Hell, you see this stuff in movies, but you don't expect it right in your face." Brinley sipped her coffee and shook her head. "Maybe this is why Dean asked us for the audit."

"Honey, you know I don't want to come out and tell you what to do, but if there's any truth in those movies, it's that you shouldn't take this lightly. No one launders money for a pack of nuns. These are bad people, and you need to get out of there. This isn't something you can take a chance on."

"You don't think I'm in danger, do you?" Brinley shook her head without a lot of enthusiasm. "I actually thought about it briefly, but I'm a nobody. The nobody only gets killed if they're in the wrong place."

"Or they see something they shouldn't. This doesn't feel right to me." Wilma placed her hand on the box of files. "Not to knock your skills, but I don't understand why they put you on this as your first assignment. Internal audits are usually done because you're trying to find theft—not because you're rolling in cash. That's the other thing that makes no sense. As to your other theory, there's no way in hell your boss doesn't know what's going on."

"Do you have any theories?" Brinley was sure of her skills, but her mother had way more experience.

"I'm sure I'm wrong, but this assignment seems like busywork. It's like they're trying to prove something they already know. An audit seems to me like a total waste of time."

"That's true too, but quitting now might ruin my chances of getting another job somewhere else. I don't want to come off as some kind of flake."

"All you need to do is look for something off the Strip. There's enough of a variety of industries here for you to find a place without all this going on. Think about Finn. You don't need to put yourself in danger for a paycheck."

Brinley stood and put her arms around her. "Thank you, and as always, you're right. Let me get all that stuff back to them and break the news. I'll tell them I have a family emergency I have to deal with, and I don't want to hold them back. The only thing I'll miss is my friendship with Naomi, but I'll call her in a week or so and touch base."

"I love you, and I think you're making the right choice. We don't really know any of these people and we can't guess what their motives are."

Finn came out of his room and screamed in delight when he saw her. Brinley knew her mom had missed her, but she had a special need to see her grandson, and she couldn't blame her.

"Hey, cutie," Wilma said, scooping him up and kissing both his cheeks.

Brinley smiled and fixed a cup of juice for him. "Why don't you take a nap, and I'll get him ready. Today's his first day at the new day care, and I don't want to lose my spot. Harvard would've been easier to get into, and I think it'll be a place he'll like when I go back to work. Once I'm done today we'll come back and take you out to lunch."

"I'll take both of you out to lunch, so hurry back."

"This shouldn't take long at all."

"Do you understand what I'm asking for?" the client asked Reed. It was the second call of the morning to give the final instructions for what they needed done.

Reed hated men who spoke to people as though they were better than anyone around them. She kept her tone even. "I understood you the first time, so send me a picture and address and it's done."

"It'll be in your messages as soon as I hang up."

Reed held the phone, waiting for the text that would mean a two-hundred-thousand-dollar payday. Why Robert Wallace would spend the cash on someone who was basically a nobody made her curious, but she figured Little Bobby was making an example of whoever this woman was.

Little Bobby's fixer, Alex, had called the night before, following the directions she'd insisted on when he'd called at the diner, and she recognized his voice from their previous conversations about other jobs, even if Alex had no idea who she was. Robert Wallace had fucked up so many times, he could be her only client if she took every contract. This could be another one of his screwups, and if the woman had stolen from Wallace, she understood punishment, but this was a bit excessive. Whatever the reason, all that mattered was it was Little Bobby's dime.

Her phone buzzed and she studied the picture of the blond woman. She was beautiful despite the awful employee ID photo, which was a waste, but that had nothing to do with the job that had to be done. The address wasn't far from where she was. She planned to make the hit look like a car accident.

"Must be my lucky day," she said as she took a left and headed over a few blocks to the nice apartment complex. "Oscar." She parked outside the gate.

"Did asshole Alex give you a name, finally?"

"Brinley Myers, and unless I'm wrong, that's not someone in management over there."

"Give me a second." She heard him tapping keys rapidly. "Ms. Myers is driving a navy blue Toyota 4Runner with Louisiana plates. That should be easy to spot even if in an apartment complex."

The vehicle *was* easy to spot as it turned right out of the lot, and she didn't take any precautions as she started following, figuring the woman wasn't expecting anyone to be doing so. "What's the story on Myers?" She kept driving but Myers wasn't headed to the Moroccan, and if she was, she'd picked the strangest possible way to get there.

"I don't know what she could've done that would've landed her on our radar," Oscar said, his voice fading away as if he was distracted by something.

"What's that mean?" she asked as they made another turn. "And where the hell is she going?" Myers took a few more turns, and the only explanation she could think of for this circuitous route to the casino was that Brinley Myers was new to town and had the directional sense of a confused homing pigeon.

"She's been at the Moroccan, like, a week and a bit, and she's only been in town three weeks. What exactly could've gone wrong in that amount of time? That doesn't sound like someone Little Bobby would waste his time, much less money, on."

"You're right." She slowed when Myers made an unexpected turn, and for a second she thought she'd been spotted and Myers was stopping to confront her. "You got anything else?"

"That's it. Brinley Myers is an accountant who obviously pissed off the wrong people in record time. She should've stayed in New Orleans with her—"

"Child," Reed said when Brinley got out, reached into the back, and carried out a toddler. "Fuck." That could've been her and her own mother a million years ago, if her mother had actually been a responsible adult.

"What, you don't have a shot?" Oscar asked, and she had no good answer. Caring about any mark wasn't supposed to happen—not ever. That rule was sacrosanct, but shooting a woman holding her kid…that was out of the question.

"Let me call you back." She punched the steering wheel hard three times.

All the contracts she'd taken were easy, they'd always been easy. She aimed, she fired, she drove away to get paid. None of those marks clouded her mind or haunted her dreams because none of them mattered. They were, in a way, all like Victor in that they did bad shit for most of their lives, so their deaths shouldn't have been a shock to them.

This woman, though, was different. She looked innocent, and that Reed had no experience with. Killing an innocent wasn't in her makeup, and she couldn't make herself aim and fire. She might've been emotionally stunted, but she wasn't dead inside.

That rash decision had the potential to blow her world to shit. You couldn't lie, collect the fee, and send the supposedly dead person back to their lives. The truth always came out, somehow.

Brinley Myers glanced back and held her kid tighter when Reed sped across the street, her tires squealing, and slammed to a stop next to her. The way Brinley's eyes widened when she saw the gun in her hand was expected, but her turning away from her when she raised it was not. It was as if Brinley was protecting her kid from what was about to happen. It was foolish and courageous, but they were in the game now. She parked her car and got out.

"Put him back in his car seat and make it fast. Don't make me say it again." She lowered the gun to not attract attention, and watched as Myers did what she asked.

Brinley threw the diaper bag in the back seat and strapped the kid in as she kept glancing back at her. Her expression was one of fear and it was obvious she was trying to figure out what to do.

"If you want, take my purse and go. I don't have much cash, but you can take my credit cards."

"Less talking and more buckling." She got into the driver's seat and pushed it back to accommodate her legs. "If you don't want me to leave with the kid, get next to me when you're done, and it's no time to get cute. Don't yell, and hand your cell phone over."

"Why are you doing this?" Brinley asked when Reed pulled into traffic. The kid was surprisingly quiet in the back, but Reed could hear him kicking the seat rhythmically.

"Shut up and let me think." She took the streets that would avoid the Strip and started making her way out of town. Maybe by the time they got where they were going, she'd come back to reality and finish the job.

The desert outside Vegas had plenty of mythology to go with it, and a lot of it was on the money. This was a place where you could bury either your secrets or your mistakes, and the elements would erase all trace of them. Once they'd gone about fifteen miles, Reed turned off and drove down one of the county roads until she couldn't see the highway. The deserted spot had a line of boulders, and from experience Reed knew these areas were only popular with off-roaders.

Reed put the car in park and placed her gun back in her shoulder holster. That didn't seem to bring down Brinley's freak factor. "Look—"

"Please, whatever you're going to do, don't do it in front of my son. I'll give you whatever you want if you don't hurt him." Brinley's tears were falling, and her emotions seemed to be in overload as she sucked in breaths between words.

"Mama," the little boy said, as if he realized how upset his mother was.

"Ms. Myers, not to sound like some cheap hustler, but if I wanted to hurt you, you'd be dead and already lying out there bloating." The way she put it made Brinley cry harder. "Look," she said louder, and the kid start crying too. "Oh, fuck me."

Reed took the keys out of the ignition and got out. She slammed the door, walked to the back of the vehicle, and glanced at the dust that still hadn't settled on the road.

How any animal or plant lived in this misery was amazing, and the fact that she was out here thinking about fucking minutiae instead of completing her contract meant she was losing her mind. Killing this woman would've been easy if Reed didn't have a mental image of that kid ending up in foster care. Oscar hadn't mentioned a father, so killing his mother probably meant the kid would be in the same spot she was in, years down the line. If he lived that long.

She went back and started the car again since the few minutes of her being outside had raised the temperature to uncomfortable. "Stop crying," she said in a gentler tone.

"I'm sorry," Brinley said, her voice hoarse but her tears still falling.

"What did you do for Robert Wallace?"

"Who?"

Reed clenched her jaw and made a fist. "If you start off lying, this isn't going to last long, and believe me, you're really not going to like the ending."

"I've been here less than a month, and I don't know anyone named Wallace."

Reed tapped on the steering wheel and exhaled as a way to regain her patience. "He's the CEO of the Moroccan, and you work there." She turned slightly to face Brinley, and Brinley plastered her body to the passenger door. The move made her laugh. "You can see why your answer of *Who?* makes me think you're full of shit."

"You can believe me or not, but I really haven't been in town that long. I do work at the Moroccan, but my boss is Dean Jasper, and I work with Naomi Williams. Robert Wallace might run the place, but he's never been to accounting, and we've never met." It sounded truthful since it took Brinley forever to get it out through a fresh bout of tears and shuddering breaths.

"Could you stop crying, for fuck's sake?" She pressed two fingers to her forehead on the spot where a headache was beginning. Hysterical women weren't part of her norm—ever. Add to that a screaming kid, and Reed had entered the twilight zone.

"Why are you doing this?" Brinley asked, and that got the kid really going with his shrieking.

"Fuck me," she said softly, not able to think because of the noise. It was time to crash back to reality and get this over with.

"Please," Brinley said. "At least tell me why."

"I'm not the answer person, lady, I'm only fulfilling a contract. You must've done something, and if you don't want to admit it, that's your problem. You can take it to your grave." She lifted her hand and wrapped her fingers around the butt of her gun.

"Wait!" Brinley opened her door and got out, but didn't run.

It was the act of a good mother, or what Reed assumed a good mother did. "It's not personal." Reed walked to the passenger side and unholstered her gun. "It's just a job."

Brinley fell to her knees when she raised the weapon and aimed it at Brinley's head. She pulled the trigger without any more thought, wanting it over—and then it was.

CHAPTER TEN

Hugo Padilla followed Mano into his office and closed the door. There was a coffee service set up along with some breakfast pastries, and Mano waved his bodyguard to the table. "I got a call from my pal on the force this morning," Mano said. He took his jacket off and threw it on an empty chair. "Sounds like we have more drama going on, and the cops can't figure it out."

"If you're talking about the Moroccan crap, I can't explain it either," Hugo said, shoving half a guava and cream cheese pastry in his mouth.

Mano didn't know where his secretary found the Cuban treats, but they rivaled any in Miami, or the ones they had specially made in New Orleans. "Victor I can kind of understand, considering his position, but an accountant who has no ties to upper management? I don't." He glanced at his phone and scrolled through the messages. Nothing seemed out of the ordinary until he saw a voicemail from Benito Lucassi. "What's this asshole want?"

"You have to narrow that down, boss. It's been nothing but a steady stream of assholes lately." He took another pastry and Mano laughed.

"Oye, you better slow down if you want to keep those boyish good looks," he said, patting his stomach.

"You're just jealous that Sylvia limits you to one a week." Hugo flipped him off with a goofy smile.

"True, but Sylvia's someone you want to keep happy. Benito Lucassi, though, I'd be thrilled to avoid forever." He listened to the message requesting a meeting that came in at two fifteen that morning. For an old bastard, Benito kept odd hours.

"He's been trying for a couple of years to get more action here, but I've had the guys throw his people out when they got too blatant about honing in on more than he's entitled to. From what I hear, he's running book over at the Tropical." Hugo grabbed another pastry but split it with Mano. "The folks over there must not care since most of his business is East Coast tough guys who can't stand the heat in Vegas."

"It might be something more than that." He leaned back and put his feet up. "Benito's living large for a guy who's only keeping book."

"You think he's got some scam on the side?"

He nodded and pointed at Hugo. "Let's meet with him but put some of our best guys on him. Whatever his pitch is, he's someone's mouthpiece. Benito hasn't had an original idea since he was born."

Hugo nodded, stood, and buttoned his jacket. "I'll take care of it."

"Something going on, boss?" Dwayne came in and handed him some ledgers.

"Benito wants a meeting."

Dwayne sat and bounced his fist on his knee. "Do we know anything but the obvious about that guy? He's bad news, and he's a slow learner."

"How so?" he asked.

"Hugo's talked to him and his guys more than once about doing business here, but it finally took Steve threatening him with legal action if he kept trying to move in on our whales. He hasn't been back, but he was pissed enough to get even more stupid since he didn't get his way."

"I agree with you," he said, glancing at Hugo. "Make the meet somewhere other than here."

"How about at Bellagio?" Hugo asked.

"That sounds good. Make it at the high-stakes bar, and we can get the girls to meet us after at Prime."

"A good steak sounds like a plan," Dwayne said.

"Not as good as the spin Benito's going to give us, but let's play nice. Once we find out who's pulling his strings, we might be in the position to cut them for good."

❖

Detective Andrew Wamsley stood close to what was left of the burned-out car someone on a hike had spotted and called in. He and Corey Grant had caught the new case since everyone from the brass down had concluded Victor Madison's death was an accident. That was bullshit, but his supervisor had threatened him with desk duty if he didn't drop it.

"Are the CSI guys coming?" Corey asked.

The vehicle was still smoking, but Andrew didn't see any open flames. "Hopefully there's something left once they get here."

"Aside from the two dead people inside, you mean?" Corey asked as more personnel arrived. "There's no way this wasn't a professional hit."

"Don't trip over your shoes, rookie. Vegas isn't the Wild West anymore." He waved the CSI team over and gave them room to work. "You start saying shit like that and it freaks people out, and the brass is allergic to freaked-out people."

"Hey, Andy," Mike Henry said an hour later. "You ready for the perimeter report?"

"Let's start with the back seat, and maybe what I'm looking at has some other explanation." He was disgusted by the waste of human life, and whatever brought the driver to this place had definitely ended in a waste.

"Sorry, friend, but it looks like we got a dead female in the passenger seat, and a baby in the back. We're taking samples, but from this secluded area and the heat of the fire, there's no way someone didn't use an accelerant." Mike walked to the car and pointed. "If the hikers hadn't called this in, there would've been nothing left. The firefighters added a new layer of forensics we'll have to get through, but this is a homicide."

"The plates are gone, but is the VIN still viable?" Corey asked.

"One of the guys is running it now," Mike said in a tone that telegraphed he didn't appreciate anyone telling him how to do his job. "Any other suggestions for me?"

"Excuse us a minute," Andrew said, grabbing Corey by the bicep and dragging him away. "Look," he said, speaking low enough so no one would overhear, so as not to embarrass his new partner. "We all get you graduated at the top of your class, since you mentioned it more than once, but I'm your last resort."

"What the hell are you talking about?"

"No one else wanted to partner with you since they think you're a dumb obnoxious asshole. That's not meant to hurt your feelings, just the truth, so try to show some respect."

"Are you asking me not to do my job because some old dude

might get twisted?" Corey pointed to Mike, who seemed to be watching them with interest.

"The old dude is one of the best in the country and has closed more cases than all of us combined. But hey, I can see since you solved all those classroom cases you have a need to work by yourself so the rest of us don't hold you back. Go ahead and drive to the precinct, and when I'm done here, I'll ask the captain about cutting you loose to do your own thing." Andrew handed over the keys and went back to the crime scene. If he stuck with this kid, he'd never close another case.

"You lucked out with that one," Mike said as the car peeled out and fishtailed before getting back on the road.

"I'm convinced I sacrificed a virgin or something equally unforgivable in a past life and it's coming back to haunt me."

Mike laughed and put his glasses back on. "We're getting ready to wrap this up and bring it all back to the lab. They're melted to their seats, so I'm going to tarp the whole thing and tow it."

"I'll meet you there. Any hits on the VIN? With the kid in the car seat this is going to hit the media big-time." He took one more glance toward the small seat and a shroud of depression dropped over his shoulders, making him nauseous. "What kind of coldhearted bastard does this?"

"That I can't answer for you, my friend. All we can do is try to wade through the shit people pile up for us and try to make it to retirement without eating a bullet," Mike said.

He slapped Mike on the back and nodded. "You get an amen on that one, brother."

❖

Reed turned off another road and tapped on the steering wheel as she headed for a storage facility she had out of town. What she'd done wasn't something she wanted to dwell on, but there was still plenty left to get through before she could head home and take a cold shower. She'd been sweating a lot more than usual, but the desert was always brutal on a cloudless day. It was nothing to do with the massive fuckup she was still in the process of making.

"What now?" Brinley asked, when Reed pulled her car into an empty unit. "You keep us locked here so we can die from the heat?"

"Get out and grab the kid," she said, draping her jacket over her arm and noticing Brinley's eyes seemed to be fixed on her gun. "You and I are going to have a talk."

"About letting us go?" Brinley asked, her tears no longer falling, though she was obviously still upset.

"Lady, just move and we can get this over with, one way or another." The door sounded loud when she pulled it down but didn't lock it. The unit next door was hers as well, but this one had no door to a safe room. It had an old fifth wheel camper that was wired into the facility's electricity, water, and sewage. "Get in."

It was early afternoon and the kid was starting to get fussy, so she sat at the small table and waited for Brinley to deal with him. After Brinley fed him something out of the diaper bag, he stopped crying, and Reed closed her eyes for a moment as Brinley started singing while she rocked him.

Her assessment that this really was a good mother was right, and she had absolutely no experience there.

"What do you want to talk about?" Brinley asked.

"I lost my mind today." She clenched her fists. Her mouth had momentarily taken control of her brain for those words to have come out. Shit like that either got you caught or killed.

"Oh, good. You can let us go and we'll forget this ever happened. I've got no idea of who you are, and I don't care what you want." Brinley appeared almost relieved, as if she'd put down a heavy load.

"Slow down, and that's not what I meant." She forced her hands open and held them flat on the table. "Right now, you should be dead, and I should be collecting my fee. You may not know Robert Wallace, but he wants you dead. Letting you go isn't going to happen—just yet."

"That's ridiculous," Brinley's laugh was nearly hysterical, and Reed could tell her tears weren't far behind. "I haven't even collected my first paycheck."

"No one pays top dollar for the ridiculous, Ms. Myers." She set up the coffeepot to have something to do with herself, then leaned on the counter. "Start talking, because I have limited options here."

"What are *my* options?" Brinley rubbed her hands up and down her thighs and rocked as she spoke. "Letting us go isn't one of them, I'm guessing."

"You want honest, so here it is." She poured two cups and handed one over. She preferred milk, but she wasn't in this thing often enough to keep it fresh, so the powdered shit would have to do. "If you want to leave, I'm going to have to kill you. That isn't me being cruel, it's the truth. Killing you is the job I was hired to do today."

"Why didn't you?" Brinley sipped her coffee as well, and there was something very surreal about the whole day. It was like one of those internet dates you met at a coffee shop to make sure the other person wasn't a psycho.

"I grew up without my mom," she said, not believing these words were actually spilling out of her mouth. "I saw your kid…"

"And you couldn't do it," Brinley finished for her when it was clear she had nothing else to add. "Thank you."

"Don't thank me, lady. I'm still trying to figure out what the fuck is wrong with me." She shook her head and took a sip of coffee. "Both of us have plenty to lose now, so tell me what you did."

"My job is all I did. I was hired by Dean Jasper as an accountant, and it seemed like a great opportunity. Then my work partner and I got a new assignment," Brinley said. "He asked Naomi and me to do an internal audit, a pre-audit, really, before it went to the outside accountants."

"Did you find something?"

Brinley stared at her as if this might be the trap that would get her killed. Like all she had to do was confirm the information and she'd pull the trigger this time. "What does it matter if I did? You're going to kill me anyway."

"I'm curious, since I doubt whatever it was rises to the level of a top pay hit." Reed sighed, exhausted to her bones. Perhaps big life-changing decisions were a sign that she'd finally snapped and should consider retirement. "You can leave if you want—I'm done."

"I thought you said that wasn't an option?"

She brought the breaking news up on her phone after Oscar's text. "I didn't say you'd survive the day, but *I* won't pull the trigger." She tossed Brinley's keys on the table and stood to pour the rest of her coffee in the sink. "Little Bobby wants you dead, but you weren't the only one."

Brinley took the phone and read the article that accompanied the picture of a vehicle covered with a tarp. "Why are you showing me this?"

"By tonight the news will report on the murder of Naomi Williams and her kid. The police will swear they'll do whatever it takes to find the animals responsible, and jack shit will get done."

Brinley paled and she took a deep, shuddering breath. "They killed Amelia? She was only two."

"Now there's only one problem left, and once you're out the door, you'll be somebody else's contract." She stood still a minute longer before she pointed to the keys. "Go on, and before you get any ideas about going to the cops and bringing them here, you'll never find me again, or anything that'll lead them to me."

"Dean Jasper gave Naomi and me that assignment and said it was ordered by management. I guess it was that guy Wallace you mentioned," Brinley said, gripping the table as if she'd fly away if she let go. "After a couple of days, I dug deeper because the numbers didn't make sense. Naomi agreed and was always worried about us being overheard. My mom confirmed and backed up what I thought."

Reed sat back down and glanced at the sleeping kid before she turned her attention back to Brinley. "Your mother? Seriously?"

"She's here visiting me, and she's a CPA, so yes, my mother. Someone at the casino is laundering money, and a lot of it." Brinley pressed her hands to the sides of her head. "I don't have proof of that yet, but I was going in today to quit. There was no way I want any part of what's going on. I worked hard to get my license and I'm not losing it over someone else's stupidity."

"Are you sure that's all you found?"

Brinley stared at her as if she'd gone insane. "Believe me, I don't have anything to gain by not telling you, so that's it. My mom must be going nuts with worry by now."

"What you said doesn't sound like something you or the other woman should've died for, but Wallace isn't your average nut job. He's a paranoid asshole, so he must've feared something." She checked her watch and was ready to head home, but she'd fucked up her life by not killing this woman, and because she hadn't, she'd severely narrowed her options.

"Can I ask you something now?"

"Why the hell not." She laughed and spun the pen on the table.

"I'm glad you think this is funny," Brinley said, her anger finally emerging.

Anger in this situation was brave. "This isn't funny or fair—I get that, but life's a bear waiting to take you down. If you want to get pissed, give Little Bobby Wallace a call. All this crap isn't on me."

"Tell me the truth, and finish the story of why you didn't kill me," Brinley said gently, as if that would make her answer. "The other person didn't have a problem killing Naomi and her daughter. If you're really a professional killer, then me and my son should be dead."

"You're going to have to accept the answer I gave you. You wouldn't believe me if I told you the whole truth. Trust me." It wasn't like she got some cheap thrill from killing people—it was a job, like accounting, but with better hours and much better pay. Spilling her guts to a mark would make her not only a chump, but extremely stupid. Stupid people didn't live long in this profession.

The real problem now was not only could she not talk to Oscar about this, but she couldn't tell anyone. Silence and secrets were the only things that guaranteed your freedom. And telling Oscar would only drag him down with her. She owed him more than that.

"Try me."

CHAPTER ELEVEN

I'd give you my condolences on your loss, but I'm not that much of a hypocrite," Francesco Terzo said when Diego Moretti took a seat in Francesco's study. "The man was a piece of shit, God rest his soul, but he picked a bad time to die."

"I agree on all counts." Diego had formulated a plan for this meeting, and the most important aspect of it was not saying too much. "Victor went out of his way to humiliate my daughter, but she'll get over it and move on. We, on the other hand, have to find another way to conduct business."

"Sofia has my sympathy. First Victor, and now all this business with their sons. Poor woman has no luck." Francesco reached over and patted his knee like he was a small boy in need of comforting for a scraped elbow.

"Her sons will learn respect, or they will have to learn to fend for themselves," he said, not appreciating Francesco's willingness to talk about things that weren't any of his business. "I won't tolerate disrespect, or the hold of a man like Victor over their mother. I don't give a fuck that he was their father."

"It's the young, Diego. Things like loyalty and respect aren't concepts they understand. That you're here makes me glad for those boys. If you straighten them out now before it gets too far out of hand, they might have a chance." Francesco leaned back and spread his hands out. "You don't deserve that in your family."

"My grandsons will come to see reason, or not. That's not important to me right now," he said and Francesco smiled. "Our business and how we go forward is why I'm here."

"Your late son-in-law was vital to my future as well as yours, but we're working on something else now that he's out of the picture. I don't want you to worry, though. Whatever I work out will include you." Francesco paused and Diego figured this was where he'd get screwed. "Granted, your piece may have to be smaller."

"Why is that? We were the ones who brought you this deal, and we're the ones who paved the way with Victor." He wasn't disciplined enough to not raise his voice, but he wasn't lying down, either. "Our part has to stay the same."

"Diego, maybe it's time for you to get out of Vegas altogether," Francesco said icily "Take some time to get your family under control. After that, we'll talk again. You know it's not going to be that easy to replace Victor with someone who'll be open to what we want, someone we can trust. You have no people here, no connections, so how are you going to help with that?"

"Are you fucking with me right now? Do you think I'm some punk who's going to take shit from you because you're Francesco Terzo?" His voice finally rose to the level of screaming as he got to his feet, and the door opened.

"Mr. Moretti, maybe it's time to go," Lucan said as he entered with Paolo.

"Think before you do something stupid, Francesco. I agreed to keep my people out of Vegas, but a few phone calls could change all that. I have as much right to this deal as you do."

"Once the families back east hear about your grandsons, and how Sofia had Victor killed, you won't win that fight." Francesco stood as well and waved Lucan back. "I don't want to talk about you or your family to anyone, I want to save you the embarrassment, but a move against me is a move against the family."

"Victor was scum and you know it. Sofia had nothing to do with that except for trying to be a good wife. The police ruled it an accident."

"We'll see, but the investigation isn't *quite* closed. Take care of burying Victor, and we'll talk after that. I know you don't like Vegas, but enjoy the city for a few days and relax. All these harsh words between us will be forgotten once you calm down and think about what I said."

Diego left without another word, needing to get away from the piece of shit who was going to pay for talking to him like that. "Where's your sister?" he asked Paolo as they drove back to the house. He flexed and stretched his fingers, trying to calm down.

"Papa, do you think that was smart? Francesco and all the Terzos are assholes, but we can't afford to piss them off and have them cut us out of this deal. We need this." Paolo spoke softly so his bodyguard wouldn't overhear them.

"We'll worry about business later. First we fix what's wrong within the family, since I think Terzo was right about that." The car left the edge of the desert and headed for the gated community where Sofia's house was located. "She doesn't want to admit it, but Sofia had that bastard killed."

"Can you blame her? What he did made him deserve the death he got. I should've been the one who killed him," Paolo said, his temper up. "How he died though—if someone killed him, they were good."

"I don't disagree with either of those things, but if Terzo believes she did it and is convinced that's the truth, we've got problems. He wouldn't give a shit if Victor hadn't been in play, but Sofia fucked things up by taking him out, and Terzo will take that personally. He's going to hit us hard if someone like Wallace doesn't take over for Victor, since it'll set us back months." He moved his head from side to side to crack the bones in his neck. "And like I said, Sofia left someone out there who can hurt us if someone like Terzo needs an excuse to move against us."

"What do you want to do?" Paolo asked, and his willingness to follow orders made Diego proud.

"We clean up Sofia's and Victor's messes, then put your sister on a short, sturdy leash. She's my daughter, and I love her, but she should've left this to us."

"You raised us with pride, though, Papa. Sofia isn't one who would've forgiven Victor for the betrayals he piled at her feet."

"True, I taught you both pride—but never to choke on it."

❖

"You're not going to answer me?" Brinley asked, but the woman simply stared at her as if she could see right through her. "Why are we here and not dead?"

"The kid didn't deserve to see that," the woman said, now staring at Finn. "The kid didn't ask you to get mixed up with these people, which makes him an innocent in all this."

"His name is Finn, and he's barely one. I doubt he'd remember if you had killed me and left him alive." The memory of the nurse laying Finn across her chest right after his birth came to her. It was the happiest moment of her life, knowing that perfect little boy would be hers forever to love and protect. "And does that mean I'm somehow guilty?"

"Don't try and guess anything about me. He'd have known, and then his life would've been fucked. I couldn't do that."

There was plenty of meaning in those words, but she doubted the person hired to kill her would explain. "What's your name?"

"You don't need to know my name." They locked eyes, and she finally had to turn away from the intensity of the woman's gaze.

"If you don't tell me that, then tell me what happens next. Hopefully, it's not that you're building up the nerve to kill me," she said and couldn't help the nervous laughter. "You're probably thinking of ways to get rid of me, and want me to shut up, but I'm scared out of my mind and I talk a lot when I'm scared."

"Don't start crying again. Believe me, I'd let you go, but Wallace will only hire someone to fulfill that contract. The next person won't give a shit about Finn or you." The sigh that followed didn't put her at ease. "The other thing is, my job prospects will dry up if I *don't* kill you."

"What if I promise to leave town and never come back?" It was worth a shot to ask. Hiring someone to kill her was in no way in the employee handbook as a reprimand for management's dissatisfaction with her job performance.

"Sure, I can do that if you're willing to start a whole new life under a whole new identity. You'd have to leave everything you know behind and spend the rest of your life praying no one ever recognized you. Leaving Vegas isn't an option unless you're willing to start over someplace like a remote cabin in Alaska." The woman shrugged and placed her hands back on the table. "I'm sure they could do with some good accountants in the frozen tundra."

Brinley couldn't be sure, but she seemed a little socially inept. "But I'm no one in the realm of all this. Why would they hunt me down?" She was about to cry again but the woman's nostrils flared so she tried to control it.

"Robert Wallace is paying me two hundred thousand dollars to kill you." She tapped the side of her head. "Think about that. Do you even make that much in a year?"

"No," she said as her tears dripped off her chin. Obviously controlling her emotions wasn't her greatest talent when she was literally under the gun. It was one of those things you didn't know about yourself until you actually experienced them.

"Then you know something Wallace doesn't want anyone else to know, and he's willing to pay for a permanent solution. It's either kill you, or move you to the remote cabin, where you spend the rest of your life wondering when the next hired gun is going to show up at your door."

"I can't stop you from the killing-me option, but could you at least do me a favor?" The memory of Finn's birth and all those things she promised him that day came back to her. She planned to fulfill them as best she could even if it meant him going on without her.

"What?"

"Can you take Finn to my mother? I mentioned that she's visiting me right now, and she'll take care of him," she said with a bravery that definitely wasn't heartfelt.

"I won't make you that promise, so save your breath." That made Brinley start crying again in earnest. "Jesus, come on with the tears. I'm not killing you no matter what, so you can take care of the kid yourself."

"Oh," she said, wiping her face. Her eyes felt raw and swollen, but the discomfort reminded her that she was still alive. "I should clarify and say no matter *who* kills me. Will you make sure he gets to my mom?"

"You're not dying, so save it for something else you want."

"I should admit that I wasn't completely truthful before." She started talking faster when the woman tensed up again. "You made me panic. I should've said that I have heard of that guy Wallace before. Naomi told me who he was."

"Anything else you want to tell me?"

"I've never met or seen him, but she mentioned him. After that, and after seeing my boss having lunch with someone she said was a Mob person, I accessed information on Naomi's laptop and emailed it to myself," she said, realizing that she might be responsible for what happened to her friend. "Do you think that's why they killed her?"

"They killed her because she was working on the audit with you. There has to be something in there that Wallace doesn't want you to accidentally share with anyone. Hell, you may not have even come across it yet. And what Mob person are you talking about?"

"Someone named Caterina," she said, pinching her forehead and trying to remember. "I'm sorry I don't remember her last name, but Naomi recognized her."

"Your boss, Dean, was having lunch with Caterina Terzo?" That seemed to interest her captor for some reason.

"That's what Naomi said. She got nervous after that, so we only talked a bit more over lunch and then went back to work." The way the woman was nodding was, in a strange way, making her feel better about the situation.

"What did you and your mom find that makes you think Wallace is laundering money?"

"The only thing that jumped out at me was the consistency of their cash flow statements," she said, and it didn't seem to register with the woman. "Any business like a doctor's office, or an oil-field supply company, or anyone who does the same service over and over again usually has about the same intake of cash. Well, unless they expanded or something like a hurricane interrupted them for an extended period of time."

"Those you have experience with, I'm guessing."

"I do, but do you understand what I'm talking about?"

"I understand."

"Even those types of businesses I mentioned have some fluctuation." She put her hands down when she noticed she was using them too much. "This is the first casino I've worked for, and the nature of their business, I'd guess, shouldn't be so steady. In two years the Moroccan has almost quadrupled their business with a consistent payout percentage. That's an accounting anomaly that shouldn't happen in a real-life situation."

"The records you accessed, were they available without a password?"

"Naomi told me they have to be because of the gaming commission. If they spot-check, they have to be able to sit at any terminal and open the files." She stopped talking when the woman smiled, and it transformed her whole face, making her strangely attractive, given the situation. "What?"

"The money they're taking in probably hasn't changed, but how they've reported it has."

She shook her head. "I don't understand."

"What you accessed is what the gaming commission is looking at, but what you were working on are the actual numbers. If whatever agency got ahold of those numbers, it'd bury Wallace and your boss under a world of hurt."

"What's your name?" Brinley tried again.

"Why do you need to know?" The woman looked at her like she was getting ready to strip her bare of every secret she thought to have.

"Okay, forget that and tell me what happens next. You said I'm dead if I leave, and that we don't have many choices, so what's the way out of this?" There was nothing to lose here, and it was time to gamble and try to save her life. For a killer, her captor didn't seem rash, and hopefully that would hold.

"I make my living by precise planning that can't be deviated from if I want to stay in the shadows."

The answer probably meant the woman was going to deflect again. Brinley would ask hard questions, but the penalty shots of doing the wrong thing would be hard to overcome.

"Until today, that's been the basis of my life, so I really can't answer that question honestly. Not right now."

"I'm sure I sound repetitive, but what does that mean?" How in the world did she have this kind of shitty luck? She'd moved here for better opportunities, and she was now in an old camper with the woman hired to kill her. This was no time to lose her head, but *Jesus Christ*. This was like nothing else she'd ever faced, and one wrong answer or move would cost her more than a job.

"That's simple. I don't know."

"That makes two of us." All she had to do was keep the woman talking and thinking, and she and Finn might be okay.

❖

Wilma checked her phone again and called Brinley for what must have been the fiftieth time, but there was still no answer to all her calls, texts, and phone messages. She'd checked with the day care center every hour, but Brinley had never dropped Finn off, and Brinley hadn't shown up at work yet, either. She really wanted to call the police, but they'd only tell her to wait twenty-four hours.

"Maybe if I'm persistent enough they'll make an exception," she said as she searched for the number. It took ten minutes before she was connected to an officer and he asked what she considered to be useless questions.

"Ma'am, we need to wait twenty-four hours, but what probably is going on here is your daughter decided to take the day off. My wife calls them mental health days."

"She'd take one of those if her mother came over a thousand miles to see her?" she asked, wondering what kind of idiot this guy was. "It doesn't matter, my daughter wouldn't disappear for the day and not get in touch with me."

"I have her license number and her information, and I'll put that out. If she's not home by tomorrow, we'll take a more active approach. Did you call her work?"

"Yes, but I might head over there and talk to them," she said, done wasting time.

"Ma'am, you should do that, but don't be confrontational," the officer said.

She hung up before she really got pissed. The cab took fifteen minutes, and double that to talk her way into the accounting department. "I need to see Dean Jasper," Wilma said to the receptionist.

"Do you have an appointment?" the woman asked and when she faced Wilma, her eyes and nose were red.

"Are you okay?" Wilma asked. The woman, along with quite a few other people, appeared upset. "What's going on?"

"I'm sorry, ma'am, but one of our employees and her baby were found murdered this morning. The police just left."

Wilma hung on to the counter to stay on her feet, and she closed her mouth to keep from screaming. "Who?" she asked, barely above a whisper, and she closed her eyes as a defense against the potential hard truth. "Who?" she asked louder.

"I'm sorry, ma'am, they told us not to talk about it."

"My daughter and my grandson are missing, so tell me who it was." Her voice rose, and had there not been a counter separating them, she would've struck the woman.

"Ma'am, can I help you?" a man said, coming out of an office.

"Should I call security, Mr. Jasper?" the receptionist asked.

He shook his head. "Ma'am, what can we do for you?"

"I'm Brinley Myers's mother, and I want to know who the police came and talked to you about."

"Wait, Brinley's missing?" the receptionist asked. "Should we call the police to come back?"

"Is she?" Dean asked. "The police were here this morning, but it was about another employee, Naomi Williams."

"She's dead?" Wilma's stomach felt like it'd filled with acid, and she fought the desire to vomit.

Dean took a deep breath and nodded. "The police aren't sure

what happened or why, but they found her and her daughter early this morning." He motioned her toward his office and she followed him in a daze.

"We have to call the police and get them back here," she said, sitting in Dean's office. "It can't be coincidence that Naomi's dead and Brinley's missing, along with her one-year-old."

"Are you sure she didn't hear about Naomi and take some time to clear her head?" Dean asked and she wanted to curse him for his stupidity.

"You may not have known Brinley long, but she's not in a bar drowning her sorrows with her son along. If you don't want to do it, give me the number and I'll call."

Dean took a card from his pocket and picked up his phone. "I hope you're wrong, and she just took Finn to the park. Losing Naomi has devastated the office." The conversation with the detective didn't take long and Dean gently put his phone back on his desk as if he wanted to see any incoming messages. "They're on their way back."

"Where did they find her?" She was having trouble breathing and her head was pounding at the thought of a world that didn't include Brinley and Finn. "Naomi and her daughter, I mean."

"Outside of town in the desert. From what the police said, it was a fluke they were found this fast, but some hiker saw the fire and called 9-1-1." Dean poured her some water and sat next to her. "I'm sure Brinley's fine and she'll call when she gets a chance."

"You don't think it strange that her work partner was killed and now she's missing? I don't think Brinley's fine." She stared at Dean as all the conversations about him she'd had with Brinley went through her head. Dean, who assigned her the audit, and who was meeting with some criminal for lunch.

"We're going to do everything in our power to find her, ma'am. Brinley may be new to our organization, but she's part of the Moroccan family. She was doing important work for us," Dean said, clearly trying to sound empathetic. "Did she by chance have any files at home? She was so dedicated to her job—I'm sure she did."

"You want them back *now*?" she asked incredulously. "If you want them, we're going to have to find her. She left this morning with my grandson and a couple of boxes I assume were work she brought home."

"She didn't talk about her work with you?" Dean slightly cocked his head, like the conversation they were having wasn't an inappropriate fishing expedition on his part. "Maybe something she said will clue us in as to where she is."

"My daughter's like me, Mr. Jasper, when it comes to her job. You can be assured she wasn't discussing her duties with me or anyone else, and I couldn't care less about that right now."

"Mr. Jasper, the detectives are back," the receptionist informed them.

Dean insisted on staying for moral support, and Wilma wanted to offer him a pen and notepad to take notes, he was listening so intently. She wasn't about to say anything about the accounting issues in front of him, but she needed to find a way to tell the detectives what Brinley had told her. Instead, she answered the usual questions. "I'm not here because my daughter was having problems, Detective," she said to the young guy who introduced himself as Corey Grant. "I'm here visiting my daughter and grandson because we missed each other. When she left this morning, we made plans for dinner, and lunch if she could swing it."

"And you tried her phone?" the older guy, Detective Wamsley, asked.

"Numerous times. She wouldn't ignore that many calls and messages, so something has to be wrong."

"Let's see if we can use that to find her, ma'am," Wamsley said. "Do I have your permission to track her cell to try to narrow our search?"

"Yes, anything you need, you do it."

Wamsley placed his hand on her forearm and smiled. "I believe you that something's wrong, but if you can think of anything else, call me directly." He handed her a card and pressed her fingers over it. "You have my word we'll do everything we can to find her."

"Thank you."

Wamsley's face seemed to change when he turned his attention to Dean. "Tell Mr. Wallace we'll be back, so don't think of avoiding the meeting."

"Come on," Dean said a bit too loudly. "We care about Brinley— we had nothing to do with this."

"Two employees on the same day, from the same department?" Grant pointed at Dean. "The only other things they have in common is you, and that they're missing. In police work, that's what we call a big clue."

"If you want to come with us, Mrs. Myers, we'll get started on that phone trace," Wamsley said.

"Let's go before it's too late," Wilma said. "I refuse to believe anything other than they're okay." She looked at Dean before she walked out. "And if they're not, someone will pay."

CHAPTER TWELVE

"Tell me you're fucking kidding," Robert said as Alex told him about the police visits to their offices. "They killed some kid?"

"Both women had children, and I told the guy to make it look like an accident," Alex said calmly. "All I can think is something went wrong."

"Killing a kid isn't an accident, Alex, it's a fucking disaster. It's the kind of fucking disaster that makes people crazy about demanding the police find whoever did it." Robert banged his fist on the desk a few times before he glared at Alex. "This was an easy job. Kill the accountants. That's it."

"I know that, but I didn't kill the kids, and I sure as hell didn't order that." Alex stood and turned his back on him. "Jesus, who the fuck does that? Did he think there was a bonus for both of them?"

"Get Dean up here."

Alex walked to the door and opened it. "I already called him up since I figured you'd want to see him."

"Tell me." He hoped Dean was smart enough not to need a ton of directions here.

"The two detectives came to ask questions about Naomi first, and they seem satisfied we didn't have any connection to this." Dean's hair was out of his usual neat style, and his shirt was sweat stained. "When Brinley's mother got here asking questions, I had no other play but to call them back. Shit, guys, we killed a kid? Or two?"

"Myers's mother came here?" he asked, and Dean nodded. "I thought you both said she had no family here."

"She doesn't," Alex said. "She arrived last night for a visit from New Orleans."

"And she's the type who's not going to let this go," Dean said and told him about his talk with Wilma. "I asked if Brinley mentioned anything about work and she said no, but I think she's lying."

"No one in the building is paying you to think about anything but the books, smart guy. Telling her or the police we had nothing to do with this is like telling them we did it," he said, punching the desktop twice more. "If anyone else comes, you send them up here."

"Yes, sir. What about Brinley and her son?" Dean asked.

"With any luck she'll never be found. Let's hope our other guy dropped the kid somewhere, or this will be radioactive." Dean stood up and Alex placed his hands on his shoulders from behind. "Dean, you've been here long enough to know to keep your mouth shut, right? You letting anything slip to the police over a girl who was never going to fuck you unless she was tied down would not be healthy for you. You screw up, and we'll introduce you to Caterina Terzo's dark side, and she *will* fuck you."

"Come on, Robert. You know I'm solid."

"Get out of here and finish all that audit stuff yourself," he said and dropped into his office chair. When he opened his eyes he noticed Dean's pained expression. "What?"

"Brinley took a few boxes to finish at home since we're on a tight deadline, and so did Naomi."

"We all know Naomi's aren't a problem, but that's not true of the rest. If Myers's car gets dumped and the police get to it first, and those boxes are in there, I'm going to kill you to make myself feel better." He leaned back and closed his eyes again. If he could kill Francesco and his two evil spawn, he would. That's who was to blame for all this, since they'd pushed to expand way too fast and without a lot of planning. Francesco and his need to rush had pushed him into this fucked-up corner.

"You want me to call and have the car torched? Have him search the house?" Alex asked when they were alone.

"And invite our contractor to make some more money off me when they try to sell the paperwork back to us?" He poured himself a finger of whiskey and swallowed it. "Let's give it until tonight, and if this one did his job, the cops won't find the car."

"Then I'll check in the morning and get the boxes myself if they're in her place." Alex sat back down and shook his head when Robert picked up the bottle again. "It's no time to lose your head."

"The day can't get any worse, unless there's something else

you're not telling me." He poured a little more, but as he lifted his glass, Caterina Terzo came in with her man Leon Santiago.

"That was like tempting fate." Alex sighed and poured himself a drink.

"You don't seem happy to see me," Caterina said, motioning for Leon to stand by the door. "You put my father off, and for what?" She glared at them. "Then imagine my surprise when I watched the news this morning…Still, my phone was silent."

"You coming over here isn't going to help anything." He was starting not to care how Caterina or anyone in her family felt about how he spoke to them. None of them understood the importance of not going through life like Godzilla in one of those old movies. Rushing and smashing things that were hard to put back together wasn't his style, even if he had played his card on the accountants a little quickly. Their business had to be planned out if they wanted to keep going, but the Terzos were only interested in getting their money cleaned while everyone else took all the risks.

"Bobby, don't get ahead of yourself. When you took my father's deal, you understood what was expected of you. If you didn't, keep that to yourself." Caterina, as always, spoke like she was ordering in restaurants or talking about the weather. It was like killing and threatening people was an everyday occurrence. "Explaining now would have to take place somewhere you could scream all you want."

"Let's be honest with each other, Caterina, and admit you need me as much as I need you. This deal needs both sides, so don't fucking come in here and threaten me."

Leon got to him with impressive speed, but he didn't say anything else after the big guy took the glass he'd been drinking out of and smashed it against Robert's forehead. He blinked against the blood dripping into his eyes.

"The other thing to remember," Caterina's tone hadn't changed, "is you're an asshole we found with the qualifications to run a used-car lot and not much more. You're here because you can follow directions, not because you're a genius." She might as well be saying it might rain tomorrow.

He pressed a wad of tissue to his head. "I was at another casino, so don't try to rewrite history." He tried to turn away before Leon hit him again but the fist to the side of his head hurt just as much. He leaned against the desk, determined not to drop to his knees in front of her. "Come on, Caterina. I'm not your enemy."

"What the hell did you do?" Caterina asked, putting a finger up when Leon cocked his fist back to hit him yet again.

There was no other choice but to explain. He slumped into his chair. "I was doing research on the numbers to see how much more we can filter through this casino, since you and I both know this place is a dump. If, all of a sudden, we're dishing out millions more, someone's going to notice. You want that kind of heat on you?" He rolled his chair a little away from Leon to buy time. "Give me Victor's slot next door, and Francesco would have to triple his operation to max out capacity."

"You bring down an iron curtain on this place when the cops start to squeeze everyone for information on two dead women and their kids, and you expect to be rewarded for that?" Caterina laughed and shook her head. "Are you delusional?"

"Did you want me to leave them out there with the real picture of what we're really doing?" He hoped she'd see reason. "We needed the report to move forward, to prove to your father we couldn't handle a lot more at once. But we couldn't have loose ends when it came to who knew about the numbers."

"Get Dean up here," Caterina said and snapped her fingers, prompting Alex to dial. "Shut up," she said when Robert opened his mouth again. "You had your chance to talk, and I'm tired of listening to your long list of mistakes."

Dean arrived and explained what the audit was supposed to prove, and how it differed from the books they kept for the purpose of the gaming commission. "Robert's right in that adding much more isn't impossible, but it has to be done slowly. There's no way to hide much more than we do already."

"If this audit was necessary to prove that, why didn't *you* do it?" Caterina asked, and Robert saw how Dean swallowed hard. His pronounced Adam's apple was a dead giveaway.

"I gave him two weeks because I didn't want to put Francesco off longer than that," Robert said. "He wouldn't have made the deadline on his own. The women were expendable."

"You've got an answer for everything." Caterina stood. "Concentrate on your business and stop dreaming about the place next door. That might be a reach unless you can prove to us you can navigate your way out of this shitstorm. From what I can tell, all you can do is get yourselves into a world of hurt. At some point, I think you'll become expendable too."

"Do you want to stop moving money until the cops are finished with whatever they're going to do about our two problems?" He wiped his eyes again and his fingers came away bloody. If he needed stitches after the big son of a bitch Leon hit him, he was going to be pissed.

"If you want to keep breathing, then you'll keep working, and do whatever you can to send the cops somewhere else." Caterina turned toward the door but stopped. "Who'd you ask to help you? Their names," Caterina asked, staring at Dean.

Robert glanced at Dean and nodded slightly. "Naomi Williams was found dead this morning, but one of our new hires, Brinley Myers, is missing," Dean said, and Caterina mouthed something under her breath.

Caterina looked from him to Dean. "Were you drunk when you came up with this plan?"

"I was only looking out for our business," he said, but his stomach clenched, since now it sounded even dumber than it had before.

"It's a casino, Einstein. Laundering money through a casino isn't exactly difficult," Caterina said loudly, finally looking like she was pissed off. "But instead of doing what my father asked, you set your sights on bigger things and completely lost your mind. Now you've fucked us because the cops are going to be relentless on account of the little kid. Add another one to that, and someone has to go down."

"Naomi Williams didn't have any family except for her daughter, and she wasn't anyone important, so it shouldn't take long for the police to disappear. We went over this already." Robert didn't care how it looked—he poured himself another drink.

"What about this other woman? What's her story?" Caterina asked, sitting back down and crossing her legs again as if she intended to stay a while.

"What about her?" Robert asked.

"Dean," Caterina said, "start talking."

"Brinley started last week, and she didn't mind the workload I asked of her. When we went to lunch at Paris, she was there with Naomi. Remember, I pointed them out."

Caterina pinched her left eyebrow. "Wait, the pretty blonde?"

"That's her, but I got suspicious when Naomi started whispering to her. I'm sorry, I should've done the work myself, but I had a pile on my desk only I could do. Since no one but me ever looks at everything at once, I didn't think it'd be a problem." Dean was talking fast again, and it only seemed to make Caterina angrier.

"Will she be found?" Caterina asked Robert.

"She and her son are missing, and we answered all the cops' questions, and they left. Whatever happened to her, she's with a professional, so she won't be found." Robert slapped his hands together and stood. "We'll do what you said and go back to work. Believe me, you have my word, nothing like this will happen again."

"You used all your strikes today," Caterina said, standing as well.

Robert was sure she was ready to run back to Francesco and lobby for his death.

"Start praying your mistakes really do disappear." Caterina and Leon left, the door shutting softly behind them.

"Are we in trouble?" Dean asked. He looked even sweatier than he had when they'd called him in.

"Get back to work and try not to overshare again." Robert needed to get out for a little while and forget the downward slide his life and job had taken.

"Stop worrying," Alex said. "The contractor working the second job is the best in the business."

"For both our sakes, I hope so. Caterina's right that all this was unnecessary, but we can't kill Dean just yet."

CHAPTER THIRTEEN

Tf you decide to run, you're on your own," Reed said to Brinley as she stood next to Brinley's car.

"Are you sure this is the only way?" They'd talked to the point where it was apparent there was only one way to go and that was forward. Brinley had stopped crying and seemed to accept Wallace wanted her dead. "I'm not disagreeing with you, but I'm worried about my mom. She won't know and this will devastate her."

"Your mom—" Her phone rang. She put her finger to her mouth and answered it. "Hey."

"Are you done?" Oscar asked, and he didn't sound quite normal.

"Almost," she said, glad that the baby was in his car seat. After his nap he'd been really vocal, and it was surreal having a kid in her private space. All she needed now was a puppy and a prom date to complete this bizarre day. "I'm doing some cleanup, and I don't have a lot of time."

"How about the kid?"

That explained why he sounded off. "I didn't want to, but it couldn't be helped. Don't worry though, they won't be found."

"Are you okay?" As always, Oscar was her friend no matter what she'd done.

"It wasn't what I wanted, buddy, believe me, but I'll survive. I'll call you later today."

"Do you need help?"

"Enjoy your night." She stared at Brinley while she lied to the one person she'd never done that to. "You don't want any part of this, and I wouldn't do that to you."

"Call me, then."

"Tomorrow, Oscar. I need some time." She put the phone in her pocket and took a deep breath. "Your mom's got to sell her reaction or this won't work. I don't know her, but that gut reaction will make or break us."

"Us?" Brinley asked in a higher pitch.

"My job was to kill you. The man who hired me expects that to happen, and if it doesn't, there's no do-over. They're going to need proof. They don't just dock my pay if I don't get something done." She opened the driver's side door and waited. "The next part is up to you."

"I'm totally crazy for doing this, but let's go." Brinley got in.

"Do you have any questions?" The remark about being crazy was on the money, but Reed had committed.

"I'll follow you, but I won't tailgate," Brinley said, repeating the directions for the sixth time.

The Suburban in the space next to the camper had tinted windows, which would help for later, but the next hour would be all about trust. It was a strange concept to trust someone she'd only just met, but that was at the center of how to get out of this alive. Reed drove the speed limit and refused to glance in the rearview mirror, since doing so would convince her just how ludicrous this was.

Granted, she had enough money to sit and watch the golfers all day for the rest of her days, but she wasn't ready to retire. And her retirement plan didn't include a bullet to the head for either her or Oscar.

She slowed and turned onto the road where she'd brought Brinley that morning and stopped at the line of rocks. There was no moon, so the only light slicing through the darkness were the headlights from their vehicles. As far as the world was concerned, this was where Brinley and Finn Myers would die.

Brinley got out and stared at her with glassy eyes. The tears were close again and Reed wondered if they were from second thoughts. "Problem?"

"I was thinking on the way over here what would've happened to us if whoever killed Naomi had been hired to kill me instead. This sucks and is totally out of my norm, but I thank God you were the one sent."

"Believe me, if there is a God, he has nothing to do with me. And if he does exist, he's a cruel son of a bitch." Reed wasn't about to let this woman think there was anything good about the situation. They weren't friends. She was a mistake that Reed needed to rectify, but in a way she could live with.

"I don't see it like that at all."

"You don't deserve to die—that's all this is about." She stopped Brinley from saying anything else and walked away to get what she needed out of her car. "Leave the car seat."

"I don't have another one," Brinley said, as if she'd lost her mind for suggesting such a thing.

"It has to be there when the cops find this, so leave it. You're going to have to sit in the back and hold him. I know it's not what you want, but it beats the alternative, doesn't it? And before you ask, you know what the alternative is."

The car seat and the diaper bag were in the car when Reed rigged it to crash into the rocks. Brinley flinched when the impact echoed through the desert, but then the silence returned. "I just finished paying for that," Brinley murmured as Finn rested his head on her shoulder and stared at the demolished car.

"Sorry, but it's the only way to throw the wolves off your scent. If you're dead, the people who wanted you that way relax, and relaxation is the first step on the road to sloppy." She removed the stick that held down the accelerator and doused the car in gasoline, leaving the can in the back next to Finn's car seat.

"Is that it?" Brinley asked.

Reed hesitated before removing the switchblade. "Not quite."

"Have you changed your mind?" Brinley pulled Finn tighter to her, her eyes wide with fear.

Reed shook her head in an effort to avoid any more hysterics. "We have to do a bit more staging, so put the kid in the car." She waited for Brinley by the wrecked vehicle and tried not to make any sudden movements when Brinley joined her. "I need a little blood from you."

"That's not exactly like a cup of sugar," Brinley said, crossing her arms over her chest. The way this woman vacillated from scared to indignant was almost humorous.

"Close your eyes." The cut was fast but obviously not painless, since Brinley screamed when she made the cut to her forearm. "Hold your arm out," she instructed, pressing Brinley's back to her chest. "Relax."

"You'd have to knock me unconscious to get me to relax." Brinley held out her arm and droplets of her blood dripped into a small pool on the ground. "But tonight's been traumatic enough, so that's not a suggestion."

She put her arms under Brinley's and dragged her to the car, creating the tracks and trail of blood that would explain why the bodies weren't in the car. Brinley held her breath when she picked her up and lifted her into the front seat to take care of the wound she'd caused. "How's that feel?" she asked when she tied off the bandage.

"Thank you—it's fine."

"I'll put you in the back with the kid." She lifted Brinley and carried her to the back seat, not wanting any tracks as small as Brinley's on the ground. She forced herself not to think of the way Brinley's body felt cradled against her. It was irrelevant. Even if it felt…right.

It took over forty minutes to leave only the clues she wanted found, and she changed shoes three times while she worked. All that was left was to torch the car and drive away. By now the car she'd left at the day care most probably had been found, but it'd come back stolen and the doctor it belonged to would lead nowhere. Every job was about misdirection that led away from her. A stolen vehicle that could only be traced to an upstanding citizen was the first dead end the cops would find.

While she worked, she thought about the situation. What in the hell would have spooked the casino so badly they would order hits on women who didn't even know what they were looking at?

Reed worked through the little information Brinley had given her. If she could figure it out, there was a chance they could not only come out of this alive, but maybe, just maybe, she'd manage to get a little bit for her trouble too. Adrenaline coursed through her as she struck a match. She hadn't played a game with stakes like these in a long time.

"What now?" Brinley asked when she got in and they watched the car burn.

"I'm off script, Ms. Myers, so I still have no good answer to that. Stay down and think about what could've landed you in my crosshairs, because just knowing the numbers are bigger than they should be isn't enough. It's a casino in Vegas, and that's barely enough to make someone look up from their paperwork. Figure out what it is they think you know. That's the only real way to get out of this." She turned around and headed toward Henderson. Going home was probably a mistake, but what was one more on the pile?

"You know, I've read about people like you, but I figured I'd have a better chance at getting hit by lightning than meeting you." Brinley lay on the back seat with Finn on her chest, sounding like she was thinking out loud.

"I'm mostly a thief, a damn good one, but I do special jobs like yours every so often." She didn't speed until she was on the interstate, then motioned for Brinley to be quiet as she dialed 911. "I just saw some big fire off the county road close to where you found that lady and kid today. It was too far off the highway, and I didn't want to get shot." She hung up and cleared her throat. "Let's see what that shakes loose."

❖

"Has Francesco called back?" Paolo asked Diego after he'd returned from the funeral home with Sofia. They'd gone to drop off a suit for Victor to be buried in and to finalize the service arrangements and burial site.

"He thinks everything is settled. I know how he thinks, and to him we simply roll over and let them fuck us because I have no other choice." Diego had been in a dark mood since they'd arrived at Sofia's and it wasn't improving.

"Sofia will need us for the next few days, so try to forget all that," Paolo said, trying his best to calm his father.

"Wait until I talk to the other families and we get our shit from another supplier. Francesco was a middleman and nothing more."

"Papa, leave the business alone for now and concentrate on getting through the funeral without looking like we're happy this *bastardo* is dead." Paolo shrugged. "The funeral home wanted to know if we're covering the cost of the woman who died with him."

"Was this guy trying to be funny?" Diego asked, frowning.

"I warned him about any other stupid statements," he said, kicking his shoes off and putting his feet on the coffee table. "I asked who this woman was, and then the guy clammed up and said he couldn't discuss it. He apologized and said he'd been confused about the arrangements."

"Confused about what?" The way Diego asked made Paolo turn his head in his direction. His father seemed more interested than before. "What's to be confused about?"

"I don't know, Papa. The guy wouldn't talk about it anymore, and we finished our business. By then both Sofia and I were ready to get out of there."

"How much is all this setting me back?"

"Sofia knew better than to give Victor a world-class funeral. He's lucky she didn't settle for the cardboard box option." He rubbed his eyes, ready to get some sleep before it got much later. He'd agreed to play golf with Lucan in the morning and the fucker had chosen an eight o'clock tee time, but they had to keep a foot in the door and play nice. "She agreed to pay and said you didn't have to worry about it."

"Did she say anything else?"

"Sofia hated him, Papa, and that bullshit about working on her marriage was what she lied about. His death sounds like a legit accident, proving Victor was an asshole until his last breath." He stood up and picked the shoes off the floor, suddenly hungry. "You want a snack before I go to bed?"

"Where's your sister?" Diego asked as they left Victor's home office and walked by the front stairs to the kitchen.

"She said she was tired and went up. I think this, added to Pietro's and Gabriel's hostility, is too much to handle." He flicked the lights on and opened the refrigerator.

The kitchen was the only room in the house that wasn't an ultramodern space, and he figured Sofia had designed it. His sister was many things, but she'd always loved to cook, having learned from their mother, and he had no problem imagining her here enjoying herself.

"The sooner we put Victor in the ground, the sooner we can clean up this mess. I'm shocked we haven't heard from the girl's family." Diego sat at the breakfast bar and watched Paolo take stuff out and pile it on the marble counter. "She was nineteen, so they're probably going to hit Sofia with some kind of legal action for wrongful death because she had her whole life in front of her," Diego said sarcastically. "Never mind that she was in there partying with that fucker. It always comes down to the money."

"I'll take care of it if they try that." He made two sandwiches and heated a frying pan with butter to toast them. "They should've been looking out for her, not trying to cash in after she's dead. Besides, Ezra said she comes from a high-end neighborhood. How much more money do they need?"

"Ask Pietro and Gabriel that question." Diego laughed. "A few weeks of slumming will change their tune, but don't do anything about any of this without talking to me first."

"You know I wouldn't do that," he said and the doorbell rang. It was after ten, and their guards had let the visitors—whoever they were—through, which meant the guards had no say in keeping them out. "Stay here, Papa," he said.

"It's the cops who called the house in New York, boss," the guard said, entering before their visitors were allowed in.

"Open the door and put them in the living room," Diego said, "and keep them there."

"What do you think they want?" he asked, setting the food aside. "The investigation is done."

"They're here because they know all this is bullshit."

The detectives were studying everything Paolo had brought from the funeral home and dropped on the coffee table when they joined them, and they didn't seem to care that they'd been caught.

"Isn't it past your bedtime?" Diego asked when he took the wingback chair.

"Sorry for the late hour, but we're split between this case and another murder on the Strip," the older cop said. "This won't take long."

"What case?" Paolo asked, his eyes on his father. "My brother-in-law was an ass, but the girl had to know how old he was. I doubt he forced her."

"He's dead, but forced or no, the young woman did lead us somewhere. We've reopened the investigation to make sure Mr. Madison's death really was an accident," the old cop said.

"You think someone fucked him to death?" Paolo asked and Diego joined him in laughing. "Our family wants to put this to rest. My sister's been humiliated enough, and I refuse to let it go on."

"It's your sister we'd like to talk to," the young guy said.

"Did you not hear what my son said?" Diego asked in that cold voice Paolo had heard through the years that foretold someone's death.

"Sir, I understand you'd like to protect her, but this time it's not voluntary," the older guy said calmly.

The cop didn't project fear or any sign he was intimidated, and that solid confidence made Paolo nervous.

"If you'd like to call your attorney as a way of making you feel better, we'll be happy to wait, but I need to talk to her. I'd rather do it here and not at the station."

"Paolo, go get your sister, and let's see what this is about. My daughter has nothing to do with this and doesn't need to hide behind an attorney." Diego locked eyes with Paolo. There was nothing else he had to say to be understood. All that would happen next was them listening and not talking.

"Thank you, sir," the older cop said.

"You can stop with the act, Detective. I've got enough experience with police, and I know you don't have my best interest in mind." Diego leaned back, missing his leather chair back home. Nothing in this house was his style, and his plan was to sell it unless Sofia wanted to stay.

"Maybe that means you need to reevaluate your life if you have that much interaction with the police," the young guy said. "Most of the people we meet don't have that problem."

"What's your name?" Diego asked.

"Detective Corey Grant, and this is Detective Andrew Wamsley."

"For a man with a name I'd give a Chihuahua, you make a lousy counselor. I have no intention of changing my life." He smiled and stopped talking until his children came down.

They all looked toward the stairs as Paolo came down a little in front of Sofia. "Mrs. Madison, I'm Detective Andrew Wamsley. We realize this has been a trying few days, but we need to ask you a few questions."

It was obvious to Diego the older detective was now firmly in charge.

"If any of your questions are about the girl Victor was with, I don't know anything about her. We were having problems because he was having an affair with his secretary. I knew about it, we talked it over, and we decided it wasn't something either of us was willing to give up our marriage over." Sofia showed enough emotion to be believable and gave just enough information that it took her out of the suspect pool if there was one.

"Did you know Victor was planning to divorce you? Maybe he was in a different place than you."

The comment made Sofia flinch, but she didn't bite right away. "That's news to me," Sofia said finally. "He never told me."

"We spoke to your sons, and he'd discussed it with them. His death prevented him from filing the paperwork, which is why your attorney, Mr. Brayden, has no record of it."

"My sons aren't happy with me, Detective, and I'm sure you're aware of that since they tried to have my father and brother thrown out of here," Sofia said, and it was bordering on too much information. Diego tapped his fingers on the arm of the chair as a warning to be quiet.

"Why do you suppose that is?" Grant asked, but it seemed more out of curiosity than any kind of question to trap her.

"Their father finally took an interest in them, but only to complain that I'd ruined his fun. I didn't want to badmouth their father, and I won't do that now. Eventually we'll resolve our problems and move forward after all this."

"What do you think was Victor's biggest problem?" Grant asked.

Wamsley stared at Sofia long enough that Diego spoke up. "I haven't heard a question that justifies you coming here so late."

"We're working up to that, Mr. Moretti," Wamsley said.

"Do you need me to repeat the question, Mrs. Madison?" Grant asked.

"He died with a woman who wasn't his wife, Detective. You can work your way down from there," Sofia said.

"The woman Victor was with, did you know her?" Wamsley asked.

"Like I said, I have no idea who she was. What does that have to do with anything?" Sofia asked and Diego slightly shook his head.

"Her name was London Emerson," Grant said, producing a picture of a pretty blonde. "Do you recognize her?"

"I've never seen her before in my life. Are you here because of her family?" Sofia looked again, but only for a second. "I had no idea my husband was capable of such bad judgment. The cheating was bad enough, but drugs too. Maybe it was this woman who forced him to do that." Sofia handed him the picture back like it could burn her if she held it much longer.

"Mrs. Madison, our tech people went through Emerson's phone and found quite a few references to you," Grant said.

"She was sleeping with her husband, so that's no surprise," Diego said. "What were the texts about? If you're only here to add to my daughter's humiliation, you're free to go."

"That's not what this is about at all," Wamsley said, putting his hands up. "From a string of texts, it appears that London Emerson and your late husband"—he nodded toward Sofia—"were making plans to have you killed."

"What?" both Diego and Paolo said together.

"Is this a joke?" Sofia paled. "Victor and I were having problems, but nothing bad enough to kill me over."

Andrew handed over a few pages for her to read, but the names had been redacted, making it hard to tell who was saying what. "Why did you do this?" Sofia asked, handing the pages to Diego when he motioned for them.

"Read them and we'll talk about that," Wamsley said.

Sofia took them from Diego one by one as he made his way

through the pages. "Victor didn't write these," Sofia said when she was done. "For some of the sex mentioned here, Victor doesn't qualify."

"You're right, but since this is still an open investigation, we can't comment on who Emerson was exchanging those with. Victor was in total agreement with her, as you can see from the last page. Lucky for you he died before he was able to carry those plans through."

"What's your question then?" Sofia asked, her grief seeming to be on hold for the moment.

"No one would blame you for having Victor killed." Grant smiled. "The court would probably consider it self-defense."

"Do you?" Sofia asked and Diego leaned forward, ready to interrupt her. "The only problem with your theory is, I had no clue this girl existed until she died with Victor. The only intrigue I'm involved in is where to have lunch with my friends." Sofia seemed like she was about to cry, and Diego almost laughed. "I've had a hard week, and now you tell me Victor wanted me dead. Don't add to that by telling me you think I'm a suspect."

"Are you sure we won't find any clue along the way that would connect you to all this?" Wamsley asked, placing the papers back in his folder. "This is your chance to come clean."

"If that's all, you're free to leave my house," Sofia said, and both men hesitated, then followed Paolo when he led them out.

"Cara, I hope you understand now what I've been trying to tell you. Just because Victor's gone doesn't mean you're out of danger," Diego said. "I couldn't give a crap if you had anything to do with this, but some people might not be so forgiving."

"Victor's dead, Papa, and the rest doesn't have anything to do with me." She stared at the floor, tears sliding down her face.

He'd always known when she was lying, from the moment she first tried it when she was a little girl. There was no question now. "You've been in this damn town too long if you want to take a gamble that big."

CHAPTER FOURTEEN

Reed drove through the car wash before she went home. Once the garage door came down, she told Brinley she could sit up. The windows were tinted enough that Brinley could have sat up safely for the entire ride, but Reed didn't want her to know where they were going. This was the only place she was willing to bring her that wouldn't compromise her safe rooms.

"Is this your home?" Brinley asked as they entered through the kitchen.

"The house is where I live, but I've never considered it home. That place hasn't existed for a long time." She managed to keep from saying anything else. "Do you need anything for the kid?"

"We're going to need some diapers and other things pretty soon, but I'll make you a list." Brinley followed her to the den and seemed to be trying to memorize the space.

She glanced around briefly and wondered what Brinley thought. The house had been the model, and she purchased it as it was. All the furniture and decorations had been professionally done to entice people to buy, and she really hadn't added anything else.

"I'll take care of it, but we need to talk." She pointed to the sofa.

"I know you said you didn't know, but what exactly do you plan to do with us?" Brinley asked as Finn wriggled in her arms. The little boy appeared ready to explore the new space, and considering he'd spent the day fairly confined, she couldn't blame him.

"Let's be honest with each other," she said, taking Finn from Brinley and standing him next to the sofa. "He'll be fine."

"I don't want him to break anything."

She laughed. "What are you worried about? You think I'll kill him?"

"That's a weird thing to joke about considering the situation, but I'll take your word for it."

"I own everything in here, but none of it's mine," she said, smiling at the little boy when he slapped his hands on her knee. "Do you understand me?"

"I think I do, and if you didn't understand me before, thank you for what you did." Brinley raised her hands to her face as if the horror of the day pummeled her again.

"Don't cry anymore," she said as Finn rolled the marble balls on the coffee table toward the sliding glass doors that led to the pool. "I told you I won't fulfill my contract." This was the first time anyone had been here, besides Oscar. Having Brinley and a little kid here was as bizarre as winning the lottery twenty times in a row. She tried but there was no reference in her experience to define her feelings.

"Why would someone hire me to do a job, then order someone to kill me? I'm sure that might make sense to you, but believe me, that's not something I can wrap my head around."

"Alex Bell called me and placed the order." She raised her hand when Brinley opened her mouth. "Alex Bell is Robert Wallace's assistant and fixer. Wallace would never make that kind of call himself, but I've dealt with Bell before and recognized his voice."

"Did he say why?"

"No one like Bell will give me that. If he did, I could use it against him, but he wants you and whatever you know to die with you. Whatever he—or I should say, Wallace is afraid of, it was something you and the other woman knew. They sure as hell wouldn't tell anyone else." She stood and got Brinley a paper towel from the kitchen. The last time she'd experienced this many tears, a new girl in the foster home she was in had watched her father kill her mother.

"I can go over it again from the beginning. I got hired in accounting, and on my first day, Dean asked Naomi and me to start an internal audit. Usually you do that when management suspects—"

"Embezzlement," Reed finished for her. "But no one pays me a couple hundred grand as a reward for you finding evidence of someone stealing from them. What did you find?"

Brinley explained the daily take and payout ratios for the past couple of years. "At the beginning of this year that changed." She explained the jump in the numbers and the payout percentages. "I don't know enough about casinos to tell you more than that."

"So for pretty much this whole year they paid out a consistent percentage?" The question was a way of connecting some very fuzzy pieces that were still out of focus.

"Yes, remember we talked about how it shouldn't be consistent? Unless you have a steady business, like say a baker with a contract to a restaurant that always buys the same amount of bread every day for years, your numbers are never going to be the same. It's not impossible, but it's not normal." Brinley glanced at Finn, who was still engrossed in the marble balls. "Are you sure he's okay?"

"Do I look like someone who bought those?"

"Maybe I can add some toys to the list," Brinley said softly.

"Sure, but can you think of anything else about all this? Anything bigger than consistent numbers? I'm sure you don't want to be locked in here with me forever." She got up and took a pad and pen from the kitchen drawer.

"My mom came to visit me, and I talked to her about it since I was starting to have major second thoughts. She thinks the only logical explanation is they were laundering money and plenty of it." Brinley started writing so Reed turned the television on to see if Brinley's car made the news. "We talked about what kind of people launder money, and she convinced me to give notice before I attracted trouble. I guess I was too late for that."

"Your mom's probably right, but it still doesn't explain your contract. Wallace wanted that audit for a reason, and something spooked him. That knowledge alone wouldn't have gotten you killed." Her phone rang and she stepped outside so whoever it was wouldn't hear the baby. "Hello."

"Bell was happy and made the transfer," Oscar said.

"Good, did he say anything else?" She glanced at the golf course and back at Finn, who was slapping the glass doors to get her attention.

"He did ask a weird question about the vehicle. He wants assurances that it'll never be found, and if there's a chance it could be, then there's some money in it for you to torch it."

"Did anyone find her car?" She grinned at the little guy still slapping his hands on the glass. "I went far enough out of town that it should stay hidden, but I want to be sure."

"Keep whatever car you used out of sight. Someone called it in and the sheriff's office reported that they were responding to the scene. I heard it on the scanner, so they've found it."

"Thanks for the heads-up, and no bonus for us since I already torched it. The desert is getting more crowded than we thought." She almost laughed when Brinley sprinted across the room when Finn picked up one of the marble balls and was about to bang it on the glass door. "Anything new on the books?"

"You get the week off, but there's all kind of shit happening around town, so keep your phone on."

She turned toward the golf course at that statement and spoke softly. "What shit?"

"That woman you took out worked at Moroccan, but so did the other woman found barbecued in her car with her kid. I asked around, but discreetly, so don't flip out. They were work partners so they must've known or found something Little Bobby wanted kept secret."

Things she already knew, but she couldn't share that with him. It irked. "That's a dead issue now, and none of our business."

"True, but shit like that has a way of boomeranging on you when the shit gets deep and people like Wallace and his pet Alex need a way out."

"He knows better, and I'll finish with Sofia and take some time off. This last job was enough for a while, which means don't accept anything new without talking to me first." If the investigation was starting to look at Brinley's and the other woman's work connection, there was a chance something would shake loose from Bell or Wallace. They ordered Brinley killed for a reason.

"No worries, buddy. I could use some days off myself."

She went back in with the realization that Brinley and her kid would be with her for a while. "The sheriff's office found your car."

"My mom must be out of her mind." Brinley's lips trembled as if she was going to cry yet again. "I hate hurting her like this."

"Brinley," she said, and Brinley stared at her with an open expression that confused her even more. "Her grief and her reactions have to be real. You might not believe me, but I don't want to kill either of you. If we tell her, or I let you go, you'll be dead before you can enjoy your reunion."

"What if I go back to Louisiana? Maybe they'll forget about me."

"Think about your kid and that other woman—the one you worked with. The chance they'll forget about you, or that you don't run into another me, is nil if they find out you're still alive." She sat back down and accepted all the things Finn brought her that he took from the surfaces he could reach. "Then there's the fact that I've accepted payment for killing you."

"Can you at least promise you'll let me contact my mother when it's safe?" Brinley seemed like a reasonable woman, but it could all be an act to get her to lower her guard. This was as far as she could go though. If Brinley ran, she fulfilled the contract, and learned a lesson from it.

"The police will push her hard for maybe a week, but hopefully after the bodies are never found, they'll move on to what's really important in this case." Finn brought her the marble balls and handed her one before pounding the other one on the coffee table with enough force to make a divot in the wood. "He's a strong little sucker."

"I'm so sorry."

"Don't apologize for that. He's fine," she said. "Do you agree to wait until the pressure's off your mom? Like you said, I could let you go, but then your mom will follow you home, and that's going to alert the cops and Wallace something's off."

"This is so fucked up." Brinley covered her mouth with her hand. "Sorry, but it's been the strangest day of my life."

"I have to agree but for different reasons, I'm sure." She tried her best to empathize and smiled. "If you make your list, I'll go get the stuff you need."

"For a hired killer, you're really nice." Brinley said it softly, as if not to make her angry. "What you've done—it doesn't fit, you know."

"You caught me on an off day."

❖

Hugo handed Mano the envelope he'd paid a thousand dollars for, then sat in one of the chairs across from his desk in his home office. "A little birdie told me we have some more visitors from the East Coast, and I'm talking a lot more to my contact in the LVMPD."

"Does this have anything to do with that?" Mano held the envelope up and tapped it against the side of his head.

"According to our source in the department, those two detectives that came by the office the other day paid Diego Moretti a visit last night and showed Sofia a redacted version of that." He nodded at the envelope. "The only thing marked out were the names, but none of the information."

Mano opened the envelope and flipped through the pages, reading them twice. "Caterina really was trying to have Sofia killed. Does Diego have any idea that's who's in these text messages?"

"He's pushing, but you need friends in the police department for that to work, and there's only so much he can do to strong-arm the unredacted copies." Hugo got his phone out and handed it to him. "I'm sure the police will concentrate on London Emerson next, along with Caterina."

"How the hell did Caterina find this woman?" Mano asked as he studied the picture of the Emerson girl.

"That's the next wrinkle," Hugo said.

"Bigger than Diego Moretti trying to obliterate the entire Terzo family for trying to kill his beloved daughter? That must be some special wrinkle because there's no way in hell old man Terzo didn't know about this plan."

"You probably don't recognize the name of the girl in the photo—I sure as hell didn't," Hugo said and Mano glanced at the picture again. "Sorry, I don't have a paper copy yet, but our guy couldn't afford to take it out of the file."

"If you're talking about London Emerson, then I don't recognize her."

"How about Benito Lucassi?"

Mano put the phone down and slid it back to Hugo. "How is that bookie jackass involved in this? I'd have asked him, but he canceled on me the other night."

"Benito's only daughter married a guy and they had one daughter."

Mano shook his head. "London Emerson is Benito Lucassi's granddaughter? Are you kidding?"

"I wish I were, and I'm as shocked as you are. Lucassi is mostly unknown outside of his main job as a bookie, since he deals pretty strictly with the East and West Coast guys that have nothing to do with our business." There was noise outside, and Hugo stopped to wave to Sylvia and the kids as they headed for the pool. "He met with Victor for some reason before he died."

"You think it was about his granddaughter?"

Hugo shrugged. "I don't think that was it. If Benito had known, I'm sure he would've gone with some backup to break Victor's penis into three pieces."

"Give me an hour and then we're going out." Mano stood and rolled his sleeves up. "I have a few calls to make, but I want to spend a few minutes outside."

"I'll be waiting, boss."

Mano made two appointments before going and watching his kids swim. Tres was on the diving board and Sylvia was in the water waiting on him. "You guys don't stay out too long. The sun is brutal today."

"Do you have to go out?" Sylvia asked.

"I'll be back and take you all out for dinner. Wherever you guys want to go is what we'll do, so take a vote." He crouched down and took Sylvia's hand that she held up to him.

"Be careful, okay?" Sylvia said. "After watching the news this morning, I'm afraid for you. That poor woman and her son are still missing."

"I'll be okay, but I need to take us out of the war I have a feeling is coming, since it's got nothing to do with us."

She nodded, as usual leaving questions unasked. She trusted him to take care of their family, and he'd never let her down.

He left once Hugo told him the people he wanted to see were expecting him. "Who's first?" Hugo asked. They'd had a heated discussion about bringing more people with them, but he didn't want to escalate this by showing up surrounded by armed guards.

"Let's go by Benito Lucassi's first. We might get some idea of how to handle Diego if Benito's in a talkative mood."

Lucassi's house was right outside of town, in a section that was mostly upper middle class, and Benito had considerably overbuilt for the area. The place reminded Mano of a style of house you'd find in New Orleans, which was a change from the ranch homes around it. There were so many cars lining the street that Hugo double-parked in front of the driveway, but no one said anything when Mano got out.

"Keep your eyes open," he said as they walked to the door. "I'm curious who's going to do their best to make this go away. It's the fastest way to make this mistake a memory, but Lucassi isn't about to let that happen. He's never going to see his granddaughter as anything but an innocent in all this."

"Caterina will probably try to cover it up," Hugo said as he rang the doorbell.

"She does that, and it'll be like admitting guilt. If she tries anything, it'll be through a surrogate."

"Mano," Benito said, answering the door himself. "Thank you for coming."

"Benito, you have my condolences, my friend." He embraced Benito and followed him to the back of the house. His daughter was crying and was surrounded by women who appeared uncertain how to help. "I'm so sorry for your loss," he said to the distraught woman.

"Thank you." London's mother clung to him and started sobbing until Benito helped her sit back down.

"Let's have an espresso," Benito said once his daughter was calm again.

He sat in Benito's sunroom and stared at the pool as his host ordered their coffee. There were more people lingering out there than in the house, but Mano didn't recognize anyone. They appeared to be the spouses of the women comforting their friend. He couldn't tell for sure because he really didn't know Benito's family well, but none of these guys seemed too upset, which meant London's father wasn't here.

"I came to offer my support," he said when Benito handed him a demitasse cup.

"The only person I want to kill slowly is already dead." Benito gulped the hot coffee down like it was a shot of whiskey. "That goddamn Victor killed my grandbaby, and dying the way he did was too good for him." Benito sounded angry, but also broken.

"Did you have any idea London was involved with Victor?"

Benito stared at him as if he was trying to decide if he was going to hit him for asking the question. "That fucker must've seduced her, and she got in over her head."

"Is your son-in-law here?"

"That loser hasn't been around since London was six, and he realized my money wasn't going to fund his lazy ass. I've taken care of London and my daughter ever since. London was always a headstrong kid, but she was a good girl," Benito said like he truly meant it.

"Have the police come by and told you anything else?" The tiptoeing to get information wasn't working, so a more direct route was needed.

"Mano, I know we're not great friends, but we are friends," Benito said, his hands in fists. "You got something to say—spit it out."

"I'm not hiding anything from you, Benito, but the two detectives assigned to London's case came by my office."

"What the fuck for?" Benito's voice and temper rose predictably. "They think you had something to do with this?"

"Like you said—we're friends. There's no reason for me to go against your family, and my father would never allow anyone to harm, much less kill, someone so young who has nothing to do with our business," he said placing his hand on Benito's forearm. "My family has too much honor for that."

"I know your father—known him a long time. You and Remi are a lot like him, which means I believe you." The sad calm returned and Benito seemed to deflate. "Why'd the cops hassle you?"

"When things like this happen, they come and ask inappropriate questions because they think it's their right. It's like one dead fish is bait to catch as many live ones as they can put in their net." He got up and poured a bit of brandy for Benito. "I'll admit I didn't realize it was your granddaughter with Victor then, but then I got curious once I found out."

"She was in college but got reprimanded a few times recently," Benito said, almost absently. The facade of the young innocent schoolgirl was starting to fall away from London like feathers off a tattered boa. Mano wondered how the whole truth would sit with him. "It was like she was in trouble and she didn't know how to tell us."

"You can't take the blame for this." Death and its permanence was something he wasn't familiar with. His family had taken some losses, but they were in Cuba, and for him and Remi the death of unknown relatives wasn't something they'd suffered through since they'd left so young. You couldn't really mourn someone you didn't know at all. They'd watched their parents grieve the loss of their own parents, though, which gave him the idea of what Benito was going through. "Perhaps there is blame here, but you and your daughter share no part of it."

"I met with that son of a bitch right before he killed my angel," Benito said. "That was something I didn't tell the cops because I'd have to explain why."

Mano poured him more brandy since it seemed to soothe him. "Was he asking you to handle some action?" It was football season, but Benito didn't make house calls at any of the casinos. He had flunkies for that. "Is there something I can help you with?"

"Can I trust you, Mano?" Benito seem dazed, which meant he'd indulged in more than two small brandies.

"I'm here because I believe your granddaughter deserves justice. Our families may have to live with what we do, Benito, but honorable people never touch an innocent. When that happens, the penalty is blood, and enough of it that no one ever dares to do it again."

"But Victor's dead," Benito said, appearing confused. "Sofia and her sons bear no blame here."

"Before you become too forgiving, make sure your family can

live in peace." It was too much of a cryptic comment to say to a drunk grieving man, but slow-burning fuses were sometimes best. "Why did Victor want to see you? That is, if you can tell me."

"Francesco Terzo wanted me to deliver a message."

A message and business opportunity coming from Francesco Terzo probably meant Victor and Robert Wallace would've been forced to work together. The only way to make that partnership work was the scheme that would eventually lead back to Caterina. Once Benito sobered up and figured all this out, he was going to blow Vegas to shit with a few phone calls. Benito wasn't just a bookie, he was New York connected, and the main guy loved him.

"I understand completely. Your discretion is why you've been as successful as you have through the years." That part was totally true. Benito wasn't a man who spoke about anyone's business, which was why Mano allowed him to work out of the Gemini, within certain parameters, when Benito had a need. "As your friend though, I should tell you my contacts have told me they're reopening the investigation."

"What?" Benito seemed to sober instantly. "Why?"

"That I don't know." He almost laughed at the suspicion on Benito's face. "You've been here a lifetime, Benito, and I know the long list of friendships you've made. Some of those have to be cops."

"Why are you here, really?" Benito asked after he stayed quiet for a few minutes.

"My little girl will be nineteen one day," he said, and Benito nodded. "Perhaps if she falls for someone I'd never approve of, but it's for love, I'll rage but eventually understand." Benito nodded again. "But if she's lured to do someone's bidding like an unpaid prostitute, then whoever sent her will roll snake eyes. Do you understand?"

He and Remi were twins, Remi the older by less than thirty minutes. And they'd been born with unique eyes. They each had one green eye from their mother and one blue from their father, but they were mirror images. When he stood at Remi's right, and their eyes were level, the two middle were the ice blue of their father, Ramon.

A tattoo of their company logo was inked on their shoulders, each bearing half the hooded king cobra with dice for eyes. Only when they stood together did the whole picture appear, cementing the nickname they were known by on the streets. Snake eyes.

Benito said, "Snake eyes is something everyone understands, Mano. It's been a while since anyone has had that unique experience, from my understanding, but everyone remembers."

It was true that to see that tattoo in its entirety meant it was probably the last thing you saw, since he and Remi took care of their bigger problems with very permanent solutions. "Anyone who threatens our families will find that we can still teach important lessons."

"Are you saying your family's in danger?"

"I'm telling you to make those calls not only to the police, but to your friends back east, and give London the peaceful rest she deserves."

"Something tells me you could give me those answers right now if you really wanted to."

"There are battles we look for, Benito, and some that have nothing to do with my family's business."

"Those are the ones I imagine you don't want to be dragged into," Benito said.

"Exactly." He stood and buttoned his suit jacket.

"That only happens if I do something stupid with what you say. I haven't lived this long by being stupid." Benito stood as well and took his hand. "If you know something, I'll be in your debt. Thank you for letting me know I should look a little deeper."

"Promise me you'll call before you do anything."

"You have my word."

He handed Benito an envelope with the text messages in it and shook his hand with both of his. "Your granddaughter bears no blame in this either, my friend. I may have never met her, but she's the good girl you'll always remember."

"Thank you, Mano." Benito placed the envelope in his pocket. "Is Remi coming to town soon?"

"She'll be here for the service." A small white lie never killed anyone.

"That's generous," Benito said, his eyes becoming glassy. "Your friendship is appreciated, and I might need it going forward."

"It's why I'm here. Snake eyes isn't something you have to fear." Mano left knowing he'd planted the seed. The Terzo family had grown fat and powerful with the money they were making off drugs, and it would be suicide to hit them directly. Giving Benito the information about Caterina was like loading a cannon and aiming it right at the Terzos.

His father always said that sometimes the smart play was letting someone not only take out your trash but having them be grateful once the cleanup was done.

CHAPTER FIFTEEN

Reed returned with more shopping bags than she'd ever put in her car at once and found Brinley and Finn asleep on her sofa. The stress of the day before seemed to have caught up with them, and the silence gave her a minute to think. Not killing these people had been the right thing to do, but keeping them here long term wasn't something she was prepared for.

She put all the stuff Brinley had requested on the counter and in the refrigerator and took the time to unbox all the toys she'd gotten for the kid. With any luck her windows and doors would survive if he had something softer to play with. She left everything on the coffee table and went upstairs to the bedroom to shower and change. She felt like she'd been wearing the same clothes for a week.

The house was still quiet when she put on a pair of sweatpants and a T-shirt, so she closed the door to the bathroom and called Sofia. There was no reason to keep her waiting any longer since she had new things to handle.

"Hello." Sofia spoke softly, and she seemed to be alone since there wasn't any noise from her end.

"Mrs. Madison, I believe our business is done, and it's time for us to move on." Reed stared at her reflection and made a mental note to get a haircut.

"Why didn't you tell me that bastard was planning to kill me?" The rage was easy to hear, but it was misplaced.

"He's dead, so what does it matter?" She came close to laughing when Sofia let out a strangled scream. "I read the woman's texts, or should I say *really young* woman? She was more than a bedmate—she was an enticement to talk him into killing you. That I didn't know until they were both dead."

"You read her texts, or you overheard them talking?"

"Believe me, their conversation was limited and had nothing to do with you." She heard Finn's muffled laughter from the other room. He'd found his new stash.

"Why didn't you take her phone, you idiot?" People like Sofia who'd grown up wanting for nothing were all the same. Their mouth engaged with no thought of consequences, because up to now there had been none.

"Mrs. Madison, you asked for your husband's death to look like an accident, and that's what you paid a tremendous amount of money for. A nineteen-year-old with no cell phone makes people suspicious, and suspicion erases the odds it was an accident."

"A death plot outlined on the phone makes me a suspect, which in no way is what I asked for. But since that's what happened, go ahead and cut your fee in half." Sofia barked orders as if she already had her inheritance and could actually carry out the threat.

"The police still think you're a suspect after they saw who that kid was taking orders from?" The police telling Diego Moretti that Caterina Terzo had tried to goad Victor into killing Sofia so Victor would do Caterina's bidding was an invitation to start a war they'd quickly lose control of. A slew of murders triggered by that information would make the original crime hard to solve, if suddenly the authorities had fifty murders instead of the one—well, the two. It was no wonder the investigation appeared to be moving at a snail's pace.

"You're about to lose the other half of your fee if you know that and haven't told me." Sofia was truly angry now, and it was the only explanation for the stupidity spewing out of her mouth at top volume.

Reed hung up and turned the phone off even though Sofia didn't know the number. Her days of taking shit from people who considered themselves superior to her in every way were over.

She called Oscar and gave him the rundown on what happened, and he laughed. "Start monitoring what's going on in the house and call me if you hear anything about us."

"What a stupid bitch."

"We both know the world is full of them." She heard Brinley's voice, so she had to cut this off before her guests came looking for her. "Call me, and tonight might be a good time to go back to Victor's love nest and search for the treasure I'm sure he left us."

"You don't think they've cleaned it out by now?"

"Whatever he left isn't in plain sight, and it's a crime scene. It'll be another two days or so before they release it to the cleaning crew, which means it's still there. If we go late enough, it shouldn't be too hard."

"Okay, I'll book a room and let you know when I'm set up to go."

She walked across to the guest rooms to see if they were habitable. Aside from the house tour, she'd never been in them, and she didn't want to spend another night downstairs in the recliner keeping an eye on Brinley.

When she got back to the living room, Finn was playing with the trucks and cars she bought for him, and Brinley was smiling as she watched him. It hit her how unfair life was, but she was glad for the kid. He was obviously not only loved, but wanted.

"Thank you," Brinley said with a smile. It was a change that made her stunningly beautiful.

"I figured this way you didn't have to chase him the entire time." She glanced down when Finn drove his truck over her foot. "Are you hungry?"

"I shouldn't be, but I'm starved."

She took out two frozen meals and Brinley appeared amused. "I don't cook, so it's either this or nothing."

"I can make you another list since I do cook, but that might be too domestic for you." Brinley sat at the counter and rested her elbows on the surface. "Do you own any pots?"

"If they came with the house, I should, but you don't have to go to any trouble. Maybe if I work fast enough, you and the kid can leave." She placed Brinley's meal on a plate and took the plastic off the top. "You'll probably have to move once I'm done, but I'll do my best to take you permanently off the radar of whoever wants you dead. Unless you've changed your mind about the cabin in the woods."

"Wall-to-wall nature isn't my thing. Why do you think Dean would've set us up like that?" She concentrated on the microwave while Brinley cut up a piece of chicken and blew on it. "Naomi was a nice person with a little girl, not someone who was working to bring anyone down. I still can't believe she's gone."

"I wish I had all the answers for you, but the people you went to work for aren't exactly the moral upstanding citizens you're probably used to." Standing across from Brinley was obviously an invitation for Finn to use her feet as an obstacle course for his trucks.

"I can hold him if he's bothering you," Brinley offered.

"He's okay." The little boy had a joyous laugh, and she couldn't help but give him a small smile. "Where's his father?"

The question made Brinley hum for some reason, but the sound didn't seem like something joyous. "His father's serving a very long prison sentence for selling drugs. We all make mistakes, and he's mine, but he did give me the greatest gift I've ever been blessed with."

"Does he give you problems?" A small but persistent voice at the center of her brain told her it was a waste of time to find out anything personal about Brinley.

"I wanted to give Finn the best life I could, and Jarrell and his mother thought I'd make an easy mark for money. I'm not rich, but I have a steady job like a normal person, and they thought I was stupid since I didn't want to spend what I made on drugs." Brinley glanced down and smiled at Finn as he ran his trucks over her feet as fast as he could move them. "That's all they cared about, so I didn't list him on the birth certificate."

"The kid's lucky to have you," she said before taking a bite of her meal. Like always, though, it tasted like sawdust in her mouth.

"What's your name?" Brinley asked, clearly not giving up on that one.

"Planning to give a complete story to the police?"

"I'm sure you aren't going to believe me, but I'd never do that. You could have killed us, and you didn't. Because of my son, I'm going to do whatever you want." Brinley put her fork down and placed her hands on the counter. "What you did is a gift to me and Finn."

She stared at Brinley and she believed her. "Reed." Usually in a situation like this she gave the name Rebel, the name she'd been born with. At least in the eyes of the law, Rebel Jones had died years before and was thus untraceable back to her. Why she'd just given Brinley her real name was baffling.

"Thank you, Reed," Brinley said and briefly touched her arm. "Whatever you need me to do to help you, just tell me."

"The best thing until I come up with the plan is for you and Finn to lie low. Robert Wallace is a savage, and he isn't the kind of man who thinks things through very well."

"What do you mean?" Brinley started eating again, which broke their eye contact.

"He hired you, got you to do a job, then decided to kill you to keep you quiet. That's not a great plan to begin with, but when you add two small children, you weaponize the cops to take you down." The way Brinley was nodding made her want to laugh. Considering where they'd begun, Brinley was taking things pretty well.

"What kind of person kills a small child? And how does this Wallace guy know anyone like that?" Brinley asked as she watched Finn abandon her feet and head back to the glass door.

"Vegas is much more corporate than the old Mob movies, but that doesn't make it tame," she said, throwing her dish away.

"I get that, since the accounting department at Moroccan was like any other place."

"What you have to understand is the Mob is something of a corporation now too. They're not about tacky suits and back rooms anymore." She started a pot of coffee and sat next to Brinley as it brewed. "Wallace might not be total family, but he must be, like, a distant cousin at least."

"Family?"

"Every segment of organized crime is ruled by a family. We simply have to find out who controls Wallace's world and it might get us somewhere." Brinley nodded when she held up creamer and sugar once the coffee was ready. "No respectable family would've sanctioned what happened to your friend and her kid."

"The problem is, I've never met Robert Wallace," Brinley said, following her back to the den.

"Who was it who hired you again?" She remembered the name. She never forgot details. But it didn't hurt to hear it again. Maybe it would shake something loose.

Brinley slipped her shoes off and folded her legs under herself. "Dean Jasper. He's the head of the department. From what little Naomi told me about him, he's been there for a while."

"Jasper might be a good place to start, but I've got to finish something else tonight."

Brinley stared at her intently again with an unreadable expression. "You're not going to kill anyone, are you?"

She laughed at the stilted question. "Granted, I was hired to kill you, but that's not my usual line of work. I may be exceptionally talented at it, but I'm more of a thief. That isn't legal either, but I'm not out there trying to up my body count."

"I'm sorry, I shouldn't have asked you that."

"No problem." She finished her coffee and motioned for Brinley to keep her seat. "If I promise not to shoot anyone, will you stay inside?"

"I give you my word, if you make one more deal. We'll stay here, and you go to the grocery store again." Brinley smiled. She really was beautiful. "I'll make you another list while you get ready."

"Sure, and don't call anyone either." She knew she'd have to leave the house behind if Brinley decided to be stupid, but it could be much worse.

"Go and we'll be good." Brinley held her mug with two hands and sat back.

Reed got up to get dressed and decided to stop worrying about things she had no control over. The job would require another walk through the casino, so she changed into slacks and a dress shirt. Brinley was on the floor with Finn when Reed came back down, and she accepted the bundle Reed handed her. They'd have to do something about clothes for both of them, but there was only so much shopping she was willing to do.

"The room on the left at the top of the stairs is all set if you want to get some sleep. That T-shirt should do if you want to be more comfortable out of those clothes."

"Thank you, Reed, and I meant what I said. Whatever you need, you let me know, and I'll do it." Brinley stood up and walked to her. "I'll do it not only for Finn, but for Naomi and her daughter."

"Do you have any of the information from the audit you were doing for your boss?"

"The boxes in my car," Brinley said, clearly disgusted. "Damn, I should've saved those."

"I did," she said, picking up her keys. "They're all back at the storage unit."

"It's a start." Brinley seemed almost shy when she handed her another note. "And here's another start—to stocking your pantry and refrigerator."

"Maybe it's a start for both of us, but if not, we'll figure it out."

❖

Sofia held the phone in disbelief that the bastard she'd hired hung up on her. She had to get her hands on the money since there was hardly any in her and Victor's joint accounts, and life insurance would take a while. This was the problem with not knowing who was working for her, but she'd have no choice but to wait him out.

"What's wrong?" Paolo asked when he joined her outside. The sun was starting to set but the temperatures were still stifling.

"Nothing." She didn't want to hear another lecture from her father or her brother.

"Sofia, come on," he said, putting his head on her shoulder. "I'm still the guy you used to sneak out with, and the one who's always kept your secrets."

"You wouldn't understand." And he wouldn't. Every man in her family was a little like Victor when it came to women. They did what they wanted, with whomever they wanted, and there was never a consequence.

"I do understand, and more importantly, I'll help you explain it to Papa. What Victor did, how he died, isn't how a real man conducts himself. You had him killed, and he deserved what he got." He shook his head before leaning down again and kissing her cheek. "The only thing I'm pissed about is you not calling me and telling me what he was doing. If you did take care of it, believe me, it's going to be fine."

"How can you know for sure?" Paolo had truly been like a friend her entire life, and it made it hard to hide anything from him.

"Because no matter what you face, you're no different from me. We were raised the same, and we tolerate no disrespect." He sat next to her and unbuttoned his shirt a little so he could run an ice cube from his drink along the top of his chest. "You need to be honest, though. There's more to what happened than what you've said, and we need to plan for the fallout from all of this."

"You and Papa keep talking about fallout, but all I see as a downside is that I'm a suspect."

"You have to know that people like us and the Terzo family were going to use Victor for something, considering what his job was. And no one kills someone like that, no matter what kind of scumbag he was, without permission," Paolo said, and he sounded reasonable. "There's going to be fallout between the families, Sofia, and only by telling us what you've done can we keep you safe."

She stared at him, realizing her mistake might cost her more than Victor's money if her asshole husband was working for her father and God knows who else. Telling the truth would confirm her stupidity, but her father would never allow anyone to harm her, of that she was certain. But not telling the truth could also put her family in danger, and then she'd be as dead as Victor, so she had no real choices here.

"Let's go inside," she said, placing the burner phone in her pocket. "If I have to confess to my sins, I might as well do it only once."

"You hired someone without meeting them?" Diego asked twenty minutes later when she told them the entire story. "Why would you take that kind of chance?"

"Because I asked a few people, and this guy is the best anyone with connections uses. Hell, even I believed this was an accident. I don't know how he did it, but everything was perfect."

"Yes, it was, but whoever this guy is now has your money."

Her father spoke with an eerie calm that worried her. Rage and screaming she understood, since that's what she'd seen all her life.

"And he knows who you are, and who your family is. If you don't see that as a problem, let me tell you—it is."

"It's done, Papa, and all I need to do is get the account numbers to finish this."

"That *is* what you need to do, but you talked to your guy like he's a punk, and he called you down for it." Diego lifted his hands as if he couldn't understand her stupidity. "Let Paolo handle it from here on out, and he'll get it done and find out who this bastard is. He's a problem we'll have to take care of."

"What about the rest?" The fact that she'd killed Victor before he got the chance to kill her would have made her laugh, if she wasn't still worried about that being a possibility.

"Rest of what?" Paolo asked.

"The cops came here last night and showed us those texts. My contractor saw the cell phone and knows the names that go with the messages. He knows who wanted me dead." She spoke without trying to let too much anger bleed into her voice. "I'd like to know who was trying to talk Victor into killing me, since you both keep going on about keeping me safe."

"I'm working on it, cara, but this town doesn't know us. I've got to call in some favors, and we have to ask the right people." The bell for the gate sounded and they all glanced at each other before Paolo got up and answered it. "If it's those cops again, go up and don't come down no matter what they threaten you with," Diego told Sofia.

"It's Mano Jatibon, Papa. He called, remember?" Paolo said.

"What does that slick son of a bitch want?" Diego asked. "Ramon and his kids are way too smug for my taste."

"He came because of Victor, he said," Paolo answered.

"If he's mourning that piece of shit, he's a sick fuck."

"I doubt that's it," Sofia said. "Mano doesn't strike me as the type."

"That's because you don't know that fucking Cuban prick like I do," Diego said. "Ramon doesn't believe anything or anyone, and that makes him a prick as well as a dangerous man. He taught that to those twins of his, and they have no respect for anyone but themselves." He stopped talking when the door opened but he didn't stand.

"Sofia," Mano said when he entered and took both her hands. "I came to tell you that my family and I are at your disposal if you need anything."

"Thank you, Mano," she said with a small smile.

"Mr. Moretti," Mano said, shaking Diego's hand next. "It's nice seeing you again, and my offer of help extends to you too."

"And what do I need help with?" Diego asked, and it was hard to miss the sarcasm in his tone. "Believe me, I've got everything I need."

"Then I'll go ahead and leave. Sofia, you have my condolences on more than Victor's death, and I wanted you to know I'll have to miss the services." Mano spoke right to Sofia and totally ignored her father and brother. "There's another funeral I have to attend tomorrow, but I did want you to know that I'm available if you should need anything."

"Who else died?" Paolo asked before she had the chance. It was strange that Mano would announce something like that for no reason.

"Benito Lucassi's granddaughter," Mano said and nodded for his guard to open the door.

"Lucassi had a granddaughter?" Diego stood up and started for Mano, but Mano was on his way out.

"He did." Mano stopped by the door. "Beautiful nineteen-year-old, so you'll understand why we won't make it tomorrow."

"That's all you're going to say?" Diego asked.

"You don't need my help, and I won't insult either of us by offering again." Mano walked out and Sofia saw that only his man looked back.

"Papa, I know you run the family, but all the answers we want just walked out the door," Sofia said, and Paolo nodded slightly as if agreeing with her admonishment.

"I don't want his fucking help. He acts like he's doing us a favor by his charity."

Sofia sighed and didn't say anything else. Paolo, though, seemed to understand the significance of what Mano had said. "If the bitch with Victor was Lucassi's granddaughter, that's going to be a problem for us, Papa. He's an old bastard, but the families back home love him," Paolo said.

"Do you both remember the dead sorority girl was planning to kill Sofia?" Diego asked, sounding like a petulant child.

"She wasn't planning it alone, and the answer to who else was part of that plan was something Mano knew—you could tell. Now, though, he'll die before he shares that with us." The threat to her life might be still there. And if whoever it was hired someone with the talent of her contractor, she was as good as dead.

"We need to find out who London Emerson was working for, even if it takes begging Mano Jatibon," Paolo said, and on that she was in total agreement.

"Don't fucking worry about that. I'll find out, and if you beg that asshole for anything, I'll kill you myself," Diego said. "All we have to do is find Sofia's contractor and we'll have our answer."

"Let's hope you're right, Papa," she said as she started to leave. There was an overabundance of testosterone in the room and she couldn't take it any longer. "Vegas is another planet compared to what you're used to, and the people here won't bend to your will simply because they fear the name Moretti."

CHAPTER SIXTEEN

Reed stood in the gardens right past the check-in counters in Bellagio and watched people taking selfies from every angle. Las Vegas had a way of attracting people who had an incessant need to chronicle every step of their trip to this cornucopia of sin. She smiled at the number of fanny packs and garish T-shirts and thought she was overdressed.

"Are you sure you don't want to wait a few days?" Oscar's voice came through her Earwig and she chuckled at his cautious nature.

"Are you ready to make me as invisible as David Copperfield in his show down the street?" She started walking at a leisurely pace so he could keep up electronically.

"I'm ready, but if you think he'd hide whatever this is, what's the hurry?"

"Oscar, think a little about who Victor was." She entered the beginning of the gardens where the private villas were and slowed even more to scan the area for more people.

"What do you mean?" Oscar was typing and talking fast.

"Forget for a minute he was Diego Moretti's son-in-law." She stepped into the foliage that fronted Victor's villa and tried not to make noise. If there was a guard posted, it'd make this harder, but not impossible. "Forget London Emerson and what she was trying to talk him into at Caterina Terzo's direction."

"That's a lot to forget, and not a hell of a lot to remember."

The place appeared deserted but there was no reason to rush. "If he killed his wife, Diego would've hit him hard, so he must've believed in his dead black heart he'd found a bigger shark to protect him. Who do you think that could be?"

"Caterina's got clout here, but not enough if the families back east united against her for killing someone like Sofia without permission.

The oath of the Cosa Nostra isn't some legend told in movies. Those guys take that shit serious."

"I know all that, and I agree about Caterina. But we know she was the one in the texts, and we know she's not at the top of the food chain in the Terzo family. We don't know who Caterina was working with, if anyone, but that's the person who wanted Sofia dead."

"Then who did it?"

"I'm narrowing it down as I think about it, but I don't know for sure." She went around back to the private pool and picked the lock on the sliding glass door. "Francesco might be a good bet."

"Why do you think so?"

"He's from New York, which means he's not an outsider, so he's someone the families would expect an explanation from before they cut him into small pieces." She stood at the center of the main room and allowed her eyes to adjust to the dark. "There's that, and he's become the biggest dealer with a pipeline from the Mexican border to the Statue of Liberty. Sometimes forgiveness comes when the money's too good to kill the goose."

"True, but it's still Diego Moretti we're talking about. He's not going to sit on the sidelines if he knows Terzo ordered the death of his daughter. The fact that she's still alive is going to be lost on him in the fog of rage. And why Sofia? It's not like she was useful."

"Money makes people do stupid shit all the time. Sometimes people kill kids if the payday is big enough." She wondered who'd been assigned to Naomi and her daughter. That idiot deserved killing.

"It couldn't be helped, though, right? When it comes to the person I love—today was an anomaly."

"Thank you, Oscar, and you're right. Today was not like me at all, and I'm going to do what I can to atone for my mistakes." She took a walk-through to plan her strategy. "Keep a lookout. I don't want to get interrupted by an overzealous CSI crew."

She started in the small den area and knocked on the walls, waiting to hear a hollow spot. The pictures came off the walls next. Nothing. There was nothing in the bedroom, so she concentrated on the bathroom. That'd held the jackpot in his office, and Victor didn't strike her as an overly imaginative man.

"Anything?" Oscar asked, and she stood in the doorway of the bathroom before she moved on.

"Unfortunately, there's no tacky velvet painting in here, but there's a really nice copy of Botticelli's *Birth of Venus*." She checked all the corners and it wasn't rigged in any way. It also didn't hide a void with a safe. "What other painting was Botticelli known for?"

"Something about spring. Do you want me to google it?" She heard keys again so he was doing it anyway. "They're both in some museum in Florence."

"Yes, I've seen them. Remember that trip I took to try and break out of the sameness of our everyday lives?" The den had a copy of the other famous painting, but that was another dead end.

"You never mentioned that, but you like to disappear on me every so often. Did you learn anything?"

"What we've known all our lives, buddy." She studied the room again and saw the small model of the Uffizi, the museum that held the two famous paintings in Florence. It was on one of the shelves of the built-in bookcases. The rest of the room held the usual stuff you found in places like this, put there by professional decorators.

"What's that?" Oscar asked.

"You can't outrun your past, not even when you surround yourself with pretty things." She tapped the back and it felt solid.

"We can change our perspective though. The past can't be changed, but the future's uncharted."

She chuckled, since that was certainly true. "We've proven that by beating the odds those losers at the group home gave us, and there's no going back." They picked some weird times to have these heart-to-heart chats. She took everything off the shelf and made sure there was nothing in each piece. A small key fell out of the Uffizi and she stared at it in her gloved hand. "What the hell does this open?"

"What's it look like?" Oscar asked.

"Small key that has more detail than one that opens something like a diary." Nothing else appeared to need a key, and she sat for a minute to think. The shelf was third from the bottom, and that didn't seem to be the height someone like Victor would've chosen as a hiding place for something important.

"If he hid it in a book, it's the only one he's opened since high school," Oscar said, making her laugh.

"I don't see any books, but I'm guessing the next best thing." The shelf came out easily, and it seemed heavier than it should have been. On the very back she found a slot for the key. "Very good, Victor," she said as she turned the key and the back came off. "You're more creative than I would've guessed."

"What is it?"

"This guy had a thing for diamonds." A bag with quite a few large stones was stashed with a few ledgers. "Did you see anything else in those first ledgers, aside from where he'd hidden his money?"

"That's all I found, and they're useless now that I've moved the total amounts to different accounts."

"He's got another set." She emptied the hiding space and replaced it. The fact that there was one meant she had to take the time to check the rest of the shelves. "What's it looking like outside?"

"The area is clear, but I'm watching out for you. Go ahead and finish, then come upstairs. I've got something you need to hear."

"I'm almost done." Her search landed her one more carved-out shelf holding a thick file that had pictures to go along with whatever the writing was. The only thing she recognized right off was the picture of two people having sex, and it appeared to be Lucan Terzo's wife and her lover. They were similar to ones she'd taken of the same couple. What Victor was doing with all this was another mystery. "Can I move?"

"Go ahead, and I'll let you know if you have to stop."

The walk to the elevators was relatively clear, and she glanced at her watch, wondering if Brinley was getting restless. "Are you staying the night or heading out?" she asked when she found Oscar packing up.

"Heading home. I wanted to go to Reno for a few days, but there's been plenty happening at the Madison place." Oscar gave her a rundown of everything from Sofia's confession to the visit from Mano Jatibon. "The situation seems like something we need to clear off our books. These people aren't the forgiving kind."

It was the moment to tell him about what she'd done or, more accurately, not done, but she felt the need to keep her secret. Not that she cared about Brinley, but the only way to keep her and Finn alive was to let them stay dead. Plus, she wanted to keep Oscar far away from any blowback from her actions. He deserved better than to get hurt or get killed because of something she'd done. "Send the feed from those wiretaps to me and stay in touch. It sounds like Sofia is planning to double-cross us, and that's not going to end well for her or her thuggy family."

"You want to come with me?"

They traveled together at times, but she knew Oscar enjoyed his solitude as much as she did. "Have fun, but I'm going to pass and see what all this stuff is about." She pointed to the stack of items she'd found. "Once I get through it, we can put all this crap behind us."

"Are you sure you're okay?"

"I'm fine, but tired," she said, placing her hand on his shoulder. "Be careful."

"I always am," he said and laughed. "I'm the backroom guy, remember?"

"Yes, I do remember, but be careful anyway."

"You follow that advice too."

"The two of us will do something no one expected us to do, and that's grow old." She smiled and squeezed his shoulder before walking out. The trip to the parking lot was faster since all she ran into were people anxious to lose their money inside.

It took her another two hours to get through the shopping list Brinley had given her, and once again the bags filled up the back of her SUV. Buying groceries for a woman so she could cook a nice meal. Who would have thought? She wondered if it would be okay to enjoy it, just a little, before it disappeared like smoke. Now was the time to pull her head out of her ass since that wasn't a question to even wonder about.

As a precaution she slowed down when she got close to her street. Maybe Brinley had been waiting for a moment alone to call for help. In a way she wouldn't blame her, but Brinley would only kill both herself and Finn by resurrecting herself. Everything was quiet when she got closer, and it didn't appear to be a trap, so she drove into the garage.

"Did everything go okay?" Brinley asked. She was waiting for her in the kitchen.

"It was for another job, but let's talk about yours."

"What do you want to know?" Brinley appeared sad and Reed could tell she'd been crying again.

"Everything."

❖

Caterina parked outside Lucassi's house and leaned her head back. The last thing she wanted to do was to go inside, but her father had sent her as the family's representative in some bizarre exercise of kissing the ring of some dinosaur who was nothing but a joke. The only reason she'd agreed was her contact within the department told her Lucassi had no idea about her involvement in London's death, and she wanted to confirm that.

She still wasn't sure why the cops hadn't come to chat with her about the texts they'd surely found on London's phone, and she wasn't entirely sure how she was going to play it when they did. It had been a stupid mistake, texting London and leaving a trail, but there was no changing that now. For now, she'd do as she was told.

"Are you ready?" Leon asked from the passenger side. Lucan had wanted to come with her as well, but she convinced him to stay home. No one except Lucan really knew about her relationship with London, and she knew the consequences of anyone finding out, even if they were part of her family. Leon, though, was a reality she couldn't escape. He was supposed to be her bodyguard, but he'd been her father's choice, not hers.

"Wait in the car. This won't take long."

"Your father doesn't trust Lucassi, and he doesn't want you alone with him." Leon got out and closed the front of his jacket to conceal his gun. He cocked his head to the right and cleared his throat. "Lucassi's got company. Are you sure you don't want to come back later?"

"That kind of company might be good, since we have nothing to hide. I don't want to stay long." It was time to find out exactly what the cops knew and start planning to get out of it if it incriminated her in any way. "Please tell Benito we're here." The guy who'd opened the door wasn't anyone she knew, but he wasn't some caring family member, based on the gun and attitude.

"Have a seat in the office and he'll be right with you." The man walked as if expecting them to follow him like they were some kind of well-behaved puppies.

"I don't like this," Leon said, obviously having noticed the number of men scattered throughout the house. "What the hell is going on?"

"Benito is one of those people none of us understands, but the old guard love him, and all this is about showing the kind of respect he really doesn't deserve."

"Obviously someone thinks he deserves it," Leon said, arranging his jacket as if to make his gun more accessible.

"He's a goddamn bookie who started in New York and moved out here once the heat turned up in the city. That's all he is." She sat down and stared at the group of people out by the pool. Most of them appeared to be college students who were probably friends of London's, but the woman talking to some of them could've been London in twenty years. "The grieving dutiful mom," she said. That was laughable, considering how easily she'd seduced London into doing whatever she wanted. Parenting obviously wasn't London's mother's strong suit.

"Why, exactly, are we here?" Leon asked, gazing where she'd pointed.

"My father thinks this is beneath him, and Lucan's keeping Paolo happy on the golf course. We drew the short straw when it comes to upholding the family name."

"For only a bookie, this guy's got a lot of muscle around, and I don't want any kind of misunderstanding."

"Relax, this won't take long, and Benito knows better than that." She glanced around the room, noticing all the pictures of Benito with a number of bigwigs from New York, all of whom she recognized.

"You might want to change your assessment about that," Leon said, making her look outside. This group she recognized as well.

"What the hell?" The tall woman holding London's mother as if she were her lover was Remi Jatibon, Mano's sister, and the beautiful blonde looking on was the actress Dallas Montgomery, Remi's partner. Why did people like naming their children after places? It was so incredibly annoying. "How very touching."

"The Jatibons know Benito that well?"

"The Jatibons hate Benito and everything about him, but they're also opportunistic whores." She took her phone out and sent Lucan a text. He had to do his best to get some information out of Sofia's idiot brother.

"It sure doesn't look like that."

"That's why it's your job to sit and keep your mouth shut. I've been waiting a few years for Mano's power play to get us to back off the Strip, and this might be it. Of course he needs to hide behind his sister to do it." Benito was out there acting like his family was getting a visit from the president, and that he'd gone to Remi first showed her where they rated.

"Mr. Terzo's not going to like this. He's going to want to know right away if the Jatibons are planning something."

"Let's find out what this is before you lose your head." She took a deep breath and tried to center herself.

"Do you want me to step out and call? He may not like us waiting to tell him," Leon said, and she felt like slapping him.

"Leon, I heard you the first time, and I'm not going to tell you again. Sit down and shut up. I'll be the one to talk to my father. I know it's your dream to be assigned to him, but you have to realize one glaring fact. My father already has his trusted guard, so cool it. Either way, after today you'll get what you want, and that's away from me."

"You know I work for you." He spoke fast as if trying to save his job. "I'm loyal only to you."

She brought the annoying conversation to a halt when Benito opened the door. Leon's stupidity had made her miss the end of the meeting outside, and now she was caught by surprise.

"Caterina," Benito said, walking straight to his desk before she could get on her feet and embrace him. "Thank you for coming."

"Of course." She was happy she didn't have to touch the old man. "Papa sends his condolences and wished he could have come, but he's not feeling well."

"I appreciate *you* coming." The way he emphasized the word made her lean forward a little. She felt the crack in her facade and struggled to pull it back.

"Is there a problem? Something you're worried about?" She motioned around them and didn't lose eye contact with Benito. "You have a lot of muscle around for such a sad occasion."

"They're here for my granddaughter's service. All of them are friends, so I don't think of them that way." Benito lost his smile and stood.

"Is there something we can do for you?" It was probably her imagination, but Benito's expression seemed one of hatred. Had the old fool figured out her relationship with London? Had the cops told him before confronting her? There was no way…but something was really off.

"There's nothing you can do for me, Caterina, nothing, but thank you for coming. I've got a lot of friends and guests to attend to, so if you'll excuse me."

"So the friends you need are Remi Jatibon and her family?" The question wasn't smart, but she wanted to know. If her downfall was coming, she wanted to know who to strike out at once the attempt was made. With any luck Remi and Mano would be in her crosshairs, along with Benito. Once they were dead, no one could blame her for protecting herself.

"She's someone who doesn't need to ask things like that. Dominic will show you out."

The door closed with a bit too much force, and she tried to write it off to grief. "We need to meet with the Jatibons." She tried to ignore the urge to run to a safe place. That kind of fear was something she detested in anyone, much less herself, and she wasn't about to fall into that trap.

"You know how Mr. Terzo feels about Ramon Jatibon."

"I didn't say my father, Leon. Try and keep up." She was tired of being questioned by someone beneath her. "Drop me off at home, then take the day off."

She didn't wait for anyone to show her the door, and she got into the car and let Leon drive. She stared at the deputies down the street, and they seemed to be staring right back. What exactly were they doing here?

Two low men on the law enforcement totem pole seemed out of place compared to the only real company her family usually had, the guys who lurched about in vans like mobile cockroaches. The Feds were never this open in their surveillance, and then they only concentrated on her father and sometimes Lucan. She still had the freedom to go out without any type of shadow.

They were a block away from home when the flashing lights came on behind them, and Leon cursed. "Shit," he said punching the steering wheel. "Let me do all the talking."

"Are those the same guys from outside Benito's house?" She glanced in the side-view mirror, wishing she'd paid better attention.

"It's no time to start losing your grip," Leon said and smiled. It faltered when she glared at him. "Come on, I'm kidding, and I was speeding. You know, no matter what, I've got your back."

"Step out of the car," a man said over a loudspeaker.

"What the hell?" Leon looked in the rearview mirror.

"Don't make me say it again," the guy said.

"Wait," she said when Leon reached for the door handle. "Let me think." There was something not right about all this, and that feeling had started back at the Lucassi house.

"Let's not provoke these assholes into doing something we'll regret." Leon got out and walked to the back of the car and right into a blind spot where she could only make out the sounds of talking.

"Shit." She said it loud enough to bleed out some of her panic, but the man who tapped on her window scared the hell out of her. He motioned for her to roll her window down. "Yes?"

"Step out of the car."

"I wasn't driving." The sounds of a struggle made her want to lock herself in, but there was no way to defend herself if this guy opened fire.

"You really want to do this the hard way?" The cop smiled as if hoping she'd go with exactly that option. "This has nothing to do with driving."

She stepped out and he immediately turned her around and slammed her against the car. He forced her hand behind her back, and she felt the cuff go on, which made her resist before the other one went on, but it was no use. Both she and Leon were restrained, and she cursed herself for her own stupidity. She'd dealt with an inexperienced idiot, and London's immaturity in everything but the bedroom was coming back to bite her.

"What's this about?" she asked as he frisked her.

"You have the right to remain silent." He read Caterina her rights and in a way it relieved her that these guys were exactly what they appeared to be. The families had other ways of dealing with anyone they blamed for the death of an innocent. That London was considered innocent was laughable, but the little idiot *was* dead. Since she'd put her in that situation, she'd be blamed and, in turn, pay the price. It was a monumental fuckup, and she wasn't sure how to get out of it.

She wanted Victor alive and Sofia dead so she could keep him under her family's control, show him they were the ones with the power. It would have cemented her place at the top when she showed some initiative that worked in their favor. Instead, Victor was dead, and now she was going to pay a huge price because the woman she'd set him up with was dead too. That the fucking moron had contacted her at every opportunity wasn't going to help her plead her case to either the police or the other families. London Emerson was completely on her.

"Let's move, since I'm going with that remain silent thing." She hoped she sounded less rattled than she felt.

He laughed at her comment just before bits of his brains and blood splattered her face.

"Fuck," she said as the other officer went down before he could radio for help. "Fuck, fuck, fuck."

CHAPTER SEVENTEEN

"Did you find something?" Brinley asked, moving closer to Reed. "Not necessarily, but my work is starting to get stranger by the day, and I'm at a loss as to how to make sense of it." Reed pointed to the den and opened the bar next to the fireplace. "Do you drink?"

"Mostly wine, but the way my life is going lately, I'm thinking anything sounds good." Brinley sat with her legs on the sofa and smiled. She wasn't relaxed, but there hadn't been any talk of killing her or anyone else in a while, so there was no reason to have every shield up.

Reed poured them two glasses of Frangelico and added ice. "This is something my friend found when we were both old enough to drink, and we kept up the tradition of ending hard days with some, even if we shared it over the phone most nights."

The comment was surprisingly personal, something Reed had never done without prompting in their short time together. Brinley had tried to express her gratitude at every opportunity, but this might be another chance to get to know Reed better. If Reed saw her and Finn as people and not marks, it upped their chances of surviving this craziness. She'd watched enough ID TV to know that.

"That sounds nice. I do that sometimes with my mom."

Reed nodded and sighed. "There's a room upstairs for you and Finn." She took her shoes off and yawned. It looked like the fatigue of the last few days was catching up to her. "Did I tell you that?"

"You did, but I wanted to wait for you and didn't want to find Finn skiing down the stairs if he woke up alone. He's a handful, so I let him fall asleep down here." Brinley took a sip of her drink and closed her eyes. "What do you find strange about this work? If you can tell me."

"Do you really want to know? You've got enough problems."

Brinley laughed. "I was planning to quit my job before I found out anything I couldn't ignore, and someone put a hit on me. Since that plan didn't work out for me, I'm thinking anything you have to tell me won't make things worse. And I'd rather keep my mind busy than sit here thinking about being afraid of death all day long."

"You're an interesting person, Ms. Myers." Brinley handed over her empty glass, so Reed poured them some more. "I thought you'd be screaming to be let loose no matter the consequences."

"Oh, I'm freaking out, but I'm trying to do it quietly since you don't seem to have a lot of experience with hysterical women," Brinley said, and it made Reed laugh. "No matter, though, we're stuck together, and the best thing is to help each other."

"Hold on." Reed stood and went out to the garage. She came back and put a stack of stuff on the coffee table, then watched Brinley stare at it. "Your contract came through right after I finished something similar."

"You killed someone?" Brinley asked and tried her best not to appear horrified. From the way Reed was staring at her, that plan had not gone well. Considering what Reed had just said, a poker face wasn't easy to pull off.

"I'm not a nice person, and if the price is right, I do take those contracts. That's as simply as I can explain it."

"Reed, I'm not going to judge you, but let me ask you something." Brinley wasn't exactly sure how to handle that information. It wasn't like playing house when you were a kid, but the other person left after you made the mud pie so they could go out and kill people.

"What do you want to know?" Wariness radiated off Reed like heat from a furnace, and Brinley didn't want to make any wrong moves.

"This other job you had, was it someone like me?"

Reed smiled and shook her head. "Are you trying to explain away what I did? Believe me, you don't want to do that."

"Just answer my question," Brinley asked forcefully.

"It was someone who was your exact opposite. He was an evil bastard, and I made a lot of money, but I should've turned it down. Damn, you're like truth serum."

"Why do you think you should've turned it down?" Brinley's voice was soft, and Reed seemed to suddenly become alert.

There was no way Reed would be taken down by this kind of seduction—not after everything she'd supposedly done. Not that seduction was on her mind, obviously. But Brinley had to find a way to level their situation. If she had something to offer, then it would be harder to get rid of her. "No reason." Reed finished her second drink and stood up. "Do you need anything? I'm going to bed."

"Oh, go ahead." Brinley was confused at the abrupt retreat. "I'll stay here if that's okay."

"Sure, but remember not to call anyone."

"I already promised I wouldn't. You have my word, and you don't have to leave."

Reed picked up the stuff she'd brought in and stared at Brinley. "Maybe tomorrow we can figure something out that'll get you back to your life sooner."

"Reed," Brinley said, stopping her from going. "Today was another strange day, but while you were gone, I figured something out."

"What's that?"

"We got here because you didn't fulfill your contract, but now we really are in this together. I believe you when you say we're not safe." Brinley stood as well but didn't move from the sofa. "You have to know there's nothing I wouldn't do for my son, and nothing I'm not willing to accept to keep him safe. Do you understand?"

Reed shrugged. "Not really, but I'm not going to stop trying to help you if that's what you're worried about."

"I believe you about that as well, so I'm not worried." Reed nodded and turned to go. "Reed," Brinley said her name again, trying to make the connection that would keep Reed on their side.

"Yes." She kept her voice low, as if being careful not to wake Finn.

"You need to forgive yourself."

"You don't really know me, so how can you say that? We both know the outcome would've been very different if Finn hadn't been with you."

"I do know that, but thankfully he was, and that means you shouldn't dwell on what-ifs. You need to forgive yourself." She wasn't sure if she meant it but felt like it needed to be said.

Reed turned around and faced Brinley. "Forgive myself for what?" She crossed her arms and tilted her head.

"Whatever it is that brought you to this place in your life, that makes you ache. I may not know what it was, but I have a feeling you're not to blame." That part, at least, she knew was true. She'd seen Reed's humanity. She'd seen the way she smiled at Finn, and she'd taken the time to do what she could to make them comfortable. She might be complicated, but there was more to her than just a thief and hired killer. The thought was surreal, but that's what life was these days.

Reed simply stared at Brinley for a long moment. "Thanks." There would never be that kind of forgiveness for her, but it was generous of Brinley to suggest it considering the circumstances. She nodded and left, not wanting to expose any other weakness that Brinley seemed to see so easily.

Another shower was good, and she sat naked at the small rolltop writer's desk in her room and opened the books and files she'd taken. If anything, work would take her mind off Brinley.

The ledger seemed to be a record of all the transactions Victor had done for Robert Wallace. There weren't that many, and all she could think was they were test runs, considering the comparatively small amounts for each one.

"What the hell were you doing?" Reed tapped her pen on the ledgers. Wallace and Victor's business dealings had started about six months prior and there had to be more of a paper trail than this, but it wasn't in the villa. "It's not in the office, and not in your little love nest," she said, closing the ledger and opening the file. "That leaves the house if you have anything else."

The file concentrated on Lucan's wife, Mandy, and her affair with the lawyer from the firm Reed had scrubbed of Victor's divorce plans. The private eye had gotten some great photos. They were good enough to earn Mandy and her lover a grave somewhere they'd never be found if Lucan ever figured out the affair was going on. The question was, why had Victor cared?

"I'm too fucking exhausted to care myself," she said in her old habit of talking to herself. She'd started doing it as a way to fill the silence she'd lived with for so long, but also to actually use her voice. The only person she'd had to talk to for a long time was Oscar, and she didn't like bothering him with her insecurities.

She checked her computer before she got into bed, and there were no new work orders in the private email account. Not that she was looking for any, but she was curious as to what else would come up, considering what was happening around town. "Thank God for that."

The darkness of the room relaxed her into sleep, but she found Penny waiting for her in her nightmares.

"Here." Penny gave Rebel five dollars and shoved her away. "Stop all that fucking crying and go get me some cigarettes." The order was

slurred, and Penny stumbled. "Stop it or I swear I'll give you something to cry about," Penny yelled, grabbing the sides of her head like she couldn't stand the noise.

Rebel put her shoes on and wiped her nose on her arm, trying desperately to swallow her emotions. She was hungry since there'd been nothing in the apartment for two days and her mama had been too sick to notice. The problem was, she knew better than to complain. Mama didn't like it.

"You deaf, you little shit? Go get me some cigarettes." Penny whipped her hand back and slapped the top of her head.

She ran out and tripped going down the stairs, catching herself, but not before hitting her head against the railing. There was blood on her fingers after she touched her forehead, but it would be worse if she didn't get the cigarettes, so she kept running.

The clerk at the convenience store hesitated like he always did, but he handed over a pack and gave her thirty-eight cents in change. It was the same amount every time, and she was planning to keep it like she did every time. She really didn't know much about money, but all those coins were hidden in her room, and when she had enough of them, she was going to run away.

She took the money and the smokes, ready to run back, when the clerk stopped her. He was an old man, but he was nice to her. "Here, kid." He peeled open one of the ham sandwiches from the cooler and handed it to her. "Eat it before you go back."

"Thanks, mister." She took it and ran, not wanting to stay too long. Mama said if she did, that someone would take her away and not bring her back.

The dumpster behind the apartment building was her quiet place, so she sat and took big bites of the food. There were new kittens this time, but she was too hungry to share like she usually did. A car door slamming made her jump to her feet and peek. It was the man who came sometimes to get in bed with Mama, and when he did, Mama made her hide. Those were the times Mama screamed about how she couldn't fucking believe she had her, and how she was fucking ruining her life.

That he was here meant she could stay longer and breathe. She sat and played with the kittens, figuring it would be better than hiding in the dark closet not making a sound until Mama yelled it was okay to get out.

When she woke up it was dark and the man's car was gone, so she took her time going up the stairs, though she'd much rather stay with the kittens. Mama was sleeping with no clothes on, and she put the cigarettes next to her and kept quiet so as not to bother her. She hid her coins and lay on the sofa. The slap across the cut on her face woke her up and she tried to roll into a ball to protect herself.

"Where the fuck were you?" Penny screamed as she hit her over and over. *"I should have gotten rid of you. I should've fucking gotten rid of you "*

Reed woke with a gasp and her arm over her head, the echo of the slap and her memory of the pain still viciously clear. It was a toss-up as to what hurt more, Penny's beatings or her words. She'd mourned her mother even though Penny had been nothing close to a parent. The idiot had died not long after that day, and Reed's only inheritance had been the thirty-eight cents she still had on her from her last trip for more cigarettes.

The coins had been in her pocket when Mrs. Speck had driven her away, and she'd managed to keep them even through all those years of misery in the system. She'd had to leave so fast, she never got a chance to get the rest. Hopefully whoever got them understood the complete misery that had gone into that pile of coins.

"Fuck me, Penny, why don't you just stay dead?" Reed sat up, knowing sleep wouldn't come now. "Might as well get something done." She got dressed and wrote a note and left it for Brinley. Years of experience got her through the house and outside without waking anyone up.

It was one thirty in the morning, but she still had plenty of time for what she had in mind. "Let's see what you know, Dean Jasper."

❖

Yankee Balboa sat in one of the villas at the Bellagio and waited. When Benito Lucassi had called him and placed his order, he'd almost laughed the old guy off, but the amount of money the fucker offered made him agree. Between this job and the bitch with the kid, he'd be able to go to Cabo for a few months and enjoy some fishing and plenty of fucking.

"Come on, man, is it broken?" he asked the big dude he had tied to the bed. "You got two of those pills in you so you should be hard as stone by now. Don't tell me it's performance anxiety. It's not like I'll be taking notes on what you're doing wrong."

The guy moved his head from side to side and moaned, but he couldn't get too loud because of the gag.

Caterina Terzo was next to him, but she still was out from the shot of heroin Yankee had given her, and he had to laugh at what came next. "Whoever the sick fuck is who thought of this scenario is a genius."

Caterina moaned but her eyes didn't open.

"She really fucked that chick Victor was with?" He pointed to Caterina, and the big guy shook his head some more. "Don't lie, big man, you know she did, and now that girl's dead after your boss tricked her out. Her family's pissed about that, and you need to ask yourself if you want to stand between this bitch and justice."

Thankfully the guy's dick was starting to get hard and he could finish this.

"Stop moaning and listen," he said, grabbing the guy by the chin. "You want to walk out of here?" The guy's eyes widened, and he nodded much more enthusiastically, or as much as he could with his chin in Yankee's grasp. "Good boy. All you need to do is fuck your boss, and it's your ticket out."

The guy stopped moving and stared at him, his expression one of disbelief.

"Stop bullshitting me and tell me you haven't thought about it. Someone like Caterina Terzo needs to be put in her place, and if you're the man who does it, you get to walk out and brag about it."

It took a moment, but the guy shook his head again.

"Are you fucking kidding me? You'd rather die than fuck this loser?"

The guy shook his head and blinked rapidly.

Yankee guessed dying from fucking Caterina or from Francesco finding out what he'd done were one and the same. "I'm going to untie you, and if you make any move other than what I'm asking, you're going to join those cops in a closed casket funeral. Understand?" he asked as he cut one leg loose.

The way the guy resisted when he tried to roll him over onto Caterina made Yankee believe he really did fear Francesco more than him. The idiot stopped struggling when he jammed his gun to the back of his neck. Finding Caterina with this guy's dick in her was the last piece of the tableau that Benito wanted the police to find, but there was only so much he was willing to do for a job. He wasn't going to sit there and try and shove the damn thing in.

Whatever reaction Francesco Terzo was going to have didn't seem like something Benito was worried about. That wasn't his problem, and he shoved the dildo in the guy's ass none too gently.

The move made the guy buck a few times as if trying to dislodge it before he slumped bonelessly onto Caterina. His weight made her open her eyes and say *fuck* once, before Yankee forced a pill down her throat and slammed his hand over her mouth and nose. The thrashing and gulping that followed made Yankee confident she'd swallowed it, so he sat on the bed and waited.

Caterina Terzo died with her eyes open and her bodyguard on top of her, making it look like they'd been fucking, and that was close enough. It was the revenge London's grandfather had wanted for her and had gotten permission to mete out. Benito's guarantee of New York's okay was the only way he'd accepted the job. He wasn't an idiot, and he wasn't about to get caught in the crosshairs of the warring mob families.

"Hello, sir," Yankee said, packing away all the ropes and cuffs he used. "It's done."

"The way I wanted?" Benito asked.

"Exactly that way, sir. Give me twenty minutes and you can have someone call it in. Terzo paid for the loss of your blood with her own."

❖

"I'm telling you," Alex said as Robert got undressed. They'd had a few late nights trying to keep the police out of their business, and trying to keep the media from reporting from the front of the casino. All the attention had Caterina Terzo on Robert's ass and he was getting damned tired of it.

"Alex, I'm not interested in talking about it again." He folded his pants and placed them on the chair in his room. "I'll tell you what I've said to Caterina a million times. The only thing we can do is wait it out. If we try to shut down the cooperation we've shown, the cops will only ramp up the pressure."

"Why do they keep coming back?" Alex, at least, seemed more relaxed now that he was in his underwear.

He pointed at Alex's pants and lay down. "Because we had to kill those two idiots Jasper hired, and our contractors were even bigger idiots by killing those kids. At least the other guy got rid of the bodies, but he accepted the money, so they're dead. No one's stupid enough to collect the fee if the job's not done." He put his hands behind his head when Alex got naked and took his time putting his hands in his boxers. "The kids are what's going to force us to be patient."

"I hope you're right."

Robert exhaled when Alex finally shut up and sucked the head of his dick in. His phone ringing wasn't anything he wanted to deal with, but it wasn't the time to let anything slide.

"What?" He was glad Alex didn't stop.

"Mr. Wallace, it's Rick."

"Who?" He put his hand on Alex's head to get him to slow down.

"Rick, I work security at Bellagio. You told me to call you if I saw or heard anything strange. Remember that?"

"Yeah," he said, stopping Alex since this guy seldom called. The last time was when Victor had been found, and he'd paid him five grand for that information. "You have something for me?"

"The police just called for us to check out the villa next to where they found Madison, and I just left there. Once the cops showed up they threw everyone out."

Robert sat up and pushed Alex aside. "What did you find?"

"The same kind of shit we saw when Madison died, but this time it was Caterina Terzo and some guy named Leon Santiago. It was the same thing, right down to Caterina and the guy dying while they were fucking. That's what they told me."

"Caterina Terzo's dead?" he asked, which made Alex sit up as well. "You sure it's her?"

"I didn't get to take any pictures, but I'm telling you, it's her. She doesn't come over here often, but I've seen her."

"Rick, come by the office tomorrow and I'll have something for you. Remember that there's always going to be a payday if you keep calling." He hung up and smiled. "Can you believe it?" he asked Alex. "The bitch is dead, and she was offed the same way Victor bit it."

"Who do you think had the balls to do that?" Alex said, standing up and pouring him a drink. "Francesco is going to be insane until he finds out who."

"This is nothing but good for us. If Francesco and Lucan spend their time looking for her killer, it takes their eye off us." He enjoyed the burn of the whiskey. "Shit, if this had come sooner, we could've saved ourselves the contracts we had to take out. Caterina would never have found out."

"Not really, lover. There's no way you could've left those women out there knowing what they did."

"No sense in worrying about it since we'll be rolling in cash before Terzo and his partners figure it out." Now was the time to get in touch with his new contacts and finish their business. "It's time to start celebrating."

"Not yet," Alex said, going back to what he'd been doing, "but soon."

CHAPTER EIGHTEEN

Reed silently went through Dean Jasper's home office and collected a box full of files she was taking with her to show Brinley. Jasper was a weasel, but it appeared he was smart enough to have backups of everything he'd ever done for Wallace. From his notes, Wallace was indeed a cleaner for Francesco Terzo, but she'd need Brinley to interpret the numbers. Dean had been nice enough to outline Wallace's business with the Terzos, which, as it turned out, wasn't an exclusive arrangement.

"I doubt old Francesco knows that, though," she said as she slipped the cover on the box. Wallace was branching out and going to work for the cartels directly, and he'd risked Terzo's anger to get his hands where the real money was, by cutting the old man out and taking a bigger cut from the cartels.

Jasper was sleeping naked on satin sheets and she wanted to laugh at the pathetic sight of the porn magazines scattered on the bed next to him. His toupee sitting like roadkill on his nightstand must've been a huge turn-on to any woman stupid enough to find herself here. Reed twitched her top lip since the moustache she'd put on was a little itchy, but all she wanted Dean to remember was some kind of biker dude attacking him.

She slapped him and pressed the big hunting knife she'd brought with her right under his balls. The cold bite of the metal made Jasper go from confusion to total stillness. "You move and I'm going to cut this little thing off and choke you with it. You get me?" she asked in a gravelly voice.

"Yes," Jasper said in such a high-pitched voice it made it sound like she'd already cut his balls off. "Take whatever you want."

"I already did, dumbass, but I'm not done." She rolled him over and positioned the tip of the knife at the bottom of the scrotum. "You and I are going to have a talk, and honesty really is the best policy now. Lying will come with huge penalties."

"What do you want?"

"You work at the Moroccan, right?" She pressed the knife down hard enough to break the skin, and the move seemed to break Jasper as well.

"Yeah, I do, but I don't have a lot of money here," Jasper said, trying to press his groin into the mattress to get away from her.

"Your boss already paid me a lot of money to kill some bitch and her kid, so I don't need no money." She smiled at the way he sucked in a lungful of air. "Now I'm here, and I think you're smart enough to know why."

"Robert knows I'd never talk," Jasper said and his pitch went up even more. "Call him. You don't have to do this. I know I didn't agree with what happened to Naomi and Brinley, but I'm not stupid enough to talk."

"That motherfucker killed two kids, and now he's cleaning up," she said, glad that Jasper was making this a lot easier than she expected. "You're a loose end, and I'm going to dump you next to Brinley Myers and her little bastard."

"Wait—just wait," Jasper said, and she could hear the snot draining out of his nose once his tears started. "You don't have to do this. Really, call Robert and let me talk to him."

"He was right," she said and pressed down harder. "You really are a dumb motherfucker. The deal's been made, asshole, and you're dead."

"You kill me, and everything I know will come out," he said, crying louder than Brinley when she'd pointed her gun at her. "You do this and he's going down, so make sure he knows that."

"You got something on Wallace?" She let up on the pressure as if rethinking killing him. Jasper's self-preservation was strong enough to get her somewhere. "You think it's worth more than fifty grand?"

"Way more than that," Jasper said, sounding euphoric. "Let me go, and I'll give you a copy."

She pressed down again, making him yelp. "What are these worth to you?" The knife sliced in a little more and Jasper stopped breathing. "You think these are worth more than a copy?"

"Okay, I'll give you the originals. The stupid bastard insisted I keep them here and only the two of us know the combination. We keep updated versions of the files we give Francesco Terzo every week to prove we aren't ripping him off. I'll be goddamned if I let Wallace end up with them." The bed shook a little when Jasper slapped it with his open palms in apparent anger.

"I'm curious," she said leaning into him, which pushed on the knife. "Why kill those women? I don't usually off little kids, but a quarter mill was too good to pass on. He's getting you for a bargain."

"Son of a bitch," Jasper said loudly.

"Focus, scumbag. What put a kid in my crosshairs?"

"Wallace wanted an audit. He told me to do it, but I didn't have time." He started talking and told her what he knew in a torrent of words and sobs. "The women saw the real numbers and compared them to the fake ones, and no one asked them to do that. They could have figured out what was really going on. Robert got nervous and ordered them killed. He couldn't afford them talking to anyone."

She sat up again, not believing a mother and her young daughter had died because this asshole was too lazy to do the job Little Bobby ordered him to do. "Why'd you give them access if they were going to get killed for it?" A truthful answer wasn't something she expected, but people surprised her every so often, especially when their balls were bleeding.

"I couldn't finish in time, so I had to chance it. Neither one of them had access to the entire picture. Really no one at the casino has that but me, but they accessed the information without asking me first. You got to believe me that I never thought Robert would kill them."

"Come on, and think before you get really stupid. Get me what I want."

He walked to his kitchen and opened the pantry. The trapdoor hidden behind a load of cans would've taken her a while to find, but Jasper turned the dial on the safe behind it and swung the door open. He reached in and was howling on the floor seconds later, when he'd reached for the gun on top of the large briefcase. She'd driven her knife into the top of the hand he'd braced on the wall before he could draw the weapon.

"I was wrong about you, asshole." She watched him press his wounded hand between his legs, smearing blood all over the floor. "Those balls really aren't that important to you, and I would've bet my fee they were."

"Please—I was just afraid. I don't want to die for doing my job."

"Shut up before I kill you for being such a dumb bastard." She moved behind him and placed the knife against his throat. He wasn't willing to die for doing his job, but he was willing to put Brinley and Finn in the crosshairs because Brinley was doing hers. "What was that audit really for?"

"What do you mean?" Jasper spoke softly as if not wanting to startle her into slicing his throat open.

"Did I stutter? What was the audit really for?" She quickly moved the knife from his throat to his chest and sliced across his nipple. "I'm not an idiot, and there's no way that story of yours is the whole truth. I need the whole thing, or I swear I'll kill you."

"Please don't hurt me anymore." The sound of the knife slapping against his wound was instantly drowned out by Jasper screaming.

"Then start talking."

To her amazement, he did. "Robert wanted the pre-audit for two reasons. He wanted to buy time with Terzo, and to prove to the cartels the amount he could handle." He kept talking like he was in a confessional and was praying for absolution.

"Shit." She closed her eyes for a minute, processing as fast as she could. "Here's what you're going to do if you want to live."

❖

"Mrs. Myers," Andrew Wamsley said as Wilma busied herself making coffee the next morning. "Please sit."

"Jesus." Wilma gripped the edge of the counter as tears fell slowly down her cheeks. "Don't tell me they're dead."

Andrew could almost feel the pain she was in. "Sit for me and let's talk," he said, placing his hands on her shoulders. The captain had forced Corey back on him for the moment, but he'd left him behind for this visit since Corey's social skills needed work. "We haven't found either of them, but we might have to consider the reality they're both gone. It's different than how we found Naomi and her daughter, but it has to be connected to what happened. I'm going to do my best to prove it, but finding her car and the blood at the scene probably isn't a good sign."

"Why is this happening?" Wilma asked, sounding weak. It was as if all her hope and will had disappeared along with Brinley and Finn.

"I don't know that yet, but I'm working to find answers. There aren't any of those yet, but I didn't want you to think I'd forgotten about you."

Wilma nodded. She didn't appear to notice he was holding her hand. "She moved here because of her ex-boyfriend, but this is so much worse. Jarrell was a pain in the ass, but he never tried to hurt Brinley or Finn."

"The world isn't a very nice place, at least from where I see it, but you have to be strong." His phone rang and he wanted to ignore it, but with the kind of shit blowing up around them, he couldn't. "Sorry," he said as he answered. "Wamsley."

"We got another one," Corey said, sounding like they'd hit the lottery.

"Another what?" Andrew stood and moved away from Wilma. He didn't want her to find out they'd found her family by overhearing it on the phone.

"Another case, and you're not going to believe it."

"Where are you?" The pictures on the refrigerator made him smile. Brinley really was a beautiful young woman who seemed happy in each shot with her cute little boy.

"The villas at Bellagio, and I've sealed the scene until you get here."

"I'm on my way, so keep everyone out." He hung up and turned to find Wilma staring at him, wide-eyed and pale. "Don't worry, this is about something else, but I do have to go."

"Will you let me know if you find anything?"

"You'll be my first call, but remember what I said. You have to stay strong."

He placed the blue light on his car and sped toward the next weird scene. At least, it was probably weird considering Corey's reaction, but with any bit of luck, it'd provide some kind of answers to the swirling mess that seemed to involve a whole lot of powerful families. He parked close to the entrance where the villas were located, having learned his lesson from the last time when he'd had to walk the entire property.

"Jesus Christ," he said once he'd put on booties and gloves to enter the space. "Is that Caterina Terzo?" If it was, there was a war coming, and they'd get more than their share of cases when Terzo started killing people for this. He knew Francesco well enough to know this wasn't going to go unpunished.

"Caterina Terzo and Leon Santiago," Corey said, holding up the guy's wallet. "Does this scene look familiar at all?"

"Down to the dildo and, I'm guessing, fentanyl." He walked around the room, but there wasn't much there except for the tremendous amount of shock value. "This might have something to do with either Lucassi or Diego Moretti finding out who was texting London Emerson all those instructions. What happened to that kid gives a few people motive for revenge. The captain wanted to put off bringing Caterina in until we had enough to hold her without some attorney getting involved, but I thought that was happening today."

"It was, but something must've gone wrong. The brass only sent one car so she wouldn't get defensive, but then this shit happened."

"It looks like someone wanted to send a message."

"How do you want to handle this?" Corey wasn't his usual sarcastic self, so maybe the kid had the ability to learn.

"Get Mike and his CSI team in here and tell him not to miss a surface. Let's see if this guy can leave two perfect crime scenes." He waited for Corey to get off the phone before pointing to the flecks of blood that appeared smeared on Caterina's forehead. "Where'd this come from?"

"I told Mike to check it out since neither of these guys seems to have an open wound."

"Let's go do the worst part of this job, kid."

"What?" Corey asked, staring at the bodies as if memorizing them.

"The death notification, and this one should be especially interesting since it's the Terzo family." He hadn't dealt with the connected families much in his career since they fell under the jurisdiction of the Feds, but he hated these bastards. It was hard to dredge up any sympathy for those who lived to piss on everything he stood for. When he saw horrible shit, like the situation with Naomi Williams and her child, he sometimes thought it would be better to let the bastards kill each other off. It would at least save the taxpayers. He couldn't bring himself to break the law though—it just wasn't who he was.

"You think Mr. Terzo is going to retaliate?" Corey stepped back as the forensic team started setting up.

"Is it fucking hot in Vegas in August?"

CHAPTER NINETEEN

Brinley opened her eyes and blinked against the morning sun shining through the curtains. The house was quiet and she wondered what the day would hold. It had to be better than the last few, and with any luck, Reed would let her call her mom. She also wanted to get to know Reed better, which sounded ridiculous, but there was something about her that she felt she could help with. Considering Reed had kept them alive, it would be her way of returning the favor.

Perhaps she was being naive, but Reed seemed like someone who'd done their best to survive the hand she'd been dealt and had gone off in a direction not everyone would choose because it was her only perceived option. Maybe if she could get Reed to let go of the violence she'd embraced, and show her another way to live, there'd never be another mother and child in her crosshairs.

Granted, survival was her main goal, but Reed deserved to have the pain that had penetrated her soul eased—like taking a thorn from a lion's paw. When they parted, and they would eventually, they could both find something good in all this, and that would help them each get back to something normal and safe.

All she had to do was stay calm and keep Reed talking, and they might get back to where they'd started, but changed for the better. There was no way there wouldn't be repercussions that would follow her out Reed's door when that time came, but that she could handle. Being alive with the ability to run was the only way to keep moving forward.

Finn was still where she'd put him, but he'd thrown off the blanket she'd taken off the sofa and covered him with. "We're going to be okay, big boy," she whispered as she gazed at him.

A noise made her look up, and her knees went weak.

She looked around for something to defend herself with when

she saw the guy coming in. Whoever it was had either broken in or had a key, but Reed hadn't mentioned any visitors. The only thing she could think of was the baseball sized marble balls she'd hidden in the sofa to keep Finn from breaking anything, so she reached into the sofa cushions and armed herself. With the way she was shaking, she might not have very good aim, but she had to do something.

"Hey," the guy said, and the voice was familiar. "You're not thinking about clocking me with a knickknack, are you?"

"Reed?" she asked, staring but still not believing it was her. This was the kind of guy who made you cross the street if you saw him heading toward you. "Wow, you must really rock Halloween."

"It's a way of confusing live witnesses who need to be convinced it's in their best interests to talk. The bushy mustache and long hair do most of the work for me since people think I have a biker gang waiting outside if they don't cooperate."

Reed placed a briefcase on the counter and smiled, showing off two gold caps Brinley hadn't noticed before. Of course there hadn't been a lot of smiling since they'd met, but that look seemed to be out of character.

"Did I wake you?"

"I was too nervous to sleep, I guess." She stared at Reed's face, resisting the urge to touch it. "Did you have the same problem?"

Reed's phone buzzed before she could answer, and she nodded when Reed put up a finger. "Hey, Oscar, how's Reno?"

She stayed where she was since Reed didn't ask her to move. The call let her study the disguise, and she had no problem imagining there was a man standing before her. If Reed's success came from blending in, she'd have a long career stealing and completing contracts on people's lives. It was a thought she kept pushing away, no matter how insistently it clamored for attention. The time now was to accentuate the positive since the negative could lead to a bullet in the head.

"Let's meet at the same café as before."

"Is something wrong?" she asked, following Reed to the garage door. It didn't seem like she was leaving again, but Reed wasn't exactly communicative.

"Just a friend who likes to run around yelling about the sky falling. I'll have to go out later and talk him off the ledge." Reed carried another box in and placed it on the kitchen table. "I did get some answers for you, though."

"What is all this?" She put her hands on the box but didn't open it.

"Dean Jasper had a trove of information, but more importantly, the answers to what put you and Naomi in danger." Reed brought in the briefcase and placed it next to the box. "He's a strange little guy."

"Is he dead?" That question was getting repetitive, but no less horrifying.

"Remember, that's not my only job," Reed said, sounding tired. "There's only so many answers we can get from the small slice of the pie you have. Those files you kept aren't going to help you, so it had to come from someone like Jasper, and he was in a talkative mood. He had all the answers in his house."

"Really?" She sat next to Reed and gave in to the urge to touch the droopy mustache. "That feels real."

"It has to if it's going to work," Reed said, not moving and barely breathing.

"And it worked on Dean?" she asked, and Reed nodded as Brinley put her hand down. "I'm not surprised. He always struck me as a weasel."

"Like I said, he had an answer as to why Wallace wanted you both dead. Our conversation was stressful for him, but I wasn't planning to kill him. He didn't know that, though."

"What did he say?" Brinley wouldn't readily believe anything Dean said only to save himself.

"The audit had two purposes—to buy Wallace time, and to set up a new deal with the cartels. That was all. You and Naomi were setting up his proof that he could handle the money side of it, and he was gunning for the product end too. The only way to get that was to cut Terzo out and get a sweeter deal with his new partners. You were right on about the money laundering operation, but it was bigger than that."

"And we paid for that with our lives? Well, at least Naomi and her daughter did." She covered her face with her hands at the terrible reality that someone would think so little about the life of an innocent woman and her child.

"That's the reality." Reed got up and got them each a bottle of water. "The woman you saw with Jasper the day you had lunch with your friend is Caterina Terzo, and her father is one of the powerhouse Mob guys in town. That's who set Wallace up at the Moroccan, which means he owed old man Terzo. The problem is those types of debts don't ever get canceled, except by death."

"Okay," she said, wanting Reed to talk faster. "What does that have to do with me?"

"Dean Jasper should've done the audit since it involved their real numbers, but he said he was swamped. Without Wallace's permission, he gave you and Naomi the assignment. When you noticed the difference between what they were reporting and what they were actually doing, that signed your death warrant. Wallace couldn't risk having people out there who knew exactly how much money he was moving for the Terzos, and his plans for upgrading his bosses. The buzzards in the desert would've been full for days if Terzo had found out Wallace was getting ready to double-cross him. For all he knew, you would go and tell Terzo. Paranoia breeds in bastards like Wallace." Reed drained the bottle as if she wasn't used to talking this much.

"Why *didn't* you kill him?" she blurted out. She wasn't a violent person, but Dean deserved to die for what he did. His actions not only caused the death of her friend and an innocent little girl, but he'd also blown her world to hell. Now she didn't see a way back to it, since these were the type of people who wouldn't ever let her live.

"Because you asked me not to, but he's not going to keep the life he's used to." Reed stood again and motioned her up. "Will he be okay?" Reed pointed to Finn.

"At six thirty he'll be wild, but until then he'll sleep through a stampede." She smiled at the way Finn slept with total abandon. She'd long lost that ability herself.

"Come upstairs so I can take all this off and we'll finish talking."

She followed Reed to her bedroom, noticing the same tasteful decorating that held no personal touches that would distinguish it from a nice hotel room, although the bathroom had some things that weren't the small bottles that would've made it seem like a resort. What had Reed said? *I own everything in here, but none of it's mine.*

"Have you lived here long?" She sat on the lid of the toilet and watched Reed strip off the wig and smear something around her mouth that removed the facial hair.

"A couple of years," Reed said, rinsing her face with water. "I had a condo for a few years, but I like the quiet of this place."

"I don't play golf, but you've got a great backyard." There was only so much small talk she could come up with, and she was running out.

"I don't play golf either, but it adds to the quiet."

Reed unbuttoned the denim shirt she was wearing and threw it in the hamper. Thankfully she had a T-shirt underneath, since she didn't seem shy and Brinley wouldn't have been able to keep from staring.

Not that she was terribly successful now, either. Reed's physique was impressive.

"Back to your problem."

Brinley chuckled. "You're a good problem solver, aren't you?"

Reed stared at her like she was dissecting her brain. "What do you mean, besides the obvious?"

"You're certainly laser focused." She stood to put a little distance between them and waited to see how Reed would respond to her observation.

"That's my job," Reed said. "It's what I'm good at, and all I know."

"I'm sure, but I don't see a way out of this one. This guy Wallace knows I'm walking around with knowledge I shouldn't have, even though he hired me to do it. No matter how focused you are, nothing will change that."

"There are always more solutions than the obvious." Reed never seemed to get overly upset or unhinged, but then, she was the predator in most situations.

"I don't want you to kill for me, Reed. I'd never ask that of you." She thought Reed would if she asked, but she couldn't live with that on her conscience.

Reed nodded thoughtfully. "That would be the easiest route, though. If I kill the guys who hired me, it kills the contract."

"What's the hard way?" In what world was murdering people the best option to keep her and Finn safe? The thought was chilling.

"A good game of domino drop." Reed made a flicking motion with her index finger, but Brinley still didn't understand. "All we need to do is line them up correctly, and all of them will fall once the first one goes down."

There was more of that logical talk, and it was the matter-of-fact tone that undid Brinley. That same casual manner was probably what the guy who hired Reed had when he'd ordered her death. And Naomi's.

"What's wrong?" Reed asked.

She started crying and it didn't take long for her to become hysterical. There really wasn't any way out of this, and it wouldn't matter as much if she didn't have Finn, but she was totally screwed. Her tears continued, and she was surprised when Reed didn't push her away when she practically fell into her and hung on to keep from drowning in her fear.

"I'm sorry," she said much later when the emotions burned off like dew in the Vegas heat. Reed was still holding her, and her T-shirt front was wet.

"Did you forget our promise?" Reed asked softly. She might've been a hardened killer, but she was solid and smelled good.

"I know you're not going to kill us," she said, not moving.

"I promise I won't let anyone *else* kill you, either." Reed hesitantly placed her hands on her back and held her. "You may not believe me, but I promise you and Finn are safe as long as I'm breathing."

"This is so bizarre, but I do believe you." She inhaled a few times before stepping back. "What are we going to do?"

"That's easy," Reed said, opening her mouth and taking the gold caps off her teeth. "I sent Jasper running for his life, and his panic should make Wallace and his people easier to handle."

"I'm sorry, what?" Moving away from Reed made her cold, which could only mean she was losing her mind.

"I convinced your boss that Wallace had taken out a contract on him, but I traded his life for the information he gave me. Jasper thinks that's the only reason I let him live," Reed said, running her tongue over her teeth. "The other part of the deal we made was for him to leave town. He thinks I'm going to use all that stuff downstairs to shake Wallace down for more than the contract amount."

"I'm not sure why you're doing all this, but thank you again."

Reed smiled, and the little lines around her eyes crinkled. Her smile softened her, made her look like someone Brinley would gladly have met for a date sometime.

"You know, I'm not sure either, but it is what it is. You don't have to keep thanking me for it."

"Is there something I can do for you?" She wanted Reed to answer yes, though she wasn't totally sure why.

"Don't give up." Reed lost her humor and Brinley knew the reason lay in Reed's history. "You quit, and people like Wallace and Jasper win. I'm no saint, Brinley, but there has to be a limit in a life like mine, and for me, you and Finn are it. You should've never been placed in a situation that cost you everything."

Brinley had lived her whole life playing by the rules, and Reed exemplified the complete opposite of that. In a black-and-white reality, Reed was no different than Wallace, Dean, and everyone else who'd put her in this situation. There was a difference though—a thin line that separated Reed from the total evil she was facing. She caught glimpses of it even though they weren't readily apparent. Reed had a code, and she stuck to it.

The deeper truth was, no one who was totally detached, vicious, and rotten would've held her the way Reed had, and they wouldn't treat Finn the way Reed did. In a very strange way, Reed was the most genuine person she'd been around in a long time.

"Believe me, I'm doing my best."

❖

Sofia stared at the two detectives and couldn't believe what they were saying. Even if the police eventually believed she hadn't killed Caterina, Francesco wasn't ever going to buy it. She was dead, which would give Caterina what she wanted, even if she wasn't around to see it.

"Are you accusing me of something?" she asked as her attorney placed his hand over her forearm as if in warning.

"Mrs. Madison, let me handle this," Ezra Brayden said. "Detectives, is this a criminal matter?" Ezra asked, but Wamsley and Grant didn't say anything. "Either answer the question or we're leaving."

"This is only a fact-finding session," Wamsley said and shrugged. "We're not accusing Mrs. Madison of anything. It's just that discovering two other people dead in the same exact way as Mr. Madison and his young mistress makes us curious. Both of you have to admit it was a bizarre way to die."

"Why would I kill anyone?" Sofia asked, and Ezra squeezed her arm again.

"I'm sure you remember our visit the other day." Wamsley tapped his finger on the file he'd brought to the house. He took the sheets with the texts on them and fanned them out. "Your husband was planning to kill you."

"Mrs. Madison had no prior knowledge of that," Ezra said. "The first she knew of it was when you showed her those pages, and you redacted the names."

"Are you sure?" Wamsley asked. "My problem is that Victor was planning Mrs. Madison's murder with Caterina Terzo, and now both are dead. Not only dead, but killed in the same manner."

"If she had no knowledge of Victor's intentions, how in the hell would she know Caterina Terzo was helping him?" Ezra asked.

"And why in the hell are we just hearing about this now? If Terzo was planning something against my client, we had a right to know."

"We were building a case against Ms. Terzo, but there was no proof Mr. Madison had actually hired anyone to make a hit before his death. There was no imminent danger."

Sofia needed to get out of the small room. The walls were getting darker and closer.

"Are you arresting me?" Sofia asked a bit too loudly, so she took a breath and closed her eyes.

"We're talking, Mrs. Madison, that's all," Corey Grant said.

"If you'd like to talk to her again, you'll have to go through Mrs. Madison's new criminal attorney. I'm here in her best interest, but criminal law isn't my purview." Ezra stood and helped her up. "Unless you're legally holding her, we're leaving. Mrs. Madison is still in the process of laying her husband to rest, and today's command visit wasn't appreciated."

Ezra shook his head when she went to say something, so they moved to the car and he gave her a ride home.

"What the hell happened, Ezra? Caterina Terzo is really dead?" The police had picked her up at the mall as she was shopping for something black to wear to the funeral, and they'd made it sound like she had no choice but to go with them.

"I had my staff start investigating after your call, and not only is she dead, she was killed exactly like Victor and his girlfriend. Only this time it was Caterina's bodyguard who died with her. The only difference was he was on top of her but not intimately locked to her, and it doesn't look like they actually had sex."

"Shit." She'd be lucky to live out the week. "Those cops came by the house and showed me these texts between that girl Victor was with and someone else. They blacked the names out, but if Caterina is dead, she was the other person," she said, anxious to be alone to call her contractor. "Fuck."

"The cops never divulge everything, but you're going to have to talk to your father. Francesco Terzo isn't someone who'll be quick to forgive, and if he thinks you had something to do with this, I don't have to explain what'll happen."

"I had no idea Caterina wanted me dead, so it makes no sense I was planning to return the favor. I'm not that stupid." Fear was swamping her, and it pissed her off. "Why aren't they talking to Benito Lucassi?"

"What does that geezer have to do with anything?"

She finally laughed. "Careful, Ezra, that's like insulting the pope. London Emerson was Victor's little fuck buddy *and* Lucassi's granddaughter. If anyone might want Caterina dead, Benito is a better candidate as a suspect."

"Interesting," Ezra said, turning onto her street. "Interesting—like all the traces of Victor's divorce discussions disappearing from our firm."

So he'd made the connection. It didn't matter. "Ezra, coy isn't tolerated in my family—remember that. You keep that to yourself, and I'll promise not to tell my father you forgot to mention that interesting fact when Victor died. Don't forget your firm represented Victor, but the real client who paid your ridiculous fees was my father."

Sofia picked at her cuticles, desperately trying to think of the right words, the right phrases, that would get her father to believe she had nothing to do with Caterina's death, even if there was something satisfying about it, since the bitch had wanted her dead. She trembled as they made their way up to her home, a place that definitely didn't feel safe anymore.

"Ezra," Diego said when they entered the house. "Wait out here."

Sofia followed him to the main office where Paolo was on the phone in an obviously serious conversation. "Caterina Terzo is dead," she said.

"She *is* dead, and your contractor killed her," Diego said, pointing at her as if she ordered the hit. "Those fucking Terzos are going to do everything they can to kill every one of us."

"Francesco isn't that stupid, Papa."

"Cara, I love you, but get your head out of your ass."

"Papa, I had nothing to do with Caterina, but the cops are my first concern. Obviously, Caterina was London Emerson's mentor. She was the other person in those texts." They'd finally confirmed what Mano Jatibon had said about her being Lucassi's granddaughter when they'd read her totally bogus obituary in the paper. From what the family had written about her, anyone would swear she was a Girl Scout. "I didn't have anything to do with it, but I'm not sad she's dead. Not when she was trying to get Victor to have me killed."

"Are you sure?" Paolo asked after ending his call.

"That old detective kept tapping on the printouts with the texts, then asked if I had anything to do with Caterina. I'm not an idiot, and I can put two and two together. Caterina was killed over what happened to Victor and London, and I'm not at all upset about Victor's death, and I didn't give a shit about any of the women he was with. Who does that leave?" Sofia was relieved when her father started nodding. "The upset party here is the little slut's family. What I don't get is, why me? What would Caterina gain by killing me?"

"She'd gain Victor's undying loyalty," Diego said. "That fucker was a coward who would've done anything to not only get rid of you, but to keep himself out of jail."

"So what now?" After all this, she wished her contractor had spent the night cutting little pieces off Victor until he died in extreme pain.

"Paolo, call Lucan," Diego said. "We'll guarantee your sister's safety and peace between our families through him."

"Lucassi would've had the balls to do this?" Paolo asked.

"He blamed Victor, but someone told Benito it wasn't an accident, and he managed to trace it back to Caterina. It was his chance to take revenge, and he obviously hired the same contractor to make a point," Diego said. "To me it makes that fucking contractor not that hard to find."

"You think Francesco will understand that?" Sofia asked.

"We need to do one more thing, and that'll make him understand," Diego said.

"What?" she and Paolo asked.

"We hire your contractor for one more job."

❖

"The police put Sofia and her family on the scent with that visit," Oscar said as a waitress poured them some coffee. "The bread crumbs must've been good enough to follow, and now Caterina's dead."

"Either that or someone gave Lucassi a rundown of what happened. His granddaughter wasn't exactly an innocent bystander, but she was Lucassi's blood." Reed stirred cream and sugar into her cup and shrugged. "We don't know if it was Lucassi or the Morettis who did this. We just need to be careful and not have any of this blow back on us."

"You think Caterina's death is going to be a problem?"

"You play and lose sometimes. Caterina grew up knowing that." The cars were starting to arrive at the church across the street, and Reed wondered who was bothering to pay their respects to such a big asshole.

"You don't get it, Reed," Oscar said, leaning in and whispering.

"From what my contacts at LVMPD told me, Caterina and her bodyguard died in the same position you left Victor and London in, and I mean *exactly*."

"What are you talking about?" She stared at Oscar and reviewed what he'd said.

"I'm telling you I was monitoring the scanner, and the cops got called back to the Bellagio last night. At first I thought it was because of your trip to Victor's place. I stayed home to check it out just in case, but everything shut down over the scanners when they found the new bodies."

"Where'd they find them?" If someone replicated her hit, then they were trying to set her up for something, and the only person who came to mind was Sofia. Was this her revenge for her not turning over the money? She'd put it off only because Sofia had shot her mouth off at her and it'd pissed her off. The lesson in civility she'd tried to teach Sofia might've backfired in spectacular fashion.

"The villa next door to where you were last night. Did you go anywhere after you searched that villa?"

The only way to answer his question would have to come with the explanation of why she was shaking Dean Jasper down. That was the truth, but she couldn't say anything because she wanted to keep Brinley and Finn a secret as long as she could, even from her best friend. "I didn't need to go out last night, Oscar. Stop looking at me like I did this, because I sure as hell didn't."

"I'm not accusing you, but the way Terzo died will definitely put us on her batshit crazy father's radar."

"The fact is, I'm not the only hired gun in Vegas, and the way I left Victor was strange enough to have caught someone's attention. They might've copied me, but we need to know why."

"I'm trying, buddy, but like I said—the cops shut down all radio communication once they found Caterina." Reed's phone dinged with an email, and she checked it since it was the work account. "What is it?"

She read the short note, and reread it to make sure she understood. "He must have sensed us talking about him. It's from Francesco Terzo."

"Caterina's not even cold yet, so that's fast," Oscar said, nodding subtly as three black SUVs drove by and pulled up to the funeral home door. Sofia and her father had ridden together, and her brother and the rest of their men had exited the other two. "What does he want?"

"He wants Benito Lucassi's head on a pike," she said, wondering why Benito would've taken the chance to move on the Terzo family. Lucassi had to know there was little room for forgiveness once Caterina was dead.

"Why?" Oscar said but pulled his laptop out and started typing as soon as it powered on.

"I haven't understood anything in the last couple of days, but one lesson is always crystal clear. Revenge has a way of boomeranging on you, so you should keep your head and wait until the heat is off, so you don't put a big flaming arrow over your head. Lucassi must've blamed Caterina for London's death, and now it's time to volley the ball back into Terzo's court."

"I guess Benito thought his granddaughter deserved justice, and you can't really blame him."

"You're right," she said, knowing she was in the middle of a shitstorm now, and it had nothing to do with Brinley. "Why would Terzo chance pissing off New York if all this started with Sofia Moretti, though?"

"We killed his granddaughter, and Benito obviously condemned Caterina for it. His message is loud and clear, right? I mean, in the way it was staged. Now it's like a gangland shooting, and revenge plots will start popping up until everyone involved is dead."

That sounded like a reasonable answer, but it was too easy. "Nothing in life comes together this snugly when no one knows anything for sure."

"What do you mean?"

"Oscar, that night with Victor was all about making it look like an accident. The only person who could've said otherwise was Sofia, and from our bugs, we know the only people she told were her father and brother." She stopped talking when the waitress came over and winked as she placed the plates down. "You heard Diego. He told her to shut up about it and do whatever it took to get me to turn over that money."

"What are you saying?" Oscar poured way too much salt over everything on his plate.

"I'm saying I don't know for sure, but none of this sounds right."

"Are you going to do it?" The only answer was going to have to be yes, since Terzo wasn't someone she wanted to piss off.

"I'm going to have to think about it. Terzo isn't someone I want as an enemy, but Benito's connected to some unrelenting guys. Let's play this one smart, Oscar. Head to Reno. Just because we set up our business to stay invisible doesn't mean we can't be found." She put thirty bucks on the table and touched his hand. "We need to be really careful."

"At least let me know what you're doing. I worry about you sometimes, and you're all I've got."

"I'm never leaving you behind, so go have fun. I got us into this and I'll get us out."

She walked out and read the email again before she started the car. No job came with such step-by-step instructions, but Terzo wrote that he wanted Benito to know who was responsible for his death. *One more, and then maybe it's time to quit.* That was a pipe dream, since she'd go insane within a week without something other than her life to focus on. And it wasn't like she was the settling-down-with-a-family type. An image of Brinley playing with Finn crossed her mind, and she pushed it away, but she couldn't ignore the ache it left behind.

CHAPTER TWENTY

T his isn't something Terzo's going to ignore," Remi Jatibon said as she sat in her brother's home office. Mano had built a life in Vegas developing the casino they owned through a surrogate partner. With their family's reputation, there was no way the gaming commission would've granted them a license, so they'd found someone they trusted implicitly.

Mano took the pictures of Caterina's crime scene and shook his head. "I guess Benito couldn't ignore Caterina's part in this either."

"Are you sure Benito is going to keep quiet if someone squeezes him about where he got those text messages? Terzo thinks he's the big fish here, and I'm not worried enough to try and explain things to him, but I also don't want any unnecessary complications."

"Benito admits to that, and he'll have to follow it up with who's responsible for Caterina." Mano opened the locked drawer in his desk and placed the photos inside. She'd been impressed he'd gotten copies so fast, but Hugo had come through right after the images showed up at the station. He moved to sit next to her on the sofa that had a great view of the yard. "That's not what we should be talking about."

"What else is there?" Remi smiled when she saw Dallas heading out to the pool with Mano's kids. After over a year together, Tres and Lilia loved their aunt Dallas as much as they loved her.

"Robert Wallace is becoming a problem, if my information is true."

"Robert Wallace won't be a problem for long because the cartels' plans won't turn out like they want. Granted, they're obviously bringing their crap through here, but Vegas isn't the kind of place to turn a blind eye forever, like they do in the border towns on the Mexican side." She'd heard the rumors as well, and Wallace seemed to have crawled into business with a pack of animals. "The first time a bunch of headless bodies show up here, so will an army of law enforcement and FBI. What we need to do to avoid that is tip over Wallace's cushy new life."

"He's pushing for Victor's old spot, and if he gets that, he'll shut down everyone else doing business on the Strip with the help of his new friends," Mano said, and that was probably right.

"Let's go and pay our respects to the Lucassi family, and then hopefully Benito will meet with us and tell us a story." Remi stood and grabbed her jacket. They were attending the funeral service for the young woman, but they weren't subjecting the rest of their family to the day. "Give me a minute."

Remi stepped outside and found Dallas having lunch with the kids, and they were talking excitedly about what seemed like every single thing that had happened in their lives since they'd seen them last. She and Dallas had talked about having kids one day, and Remi couldn't wait to share that with her. They'd had an interesting beginning, but they'd built a life together that made them both happy.

"You guys promise to take care of my girl while we're out," she said, and the kids got up and hugged her.

"She'll be safe with us, *Tía*," Tres said.

"Good man," she said as Dallas joined the kids, putting her arms around her. "Keep her out of trouble and I'll take everyone out for dinner."

"Finish up, you two," Dallas said, pressing closer to her when the kids sat back down. "I love you."

"I love you too, and it's killing me that I'm leaving you here in this bathing suit," she said, smiling at the athletic bikini Dallas had on. "Don't fall for any of Tres's lines while I'm gone."

Dallas laughed and slapped her side. "I'm a one-girl kind of girl, so you're safe, but dinner had better be good if you don't want me to run off with your charming nephew."

"*Our* charming nephew, and you're the best thing that's ever happened to me," she said and kissed Dallas.

"You're so sappy, baby, and I love it. Be careful, and make sure you don't put off your talk with Mano about what you told me." Dallas stood on her toes and kissed her again.

"I will, but help me out by buttering Sylvia up for me."

She waved and joined Mano by the door where her guard Simon was waiting with Hugo. "Let's go do our good deed for the day."

"Do you think whoever killed Victor and London realized how old she was?" Mano asked as they sat in the back together.

"I've seen the pictures from the security cameras that were part of your police file. I'm not defending Victor, but there's no way he would've pegged her at nineteen. What exactly did Caterina have in mind with all this?"

"You know what I know, and I can only speculate that she wanted Victor under her thumb. By using London Emerson to get Victor to kill Sofia, Caterina would have the ammunition to blackmail Victor to do whatever she wanted. There's nothing like hanging a murder rap over you as a motivation to be a good boy."

"There's more to it than that, and one of the people who could tell us is dead," Remi said as they stopped in front of St. Joseph's church. "I'll help you find the answers while I'm here, and then I'm looking forward to spending more time with you. I miss you, *hermano*." She smiled. She doubted anyone actually realized *Mano* wasn't his given name, but her childhood nickname for him because she couldn't pronounce *brother* in Spanish.

"I miss you too." He reached over and took her hand. Their relationship had always been close, and she really did miss him, but he'd volunteered for the Gemini assignment and he'd done a great job making it a powerhouse on the Strip. "Do you think I made a mistake with Benito?"

"The old guy deserved his revenge—if Lucassi was the one who killed Caterina. He might not be a good friend, but his family deserved better. That, and there's no way he did the hit without some major blessing from someone able to give it."

"What do you want to do?"

"The only real option is to finish what Benito started and put the Terzos back in their sandbox. We need to make sure the New York contingent here in Vegas won't have a problem with us doing that, though. I'm not looking for a war, even if we have good friends that assure a win for us."

"None of the Vegas players are exactly our biggest fans."

"I'm not looking for friends," she said, getting out and smiling at the row of vans across the street that weren't full of mourners, but Feds. "We're here to help them come to the same conclusions we do, and that's that no one who can't keep control over their business belongs in Vegas. Terzo has lost his way, and lost control. He's ceded it to the drug cartels that are driving away business with the way they handle all their problems. Nothing drives away the tourists who keep us all in business like the streets running with blood. The big daddy in charge from New York has to know Wallace's new friends will never be controlled."

❖

"Did you leave?" Reed asked Oscar later that afternoon. She'd gone home and found Brinley poring over the ledgers and other information she'd gotten from Jasper, and she was getting the full picture of what Robert Wallace was up to. She put her Earwig in to keep her hands free and gathered what she needed for her afternoon.

"You know I'm not going anywhere, if you're out there trying to do something you probably don't want to." He'd been with her for years, but he still had the ability to amaze her. "I'm not abandoning you."

"I thought about it today, and I don't think we have a choice in this contract. To save what we have, I'm going to have to take this job." She'd taken every precaution and worn a wig and used some other tricks to hide her identity, then drove to the location where Benito's family was hosting a gathering for their family and friends after London's funeral, since his house was too small.

"Where are you?"

"I'm on my way over to the banquet hall on Sahara. That's where Terzo's directions said he wanted it done. It's cold, but he wants Benito offed surrounded by family at his granddaughter's funeral." She parked a block away and took the small bag she'd brought with her holding the rifle. This had to be done fast, so she could get out of such a busy area with as little problem as possible.

"Wait for me," Oscar said, and she could tell he was driving. She was glad she called since he might've been on his way to her house. "I may not know how to shoot, but I can watch out for you."

"The job doesn't need any of your special talents, Oscar, so head home."

"Dammit, wait for me."

"Are you close?" She walked as if she was on her way somewhere.

It was the easiest way for people to forget you—if you appeared to know where you were going. "I don't have a lot of time."

"Give me ten minutes and I can spot you."

The building across from where Benito supposedly would be was high enough, so she headed to the back in search of the fire escape. "I'm on my way up."

The sudden searing pain in her side was enough to knock her flat.

"Oscar," she said breathlessly. "Hurry." A few more shots pinged into the metal and concrete around her and she started moving, her pulse hammering in her head and the world around her narrowing to nothing more than this moment.

With the last of her energy she rolled behind a dumpster and took the pistol out of her holster. The shots had to have come from one of the buildings in the next block, but there was no way to pinpoint where the shooter was.

"Where are you?" Oscar asked.

"I'm in back of the building on the corner, behind the red dumpster, but make sure you stay low, and come in from the east." She sat with her gun in one hand and her other over the hole in her left side. From the pain and the growing wet spot along her back, the only good thing was the bullet had traveled completely through, and she hoped it had missed anything important. She waited, counting breaths and willing the pain to ease from scorching to throbbing. The shots had stopped, but she knew they were just waiting for her to move.

"Get in!" Oscar screeched to a stop close to where she was hiding. The windows shattered under the barrage of gunfire, and she dragged herself into the back seat.

"Go, but turn left at the corner and hug the side of the building. Stop in a shadow, if you can."

"We need to get you to help." Oscar sounded close to hyperventilating.

"Stop, Oscar, I mean it." She sat up a little and took a deep breath. This wasn't the time to pass out.

"What are you doing?" Oscar's voice went up another octave when she opened the door.

"I'm getting out of here without a tail that we'll never shake, and no one shoots me without paying some kind of penalty." She was sweating, but she got out and pressed herself to the building. Whoever was up there was probably waiting for them to drive by so they could take another shot. Once the shooter figured out they weren't going to drive by, they'd have to come down. "Wait here," she said, wiping her face on her sleeve.

It took about four minutes, but she finally saw someone coming down, facing the building as they clung to the stairs. The alley was empty, and she waited until he was halfway down before she set herself, then fired. If she hadn't been injured, she wouldn't have aimed to kill, and she'd have talked to the guy to find out why he was trying to kill her, but she couldn't take any chances. The guy fell, but he got caught in the ladder and was hanging upside down, very much dead with his automatic weapon hanging from his neck.

"Get back in," Oscar said loudly.

"We need to erase all traces of me before we go anywhere," she said as the pain intensified and she fell into the back seat. "And we need to see who that asshole was. It's obvious he isn't a pro, since he shoots for shit, but he was here to kill me."

Oscar quickly took care of the droplets and smears of blood she'd left behind with the kit they kept in their cars for just this purpose. When she'd decided on this life, she'd done everything she could to learn how not to ever have the spotlight shine on her. Oscar zoomed in on the guy's face and took a picture before he drove back to where she'd been shot and got rid of that blood as well. The spot was secluded, but they couldn't take any chances that the cops were on their way.

"Who is it?" Blood oozed through her fingers as she tried to slow the bleeding.

"I can't be sure, but I think it's Paolo Moretti. This was nothing but a double-cross, and the stupidest move they could've made. He must have sent the text as Terzo to get you out in the open. And when the police found your phone with the message, Terzo would go down. The Morettis would be in the clear." Oscar pounded on the seat next to him.

"Oscar, take me home," she said softly. Her vision was starting to dim, and she tried to hang on. "But before we get there, I have to tell you something."

"Stay quiet and save your strength."

"Listen," she said, and groaned when he turned onto the interstate. "Brinley Myers and her son aren't dead."

"What?" Oscar looked at her in the rearview mirror, his eyes wide.

"I couldn't kill that woman and leave that kid alone. Don't be angry, but I couldn't do it after what happened to us." Fuck. She couldn't protect Brinley if she was dead. She'd break the promise she'd made her. The pain combined with frustration, and she squeezed her eyes shut.

"Where is she?" he asked.

"My place. Make sure she's okay." Confession time was over, and the pain stopped as the world disappeared.

CHAPTER TWENTY-ONE

Brinley sat with a fresh cup of coffee and glanced in the den to watch Finn play with his new trucks. Reed couldn't have found something better for her son, since he loved anything that rolled. She heard the garage door engage and got up and took another mug out of the cabinet to pour Reed some coffee. Hopefully she'd enjoy the meal she'd prepared with the groceries Reed had shopped for. She couldn't be sure, but Reed hadn't seemed like she wanted to leave a few hours ago, and the meal was her way of saying thanks for what Reed had done for them so far.

"Hey," she said when the door opened. She dropped the full cup when she saw the smallish man whose shirtfront was covered in blood. "Who are you?" There was no way this was Reed in another disguise.

"Oscar," the man said, and his voice was soft and almost feminine. "And you need to help me." He motioned her toward the garage.

She gasped when she saw Reed sprawled across the back seat in a pool of blood. It still seemed to be oozing from under her shirt, and Reed was motionless. "What happened?" Oscar didn't stop her when she crawled in and touched Reed's face. It was sweaty but cold.

"Some asshole shot her and we need to get her inside. I've got someone I can call, but he can't work in the car." Oscar pulled on Reed's legs and got her almost to the point where she'd fall on the floor. "Can you get her shoulders?" He pulled a little more.

It was a struggle, but they were able to get her in the house and onto the kitchen counter. Even with all the jostling, Reed never woke up or made a sound. Brinley pressed her fingers to her throat and Reed's pulse was barely there. "Who are you calling?" she asked, stopping

Finn from coming in and walking through the trail of blood they'd made.

"There's a guy who takes care of things like this," Oscar said, taking his phone out. "She's not going to like anyone coming over here, but we've got no choice."

"Are you sure we shouldn't take her to the hospital?" They worked together, pressing kitchen towels to Reed's back and front. "She's barely alive."

"The last thing we need to do is go somewhere she'll have to explain the gunshot wound to the police. Trust me, I know what I'm doing."

"I hope your guy hurries. She has to be okay." They stood together in silence until the doorbell rang. Her last chance at freedom or a life without looking over her shoulder was bleeding to death on the granite countertop. Up to now she'd feared Reed, mostly, but if Reed getting shot had anything to do with her and Finn, it meant she'd been willing to make the ultimate sacrifice. Of course, with the kind of life Reed led, the situation might have had nothing to do with Brinley at all. That released another bout of fear, but this time it centered on Reed and how she couldn't lose her.

"You need to go upstairs and take the kid with you. I don't want this guy seeing you." Oscar washed his hands and shooed her out of the kitchen. "As soon as he's done, I'll come up and get you."

"Please tell him to do whatever it takes to save her." She pressed her palm to Reed's cheek and begged whatever higher power was listening to make her okay.

"Go." Oscar waited until she'd picked up the kid and made it up the stairs, but she watched from the shadows as a young guy in scrubs with the name of a vet practice embroidered on the front came in and immediately moved to Reed and started working.

Brinley peered down at them. Oscar caught her watching and waved her back into the bedroom, but she just moved deeper into the shadows. There was no way she was going to wait in another room. It took over an hour, but the medic got the bleeding stopped and put in stitches.

"She's going to have to rest for at least a week, since she lost a shitload of blood. Make sure you change the bags of fluids when they run out, and use the whole box I left you. When she wakes up, start giving her these." He handed over a bottle of antibiotics.

"Let me go upstairs and get her bed ready. Stick around because you're going to have to help me carry her up there," Oscar said, running up and herding Brinley and Finn into the other bedroom. "Make sure the kid stays quiet until I pay and get rid of this guy."

"Is she still alive?" Brinley had never felt so lost.

"It'll take the both of us to take care of her, but she'll be okay. Don't worry, Reed's been a fighter from the day she was born." He went downstairs and Brinley moved to the shadows at the top of the stairs again so she could listen.

"Be really careful moving her. I don't want those stitches popping," the guy said. "You take her feet, and once she's settled, just remember to change her bandages at least twice a day. I left you enough stuff to get you through the week."

"You'll forget this address, right?"

"My business is all about discretion, so don't worry about it."

"This one might make the news, and if you give her up, I promise you the money you make today won't get you very far," Oscar said.

"That's the reason for the discretion, man. I'm still alive because I don't talk about my clients." The medic took his fat envelope and left with another warning from Oscar.

Brinley went back to Reed's room and watched her shallow breathing. This was what life with someone like Reed was like. This was what you could expect. So why did her heart ache? Why did she want to cry, and rage, and do whatever she could to wake her up? She moved to the head of the bed and gently lifted Reed's head onto her lap. "What happened?" Brinley said to Oscar when he came back in, not letting Reed go.

"Our job snowballed and we ended up here," he said, sitting on the other side of the bed and giving Finn a small smile when he ran his truck up Oscar's shin. "She told me to take care of you."

"The world's become a crazy place," Brinley said, glancing up at him. "Please don't turn us over to the people who want to kill us."

"I do that, and that medic who fixed her up wouldn't have enough to patch up once she was done with me. We'll be fine, and now you can tell me why you're here."

"I'm an accountant and I was too good at my job." That was the simple truth, but it felt like the weight of the world sat in those too-easy, vague words.

Oscar laughed. "That's a start."

❖

Sofia smiled as one of the older men in from New York spoke to her about Victor and what a great time he'd shown him and his family when they were last in town. The people lingering after the funeral were starting to get on her nerves, but her father said they had to keep up the facade until Paolo came back. Hopefully her brother was searching the house of the asshole holding her money.

"Do you think you won?" Pietro asked as he stood right behind her.

"Won what, exactly?" She didn't turn around, tired of both her sons' childish behavior. She'd given birth to them but obviously hadn't bothered to teach them respect.

"He's dead and you think you're keeping everything." Pietro laughed. "There isn't anything left and you're going to end up with nothing. He was leaving you—I hope you know that."

"What exactly did I do that you hate me so much?"

"You made Dad miserable. He told us about all the shit you pulled."

"I get it, you hate me for demanding he not cheat, that he respect me. Your father was good at spinning stories, but you're right, he's gone. My last favor to him was the service today, and now I'm done." She put her drink down and faced her eldest son. "You can carry on his name, and his legacy, while you have fun with your grandfather. I'm not going to force you to live with me."

"You're dropping us too?" Gabriel asked, and Sofia had no problem hearing the sarcasm.

"I'm not the one who dropped anyone, and you two have made your intentions clear. If you're waiting for me to beg, then you haven't paid attention to who I am," she said and smiled at her father. "That you think I'd tolerate what your father was dishing out makes me laugh. I'm your mother, but I'm not willing to put up with that kind of treatment from you, either."

"He spent it all, so at least he had a great time while he was here," Pietro said. "You got to respect him for that."

"True, he's left us all with nothing, but it's where we end up that matters, isn't it? All I wanted was to be a family, and it's not too late for that. If you two can learn to accept there are two sides to every story, you'll have a place with me and your grandfather." She pointed toward Diego, and he peered at her as if asking if she needed rescuing, so she shook her head. "He'll give you a place and teach you some manners."

"We'll see, Mother dearest," Pietro said and stared at the door as the police detectives came in. "It could be that we'll visit you in a better place."

"Pietro, you're still too young to be this cynical. If you don't know what that means, look it up," she said and moved to the door. "Officers, what do you want?"

"Can we see you and your father somewhere more private?" Andrew Wamsley asked.

"It can't wait? I have a houseful of people here to celebrate my husband's life. The day's been hard enough without you adding to it." She saw her father heading toward her, dragging Ezra along with him. The detective tilted his head but didn't respond. "You're not leaving, so let's go into the office, but make this fast."

"Is it true she killed our father?" Pietro asked the detective and smiled at Sofia. "We can help with that, if you need us to."

"Not now," Diego said as he led the cops away and slammed the door on the boys when they tried to join them.

"Sir, we really don't want to intrude, but we wanted to come and talk to you about your son," Wamsley said.

"What about my son?" Diego said with an edge in his voice.

"He was found an hour ago," Wamsley said and placed his hand on Diego's arm when he grasped the desk.

"Found, what do you mean found?" Diego said, not shaking the cop off.

"He was killed, Mr. Moretti," Wamsley said.

"What?" Sofia whispered, her legs nearly going out from under her. "How is that possible?"

"He was found hanging from a fire escape a block off Sahara. Someone shot him through the head, his gun's clip had only three bullets remaining, and we found an empty clip in his coat pocket. We found shell casings on the roof of the building where he was found, which means he was shooting at someone," the younger cop said.

She couldn't remember his name, and more than anything she wanted to hit him until he stopped talking.

"Does either of you have any idea what he was doing there?"

"No," Diego said, choking out the word as sobs racked his body. It was the first time she'd seen her father cry like he'd never stop. "He left and said he had to run an errand."

"There were no witnesses, but Benito Lucassi's family was having the service for his granddaughter a block over. Are you sure he wasn't there meeting with anyone who would've been attending that?"

"Are you some kind of dick?" Ezra asked. "You tell them Paolo's dead and you're asking stupid questions. This family is already grieving."

"Understand that we take every case seriously, sir, and we're looking for a place to start," Wamsley said. "The timing could have been better, but I didn't think the family wanted to wait to find out."

"Where's my boy?" Diego asked.

"We'll lead you to the morgue whenever you're ready," the younger cop said. "And we'll be anxious to set up and interview everyone to help in our investigation."

"Give it a rest. Not now, Detective," Ezra said.

"What's the matter, Mom?" Gabriel asked when the police opened the door and left.

"Is karma finally catching up to you?" Pietro asked, and Diego lifted his fist, making her son take a few steps back in definite fear.

"I'll teach you all about karma if you say another fucking thing," Diego yelled, and no one said another word.

Sofia covered her mouth to muffle her sobs when her father mentioned karma. She'd started this by killing Victor, and now she'd paid the ultimate price. Paolo was more than her brother. He was the one man in her life who'd never disappointed her and had always provided comfort. Because of her, though, he was dead, and it was all her fault.

"Come on, Papa, it's our turn to take care of Paolo." His loss meant her life would never be the same, and she'd have to find the strength to make it on her on. "We owe him our attention."

❖

Remi Jatibon sat close to the glass wall in the office Mano had set up for her at the Gemini as Gino Roca glanced around, seeming to study the room. This had been an especially bloody time for her competition, with the death of Victor Madison and the discovery of Caterina Terzo.

A request for a meeting from Francesco Terzo's top lieutenant wasn't what she'd expected, but she'd agreed if only to see what the old man was going to float.

"Mr. Roca, is there something I can do for you, aside from giving you decorating ideas?" she asked to see if she could get him to focus on her and Mano. They'd taken the meeting alone, leaving all the muscle in the outer office.

"I'm sure you've heard that Caterina was found dead at the Bellagio," Gino said, talking through his teeth as if he was pissed about something.

"We did, and I wanted to give Mr. Terzo a little time, but I was planning to call and offer him my condolences." The anger she understood, because Gino was like a part of the Terzo family, but why it was directed at them was a mystery.

"Are you sure you can't offer something else?" He leaned toward her a little, and Mano copied the move as if to protect her if this guy was stupid enough to attack.

"The only other thing I can offer is flowers or to donate to Caterina's favorite charity, but that's it. I'm not sure why you're here, but if it's to accuse me or my family of something, you're free to go." She tried never to lose her temper to the point of raising her voice, and Gino narrowed his eyes when she spoke in low tones.

"Cut the shit, Remi, we all know you and Mano want to corner the Strip for your operation and don't want to leave room for anyone else. Caterina was working to strengthen our share and neither of you liked that." He pointed his finger at her, and he obviously didn't have the same discipline as she did because his voice started to rise.

"Careful, Gino," she said, raising her own finger. "I'll let this kind of disrespect slide since you're grieving, but come in here and accuse me of something I had nothing to do with and it might backfire on you."

"What the hell does that mean?"

She wondered if he was there at Francesco's request after all. "It means I wouldn't move against your boss or anyone in his family because I have no reason to. Accuse me of something, then follow it up with some retaliatory moves, and I'm going to lose my temper."

"Why should I believe you?"

"I don't owe you any explanations, but I'm not at the mercy of anyone else."

"Do you like talking in riddles?"

"I'll talk slower so you can keep up. We needed a service for our family business, so we purchased a business to take care of it. As a matter of fact, we bought two, since Gemini has a twin in Biloxi. Why the hell would I care what Caterina or any other Terzo is doing on the Strip?" She crossed her legs and tapped her finger on the side of the custom-made black alligator boot. "If Caterina's death is a murder, you're wasting your time here. And I don't appreciate it, if I wasn't clear."

"I had to be sure, so don't take it as an insult that I'm here." Gino sounded like a spanked puppy, and she could guess why.

"When I speak to your boss, I'll be happy to explain it to him. Whoever made the move against Mr. Terzo's family will not be found here, or in our employ."

"Come on, Remi, there's no reason to throw me under the bus. I just wanted to give the old man a place where he could take out his frustrations," Gino said, holding his hands out as if pleading for her silence.

"Sounds like you were going to throw *me* under the bus. If you want me not to mention your lack of intelligence today," she said and Mano snorted, "then tell me what other theories you have about this. A move against the Terzo family took cojones, and no one does that without a good reason."

"That's what I'm trying to find out."

"I see, your way of doing things is to shoot blind. That's a problem." She put her hand up when Gino opened his mouth. "You have our answer, so get out of here before I change my mind about talking to the old man."

She leaned back when Gino left as fast as he could without actually running.

"We need to call Benito and set up that meeting."

"For what?" Mano asked.

"We have a lot of dead people, and we've been visited by both the police and now the Terzo family, though I don't think any of them knew Gino was coming here. Benito was responsible for Caterina, but we talked about how there was no way he did that without someone's blessing. He needed that to keep the rest of his family alive." She stood and grabbed her jacket. "Benito has to pay you back for that information by getting us a meeting with whoever his godfather is. That's the guy who'll keep us out of the fray."

"Hey," Hugo said, knocking and coming in. "Sorry to bother you guys, but there's something else."

"What?" Mano shook his head. "You come to town, sis, and all hell breaks loose."

"It's my exciting personality." She winked at Mano and waved Hugo on. "What else?"

"Paolo Moretti is dead."

"Simon," she said loud enough for her guard to hear. "Call Emile and tell him to keep everyone inside, and send some more people to the house. I don't want anything happening to the family."

"Who the hell killed Moretti?" Mano asked.

"The better question is, what the hell is going on?" Remi waved him toward the door. "We'd better find some answers before we do what I accused Gino of doing. We can't start shooting blind, but these assholes are going to bring the Feds down on Vegas, and therefore on us, with the bodies they're piling up."

CHAPTER TWENTY TWO

Brinley sat on the bed and wiped Reed's forehead. The fever had started early in the night and she'd spent hours making sure Reed was okay. She'd put Finn on some blankets on the floor next to the bed, and she was exhausted from watching them both. "You need to wake up so I can tell you all the stuff I found."

"I'm shocked you're still here," Reed said without opening her eyes. "It was your chance to run."

"Run where, exactly?" she asked, not stopping her caresses with the cool washcloth.

"I'm sorry." Reed seemed pale and weak, and when she opened her eyes, Brinley couldn't look away. They didn't hold the soul of an evil person even if Reed had done some evil things.

"For what?" She put the washcloth aside and pressed her hand to Reed's cheek to see if the fever had broken.

"That all this happened to you. You and Finn didn't deserve what Wallace had planned for you." Reed sighed and tried to turn her head but Brinley prevented her from doing it.

"You're right, we didn't, but you protected us from all that. We're here because of you."

"Still, you should run at the first chance you have to get away from me."

"What happened isn't your fault, Reed. I may not have understood in the beginning, but I don't blame you." The pain in Reed was so visible she could almost touch it. Her head told her to turn away, but her heart couldn't do it.

"I don't deserve those words."

"Tell me what happened to you, and I don't mean why you were shot. I know it's something, and like I told you, it's not your fault."

Reed stared at her for a long while and Brinley didn't expect an answer. They'd eventually part ways, and she shouldn't care, but she was alive because of this silent and imposing woman. She couldn't overlook that, no matter how hard she tried.

"I grew up with my mother until I was five," she said, then told her about her mother's overdose and her years in foster care. "After about ten placements they put me in a house with a bunch of other kids, and that's where I met Oscar. He's my only family, at least the only family that I know of. It took us years to get out of there, but we made it together."

"You survived all that?" Brinley's eyes swam with tears. The parts of Reed's story about the attempted molestations and beatings were hard to hear. That she'd become who she was felt totally understandable in an irrationally logical sort of way, and she admired Reed's will to survive. Not everyone who grew up in the system became a killer, but if you piled enough shit on a kid, you couldn't really blame them if they did. "Did you ever know who your father was?"

"Penny was too busy and too high to have ever figured it out. She always thought I was a true bastard, and in a way, she was right." Reed seemed exhausted by the time she finished, and Brinley wanted to leave her alone, but now that she was talking, she didn't want to stop.

"Reed, I don't really know my father either. I mean, I know who he is, but he left and my mother raised me. I was lucky that she did everything to give me a good life. You did it alone, and that doesn't make you a bastard." She combed Reed's hair back and put the cloth back on her forehead. "No one may have told you this before, but your life is a miracle, not something to be ashamed of."

"You don't have to whitewash it," Reed said with her eyes closed. "I've already told you—I'm not a nice person."

"Tell that to Finn, who doesn't use someone's feet as an obstacle course unless he likes you. My mom always said small children see the best in us, even when we can't see it for ourselves." Brinley touched her face again, not wanting to stop. She moved her hand when the door opened.

"You still alive?" Oscar said, walking in and stopping by the bed.

"Good work, Oscar, and I'm sorry I lied to you." Reed didn't say anything else.

"You lied about killing a small child and his mother. Those are the kind of lies that are forgivable every time," Oscar said, squeezing Reed's hand. "Get some sleep and then we'll have to talk."

Reed's eyes were already closed and her breathing was starting to even out. The couple of days had helped Reed's healing progress, and Brinley's worry eased. "Would you like some coffee, Oscar?"

"Will the kid be okay?" Oscar asked, glancing at Finn.

"He'll be fine, and if he wakes up we'll hear him, or at least I will." Brinley walked out and expected Oscar to follow her and he did.

"What's all this?" Oscar asked when they made it to the kitchen. He sat at the table where she'd been going through everything Reed had given her.

"Reed went to Dean Jasper's house and got the true books for the Moroccan's operation. The guy that runs it—"

"Robert Wallace, who put the hit on you," Oscar finished for her. "Well, more precisely, his fixer or assistant Alex Bell ordered the hit." Oscar turned around when she didn't say anything. "Reed and I are partners, but I never actually work with her in the field."

"Should you be telling me all this?" She leaned against the counter and crossed her arms over her chest while the coffee brewed.

He laughed and nodded. "Who are you going to tell? You're supposed to be dead, and if you leave here that'll definitely be the case. If you're here, though, it means Reed has some plan to get you back to your life, and the only way to do that is to work together."

"That's what she said, and I believe her." Brinley poured the coffee and sat next to him. "She told me about what both of you went through, and I'm sorry. What I'm not sorry about is meeting her."

"There were two contracts that day, and now it makes me sad she didn't get assigned both of them." He took a sip of the coffee and hummed. "When she told me she'd killed you, I think it was the first time she ever disappointed me. I was horrified that she could've done that, but I couldn't say anything for one reason."

"Oscar, I don't think we should be talking about all this," Brinley said, trying to put the brakes on whatever he was trying to accomplish.

"The thing is, Brinley, you and I have something in common. We're both alive because Reed did the right thing." He looked at her, and he had that same haunted expression Reed had when she told her the story of her life. "Are you going to turn her in if you get the chance?"

"No," she said, louder than she meant to. "You can't think that. I don't want to end up dead by running, and I owe her everything. I'm grateful I'm alive, and my son is my main concern."

"Then tell me what you found." He waved to all the books sitting open.

"Can I wait until Reed is awake? Not that I don't want to tell you, but I'd rather say it once."

"That's no problem, and not that this coffee isn't wonderful, but why don't we get some sleep while we have the chance? It should be a long week since Reed is the worst patient in the history of humanity," he said and she laughed.

Brinley placed both their mugs in the sink and went up the stairs, smiling one more time when she turned toward the master bedroom. That Oscar didn't say anything or try to stop her didn't surprise her—well, not as much as the desire to do it at all surprised her. She checked on Finn before she moved to the other side of the large bed and lay on top of the blanket.

Reed was sleeping, and she dozed off watching Reed's chest move in a slow cadence, glad that whatever had happened, Reed had survived and come back to keep her promises.

❖

"Remi," Angelo Giordano said, kissing one cheek then the other before he repeated the move with Mano. "Thank you for the gift."

They'd had to wait a few days for Angelo to fit them in, but Benito had come through after Remi and Mano had sat him down for a serious heart-to-heart. Remi's father and family had power in New Orleans and here in Vegas, especially after partnering with New Orleans Mob boss Derby Cain Casey, but Giordano was *the* guy in New York. His crew and family controlled everything from garbage collection to drugs and prostitutes, from the city to New Jersey. People like Benito and the Terzo family might live over two thousand miles away, but they kissed the ring when Angelo or his son Nicolai held their hand out because they were at the top of the food chain.

It had been Angelo who'd given his permission for Benito to take out Caterina when he'd gone to him about what had happened to his granddaughter. That order Remi had no problem with, since she agreed on a moral basis, but she didn't know if Angelo realized there might be blowback, thanks to the ineptitude of the players involved in Vegas. She watched him open and prepare one of the Cuban cigars from the box she'd brought with her, and offered him a light when he was done.

"Mr. Giordano," she said, sitting when he waved her into a chair. Mano smiled when she glanced at him with her own smile. She felt like she was in a Mob movie. Granted, they were in the same line of work, but Angelo seemed way old school.

"Remi, please call me Angelo. We may have never met before, but there's no reason we can't be friends. Am I right?" Angelo blew a stream of smoke away from her.

"Yes, sir, and it's an honor. We may be in different businesses, but my father and my family have the utmost respect for you." She covered all her bases as far as tradition, and he nodded as if she'd passed a test.

"Benito vouched for you, and I'm glad you're here. Hopefully you'll accept my invitation to visit New York with your father when you get a chance. If you make it, please bring your business partner, Casey. A meeting between all of us is way overdue."

"We'd love to, thank you. If you don't mind, I'd like to talk to you about a recent visit I got from Gino Roca, Francesco Terzo's right hand." After the visit from Roca two of their high rollers had been harassed going into the Gemini and been threatened, on behalf of the Terzo family, if they came back. Word had reached Mano when they'd canceled their reservations. Apparently, Gino's word meant shit.

"What's Roca doing visiting you? Terzo already has something set in town," Nicolai asked, coming in and hearing what she'd said.

"Nico," Angelo said, pointing to her and Mano. "Meet the Jatibons, Remi and Mano."

"Good to finally meet you two," Nico said, shaking their hands. "Are you having problems with Gino?"

"I can't be sure, but it feels like someone is trying to place the blame for Caterina's death on my family. And as I told Mr. Giordano, there's no reason for us to have any involvement because we have no business together. We have no interest in a war between the families in Vegas, and we're concerned about the very visible way they're taking issue with each other." It was as close as she could get without outright calling them morons.

"Thank you for letting me know, and we'll take care of it," Angelo said. "I'm sure you understand what grief does to people, especially if their children are involved. You aren't a parent yet, but they become the center of your world, and Francesco doesn't perhaps know how to handle the loss. Benito handled the issue as he needed to."

It wasn't exactly what she wanted to hear, but at least Angelo believed her. He seemed to, anyway. "Thank you, sir, and thank you for taking time to see us. If you have a chance before you go home, we'd like for you and your family to come by the Gemini and have dinner on us."

"We'd love to," Nico said, laughing. "Papa loves to be treated to a good meal."

"And, Remi," Angelo said, standing when she did, "I know you're resourceful, so if you find anything else I should hear about, you don't have to go through Benito. Call me directly and we'll discuss it. We've all lived through problems before, but Vegas is a place for fun as well as business. I don't want anything getting in the way of that."

"Thank you, and I'll do that."

She and Mano took the elevator down from Giordano's suite at Bellagio and stayed quiet as they walked through the front of the casino to the car. "That was interesting," Mano said, once Hugo pulled away.

"I think that last part was a clue that there's more to all this and he wouldn't mind if we found out what it is. Benito obviously works for him, as does Terzo, but what was Caterina up to when she tried to set Victor Madison up, other than just keeping him in line? And who the fuck was Paolo Moretti trying to kill? Where does that shitstorm fit in? We have speculation, but we need facts."

"How in the hell are we supposed to get to the whole truth? Both the Terzo and Moretti families are going to shut down now that they've each lost a kid." The Strip traffic was as terrible as ever, so Hugo turned off as soon as he could.

"We have to find that proverbial needle, Mano, and they'll hand us the key."

"Oh, that should be easy, since the cops have no clue."

She laughed and slapped his shoulder. "Stop thinking like a cop, and start thinking like the hardened criminal you are."

❖

"That's the only part I don't understand," Brinley said as she finished telling Reed and Oscar what she'd figured out.

Reed had slept pretty much for two days, but every time she woke up, Brinley was right next to her, and she'd taken Reed's hand when they saw Brinley's mother making another tearful plea on the news. Wilma had done a good job of keeping her family in the spotlight, and Reed had done a good job of providing silent comfort.

"That I'm not sure about either, but Victor Madison was one of those types who think the more ammunition you have, the better. What

Lucan's wife had to offer him to keep quiet about her affair, I can't guess," Reed said, flipping through the information again.

The file with the affair between Mandy Terzo and her attorney stumped her as well, but the books made sense. They were a total accounting of what Wallace had run through the Moroccan for Francesco Terzo and the cartel. If they came to light it would bring down not only Wallace, but a number of people who would become unrelenting enemies if they found out who fingered them. That had to be another factor in Wallace's decision to kill Brinley and Naomi. If his actions to hide his deception brought Terzo down, jail wouldn't have meant shit when it came to Francesco Terzo ordering Wallace killed.

"You think Lucan told his wife anything?" Oscar asked.

"Lucan barely knows anything, much less enough to tell his wife. He's not the brightest bulb. Caterina's the brains in that trust, but she was running a scam with a woman who had no business being in that situation. That makes me doubt the level of her intelligence too," Reed said, handing Brinley the file back. "The one thing this guarantees is Mandy and the lover's deaths if anyone decides to enlighten Lucan."

"Let's put that aside for now and get back to the Moroccan," Oscar said softly, since Finn was napping close by. Their lives had been turned upside down by Brinley and Finn's presence and none of them ever talked about that. This little cocoon where Brinley cooked, Finn played, and they pretended everything was normal was truly bizarre.

"Robert Wallace asked for that audit to put Francesco off while he negotiated with a few of the cartel middlemen," she said, and Brinley nodded. "On the surface, that's what it seemed like he was doing, but it was more than that."

"More than what?" Brinley asked.

"Francesco Terzo runs product from the border to all points north, but it's not his stuff. He works for Angelo Giordano. It's taken Giordano time and plenty of muscle, but he has the contacts within the cartels to get it here and transport it north." She moved a little to sit up more and grimaced from the stab of pain.

"Be careful," Brinley said, kneeling on the bed and helping her until she was more comfortable. "Now finish what you were saying."

"Terzo used his influence to get Robert Wallace hired at the Moroccan, and immediately set him up to clean the barrels of money they were making. It's a nothing job since cleaning money through a casino is about as hard as drinking a glass of water, but to keep Wallace happy, they paid him a boatload of cash. Little Bobby—that's the nickname Wallace hates—finally figured out the real money's in the product."

"I know as much about drugs as I do about gambling, which means not much," Brinley said and Oscar laughed. "You're going to have to explain that last bit."

"I think what Reed's saying is that Wallace was planning to replace his bosses and cash in on both sides of the business," Oscar said.

"That's exactly it. If Wallace becomes the supplier as well as the cleaner, he'll own Vegas," Reed said. Understanding more of the picture, though, didn't change Brinley's fate. "Would you mind if I talk to Oscar a minute? I need something done before we plan our next step."

"Sure, you want anything?"

"About five minutes, and then we can keep going." Brinley left and closed the door, even though she didn't have to. Reed doubted she'd stand outside listening in. "We might have to scrub our existence from Vegas until things cool off, but the only way out of this is to blow it to hell before we go."

"What do you want?"

"I need you to run an errand, but you need to do it without being seen. Think you can come out of the back room for once?" He nodded and listened to what she wanted and left without complaint. She heard the door close.

Brinley came back up half an hour later with a sandwich for her. "Is Oscar okay? He looked a little nervous."

She laughed and liked that Brinley came and sat next to her. "You have to realize that Oscar is nervous all the time. It's his state of being, and it changes your perspective of all things Oscar if you understand that."

"Do you have someone special in your life?" Brinley suddenly clamped her lips together and wouldn't make eye contact after the non sequitur.

"No, I don't. My life has been a repetitive kind of thing where I try to make it from one day to the next without going completely insane." She accepted half the sandwich, took a bite, and offered the other half to Brinley. The fresh white T-shirt meant Brinley had found her stash, but eventually they'd have to find her something to wear that actually fit. "Do you? Have I taken you away from some guy?"

"You don't do personal talks much, do you?" Brinley asked, and she laughed at this unexpected almost-friendship.

"In my defense, there isn't much watercooler talk in the contract killing and thievery business, so my social skills are pretty rusty, if not nonexistent."

Brinley finally glanced her way and laughed as well. "Was that a joke? I'm doing a victory dance if that was a joke."

"You're trying to change the subject and not answer my question. Don't make me get up and get my gun." She made a pistol with her fingers, and Brinley reached over and grabbed it.

"Another joke, and there's no special guy who's crying over my demise. I have Finn and he doesn't leave a lot of time for stuff like that, but…"

The way Brinley blushed made Reed want to sit up and touch her face, but moving still caused pain. "But what?"

"But nothing." Brinley's blush deepened. "I shouldn't have asked you about your personal life, so let's drop it."

"Aside from Oscar, and now you and Finn, I don't have a personal life." She took another bite and chewed slowly. "You know, before you, I never really talked about myself at all. Maybe you missed your calling by going into accounting. You should've considered law enforcement."

"My job doesn't give me much time to talk to people about anything other than their financials, usually, but I want to know you." Brinley moved closer and placed her hand on her arm.

"Why? Really, Brinley, I was serious when I said you should run away from me the first chance you get. My mother's dead, but she left some damaged goods behind, and you don't need that." She tried to move but Brinley wasn't letting go.

"The flaw in your argument is that I don't see you that way. All I see is the woman who pointed a gun at me but didn't pull the trigger even though her life probably would've been much easier if she had." Brinley moved closer and seemed to have gotten a burst of courage. "I'll never do anything to hurt you, and I don't want you to disappear even if I get out of all this."

"Even if my vanishing is what will guarantee your safety?" That she and Oscar had to go wasn't a discussion, it was a fact.

"All you have to do is take a chance."

"Maybe a long time ago, I would've had a shot at a life that maybe wasn't normal, but close to it, but I screwed that up royally." For the first time in her life, she wanted to let someone in. It was terrifying, and she couldn't stop.

"Tell me, it's okay."

Would it be? There was only one way to know. "I could've had that chance, but then I accepted my first contract and I didn't give it a second thought. I should have had some hesitation, some guilt, but I killed the bastard and met Oscar for pancakes the next morning like it was nothing. There was never one bit of remorse."

"Who was it?" Brinley's grip intensified some.

"He was a pimp whose specialty was young girls and boys. One of the guys at the house Oscar and I lived at worked for him, and they didn't see a problem using the place as a recruitment spot." The fat asshole was with a young boy when she'd put a bullet in his head. She often wondered if the kid ever got over the shock of the bastard dying on top of him. Had the kid been looking over his shoulder ever since, waiting for the bullet that never came?

"If you're asking me to judge you, I'm not going to do it. Maybe the law should've dealt with someone like that, but you can't tell me the world's not better off without him."

She nodded, not about to disagree with that. "You're right, and I did the guy who was working for him at the house for free. That was an act of mercy for all the kids he would've ruined, but that was my start. The proof I needed that I could not only pull the trigger, but live with what I did."

"Reed, I'm not going to hate you, no matter how hard you try."

"That's where I started, Brinley, but you're where I ended. That should tell you something. I accepted a contract to kill you, and I don't have an excuse for why, except that I'm no better than the people who hired me." It was the first time she'd said those words out loud, though she'd often thought them. It hurt, and she waited for Brinley to agree.

"What's that?" Brinley turned toward the window when there was a clear sound of someone running into the house.

"Brinley," she heard someone yell. "Brinley, answer me, please."

CHAPTER TWENTY-THREE

"Can you tell me when Ms. Terzo started an intimate relationship with London Emerson? And do you have any idea when she let Victor Madison borrow her, as it were?" Corey Grant asked Francesco, and Lucan slammed his hands on the table, making Francesco's coffee cup almost spill.

"Have some fucking respect," Lucan yelled, and Francesco glared at him.

"You're spitting on my daughter's grave by accusing her of things she can't defend herself against." Francesco could barely contain his rage. "My daughter was no pimp, and it insults her memory that you're suggesting it."

"Mr. Terzo," Wamsley said, holding his hands out. "The text messages to London Emerson can be traced to Ms. Terzo's phone. And before you ask, we had a warrant for that, so these messages are hard to explain unless they were in an intimate relationship. That's not at all in question. All we need to know is when it started." Wamsley placed the proof on the table and slid it over to him.

"I can't answer that since I didn't have a fucking clue about it, no matter how many times you ask me." He wanted this meeting to be over so he could drive to Benito Lucassi's house and remove his intestines slowly and with plenty of pain. That had to be who was responsible for Caterina.

"Then you also don't have any information about a plot to have Sofia Moretti killed?" Grant asked.

Francesco sucked in a breath and Lucan must've noticed his shock. "Are you slow?" Lucan asked. "If we didn't know about this girl, then how are we supposed to know about anything having to do with her?"

"Do you think either Benito Lucassi or Diego Moretti had anything to do with Caterina's death? Is that why Paolo Moretti is dead too?"

"It wasn't a death, Detective, it was murder. Someone killed my child and I want them to pay. I don't know anything about Moretti's death, but if he had anything to do with Caterina's murder, then I'm sorry I didn't shoot the fucker myself."

The younger cop sat up at that and Francesco laughed.

"I'm not suggesting a hit as retaliation, so don't look so happy. No matter what my daughter did or didn't do, she deserved a trial, not to be killed in the most humiliating way possible."

"I agree with you, Mr. Terzo, but the only way to get justice is to help us out and start answering questions," Grant said.

"This is the information about Sofia Madison I was referring to," Wamsley said, giving him some more paper he wasn't going to look at.

"Is there anything else? Any information that'll bring us closer to catching whoever did this?" Francesco said.

"That's why we're here," Grant said in a tone that held no respect.

"Then we have nothing else to discuss," Francesco said, standing up. "I have a funeral to plan, and I'm not leaving it to my wife. This has devastated my family, so I'd appreciate discretion. I doubt you'll give me that, but be careful what you share with the media. If my wife reads about any of this in the papers or sees it on the news, there will be a stiff penalty."

"Is that a threat?" Grant asked.

"A threat is me saying I'll rip your balls off and shove them in your head when I remove your eyes, but I didn't say that. I want updates on your investigation, and for you to do your job without sensationalizing it. Right now, though, this interview is over."

He left the room but wasn't worried since two of his men would escort the idiots out. His family had been his pride, but Caterina had fucked up royally with the use of such an inexperienced young woman, when any hooker would've sufficed. Victor Madison wasn't a picky man when it came to women, but putting a girl in the position to do a job she couldn't handle had given Lucassi the green light he needed to kill Caterina and get away with it.

"What do you want to do, Papa?" Lucan followed him to the other side of the house and took a deep breath when they reached Caterina's room.

"I want to know exactly what Caterina was up to, and what the hell she was thinking. If you had any part of this, tell me now. Your mother won't survive burying two of you."

"I doubt either Lucassi or Moretti would come after me."

He laughed as he grabbed Lucan by the chin. "Who said anything about either of those clowns? You and your sister think you had free rein to do whatever you wanted, but I'm telling you otherwise."

"I asked her if the girl was one of hers," Lucan said, pulling away and sitting on the bed. "Caterina never answered me, but she did say it would never come back on us."

"The lesson you should take away, then, is it did come back on her, since she's fucking dead. I should let it go since everyone will think she deserved it, but Caterina was my child—my family. No one takes what's mine and doesn't pay for it in blood."

"What are you looking for?"

"I need something that will keep Angelo off our asses when the time comes, so start looking for answers. I want to know what the hell your sister was doing."

❖

"You think he knew?" Corey asked as they walked to the car.

Andrew shrugged. Their multiple investigations now had a task force since everyone from the mayor to the governor's office was involved. This many murders in a place where people came to party and go wild had made the national news and that was unacceptable, as they'd been told with an impressive amount of angry volume. No one working the case had a fucking clue as to what was going on.

"There's one thing I do believe, and that's I'll never get the last thirty minutes back. It's only a theory, but I think Caterina had something going on that she didn't tell anyone about, and Victor's dying screwed it up." He sat in the driver's seat and glanced around at the men walking around with guns. It was like advertising a bad man lived there, but the house was so far off the road no one ever saw the small army.

"You make it sound like Victor's death was the true accident in all this, but it snowballed."

"We float that, and we'd better be able to prove it. But my gut tells me that it's possible." His cell phone rang as he started the car, and when he saw the captain's number, it couldn't be good news. "What now?"

"Where are you?"

"We just finished with Francesco Terzo, and we're headed to see Mike. His team should have some answers for us by now, hopefully."

"Save that and head out on Highway 156 toward Indian Springs."

"That's the middle of nowhere, sir," he said, not believing his boss wanted him to waste time now.

"We just found the two AWOL deputies who'd been sitting on the Lucassi house. Each of them has a bullet in his head, which explains the blood on Caterina Terzo's face. Mike got a match this morning and it came back to our guys. I have no fucking idea what's going on here." The captain stopped for a moment as if overcome with emotion. "Andy, I know you're swamped, but all this shit is related, and I need you to coordinate the scene. Highway patrol is out there now, but they're expecting you."

"Yes, sir, we'll take care of it." He took the drive faster than the goons were expecting and a few of them flipped him off.

"What's wrong?"

"These fuckers have gone too far. They killed two cops, so I hope they can handle more than the Vegas heat."

❖

"Brinley!"

The yell got Brinley to scramble out of bed and run to the door of the bedroom.

"Mom?" Brinley met her in the middle of the staircase and started crying as Wilma held her so tight she thought she'd have bruises. "How did you find me?"

"Thank God. Thank God. Thank God." Wilma finally let go and leaned back to stare at her. "I just *knew* you weren't dead."

"Why don't you two get comfortable and I'll go and check on Reed?" Oscar said as he stood at the bottom of the stairs with a smile.

She nodded and held her mom's hand as she went down. Oscar blushed when she hugged him and kissed his cheek. "Mom, have a seat on the sofa. I'm going to check on Finn. I'll be right back."

"What the hell is going on?" Wilma sounded so confused that Brinley wanted to rush the story, but there was something she had to do first.

"I promise I'll tell you everything, but give me a minute." She turned and stopped Oscar from going up. "Do you mind giving me a second alone with her?"

"I'm sure it might take more than a second, but I don't mind waiting."

She climbed the stairs slowly and thought about every conversation she and Reed had engaged in since they'd met, and how many times Reed had said she wasn't a nice person. It was a good thing Reed's mother was dead. If she wasn't, Brinley would've punched someone in the face for the first time in her life. Reed had deserved so much better.

"Hey," she said when Reed glanced her way.

"You know how I feel about you crying, so it was only to prevent any more of it." Reed shrugged and it came with another small grimace. "And she can't stay long, and you need to explain the importance of keeping up her act."

"Shut up," Brinley said, moving to sit on Reed's bed. Reed's eyes widened a little but she made no move to stop her when she leaned in and kissed her. She moved her hands into Reed's hair and simply enjoyed the feel of her lips on hers, and how Reed's breathing seemed to almost stop as if she was enjoying it just as much. "Thank you."

Reed reached up and wiped away the tears that were falling despite her happiness. "Seeing her again was supposed to make you *stop* crying."

"I'm not sure what kind of people you've been with in your life, but crying isn't always a bad thing," she said and kissed Reed again. "And the next time you tell me you're not a good person, I'm going to remind you about this."

"Go on, before she thinks I'm brainwashing you or something. If the kid wakes up, I'll call you so she can see him too." Reed's touch was so tentative that Brinley leaned in to it to show her how much it was wanted. "And you're welcome."

She nodded before heading back down and sat next to her mother, glad that her grief was at an end. "I'm so sorry." She started with that and it made her mother cry.

"Why didn't you call me? The moment they told me you might be dead like poor Naomi, I fell apart."

"Believe me, it killed me to see you on television, but this is what happened," she said, launching into the story. Wilma stared at her the entire time as if she wasn't exactly sure if she should believe her. "I know it sounds out-there, but Naomi and her daughter should prove to you that I'm not lying."

"And this woman brought you here and is helping you?" Wilma asked as if she didn't believe that part at all.

"Reed saved us, Mom. I know it sounds like total crap, but she did. I'm not going to share what she told me about her past, but she couldn't do what they hired her to do when she saw Finn. It might've started with that, but now she's doing what she can to get us back to our lives without any kind of threat to our future." She wiped her eyes again and laughed. "Who would've thought accounting could be so exciting? Reed isn't to blame. Dean Jasper and his boss Robert Wallace are the ones responsible for all this."

Wilma told her about meeting with Dean and all the stupid questions he'd asked her. "I knew that guy was no good. You and Finn were missing, and all he wanted to talk about were the files you'd brought home."

"Those files weren't enough, but Reed got what we needed to prove what we suspected but could never verify on our own," she said, pointing to the kitchen. "All we need to figure out now is how best to use them so we can move on."

"Where's Finn?"

"Brinley," Oscar called from the top of the stairs. "The tornado woke up."

"Come on." She stood and held her hand out to her mom.

She almost laughed when she saw Finn on the bed, sitting on Reed's lap, having what appeared to be a serious conversation with her. He had a limited vocabulary, but he had a lot to say. Reed was listening while holding his hand, and it was the stillest she'd ever seen her child.

"Mom, this is Reed."

"Thank you," Wilma said, moving to surprise Reed with a hug. "I owe you everything I have for saving my family."

"You don't owe me a thing, except your silence until all this is over."

"Brinley told me, and I don't have a problem with that. All I need is your promise that you'll continue to keep them safe."

Reed nodded at Wilma's request and glanced at her.

"Take a nap, and I'll be up later to change your bandages," she told Reed. "Come on, big boy."

"I don't know whether to laugh or cry hysterically," Wilma said, watching Finn run around with a truck.

"Trust me, if I decide to write a book when all this is over, it'll never be published because it'll sound too far-fetched." She glanced up toward the master bedroom and wondered if now was a good time to kiss Reed since they couldn't really talk about it. "That moment I saw her aiming that gun at my head was the absolute worst second of my life. Everything that came after wasn't much better."

"You seem to trust her with Finn," Wilma said in a tone that meant she was fishing.

"I trust Reed with Finn—and with me—because she's earned it. She gave me a list of choices at the beginning, so my being here is my idea." The fact she'd kissed Reed was also her idea, but this wasn't the time to get into it.

"What choices, exactly?"

"I could go and take my chances, I could disappear with a new identity and you would've never heard from me again, or I could stay here and let her try to set things right. This was hard on you, but never seeing you again was unacceptable, so I hope you can forgive me, and forgive her as well."

"Brin, you sound like you really like her." Wilma took her hand and pressed it against her chest. "Don't get blinded by all this. Try and remember where you started."

"Don't you think I know that?" The smart move would be to listen to Reed's advice and run when the coast was clear, but she couldn't. "I'm not that naive that I don't realize what Reed is, but I'm alive because of her. Finn isn't dead in a burned car because of her." She started crying again. "I can't forget that, and I won't be able to forget her."

"Oh, baby girl, you're going to have to force yourself to. You deserve a life where you're not constantly looking over your shoulder."

"I know that too, but it's going to take some time to convince my heart of that."

They spent the rest of the afternoon downstairs talking things through until Oscar told Wilma it was time to go. "Remember to keep taking interviews and don't let up on the cops. If anyone suspects Brinley's still alive, none of us are safe," Oscar said.

"Can I see Reed before we go?" Wilma asked. "Alone." She winked at Brinley, who frowned at her.

"What are you up to?" If her mother gave Reed a lecture about anything Brinley had told her, she was going to die of embarrassment.

Wilma turned to Oscar, ignoring Brinley's question. "May I?"

"She's awake, and I'm sure she won't mind," Oscar said, nodding.

"Don't worry, Mrs. Myers," Reed said when she came in. "I'm not going to let anything happen to her, and I'm sorry it took so long to get you here." Reed held out a phone and she accepted it. "For when you want to check in. I know Oscar made you leave your phone at home, but you can use this one. The only number on it is to another burner phone I'll give Brinley."

"When can I come back?"

"I have to get back to work as soon as I can walk without pain, but I'll make sure it's as often as we can manage. The only thing to remember is one slipup, and we're done."

"There are certain things I'm willing to gamble with, but my family is not one of them."

"Good, she'll need you once all this is over and I have to disappear from your life." The words hurt, but they were true.

"That's probably for the best, but I know my daughter," Wilma said, taking her hand. "From everything she just told me, it doesn't sound like that's what she wants."

"If life's taught me one thing, ma'am, it's that we don't always get what we desire. You need to remind her of why we met in the first place. That should convince her that this isn't a happily-ever-after kind of story."

Wilma tilted her head in acknowledgment. "Life is a conglomeration of our choices, Reed, and not so much about giving in, but fighting for the things we really want. You were hired for something you didn't do. That changes the way she sees you, and I'm not going to stand in her way if she decides to fight to keep you around." Wilma laughed. "It's the craziest thing I've ever heard, mind you, but Brinley is as stubborn as she is beautiful. If that is what she decides, I think you're strong enough to change certain aspects of your life. Or I'll do whatever I can to make her change her mind."

"I think this conversation is the craziest thing ever," Reed said, "but I won't forget what you said. You and Brinley need to remember how this started. Nothing I can ever do will make up for it, and I sure as hell can't change it."

They said good-bye and Wilma left Reed to her thoughts. It took a few more minutes before she heard the front door close again and for Brinley to appear in her doorway. "You think she'll do okay?" Reed asked.

"My mom deals with the IRS all the time, so I'm confident she can sell a story if she needs to." Brinley didn't move from the door, but Finn came in to play with his toys. "Do you want to talk about what happened?"

"About your mother, or that you kissed me?" She couldn't decide which thing was harder to wrap her head around. "Seeing the kid, and given what you told me about your ex, made me think you wouldn't be the type to go around kissing people who try to kill you."

"Another joke? I'm beginning to think I'm breaking through that tough exterior of yours." Brinley finally came in and sat on the same spot she'd kissed her from. "This isn't some kind of twisted Stockholm syndrome if that's what you're worried about. I'm more in touch with my feelings than that."

"I haven't done all this to put you in danger at the end, so I hope you know I'm not giving in either. You'll have a life after this, but it won't include me." Reed hoped Brinley would eventually see the truth of all that.

"I'm not that easy to persuade, and my ex was a big mistake in ways you don't get."

She had to laugh at the absurdity of it all. "Not to put you off, but I need to get up. It's time to start our endgame, and that starts with a shower."

"Let me corral Finn and I'll help you. Oscar's gone on and on about how much blood you lost, which means I'm not letting you stand up alone, so save the tough act."

"It's not an act," she said indignantly.

"Uh-huh, give me a minute." Brinley closed and locked the door since Finn knew how to escape an unlocked one.

"Just get me in there and I'll handle the rest."

"Are you shy?" Brinley asked with a cocked eyebrow.

It was an exercise in patience, but she stood and allowed Brinley to walk her to the bathroom and get her undressed. She wasn't shy, but she also tried to ignore that Brinley sat and watched her in the shower after wrapping the wounds to keep them from getting too wet. Surreal didn't begin to cover it.

She'd been with plenty of women in her life, but none of them had ever looked at her like Brinley was looking now. It shouldn't have felt sexual, but it did, from the way Brinley had slowly undressed her to the way she touched her. The gentleness of Brinley's hands felt like landing in some bizarre universe that she wouldn't know how to find again if she managed her way out. It was like finding unicorns really did exist.

The warm water was relaxing, but the tension was starting to build when she gazed at Brinley and Brinley smiled at her. She was convinced if she asked Brinley to join her she would, but that would only add to the pile of mistakes she was trying to wade through. Willpower was paramount now.

"You seem to be moving better," Brinley said as she helped dry her off. There was no question her hands lingered, as did her gaze.

"It's going to be at least a month before I'm back to normal. This isn't the first time I've been shot, so I've got a little experience." She stepped into a clean pair of boxers and took the shirt Brinley held up. "If I start moving around some, it'll help with the pain."

They both turned when they heard Oscar call out, and he sounded excited again. "I understand now what you said about Oscar's state of being. The term nervous Nellie comes to mind."

She laughed and nodded. "Perfect name for him. Go unlock the door and see what's got him in a twist now."

He glanced between them as if trying to puzzle something out, and she could only guess it was her wet hair that made him pause.

"Is my mom okay?" Brinley asked, shaking him out of his silence.

"She's fine, but there's plenty of money on the street for information about Victor, Caterina, and Paolo." Oscar was good at reading the pulse of the town when something big was out there, and this could either be great or the beginning of the end for them.

"Who's paying?" she asked.

"Remi and Mano Jatibon," Oscar said, two people they'd never done business with. "They found two dead cops today, and they're trying to divert the heat off them and their business. Everybody who owes anyone anything is trying to find something to tell the Jatibons since the money's too good to pass up."

"Okay," Brinley said holding up her hands in a T formation for timeout. "Who are Remi and Mano Jatibon, and what do they have to do with this?"

"Sit for a minute." Reed pointed to the bed. "The only players you know about are Robert Wallace, Francesco Terzo, and his daughter Caterina Terzo, but Vegas has more connected families than that. Wallace was working for the Terzo family, but it was the daughter of another family who hired me to kill Victor Madison."

"The head of Bellagio, right?" Brinley asked.

"Yes, and really Victor's death boils down to his wife not wanting to share the assets in a divorce. The problem is Victor's father-in-law is Diego Moretti, who's part of the New York Mob—his heir apparent Paolo is who shot me. Now both the Terzo and Moretti families have lost a child, and they're pissed."

Brinley nodded and held her index finger up. "I understand all that, but what does that have to do with these Jatibon people?"

"I'd think it's a survival of the fittest kind of thing. The Jatibons are the ones standing outside the ring of trouble, and they want to keep it that way. Remi Jatibon and her brother Mano control yet another family, but they're based in New Orleans. Technically, Remi is the heir apparent in that family, but she pretty much already runs the day-to-day stuff with her brother serving as her right hand."

"If they're from New Orleans, what do they care about what's happening in Vegas?" Brinley asked.

"They have interests outside New Orleans, like owning the Gemini next to Caesars Palace."

"I still don't understand why they'd get involved."

"Remi and her partner in business, Cain Casey, also a New Orleans mobster, are like the thinking arm of the Mob. They treat business like some kind of chess game, only in the end they shove the king up your ass and shove the queen in your eye before you even figure out you've lost. What I can't figure out is what do two dead cops have to do with any of this?" she asked, moving gingerly to her desk chair. The bed was getting tiring.

"Believe me," Oscar said, "I'm going to start looking for answers to that one, but two of those three people are our responsibility. The amount of money they're throwing out could become a big problem for us." Oscar actually wrung his hands and she smiled at the act usually only written about in old romance novels.

"Or it could be our way out," she said slowly. She might have never done business with the Jatibons, but she knew plenty about the guy who ran the Gemini. Mano, from all her information, was a stand-up guy who didn't take shit from anyone, especially people like Francesco Terzo. "Do you trust me?" she asked Brinley.

"With my life."

"Then let's get you back to what you know."

CHAPTER TWENTY-FOUR

I know, don't call anyone," Brinley said two days later as she stood by the kitchen door with her mother.

Oscar was about to drive Reed away from the house for the series of phone calls she had to make—she was paranoid enough not to want to do them from home. "I didn't say it," she said smiling.

"You were thinking it, but don't worry, we'll wait for you to get back. Can I talk to you privately for a moment?"

"Sure." She headed to the den. "What?" she asked when they were out of sight of Oscar and Wilma.

"This." Brinley stood on her toes and put her arms around her neck and kissed her. "Don't take any unnecessary chances."

"Your mother was right," she said, not pushing Brinley away. "You're stubborn."

"Good, that means you're not a slow learner."

She left her hands on Brinley's waist a moment longer and maintained eye contact. "I'm not the one having trouble understanding the reality of things, Ms. Myers."

"Go do your job and come back without the need for a medic."

Reed fought against the desire to take Brinley upstairs and make love to her right that moment. She'd been lying awake at night, watching Brinley sleeping next to her, and showering with Brinley watching had been agony. Every touch, every caress, the smell of her hair…it was insanely, dangerously distracting. She pulled away and left without another word.

"What are you going to do about that?" Oscar said when he pulled away from the house.

"About what?" She felt pretty good with the compression bandage she'd had Brinley put on that supported both her back and front. The pain was still there, but it wasn't distracting enough to keep her from doing what she had to do.

"Brinley's in love with you."

"That's crazy. She's grateful for what we've done, and once she's back home with Finn and her mom, the one thing she'll be the most thankful for is that we're no longer around. I may not know shit about love, but no one falls that fast. And not for the person hired to kill them."

"Okay, you saying that is what's crazy, but I'll drop it. We have to concentrate, or we'll really be out of her life when we're dead."

She forced herself to focus and thought of the conversations she needed to have. They drove to their diner, and she settled into the most private booth that still had a good view of the parking lot. The breakfast rush was over, so it was relatively quiet. "Do you ever get tired?" she asked, and Oscar nodded as if he knew exactly what she meant.

"The best thing about my life is you, and we have enough money to live the rest of our time on this planet without worrying about all this shit." Oscar sighed and it did appear as if he was physically and emotionally exhausted.

"You wouldn't miss it?"

He stared at her and shook his head. "Maybe what happened was karma's way of saying we've paid enough for shit that wasn't our fault. Penny wasn't your mistake, and my father wasn't mine. We got screwed in that department, but we made it. We've survived, we've succeeded, and we've got time to figure out what comes next."

"Getting the Jatibons to believe us is what comes next, buddy. Beyond that I've got no clue." She'd waved off the waitress and picked up the phone. Oscar had done his magic and gotten Remi Jatibon's cell number, and it only rang twice before someone answered it.

"Hello." It was definitely a woman, but she had a deep voice.

"Please hear me out before you hang up, Ms. Jatibon," she said as a start. That got her silence but not a disconnect. "Your people put out feelers about some information you want."

"This is a cryptic way to go about it, but do you have what I want?"

"I killed two of the three on the list, but I had a contract for one of them."

That got her another stretch of silence, but obviously Remi wanted to hear more. "Usually contractors don't like talking about their work, which makes me skeptical about this call."

"Until today I haven't talked about any contract, ever, but when you hire me, then double-cross me, all bets are off, as they say. I'll give you what you want, but then you have to give me something in return."

"What's that?"

"A life." The memories of Brinley's lips on hers could be the reward of her retirement, and she refused to second-guess it. "Actually, two."

"You want to hit the people who double-crossed you?"

"No, I want to save two people who got caught in the middle. They bear no blame in all this."

"You'll have to come out of the shadows. I want to know who I'm dealing with."

It was her turn to be silent for a moment. "I have your word you'll at least listen first before you turn me over to the wolves?"

"My word is everything to me, and you have mine. I usually take care of my problems myself, but to have someone like you call me… you must have an interesting story."

"It's one of a kind."

"I bet, and I'm available whenever you want to meet," Remi said.

"Now would be good, and as a sign of good faith, you pick the place." Oscar took a deep breath at that offer, but this time they couldn't stay in the shadows.

"Half an hour in the one place in the Gemini that has no cameras."

Reed laughed and reconsidered her offer for a minute. "I head up to the executive offices of your casino, Ms. Jatibon, and I'm sure I'll be on a set of glossies so fast I'll be famous to everyone who wants a piece of me."

"I was talking about the spa. By law, we don't record anything in there, and a good massage never killed anyone."

"Half an hour then." She hung up and gazed at Oscar. "This is it, buddy. We take this chance and there's no turning back on anonymity."

"Remi Jatibon better hope she has a good memory," Oscar said, standing up and leaving a tip for the use of the booth. "You might be changing the game, but there's no reason we can't play by some of our rules."

"How do you plan to do that?"

"You meet with her and give her everything, and I'll make you as invisible in there as I did at Bellagio. I'm not letting anything happen to you since you've got a good chance at happiness." He blew a kiss at her and laughed.

"Get your head out of the pretty clouds, my friend. I don't mind retirement for a while, but we have to give the cute kid and his mother back when we're done." She stood and placed her hand over her wound when she straightened out. It was a shame she could only kill Paolo Moretti once for the fucking annoying wound.

She couldn't go into a meeting with an Earwig, so she spoke to Oscar on her phone until she reached the spa, then stepped inside. He was working from the back of the SUV in the parking lot and giving her directions as she went. When she entered the spa, the tall woman with cowboy boots on seemed as out of place as she did, so she walked over and held her hand out. "Are you dying for a good massage?"

"I find that great conversation can be just as relaxing." Remi shook her hand and smiled. She was tall, but Remi had a few inches on her. "Let's take the manager up on her offer of using her office."

"I've never done this." Reed stared out at a rock garden with designs in the sand like someone had raked it. She supposed it was a Zen relaxation thing, but relaxed was the last thing she was. "But the way I see it, you don't have a gun in the war that's probably coming. That makes you the perfect person to negotiate for the lives of the people who really don't have a place in this."

"You're right, it's not our war, and I don't usually use contractors. If I have a problem, I like to deal with it internally." Remi poured them some juice and sat back. "Not that I'm not going to trust what you're going to say, but the reason I mentioned contractors is precisely why we're here. You trust someone for something important, and it leaves you exposed if something goes wrong."

Remi had a point, but a true professional like her was never that loose end. You could shake down a client for more, but that would make for a short-lived career. "I totally understand that, but I've never betrayed anyone's trust. The problem started when they betrayed mine. The same code we all abide by means you double-cross me, and that cancels any business I have with you."

"Then let's have an honest conversation, and we'll see what we can do to move forward, wherever that might be."

"My first contract was for Victor Madison." The story of what put Victor on her kill list made Remi lean forward and tap her fingers together. "It had to look like an accident, and humiliating if I could manage it. If I'd known the woman with him was that young or Benito Lucassi's granddaughter, I would've handled it differently. I'm not into killing innocents."

"London Emerson stretches the meaning of innocent as far as it'll go without snapping, but the fact that she was working for Caterina Terzo earns you forgiveness for that one. Benito Lucassi might not see it that way, but this is a game with serious penalties if you don't play to win," Remi said, shrugging. "London was too young to know the rules, much less how it's played."

"True, but still, I would've played it differently if I'd known." She left out the part about the theft from Victor's office but saved it in case she needed something else to get Remi to work with her to save Brinley. "I had no idea about the kid's connection to Lucassi until Caterina Terzo was found the same way I left Madison, but that wasn't me. Whoever hired the contractor for that job copied my scenario, but I had nothing to do with it."

"So Paolo Moretti was your other contract?"

"That's where the double-cross came in. When I got the contract like I usually do, the order came from Francesco Terzo. I should've figured out it was bogus when it came with an explanation for the hit. No one ever gives you that because it gives the contractor your motive."

"Leverage over whoever hires you," Remi said. "Nothing like a good shakedown after you've already paid what I assume is big money, but then Terzo has never struck me as genius material."

"The contract was on Lucassi, it had to be in front of his family, and it was for killing Caterina. The wording gave me no choice but to do it the way Terzo wanted it. Contract killing isn't something I specialize in, but it's worth the trouble at times." She stopped when Remi put her hand up.

"Do you mind telling me what your specialty *is*?"

"I'm a thief, and a damn good one. This time, though, I had no choice if I wanted to keep working in Vegas." She took a sip of the juice and held her hand over her side. Sitting for so long had made the throbbing worse. "I'm the idiot who went to the place specified in the order. Following such precise directions made me easy to find, and I paid for that mistake."

"Someone shot you?" Remi said, pointing to her side. "I doubt that's a pulled muscle."

"Paolo Moretti shot me. He was there to kill me, only I'm a much better shot."

"Damn," Remi said, straightening out. "What the hell was he thinking?"

"Diego Moretti is in town to bury Victor, and he thinks like you do. Sofia hired me, and I'm not someone he wanted hanging over his family's head, considering Moretti's connections to Francesco Terzo."

"What connections do you think they have?"

She smiled. Remi Jatibon didn't need her breakdown of the facts, but she was checking to see if she had an accurate grasp of what was going on. "The two families run drugs from here to New York and clean their money through the Moroccan's operations. From what I found, they were bringing Victor Madison in slowly to expand that part of the operation."

"Sofia killed Victor without Diego's okay, I'm guessing." Remi smiled and shook her head.

"That she didn't discuss with me, but Victor's affair with his secretary was the main focus of her anger. He was screwing around on her and turning her kids against her. She'd had enough and wanted him gone, but she wanted to enjoy the money and everything she would've lost by going to jail." The juice was delicious and the coldness of it was taking her mind off her pain, so she took some more sips. "I guess she knew I wouldn't come to a specific spot if she'd asked, so they made it look like Francesco had hired me."

"There's one missing piece in all this." Remi made eye contact with her and waited. "You've come this far, so finish it. Diego's an animal, but there had to be more to it than simply a loose end."

"Your brother and the cops alerted them to the text messages between Caterina and London. I doubt Diego cared about the cheating, but Caterina wanting Sofia dead for no good reason was unforgivable. Caterina wanted Sofia dead only to put a leash on Victor, or that's my guess. Before Diego could do something about the threat to his family, Caterina showed up dead, and there's only one explanation for that." She tried half the truth first. There still was no reason to mention the money quite yet.

"Benito beat him to it."

"Exactly, but Benito's contractor used my moves, and that put Sofia front and center for the police to indict. Even though she had the alibi of being out of state for Victor's murder, the way Caterina died made a case against Sofia hiring someone to do her wet work. It was the way that Caterina was found that signed my death warrant, but this time they couldn't use a contractor. Especially if Diego was going to pin it on Francesco Terzo."

Remi nodded and stood to get her more juice. "I understand

everything you've told me, but I still don't get who you're trying to protect."

"Robert Wallace is responsible for the next contract I took, the day after Madison."

That made Remi laugh. "You're a busy bee, but anyone that popular is someone who's good."

"Thanks, I guess. His man Alex made it sound urgent," she said, giving Remi the whole story. "Naomi Williams died with her little girl, but I couldn't kill a mother in front of her child, and I damn well wasn't killing a one-year-old." Greed was definitely one of the deadly sins and it had screwed her out of the life she knew. Victor's contract should've been enough, but the trade-off for what she was losing was that Brinley and Finn were still alive.

"According to the news, Brinley Myers and her son are presumed dead. Their bodies haven't been found, but the scene left little doubt."

"It's not smart to assume anything, and they're very much alive."

Remi sighed and nodded again. "I'm sure I'm not going to like the reason, but why would that little shit order a hit on two of his employees?"

She told Remi the rest and what Wallace's true plans were. "He must've been thinking too much about his pretty boy Alex to consider who he was double-crossing, and the money must've blinded him."

"Little Bobby isn't my favorite person, and I agree he's dense, but I can't go to Angelo Giordano with just your word."

"The woman I was hired to kill is an accountant," she said, taking the ledgers out of her bag. This was the gamble, since it was their only copy and it would prove to Remi she was serious about what she wanted. "She detailed exactly what I've just told you, and you may not believe me, but the numbers don't lie. Little Bobby made the mistake of being too good at record keeping, or his flunky running Moroccan's accounting department was too good. Dean Jasper was meticulous because he wanted leverage as well as a way to protect himself. If he went down, he was pulling everyone down with him. Tell whoever you share this with that it's the only copy I have. There's no reason for me to keep one if Brinley and her son are safe."

"And all you want for this are the lives of Brinley and her son?" Remi asked, sounding skeptical.

"You said it before, Ms. Jatibon. When you play this game, you play to win. The problem with Brinley is she didn't know she was in anyone's game until I showed up with a gun. She was a woman hired to do a legitimate job, and that's what she thought she was doing." The only thing left if Remi didn't believe her was to go against what Brinley wanted and take care of the problem herself.

"You need to call me Remi." She held her hand out again. "You being here is a figment of my imagination, but if I'm going to have an imaginary friend, I'd like to know their name."

"Reed Gable, and thank you. I need her to come out whole. No changing her name, no looking over her shoulder, and no bad surprises a few years from now when someone thinks it's safe to hit her."

"Reed, I'll do my best, and if I can't get her that, I'll give her peace on my terms. That might mean a new life somewhere no one knows her, but she'll be alive." Remi's promise was exactly what she was after. "But you're right. She bears no blame here and deserves to come out whole."

"How about Wallace?"

Remi smiled and shrugged again. "That one I can't promise will come out whole and breathing. Trying to cut into Giordano's business or trying to cut him out altogether isn't a wise career choice. His job performance review will be memorable for about ten minutes."

"I don't know Mr. Giordano, but I'll be happy to do a pro bono case for him if he needs to send a message."

"This time let's try finesse. There's nothing wrong with coming out of a situation having someone like Angelo owing you a favor."

"It never hurts to make friends, I guess." She didn't have much experience with that, but Remi seemed like someone who'd come through.

"No, it doesn't." Remi stood and accepted the bag with all the ledgers and Brinley's report. "You have my word that I'll do my best to get you what you want. All I need is a contact number."

She handed over a card and shook her hand again. "I'll look forward to hearing from you." The ledgers were in Remi's other hand and she was having second thoughts about letting them go. "Remember, those are the only proof I have, and the only bargaining chip I have to keep Brinley alive."

"You should reconsider that statement, Reed. They're the only thing you have that will kill Wallace and Bell. Their deaths will resurrect your girl."

"She's not my girl," she said, but for once it was nice to imagine that being true.

CHAPTER TWENTY-FIVE

D id he say what he wanted?" Robert Wallace asked Alex as he drove into work. He'd gone to an interview at Bellagio and was about to start singing, it'd gone so well.

"All he said was it was important, and not to think about turning him down."

He couldn't wait to put Francesco and all his self-importance behind him. "I'll go over there now, and then we can head home early. We might have a lot of celebrating to do."

"He wants to see both of us, so keep the champagne on ice. Do you have any idea what this is about?" Alex sounded nervous. "Mr. Terzo isn't a big fan of social visits, and he's never included me in any of the trips you've made over there."

"I'm sure it's a bunch of bullshit over Caterina's death, but we had nothing to do with that, so stop biting your nails." He turned into the casino and waved off the valet. "Calm down and we can go together."

"Park your car," Alex said. "Mr. Terzo's providing a ride for us. He said he didn't want the Feds to see us going to his house, and he'd heard from Lucan the police were still all over us about those two bitches from accounting."

"Shit," he said, not wanting to waste time on this today. He was anxious to get home and have Alex blow some of his nervous energy away. "When are they coming?"

"They're here and said they'd meet us in the parking lot. I'll meet you down there."

The police had come by again a few days prior, after they'd found the two dead patrolmen. He'd explained that he had nothing to do with them, and they'd left with a promise to be back. The two dead accountants were still on their radar, but the only thing that worried him was Dean Jasper.

That fucker had disappeared and no amount of searching had given him a clue as to where he was. The blood all over Dean's pantry floor made Robert wonder if someone had gotten to Dean, but there was no way the little shit would talk. He wouldn't have given a rat's ass about the vanishing act, but the books were gone as well. That he'd checked himself, and if Dean or anyone else thought of shaking him down, he was going to kill them as painfully as he could once the ledgers resurfaced.

The casino floor was dead except for a couple of gamblers, so he made it to the back parking lot fairly quickly. Alex was waiting by the door, and he was certainly not in control of himself from the way he was hurrying toward him.

"I don't like this," Alex said.

"All we have to do is humor him, and once the new job comes through, we'll put the Terzos and all the other assholes in their orbit in our rearview mirror." He put his hand on Alex's neck briefly and smiled. "Come on, this shouldn't take long. It's probably a check-in kind of thing to make sure everything is still on track here." He led Alex outside by the arm. "Francesco isn't a big talker, so keep your mouth shut and we'll be back here for dinner."

The driver locked them in and he tried not to show any fear. He'd negotiated with his new contacts and was ready to take over as far as distribution, but that didn't mean he wanted to be alone with the old man, ever. He was looking forward to the moment he was solidly behind the wall of protection his new friends promised. That he'd even contemplated this would be seen as a major show of disloyalty, but Francesco was as out of touch with the reality down here as his bosses from New York, so they had only themselves to blame.

"Wow, it must be a party," he said when they drove up to a slew of cars in the parking lot.

"It's all in your honor," the driver said. "Don't keep the boss waiting. He's in the dining room."

A guard led the way and another two walked behind them. "Are you sure about this?" Alex said.

"Calm down," he whispered harshly. That was hard advice to follow when he walked in and found the Jatibons sitting with the Terzos and someone he'd never seen before. "Mr. Terzo, thank you for inviting us. You have my condolences on Caterina. Such a tragedy."

"Sit down and stop talking," the man he'd never met said, his hand on a stack of something in a bag.

"Hey, I was just showing respect. Mr. Terzo's earned it," he said, but the way Francesco glared at him made him follow directions.

"When we put you in the job you have, you seemed so grateful, considering where you'd come from." The new guy wore a really expensive suit and appeared to be a man with few worries.

"I'm very grateful, and I've done a good job for Mr. Terzo. We move a lot of money through the Moroccan, and we're working on upping our numbers." Robert sat and tried to keep his leg from bouncing. That was his nervous tic, and that was the last thing he needed to show in this room. "If you want to add even more business than Mr. Terzo has in mind, that might take time."

"You're working on something, on that I agree," the man at the head of the table said.

"I'm sorry, who are you?" He glanced at Alex, but he didn't seem to have a clue.

"This is Angelo Giordano," Lucan said. "I'm sure I don't have to tell you who that is."

"Mr. Giordano, I'm so glad to meet you. Mr. Terzo has always spoken highly of you," he said, standing and offering his hand. When Giordano didn't take it, he got his first real clue that they'd walked into a trap.

"If you'd let me finish," Angelo said. "You're working on something, but it has nothing to do with us or improving our business."

Angelo took his hand off the bag and another man emptied it so they could see what was inside. The sight of the ledgers made Robert's nausea climb to the point he almost threw up. Jasper had fucked him, and he wasn't walking away from this.

"You wanted something that doesn't belong to you, and you cut a deal with someone who had no right to do so."

"You have to let me explain." He spoke fast, and Alex sat quietly with his eyes closed, seeming to shrink in his seat. "I wasn't working against you. All I was doing was trying to open new markets."

"You can talk all you want, Robert, but the books speak for themselves. I'm sure Angelo would appreciate whatever bullshit story you're going to tell," Remi Jatibon said, "but it'll be a waste of time."

"I'm sorry, but you don't have anything to do with this," he said to Remi.

"You were told to shut the fuck up," Francesco said. "The guy you were dealing with had something in common with you. He was way down the totem pole, and his boss didn't mind turning him over to us. You may not know this, but when someone starts cutting little pieces off you, believe me, you'll tell me whatever I want to know to make the pain stop. It only took a few fingers for the fucker to give you and your master plan up."

Sweat ran down his back and his leg jumped frantically. "Francesco, come on, we've got a good thing going here. Who are you going to believe?"

"I'm going to believe you, of course," Francesco said.

"Thank God," he said, almost wetting himself from relief.

"Yeah, you put it all in there, making it easy to believe you," Angelo said, pointing to the books. "You were going to cut us off, you were starting to pull Victor in with you, and you were going to screw with my supply chain." Angelo stood and walked behind him. "You were also dumb enough to try and cover up your screwups by killing two women and their children."

Robert gripped the arms of his chair and barely refrained from screaming when Angelo moved quickly and slit Alex's throat. The gurgle and scent of metal were something he'd never be able to forget.

"Karma's a true bitch when you order the death of innocents, but then, you had your fixer make that call."

"I was trying to protect you and Mr. Terzo."

"You were trying to cover your ass," Angelo screamed. "No real man kills women and children who have nothing to do with our business. All you managed to do was get police to crawl all over our asses until they manage to solve the crime. How exactly is that helping us?"

"If I made a mistake, I'm sorry. You should know that I'm loyal to you, though. There's no way I'd try to move in on your business." The words were falling on deaf ears and he let the tears flow down his cheeks unchecked.

"Remi," Angelo said, holding his hand out to her. "Mano."

"Angelo, we'll be waiting for your call once you're done," Remi said. She shook his hand and turned away like it was an ordinary day.

"Wait by the pool, if you don't mind the late afternoon heat—this shouldn't take long."

Remi and Mano nodded and started to walk out.

Robert had a feeling any chance of living out the day was walking out with them.

"You know I trust you to stay while I'm doing it, but none of this has anything to do with you, and there's no need for you to deal with the mess. I am, though, in your debt for bringing this to me," Angelo said.

"And the rest?" Remi asked, and Robert wondered what that meant.

"Let me finish this and I give you my word I'll take care of that as well."

The only strange thing about the conversation was that Francesco and Lucan seemed as confused as he did. All he had to do was turn Francesco back to his side. "Are we going into business with the Jatibons?" Robert asked. It made no sense if they were. The Gemini was a Jatibon property, no matter whose name was on the deed, and it was set up to do the exact same thing he was doing at the Moroccan. The Jatibons wouldn't need to go outside their own operation.

"Us? Who is *us*, exactly?" Angelo asked.

Robert stayed in his seat but watched Angelo walk until he was behind Lucan.

"If you want to be truthful here, Little Bobby, it'll save you a lot of pain in the end. You should learn that from your friend there," Angelo said, gesturing to Alex. His lover was slumped over as his blood dripped from the table to the terracotta Saltillo tile, bleeding on the floor like some kind of macabre Halloween decoration.

"All I was doing was trying to make new contacts and build the business. I know it wasn't my place, but I wanted to show initiative so I'd get the Bellagio job. You can't blame me for that."

"Little Bobby, I do blame you, and you fucked up. No one comes into this type of meeting completely innocent, but this time you gave me everything I needed to hang you for every crime." Angelo tapped Lucan on the shoulder and Lucan moved toward him. "You should be honored. It's not every day you give someone the chance to make their bones."

Before he could ask what the hell the bastard meant, Lucan placed his gun to the back of his head and pulled the trigger. Robert's last sensation was the cold metal against his scalp.

❖

"You know what to do, right?" Angelo asked Francesco and the old man nodded. "I'm leaving tonight, but forget the Moroccan for now. We'll take care of putting someone new in charge and concentrate on the operation in New York for the time being. You've got Caterina's funeral and your family to worry about."

"You can't cut us out, Angelo. This is our town," Francesco said, but didn't get too loud.

Angelo knew Francesco's men patrolled the grounds, but only his men were in the room with them. It didn't matter though—in reality, everyone in the house belonged to him. "This is *your* town? Honestly, that's what you're going to say?"

"You can't blame me for that motherfucker." Francesco pointed to Robert.

"Who else am I going to blame? You put him there, you missed all this, and you completely missed whatever it was that Caterina was doing. I know Lucan can't answer what the hell she was up to, but can you?" Angelo sat back down and cracked the bones in his neck. "She started something that has turned into this complete mess, and neither of you knew anything about it."

"Caterina was loyal to you and the family. Whatever it was, I'm sure it was for our best interest," Francesco said, shaking his fist at him.

"Careful, Francesco, that's how Little Bobby tried to defend himself, and look at him now." The way Francesco stared at him made Angelo want to break out in laughter. The old man never could control his temper, but he'd been a friend of his father's and that was the only reason he'd left him in this position. "London Emerson, though, is hard to overlook no matter what she was doing."

"That little slut is who you're worried about?" Lucan said.

"She was Benito's granddaughter. That alone should've made her off-limits. If Caterina wanted to fuck her, fuck her, but she should've known better than to pimp her out."

"What does it matter now? Either Benito or Diego is responsible for Caterina's death, and I need your okay to do something about that." Francesco sounded like he was about to rush out of his chair and stab him through the heart, not asking for permission for anything at all.

"You're not getting that. Benito was within his rights to do with Caterina as he pleased, and he's got my protection. Caterina got his granddaughter killed, and now she's dead. That's the way of things. The main problem I'm having is that you've lost control not only of your family, but of your people. That I can't afford."

"What the hell are you talking about?" Francesco asked.

Angelo snapped his fingers and one of the men opened the door from the kitchen so two big guys could drag Gino Roca in. Gino's face was a mess and he was moaning. "Your top lieutenant was out making threats against people who had nothing to do with any of this, and followed it up by threatening their business."

"Am I supposed to know what you're talking about?" Francesco stared at Gino but made no move toward him.

"Assuming you don't know about this, he visited Remi without your permission, so tell me how you're going to handle it."

Francesco hesitated but held his hand out for Lucan's gun. When he had it in hand, every man in the room aimed their weapon at his head. Angelo didn't worry, though, since Francesco knew the score. It was either Gino's life or his. "Are you satisfied?" Francesco asked when Gino was dead.

There was a sudden spurt of gunfire and Francesco turned toward Lucan.

"Not quite, but this shouldn't take long."

The sun had set hours before, but Reed couldn't sleep so she went down and poured herself a drink. There had been no word from Remi aside from her warning to be patient, but the breaking news of the day was about the fire that had consumed the Terzo home after a gas leak, killing ten people. That number included the entire Terzo family as well as some of their household staff. Someone had done law enforcement's job for them and taken down one of the Mob families in town. The only survivor had been Lucan's wife, who was out at an attorney's appointment.

All Reed had to worry about now was Sofia and Benito, but Remi had told her to be patient about that as well, and she would be, up to a point. The burn of the whiskey made her relax, but she still heard the soft footsteps on the stairs. Brinley hadn't been upset to hear about Robert Wallace and Alex Bell, but she seemed happy it hadn't been Reed who had pulled the trigger.

"Are you okay?" Brinley asked, taking the glass from her and taking a sip.

"I couldn't sleep, that's all." The nightgown Brinley was wearing made her smile when she noticed the small cats all over it. Wilma had been able to pack a bag with some essentials in it and drop it off with Oscar. "What are you doing up?"

"I was thinking."

"Is that a bad thing?" Brinley handed her glass back and reached over to comb her hair. In reality it was time for Brinley to go home. With Wallace dead, all Reed was waiting for was the okay from Remi.

They'd worked out a story to tell the police that blamed Robert Wallace for her kidnapping, and Brinley had managed to escape when he disappeared. Remi had promised Robert wouldn't be found to contradict anything Brinley said. "I should hear from Remi by tomorrow at the latest and I'll drop you off. You can make your way home after you deal with the police."

"Once that happens you're going to disappear, aren't you?" Brinley led her to the sofa and pushed her back.

"We talked about this," she said, finishing her drink and turning slightly to face Brinley. "You're free to go back to your life. I've made the best deal I could to make that happen."

"You haven't told me the whole story, but I'm sure you're sacrificing something for that." Brinley touched her face like she had so many times, and she wanted it never to end. "I don't know why fate brought us together, but I'm glad it did. You're one of the best things that's ever happened to me."

She chuckled at hearing that. No one had ever uttered those words in her presence. "Don't worry about me, and you don't have to lie."

Brinley shook her head and leaned in to kiss her. "You're so stubborn when it comes to believing the good in you." She kissed her again and carefully straddled her lap. "Let me show you."

She was going to stop Brinley from doing anything else, but she stripped off her nightgown and she couldn't bring herself to move. There was enough light in the room to see what a classic beauty Brinley was, and she had a gorgeous body with plenty of curves.

"I don't—" She didn't know how to finish that sentence. All she was used to were encounters like she'd had with women whose time she paid for. That seemed like a million years ago, and it was only about achieving relief and nothing more. This...this felt like something altogether different. And fuck, did she want it.

"What? Tell me," Brinley said, placing Reed's hand on her breast.

"I don't want to hurt you," she said, and Brinley seemed to understand what she was saying.

"Let me teach you, but I'm not afraid," Brinley said, helping her off with her shirt.

"Brinley, we shouldn't."

"You can toss me aside tomorrow, but I'm not going to make it easy for you."

The way Brinley touched her was like nothing else she'd experienced. It was gentle, and the kiss she'd started made Reed's objections die in her throat.

She opened her eyes when she squeezed Brinley's breast almost without permission and she raised her hand, not wanting to taint this beautiful woman with her need.

"Stop thinking and start seeing what's right in front of you." Brinley moved her fingers over her face as if memorizing every inch of it, and she placed hers on Brinley's hips to be safe. "I want you to touch me."

"I'm not sure I know how." Sex she knew well, but making love to someone was as unknown as quantum physics. And she was sure that's what Brinley wanted.

"We'll figure it out together." Brinley stood and held her hand out in invitation, and this was where she'd turn her down. It was the best choice for both of them...

She took her hand and followed her upstairs in a daze. Finn was gone from his spot on the floor and she glanced at Brinley, wondering what she'd done with him.

"He'll be okay in the guest room for now. Lie down."

She did, but not before Brinley took her boxers off and threw them over her shoulder. All that separated them now were the bandages on the bullet wounds, but the feel of Brinley on top of her erased all the pain. The sensation of running her hands down Brinley's back to her ass made her want to take charge, but she fought the instinct, wanting Brinley to move at her own pace.

Brinley must've sensed she'd go no further, so she sat up and swept her hair back as she straddled her waist. "Perhaps we shouldn't have ended up here, but if you don't touch me, I'm going to have to beg. That's how much I want you." She relaxed as Brinley took her hands and placed them on her shoulders. "Don't make me do that."

It was all she needed to hear and she moved down to her breasts, gently pinching her nipples until they pebbled under her fingers. That made Brinley move her hips slightly and take a quick breath. "Too hard?" she asked, lifting her hands.

"No, but you've got their attention now. It's no time to stop."

"Show me what you want," she said, putting her hands back on Brinley's soft, warm skin.

Brinley covered her hands with hers and squeezed before moving them down slowly until they were on her ass. "Look at me," Brinley said, spreading her legs a little wider. She took her hand and placed it between her legs. There was no need to motivate her any more as she ran her fingers through the wetness that was the clearest sign that Brinley wasn't asking her for something she really didn't want.

"You feel so good," she said, stopping at her hard clit. Brinley lifted her bottom a little and took her hand again so she could position her fingers.

"It's been so long," Brinley said as she guided her inside. "So long since I've wanted anyone this much."

Reed's bicep tightened when Brinley came down on her and then stopped as if enjoying the fullness. The stillness didn't last long when she moved her thumb to press against her clit, and Brinley's hips started moving. She went exquisitely slow, as if wanting it to last, but when Reed put more pressure on her clit, Brinley squeezed her other hand and started moving faster.

The way she didn't lose eye contact with her made it more special, at least until her body tensed and she pressed her hips down hard. She lifted their joined hands and caressed Brinley's breast, making her moan louder.

"Jesus," Brinley said, lifting up slightly and coming down again hard. "So good." She sounded breathless and sexy. "A little more, just a little more."

That was all she said until she relaxed and came forward to lie on her again. "Thank you," Brinley said, as if she'd just taken her to dinner or something.

"Why are you thanking me?" she asked.

"Because since the moment I first saw you pointing that gun at me, and after everything we've had to do to *kill* me," Brinley said, making air quotes, "I've been as worked up and tense as I've ever been in my life. Right now there isn't a tense part of me, so thanks."

"I'm not sure of the etiquette here, but I'm pretty sure I should be thanking you." Brinley lifted her bottom again so she could move her hand, which was a relief since the pain in her side was starting to throb.

"Learn to take a compliment, Reed." Brinley yawned and curled against her.

ALI VALI

"I'm trying my best." She started moving her hands up and down Brinley's back soothingly and it didn't take long for her to fall asleep. The weight of her was what heaven must be like. She kissed Brinley's forehead and was content to hold her. All she needed now was for her to keep sleeping to make this easier on both of them.

An hour later she moved Brinley carefully and stopped when she grumbled a bit, which was what Finn did when she picked him up and brought him back to his spot in the big pile of blankets on the floor. She took a shower downstairs so as not to wake them, then went back up one more time.

"Thank you," she whispered as she kissed Brinley's forehead again. "And I'm sorry for everything, especially this." She left the note on the nightstand and picked up the bag she'd placed in the closet. It was time to let them go and for her to get back to what she knew. She closed the door behind her and felt something break inside that she hadn't even known could be broken anymore.

CHAPTER TWENTY-SIX

"Mano, this isn't a punishment," Remi said when he didn't seem to take what she'd said well. "We've got too much going on at home for you to be here. I'm not going to force you, but I do want you to come home and think about running the casino in Biloxi, as well as a few other things."

"Are you sure it's not charity? I know I could've handled the last few months better, but I don't need you and Papi to hold my hand." Mano stared out at the Strip. The fire at the Terzo house had been two months ago, and the police had been like locusts on everyone trying to find answers, but with no luck. It was finally starting to die down so everyone could get back to business.

"Is the heat getting to you? Why in the hell would you say that? The shit that went on here had nothing to do with us. You know what our merger with Cain has done to our business. We've more than tripled our operation and there's room for expansion," Remi said, not moving from the conference table. "I either talk you into coming home, or I've got to hire someone else, and that's asking me to trust someone new. I'd rather the man running things with me be beyond reproach, and you're the one person in the world I trust as much as Papi."

"What about Dwayne and Steve?"

"They'd split their time between the studio and our gambling operations, which means a move to New Orleans as well. Papi wants everyone to start taking on more responsibility at the Pescador Club as well." New Orleans had voted in legalized gambling, but that's how Ramon had made his money for years. The Pescador Club was named after the place he'd owned in Cuba and had dancing and drinks downstairs, and a full-fledged casino on the second floor. Harrah's might now be at the end of Canal Street in downtown New Orleans, but their crowds at the club had never thinned.

"He's full of crap," Mano said and finally laughed. "We'll take him out of there in a pine box one day, and not until then."

"I knew you'd say that," Ramon said, coming in from Dwayne's office next door. "Your mother wants to start traveling, and I have no more excuses. *Mijo*," Ramon said, "my grandchildren are growing up without me spoiling them, and your wife's family is in Miami, which means you have no one here who's important. It's time to come home to family, and to the position that's been yours from the beginning. All this I've built isn't solely Remi's responsibility."

"Besides, Dallas already told Sylvia and she's packing. You can either come with them, or stay here and find a showgirl to keep you company," Remi said.

"I do that and Sylvia will fillet me with Mami's and Dallas's help. Thank you for giving me this opportunity, though. It was good building Gemini to what it is now." He embraced his father, then her. "We're not selling this place, are we?"

"I've got something else in mind, but I need to do some more convincing. I think I'm pretty good at it." She grinned and punched his shoulder.

"This wasn't convincing, it was a hard sell," Mano said, shaking her.

"Hey, if that's what it takes." She left Mano to catch up with their father and left with Simon to head back to the house. Her guest was due in an hour and it had taken a threat to get her to agree to come at all.

"Are you sure about this?" Simon asked as they drove back.

"I'm not, but what she did really impressed me. You don't often see someone who has everything to lose give it away so effortlessly to save someone she barely knows and was actually hired to kill. That shows me there's loyalty there that can't be bought unless it's to protect something she cares about."

"That's the problem, Remi. This woman has nothing she cares about," Simon said, following the GPS. "She has no family, no ties to anyone, and is nothing more than a contractor for hire."

"She's a survivor, and she thinks she owes me one. Let's give her a chance before we throw her back into the wild. And you're wrong about her not having anything she cares about. Her sacrifice says otherwise." She went inside and found Dallas with one of the studio's staff, running lines for her next project. It was slated to start in Vegas, which meant if Reed was open to what she had to say, they'd be around for a little while. "I'm back, but I've got a meeting in a few."

"Your meeting is early, and waiting in the office. She was surprised to see me, but she seems nice." Dallas stood and kissed her. "Don't take too long. We're supposed to hit the tables later so I don't look like a dork when we start filming."

"Impossible," she said, slapping Dallas on the ass. "And I won't be late."

❖

"Reed," Remi said, not surprised to find Reed sitting in a chair across from the desk but not looking at anything on it. "Thanks for coming."

"I wanted to thank you, so I'm glad you called." The time since they'd seen each other seemed to have been enough to heal Reed's wounds, based on the way she moved. "I've kept an eye on Brinley without her seeing me, and she's doing great. She's working for a tech company and her mom visits a lot. The police bought her story, and I haven't heard any chatter about her."

"Brinley *is* doing fine," she said, nodding. "I promised you she'd come out of this as best I could manage, but I also wanted to keep my word about keeping her safe, so I've had a couple of guys keeping tabs. She's under my protection as well as yours."

"Thank you," Reed said, clenching and unclenching her fist. "She's really special, as is her son, and she deserved another chance."

"She's not the only one," Remi said and winked. "I wanted to talk to you about something, but not necessarily about Brinley just yet."

"That's all we have to talk about."

"Have you taken any more contracts?" Remi asked, already knowing the answer.

"I'm thinking of retirement, but I haven't decided yet." Reed hesitated but didn't say anything else.

"Retirement is for people who think golf is an exciting day, and you don't fit that bill, Reed. What happened, though, should tell you there's more to life than living for the next contract."

"What do you have in mind? It sounds like you have a sugges- tion," Reed said, and it was a good sign she wasn't leaving.

"You seem to know a little about the casino business," she said as a start. "The way you explained Wallace's mistakes means you can spot a thief, and you're familiar with the players that are left."

"You have to remember, I *am* a thief," Reed said.

"I do remember that, but I'm thinking you'd only take something you were hired to take. Sofia hired you to take something as well as Victor's life, but this isn't about that."

A week after the deaths of the Terzo family, Diego and Sofia disappeared. The police were still investigating that as well, but Angelo had assured Remi when he'd cleaned house, it had been an all-encompassing kind of thing, even though Diego didn't work for him. That meant the Moretti family was missing but they'd never be found.

"It's a shame about Sofia, but the police have no leads," Reed said, as if knowing what happened.

"That's not anything you ever have to worry about. Whatever business you had with that family is fulfilled." Reed nodded and it was good she understood nothing else had to be said on the subject. "Knowing that, let's talk business."

"I thought you understood I'm not taking contracts right now."

"I realize that, and I'm not offering you one. What I am offering you, though, is a way out of the shadows. You've proven yourself, and it's time to start living, don't you think?"

"My life has always been about the shadows. That's where I'm comfortable."

"Your life is a testament to survival, Rebel." The name made Reed's head whip up, but more from surprise than anger or embarrassment. "I make it a point to know all about the people I want to work for me."

"Work for you how?"

"My brother's coming home to New Orleans, but we have a casino in Vegas. We're not getting rid of that since it's essential to our business, but without him here, it's going to need a manager."

"You have a manager," Reed said, sounding like she knew as much about them as she'd found out about her. "His office is a floor under your brother's, and he's the face of Gemini."

"Elliott is the face of Gemini, but he's not the brains," she said of Elliott Walsh, who'd worked for them for years but knew his place. "I need someone in Mano's chair who knows not only how to run things, but how to handle problems in a unique way. Snake Eyes can't be everywhere at the same time."

"So you *do* want me to kill for you?" Reed said, smiling.

"I want you to not waste your talents on people who don't

appreciate you. With me you can start to see the possibilities outside what you've been doing, and I'll give you a home, figuratively and literally."

"What do you mean?" The house in Henderson was already on the market and she had a tentative contract to sell.

"My family would become your family, Reed, and you're sitting in the home I could provide. Mano's not going to need it, and my girl loves room service, so we'll be happy to stay at the Gemini when we're in town." She motioned around the room. "Mano's taking all the family photos and some stuff with him, but the house comes with the job. You can't live with Oscar forever."

"You really did do your homework."

"That's what you do for people you want to take care of, and I know how you feel about Oscar. He comes as part of the package. Anyone who can make you disappear off my security system is someone I want working for me."

"Can I think about it?" Reed appeared to be confused, as if this wasn't something she'd ever considered, much less been offered.

"No." It was a chance she had to take, but sometimes pushing someone was the only way to get them to the watering hole. "I need your answer right now, and the smart play is yes."

Reed laughed and she finally looked her age. This was someone who'd carried a heavy load for way too long. "You don't fuck around, do you?"

"Not when I see someone who will be an important part of my life. You won't be happy going back to what you've known, so why not take a chance on something that could make a good change for once?"

"Yes," Reed said, holding her hand out. "And thanks for Oscar."

"Oscar would've missed you if you'd turned me down," she said and winked again. "He already agreed."

Over the next two hours they worked out the logistics of what she wanted and Reed left with a firm offer in hand. Reed would take over the operations at the Gemini, with Oscar at her side, and she and Mano would take a few months to get them up to speed. Reed might've been an unknown, but she was worth the risk. In turn, she and her family would help Reed see what good things friendships could bring into her life.

"Thanks, Remi, and not just for this," Reed said, stiffening at first when Remi hugged her. "I never imagined Sofia Madison would land me here."

"Dallas keeps telling me to throw good things out into the universe, and she'll answer by giving me good things back. Maybe you should try it."

"This is about as good as it'll get, I'm guessing."

"You need to tune your universe a little then," Dallas said when she came in. "I threw out my wishes and reeled this one in."

"Maybe one day, Ms. Montgomery, but I doubt I'll be as lucky."

EPILOGUE

Three Months Later

Reed flexed her hand after punching the idiot from Utah who'd thought it was a good idea to steal chips off one of their tables. Granted, there were people on their payroll who could've given the moron a lesson, but it was nice to get some action every so often. "Take some friendly advice. Next time, it's going to take surgery to fix those sticky fingers. You understand that?"

"Yeah," the guy said, holding a tissue to his nose.

"If I see you in here again, your fingers will be a treat compared to what'll happen to you." She motioned for the security guy to show him out. "Make sure you pass around his picture to the others and make them understand he's not welcome."

"You got it, boss."

"Anything else tonight?" she asked Oscar over the phone. It was only eight, but she'd had months of late nights working with either Remi or Mano learning the ropes, and she was looking forward to a beer and maybe a game on television.

"Elliott's working tonight and said he'd let you know if he needed anything, but everything's quiet. At least as quiet as a big crowd of people in a casino can be. Go home and don't forget about the meeting with the catering staff tomorrow."

She laughed as she waved to a couple people on the way out. It was still strange to have so many people recognize her, but it was becoming more second nature. Her first instinct was still to retreat to the solitude of the really nice house Sylvia Jatibon had left decorated for her. This job, though, was all about finesse, as Remi and Mano kept saying, and she was learning that slowly. "That's not something I'd ever expect to hear from you."

"Well, it's not going to change the fact that they'll be expecting you at one. See you tomorrow and have a good night."

The drive home was quiet and she listened to the news on the way. It was the distraction she used every night to make her not think about Brinley and Finn and what they were doing. Oscar had told her how upset Brinley had been when she'd woken up alone and realized Reed would never be in touch with her again.

That night was the closest she'd ever come to staying and trying to have something more important in her life, but she didn't have the tools for a long-term relationship with a mother and child. It was one more failure on her long-ass list. There was no way she'd subject Brinley or Finn to what she'd grown up with.

She drove by the apartment complex and saw Brinley's new car in the lot. It was her parting gift, along with a college fund for Finn. It was all Brinley would accept from her, but it'd made no dent in the money she still had from Victor's contract. With time she hoped to have better luck working through Brinley's mom to give them more to make life easier.

The street was fairly busy, so she started driving home, not wanting anyone to notice her parked and staring up at Brinley's place, and it still took some thought to turn toward the new house. Her neighbors were mostly the upper management and headliners at the various casinos, but there was plenty of space between the houses for privacy.

A note from the maid on the table by the door said she'd placed a meal in the oven, and that the pool guys would be there early. That someone was in her space during the day still made her nervous, but all her secrets were locked in the office. Plus, Remi told her every staff member was trusted and vetted.

"Shower first, then enchiladas," she said, dropping her keys next to the note. Gloria, her maid, was Mexican American and enjoyed feeding her some of her favorite recipes along with friendly advice about a slew of different topics. It was like the older woman had taken one look at her and decided she needed a mother as well as clean bathrooms, and she was doing both jobs beautifully.

The bedroom had a little light coming from it, but she figured Gloria had left the bathroom light on for her. She froze at the sight on the bed.

"You know," Brinley said, holding the sheet up to her chest, "a woman I dated for two years, who broke my heart, didn't hurt me as much as waking up and finding you gone. You touched me and left, which kind of makes you an asshole."

"I probably am an asshole, but I thought it was the right thing to do."

"Staying and talking to me would've been the right thing to do. I mean, you still could have left after that, and it would've made you less of an asshole." Brinley dropped the sheet and stood. Her gorgeous body was everything Reed remembered. "Do you think that'll happen again?"

"Not unless you want me to go." She didn't stop Brinley from unbuttoning her shirt and unbuckling her belt.

"I was the one rooting for you to stay." Her pants dropped to her ankles and Brinley dropped to her knees to take them, and her underwear, off. "And it's your house, so you'll have to ask me to go."

"I'd never do that." She almost cried when Brinley stood and pressed herself to her. The kiss of all that skin against hers was enough to make her want to rush.

"I know that too, but the problem is, I know where you live. It won't be so easy to ignore me now." Brinley took her hand and led her to the bed. "Sit."

She followed orders and sucked Brinley's nipple in, then put her hand between her legs when Brinley stood between her knees. "God, you're so wet."

"If you think you're getting away with that tonight, think again." Brinley pulled the hair at the back of her head to get her to lean away from her, and she grabbed her by the wrist to take her hand away.

"I'm sorry, I assumed…" she said, stopping when Brinley kissed her.

"You thought right, but you need to slow down." She didn't understand until Brinley knelt and spread her legs. "I need to touch you first in case you relax me to the point of unconsciousness. Think of it as cutting down your chances to revert to your asshole ways."

"I think this is just an excuse to call me an asshole a bunch of times."

"You think that's all this is about?" Brinley pushed her back and touched the bullet wound scar on her side. As she started to assure her it was fine, Brinley lowered her head and started slowly dragging her tongue from her sex to the top of her clit. It instantly made her crave more and she wrapped her hand in Brinley's hair.

"I must be doing something right," Brinley said after another swipe of her tongue. "You're not telling me it's in my best interest to go."

"It is," she said but didn't let Brinley go.

"My God, I thought I was stubborn." Brinley bit her mound as punishment and she moved back some. "That was a wrong answer. Do you really want to end up with a nickname like—well, I don't think I have to say it again. Unless it's warranted."

"You want honest, don't you?"

"I want you to sit back and let me touch you. That's all I'm asking...for now."

Brinley started again with her tongue, and when Reed thought she couldn't take any more teasing, when it felt like she'd damage something her clit was so hard, Brinley sucked her in and really used her tongue.

"Fuck," she said, needing to come. "Fucking don't stop," she said, losing herself to the orgasm that was starting. It was ridiculous, but it was like she was unraveling, and she had to hang on to Brinley or she'd fly away.

"Are you okay?" Brinley asked as she lay on top of her. She didn't remember falling back or Brinley moving but she was glad to open her eyes and see her.

"I'm fine...but not really."

"That's a confusing answer," Brinley said, running her finger along her eyebrows.

"I'm alive, but I'm not sure what you just did to me."

The way Brinley smiled made her happy. "That's easy, I loved you. It's the only way to crack that heart of yours open. Up to now it's been a tough nut, but I'm not giving up."

"You're a little insane, you know that, right?" she said, rolling over and taking Brinley with her.

"It's a quirk of mine. Not insanity, obviously." Brinley pulled her down to kiss her.

"What quirk is that?" She moved down, wanting to taste what Brinley was offering.

"I've fallen for every single person who's tried to kill me," Brinley said as she lowered her head. "So you're nothing special." She tapped the end of her nose before pointing down. "But since you're down there, get to work."

She looked Brinley in the eye as she ran her tongue through her heat, and stopped to savor the moment. In all her sexual experiences she'd never done this to another woman. It seemed like an intimate act that should be reserved for a lover, and that was someone she'd never had.

The taste of Brinley was as intoxicating as the woman herself.

"You need to put your fingers in me," Brinley said when she sped up. She lifted her head when Brinley pulled her hair again. "I've been waiting for you all night and I can't hold out much longer. I want to come in your mouth but with your fingers in me."

She flicked her tongue over Brinley's clit again as she slowly slid her fingers in, liking the way Brinley's sex squeezed them every bit of the way.

"Yes," Brinley said, throwing her head back and lifting her hips slightly. "I need you."

"Tell me what you want."

Brinley bucked her hips to keep pace with her but her movements were starting to become erratic. "Uh…oh my God," Brinley said as she sucked her in again. "Like that, don't stop doing—"

The end came way too soon, but Reed doubted it would take long for them to repeat the process. "You changed my life, you know that?"

Brinley sighed when she moved up and put her arms around her. "I think it was mutual, baby." Brinley drew random designs on her chest with her finger as she put her leg over her as if to hold her in place. "It's time to stop overthinking this and see what it could be."

"I'm not throwing you out, but don't sugarcoat it. There are a lot of demons in my past, and I don't want you or Finn getting hurt. It's not like I've gone to work for the Girl Scouts, either."

"That's true, but you haven't taken any more contracts either, have you?" Brinley pinched her nipple hard enough to make her suck in a lot of air. "I mean, you're not bringing home any other women and children you've been hired to kill, are you?"

"No, but I told you who Remi and Mano are. The job I accepted is still a kind of contract with the Mob." She grabbed Brinley's hand before she got pinched again. "You need a nice quiet life in the suburbs."

"And what you need to do is stop dwelling in the past and turn your head to the horizon." Brinley straddled her like she had the first night they were together. "You can't change anything that's happened, but you can work to make all your tomorrows your own."

"Did you read that in a fortune cookie?" She laughed when Brinley pulled away and pinched her again, hard.

"My mother told me that when I admitted I was crazy about you," Brinley said, laughing as well. "Don't shut me out. Remi and Dallas must agree with me, since they're responsible for me being here."

"We'll learn together as we go, I guess, and I promise to do my best. You need to know, though, that I've got plenty to learn."

"That's all I'm asking of you." Brinley lay down and kissed her. "All you have to keep repeating is that you're not alone anymore."

They made love again and shared the food in the oven when they finally came up for air.

When Brinley led her back to the bedroom, putting on pajamas wasn't what she had in mind. "Are you suddenly shy?"

"Believe me, I'd love nothing better than to sleep naked, but we'll have to wait a few years on that one. Six thirty will roll around faster than you think."

"That's a weird thing to say," she said, since all she was waiting on that early was the pool guy.

"Good night, baby, and if you sneak out of here before I wake up, you're going to wish you'd killed me."

"Good night." Reed pulled her close, the novelty of holding someone and knowing they didn't want to leave a wondrous thing. Brinley was beautiful, of that there was no doubt, but she was also an interesting woman with an infinite capacity to forgive. Her sense of humor, though, was going to take a little getting used to.

The sensation of something running up her leg woke her what seemed like minutes later, but it was light outside when Reed opened her eyes. For a split second she thought she was going to have to stab something when she felt the sensation again, but then she realized: Finn.

"Where'd you come from?" she asked, smiling when he moved to sit next to her. He had some more words now, but she still couldn't understand most of them.

"The guest room. I didn't have a sitter." Brinley smiled at her sleepily.

"I get the pajamas now," she said, closing her hand around Finn's when he put his in hers.

"Once he learns to knock, we can go with the naked option," Brinley said, kissing her.

"It'll be worth the wait, I'm sure."

This was as far from where Reed had started as she could imagine, but her need to run and hide was beaten back by the desire to make a new life, wherever that might land her. It couldn't be better than this.

"We'll take it slow until you adjust," Brinley said, kissing her again. "I don't want to freak you out."

"I think not adjusting my universe might be what I've been doing wrong all this time, so no need to slow anything down." She smiled, thinking about all the mornings they'd spend together, and it wasn't completely terrifying. "Six thirty sounds like a good time to start over, and we'll go from there."

"Promise?" Brinley asked.

"That's an easy one to make. The rest we'll work on together." Whatever came next, she had something to fight for and believe in now.

About the Author

Ali Vali is the author of the long-running Cain Casey Devil series, the Genesis Clan Forces series, and the Call series, including Lambda Literary Award finalist *Calling the Dead*.

Originally from Cuba, Ali has retained much of her family's traditions and language and uses them frequently in her stories. Having her father read her stories and poetry before bed every night as a child infused her with a love of reading, which she carries till today. Ali currently lives outside New Orleans, Louisiana, and she has discovered that living in Louisiana provides plenty of material to draw from in creating her novels and short stories.

Books Available From Bold Strokes Books

All She Wants by Larkin Rose. Marci Jones and Tessa Dalton get more than they bargained for when their plans for a one-night stand turn into an opportunity for love. (978-1-63555-476-2)

Beautiful Accidents by Erin Zak. Stevie Adams doesn't believe in fate, not after losing her parents in a car crash. But she's about to discover that sometimes the best things in life happen purely by accident. (978-1-63555-497-7)

Before Now by Joy Argento. The instant Delaney Peyton and Jade Taylor meet, they sense a connection neither can explain. Can they overcome a betrayal that spans the centuries to reignite a love that can't be broken? (978-1-63555-525-7)

Breathe by Cari Hunter. Paramedic Jemima Pardon's chronic bad luck seems to be improving when she meets police officer Rosie Jones. But they face a battle to survive before they can find love. (978-1-63555-523-3)

Double-Crossed by Ali Vali. Hired thief and killer Reed Gable finds something in her scope that will change her life forever when she gets a contract to end casino accountant Brinley Myers's life. (978-1-63555-302-4)

False Horizons by CJ Birch. Jordan and Ash struggle with different views on the alien agenda and must find their way back to each other before they're swallowed up by a centuries-old war. Third in the New Horizons series. (978-1-63555-519-6)

Legacy by Charlotte Greene. In this paranormal mystery, five women hike to a remote cabin deep inside a national park—and unsettling events suggest that they should have stayed home. (978-1-63555-490-8)

Somewhere Along the Way by Kathleen Knowles. When Maxine Cooper moves to San Francisco during the summer of 1981, she learns that wherever you run, you cannot escape yourself. (978-1-63555-383-3)

Blood of the Pack by Jenny Frame. When Alpha of the Scottish pack Kenrick Wulver visits the Wolfgangs, she falls for Zaria Lupa, a wolf on the run. (978-1-63555-431-1)

Cause of Death by Sheri Lewis Wohl. Medical student Vi Akiak and K9 Search and Rescue officer Kate Renard must work together to find a killer before they end up the next targets. In the race for survival, they discover that love may be the biggest risk of all. (978-1-63555-441-0)

Chasing Sunset by Missouri Vaun. Hijinks and mishaps ensue as Iris and Finn set off on a road trip adventure, chasing the sunset, and falling in love along the way. (978-1-63555-454-0)

Double Down by MB Austin. When an unlikely friendship with Spanish pop star Erlea turns deeper, Celeste, in-house physician for the hotel hosting Erlea's show, has a choice to make—run or double down on love. (978-1-63555-423-6)

Party of Three by Sandy Lowe. Three friends are in for a wild night at billionaire heiress Eleanor McGregor's twenty-fifth birthday party. Love, lust, and doing the right thing, even when it hurts, turn the evening into one that will change their lives forever. (978-1-63555-246-1)

Sit. Stay. Love. by Karis Walsh. City girl Alana Brendt and country vet Tegan Evans both know they don't belong together. Only problem is, they're falling in love. (978-1-63555-439-7)

Where the Lies Hide by Renee Roman. As P.I. Camdyn Stark gets closer to solving the case, will her dark secrets and the lies she's buried jeopardize her future with the quietly beautiful Sarah Peters? (978-1-63555-371-0)

Beautiful Dreamer by Melissa Brayden. With love on the line, can Devyn Winters find it in her heart to stay in the small town of Dreamer's Bay, the one place she swore she'd never remain? (978-1-63555-305-5)

Create a Life to Love by Erin Zak. When sixteen-year-old Beth shows up at her birth mother's door, three lives will change forever. (978-1-63555-425-0)